Eric Russell did his bit in the ⸻
fascinated by the events of that ⸻
diverse areas since then and f⸻
business journalist. *Men of Stee*⸻
experiences.

⸻ recipe for the *Men of Steel* cocktail mentioned in the book
⸻ be found on his website at www.ericrussell.co.uk.

Men of Steel

ERIC RUSSELL

Ten 10ths Books

Published by Ten 10ths Marketing Ltd
7 Sandybed Lane Scarborough YO12 5LH

ISBN 0 9545217 0 6

Printed by Antony Rowe Ltd, Chippenham

This book is dedicated to Dorothy, Kate, and Richard.

Chapter 1

May 24th.

'This is the first day of the rest of your life.'

Professor Lazio Palfrey read the cliché of the day on his desk calendar and paused.

'Coincidence or what?' he thought, as the cause of his musing knocked on the office door.

'Hi!' he said, as a well-groomed head appeared round the door. 'Come in and grab a seat. Thanks for dropping by, how's things at the business end of the university, then?'

'Busy, busy,' said James Russell, taking the proffered chair. 'Just about every academic department wants to make money out of its research just now so we're up to our eyes transferring patents, selling licences and spinning out new companies.'

'Well, it'll keep you out of mischief,' said Lazio with a twinkle in his eye, settling back in his chair.

'Thank you very much,' said James, sensing there was a double meaning in the comment but unable to decide what it was.

Palfrey loved teasing people he saw as buttoned up and unimaginative. James Russell, commercial manager for Leicestershire's Burnstone University, was the perfect foil. Short and dapper, he was the starched dress shirt to Palfrey's comfortable country check.

While Russell felt he had to maintain the professional, groomed business image at all times, Palfrey revelled in eccentricity. As Head of the Combined Engineering School at the university, he felt he had licence to be different.

'Anyway, when you've been a man of steel, researching the metal and its markets for thirty odd years, you need another

1

interest in life,' he would say to those whose life he made difficult by his unpredictable behaviour. And that was often.

But at least you could always see him coming. Most days, his ample frame was just about contained in a brocade waistcoat that clashed with the yellow of his bow tie but sat well with the grey of his hair. Best described as a shock, it was curly at the back and wildly carefree at the front. Lazio Palfrey was unafraid to promote his image as an eccentric.

'So what have you got for me now that's new?' said James, hoping that if he got down to business he wouldn't have to engage in a verbal duel that he felt sure he'd lose.

'I think I've got an idea that could be really big and I'd like to handle it in a new way. Instead of simply selling a licence, so that a commercial firm can use the technology, I want to keep this one for myself. That means setting up a new company to make and sell the equipment.'

'I see no problem with that. We've created several companies since the business development department was set up, what is it? Seven years ago now? And I like to think we've put together some good deals selling your other licences and patents.'

'Oh, yes. No complaints at all. But this time is a bit different. Although it appears to continue my research into the hardening of steel, this is an exciting new idea. I'm calling it my quintahertz machine. It's taken a lot of cash to set up and as it was something of a private venture to start with, I've used my own money throughout. So the new company will need some considerable funding from elsewhere to get the machines into production.'

'Well,' said James, 'with your reputation in steel research, money should be the least of the problems. Let's have a look at your business plan.'

'Right,' said Lazio. 'By the way, do you see what it says on the calendar today?'

* * * * * * * *

After James Russell had left, Lazio paced around his office enjoying the moment. This was a good start to the rest of his life. His latest research promised to attract a lot of attention and that pleased him no end. It also meant money, and that was equally attractive just now.

The sixteenth century manor house that was home to him and his wife matched his image perfectly, but it needed constant attention and repairs never came cheap. Not when the builder saw the size of the pile, the Maserati in the drive and was told early on how important Lazio Palfrey was in steel research.

The telephone ended his reverie.

'You know you're lecturing in under five minutes?'

'Yes, yes. I'm on my way.'

Ann Whittaker, his secretary, was well used to shepherding Lazio around his timetable - and the explosive reaction that sometimes followed. The fiery side of Lazio's half-Italian temperament was never far below the surface.

After a holiday in Sorrento, Ann had brought him back a large poster looking down into the crater of Vesuvius and pinned it up on his office wall. He never realised it, but the poster had a special significance for her and the staff.

'One day they'll both blow up. And I bet it'll happen at the same time,' Ann would tell her staff after a typical Palfrey outburst.

Lazio was born in Italy, where his parents still lived. But he almost had dual nationality. While his mother was Italian his father was English and he himself had felt well at home during the three years he had been studying at Cambridge.

His parents met while working in the Allied administration that ran Italy after the Second World War: she was a translator, he was in intelligence. The two had married and settled in the country and Lazio grew up showing his mother's Italian volatility rather than his father's steadier and more disciplined outlook.

While at Cambridge, Lazio met Helen and she had been the deciding factor when Lazio was uncertain whether to go back home to Italy to find work or to stay in Britain. Helen was English through and through and would never have considered living or working permanently outside the country. So he had to choose between girlfriend and homeland.

His leanings towards Italy were influenced by strong, inbred family instincts, as befits all good Italians. The weather compared to the British climate was another strong influence. But love was stronger and when a lecturing post was offered after he achieved first class honours in his subject of mechanical engineering, the immediate future was decided: England and marriage.

But his volatile Italian nature often tested Helen to the limit.

'You're either all up or all down,' she would say in exasperation after one of his depressions. When he was all up, he was extravagant and generous and made up for the black times. He mostly lived beyond his means anyway. That also exasperated Helen, who tended to sail through life on a much more even keel. But the marriage was still strong after thirty two years.

Ann Whittaker also knew Lazio pretty well. She had worked out that a five minute warning gave him the chance to huff and puff his hurried way down the corridor, creating an effect of importance that people sometimes thought was his main aim in life.

'Morning,' he said as he entered the lecture room. 'Hope you are all here for a stimulating insight into the economics of steel manufacture.'

His audience groaned with the collective student grief that a bright approach to the dullest subject always generated.

'Glad to see the fantastic enthusiasm the Combined Engineering school creates in its students,' he replied. 'Any connection between this lecture on making low grade materials work as well as high grade stuff, and teaching you lot, is entirely intentional.'

More groans.

'As some of you know, my quest here is to make low cost steel perform as well as high grade versions by treating the surface. This makes low grade steel very hard wearing and reduces the friction between adjacent components. Parts last longer because there is less wear on the surface and that means less maintenance is needed. Machines also need less power because there is less friction to overcome.

'The core of the component is not exposed to wear and tear, so it does not matter if it is low quality material. But it has to be sufficiently strong to withstand all the stresses that apply through the depth of the component.'

He was now talking to the tops of fifty heads furiously transferring his facts to notebooks. His determination to keep his department at the head of this research meant he drove his students, and himself, hard. So when a line of research came to a dead end, the department was hell with an electric tension that affected everyone until a way was found to move the research forward.

But his mark on industry was permanent and hugely beneficial. Britain was an acknowledged leader in the science of surface finishing, while the financial benefits to industry were enormous. Over the years, it had saved millions of pounds because components were less expensive.

He ran through the current hardening treatments describing the benefits and disadvantages of chemically based and mechanical hardening techniques, but he did not tell them that his own research was moving on to new and completely uncharted territory.

Having filled his students' heads with sufficient information for that day, Lazio asked for questions to round off the lecture.

He was answered by the lecture room door opening and Ann Whittaker signalling him outside. The students looked at each other with surprise, that sort of thing didn't happen very often.

'I'm afraid I'll have to end there,' said Lazio as he came back in, 'If there are any pressing questions, fix something up with Ann.'

He gathered up his papers and swept out leaving a bemused audience behind.

* * * * * * * *

'David Bearing's in your office now. It seems that John Fleming has had an accident with your quintahertz machine and it doesn't look too good, I'm afraid,' Ann's voice trailed off as she tried to keep up with Lazio.

Dr David Bearing was principal lecturer in the Combined Engineering School. Slim, almost a shadow against his professor, he was one of those people who, annoyingly, can eat like a horse yet keep their figure and not gain weight.

'Hi!' said Lazio as he swept into his office, 'What's all this about then?'

'It seems that the new hardening machine has laid out one of the lab technicians,' said David, 'No-one saw him take the hit but one of the students heard a great clang as the sample he was working on hit the floor and then heard a gasp from John.

'She came over to find him draped over one of the side bars of the framework. She immediately pulled out the mains plug, got some help to lay him out and called the nurse. She also got the other lab technician to call an ambulance.

'It took the nurse about ten minutes to run over and her diagnosis was that John was fast asleep. The paramedics took another ten minutes to arrive and their diagnosis was the same. They decided to take John to the hospital for a full check up, but apparently he woke up in the ambulance.

'I've just had a call from the other technician who went with him to the hospital. Apart from being highly surprised at his situation, he said he was as right as rain. The hospital's checking him out now.'

'Thank God for that,' said Lazio. 'The way Ann was going on, I thought he was going to be dead. So what do we do now?'

'Well we've got to tell his wife pretty soon. Then we'll have to look at the machine to see what went wrong. I asked the rest of the students to pull some benches across to block off the machine and said they were to touch nothing whatsoever. As far as John goes, we just have to wait and see how he shapes up.'

'OK. Well, I'll get John's home number off Ann and call his wife. Are you lecturing now, or could you start looking at the machine?'

'I'm clear till after lunch so I'll go down to the lab now.'

'Right, I'll see you there as soon as I've got this business sorted.'

* * * * * * * *

The engineering laboratory, like most university engineering departments, resembled a disorganised, wall-to-wall car boot sale with obviously home-made gizmos and mechanisms laid about on the benches, mostly connected up to computers. But there was no doubting the enthusiasm and dedication of the technicians and students who had spent hours conceiving these launch pads of tomorrow's science.

David was quizzed by the students working there as soon as he got through the door.

'The latest news is that John's fine. He's being checked out by the hospital and may be in for a day or so, but there seems to be no after effects at the moment. So, fingers crossed. Now, who saw him after the accident?'

Everyone, it seemed.

'Right, let's take some notes. First, can someone take a piece of paper and collect all the names of the students who were in the laboratory. Put down their student numbers and which course they're on as well. Now, who was first on the scene?'

He wrote down an account from the first few students, who all told the same story. No-one had seen the actual event so it was obviously only the lab technician who could say what had happened just before the accident.

'I think these notes will do for now,' David said when he'd finished. 'Can I ask you not to say too much to any other students, and absolutely nothing to anyone outside the uni for obvious reasons. Try to put the incident out of your minds as soon as possible. Accidents will happen. Hopefully this one's not too serious. It's about lunchtime now, so go and get something to keep body and soul together - and that doesn't mean several pints in the bar.'

Lazio came in as David ended his pep talk and the students wandered off in groups.

'I've quizzed the students that were here,' said David, 'so I'll get Ann to type up the notes and give you a copy.'

'Thanks, we'd better have a look at the machine then.'

Lazio's steel hardening machine was tucked away in one corner not yet ready for students to start using. Its metal framework formed a cube about two metres long on each side. Crossbars supported a shelf on one side and a box of electronics on the other. A laptop computer sat on another shelf.

Laid against the frame were several shielding panels while a nearby bench sported the test samples: rods and ingots of different metals.

'Unplug the computer first,' said Lazio. 'We'll run it up by itself to see what stage it was at when the mains plug was pulled.'

A graph came on screen.

'Look,' said Lazio, 'this first pulse shows when the hardening radiation was switched on and then there's the steady line we normally get that shows how much power was being absorbed by the sample. The graph should then fall to zero when the test is finished but there's some variations at the end that I haven't seen before.'

David hit some keys and expanded the graph at that end.

'The graph goes down, then up slightly, down again and then there's the sharp spikes as the mains plug was pulled out without closing down the system properly.'

'Right,' said Lazio, rubbing his chin, 'The first thing anyone heard was a clang, so if the sample rolled off the shelf and out of the beam, that's when the graph goes down as there's nothing to absorb the radiation.'

'Say that John leans over the bar to pick up the sample without switching the machine off. He catches some of the radiation and that's when the graph goes up. He falls over the bar, out of the radiation area, so the graph goes down again and then there's the spikes as the plug's pulled.'

'Sounds reasonable,' said David. 'I'll print off this graph and put it with the notes and we'll have to wait until we can talk to John and get his side of the story.'

Ann Whittaker came up beside them.

'The story's reached the dean and he wants the latest news. I've said you're investigating at the moment but he's jumping up and down a bit'

'Bugger,' said Lazio. 'Alright, I think I'm finished here, I'll call him from my office. Can you cover up this machine, David, and put the bench back in front of it. Keep the whole thing low profile. We'd better decide what we're going to do next. Can we have a meeting this afternoon?'

'It'll have to be after five. I've lectures and tutorials until then.'
'I don't fancy staying that late. How about tomorrow morning?'
'About eleven?'
'Go for it.'

* * * * * * * *

Lazio opened his study window and sat for a moment taking in the early morning freshness, the May scents and the birdsong that wafted in from the two acres of manor garden outside.

He straightened his yellow bow tie in the screen of the laptop computer in front of him and, as the machine started up, he settled his ample frame into a leather swivel chair.

Like the house, the chair had seen better days, but both fitted comfortably. That suited Lazio. During the fifty four years he had been on earth, his body had also seen better days.

As he finished off his report to the university dean on John Fleming's accident, his train of thought was broken when Helen bustled in with coffee.

Lazio saw she had brought in two cups so he pulled out another chair, obviously there were matters to be discussed.

'Lunch,' she said briskly, 'are you going to be in or out?'

'Out. I've some people who want to catch me during the break and anyway I don't eat so much in the refectory because the food is nowhere as good as yours.'

'Flatterer. But I can't see you eating less whatever the quality.'

Lazio pouted.

'Next: you haven't forgotten that Saxon and family are here for the weekend and you will be around for the whole time, won't you?'

'All arranged, my dear.'

'That means you'd forgotten, but don't bother to pout again even though it suits you.'

Lazio grimaced.

'And there's something that Saxon might want to discuss with you. William starts at public school in September and there might be a request for some financial assistance with the fees.'

'I hadn't forgotten that either. But it could make life a bit difficult for us, you know.'

Helen sighed. 'Well, it's traditional for grandparents to help, just see what he wants first of all. There's time for us to talk it over after the weekend. But now I'm off down to the post office and there's several people I want to see as well, so I'll catch you when you get in tonight. Don't forget to set the burglar alarm as you go.'

She kissed him and disappeared with her coffee.

Lazio thoughtfully turned back to his computer. Money, money, money.

He checked the conclusion to his report on the lab accident, plugged in the printer, ran off a hard copy which went into his safe, pulled all his papers into a battered leather briefcase and set off for the university later than intended.

* * * * * * * *

It took about twenty minutes and some wild overtaking to get to the university campus for eleven. The three litres of Maserati engine allowed Lazio to drive with style, or with what he thought was style. But his version drove other motorists mad in the same way that he could exasperate his staff. Waiting until the last minute and then giving it all you've got isn't quite the Highway Code approach to driving, but at least it ensures the adrenalin system still works.

The Maserati was light of foot, quite the opposite of Lazio, who was a bit hard pressed to get in behind the wheel nowadays. But that was no deterrent if you didn't admit it. He was still well over the speed limit as he approached the car park barrier, flashing his lights to get the barrier up so he wasn't delayed. He would make his appointment with David Bearing in time, but that was no reason to drive reasonably. Flair at all times.

'One day, no-one will be on duty at this barrier and he'll never stop in time,' said the security man to his assistant. 'And if he did, he'd never work out how to get the thing up, I don't think I've ever seen him use his entry card. Can you just whip out and make sure he can get into his slot OK, or that'll be all wrong as well.'

David Bearing was talking to Ann Whittaker in her office when Lazio walked in.

'Morning all,' He announced to everyone in general and no one in particular. 'What's new in the world?'

'John Fleming's back in the lab,' said David, 'and appears as right as rain.'

'Shouldn't he have taken a few days off?' asked Lazio in surprise.

'That's exactly what we were saying just now. But he discharged himself from hospital last evening. He said it was so depressing there that if he'd stayed, he'd have woken up this morning with something worse.'

'Well, let's have a chat about what we should do next and then I'll go down and see him,' He picked up the wedge of paperwork from his pigeonhole and went through the adjoining door into his office.

As an established expert in his field, Lazio sat on many committees, always had companies looking for advice and was always in demand for the latest information by the technical and engineering magazines. So there was always paperwork to clear.

'The dean wanted an initial report quite quickly so I drafted one last night. He's worried about compensation claims more than John's state, I think. I'll get you to have a quick look to see if there's anything that needs adding to it. So what do you think we should do next?'

'If it turns out that the radiation can harm people, we must keep it within the machine. So I think we've got to find out what material will best stop it. And say the beam misses the sample, will it go through to next door? And if it goes out of focus and spreads out, can it come through the workshield? We'll have to take some measurements.'

'This is going to be a nightmare, I can see it coming,' said Lazio.

'No, it's not going to be that dramatic. We've been playing with it for months and this is the first problem we've had. And if we can't find some expertise to draw on within this university, I shall be most surprised.

'Let's go down to the lab while we're thinking about it and have a quick look at the machine to see what other points might suggest themselves. We can also get the latest off John.'

As they went down the corridor, David continued.

'It's probably also time that we put some safeguards on the machine. We'll have to before the students are let loose on it anyway. Just standard stuff. Something like two buttons instead of one to start the machine. They'd be a metre apart and have to be pressed at the same time. This means both of the operator's hands are kept clear of the beam.

'Then we add a circuit so the start buttons aren't energised until the workshield is brought down over the sample that's being hardened. That means the radiation can't start until the machine is fully closed up.'

They went into the laboratory office. John was poring over a computer printout.

'Hi! How are you feeling?'

'Better for being back here, I can tell you. That hospital put years on me. All those old dodderers staggering about. Grim. But these analysis figures look brilliant, I've run you off a copy. These are for the sample I did before the machine bit me.'

'Thanks,' said Lazio, 'but how are you feeling in yourself?'

'Oh. No problems at all. Once I'd got over the shock of waking up in an ambulance there haven't been any funny feelings at all, and there's nothing to see either. I can just remember feeling a buzz when I was at the machine but nothing else. I'm going to see my doctor this evening just in case. I'll let you know how I get on.'

'Thanks,' said Lazio again, picking up the computer printout.

John had highlighted the key results. The surface of the sample of steel had been hardened to twice the depth that any other system could achieve; the evenness and hardness of the surface itself were also twice as good as usual; and the power used to achieve the result was far less than expected.

'I've also just run an X-ray scan,' said John 'and the quality shows no sign of regression or stress. I know the sample is only a few days old but I'm sure something would have started to show up by now.'

Lazio was lost in thought. He was adding up all the results to see what the total cost saving would be to anyone using his system.

'Well done, John, but not a word to anyone till we've sorted out the machine and fully proved the technique. I'll go and analyse these results in depth.'

'Well, we can't stop the research now,' said David as they walked back down the corridor. 'The first results from the sample look better than anything we've ever done before so we're really on to something. Even if the full results aren't quite so good, we've still got a steel hardening method that industry will pay handsomely for. We just need to hold off treating more samples for a bit and concentrate on the machine itself.'

'Let's hope you're right.'

'Oh, come on. Cheer up. Now, another thing we'll have to think about is the size of the sample. If it is very small, it won't absorb all the radiation from the hardening beam. So there will be a lot of excess power floating about that the shielding will have to absorb.'

'I think that's the lesson to be learned from John Fleming's accident,' said Lazio. 'The samples that were put onto the target bench were big enough to absorb all the radiation power. But when the last sample rolled off the shelf and onto the floor, there was nothing to absorb the beam. As John bent over this side bar, his body absorbed it instead.

'If you can start setting up some measuring instruments around the machine, to check the extent of stray radiation, we'll move forward step by step. Have a word with the electronics department to see what ideas they might have on measuring high frequency radiation but don't make too much of the machine, just keep it a low level routine enquiry.'

* * * * * * * *

'What a week,' said Lazio as he stopped off in Ann's office on his way home. 'I'm glad to be on my way for once. Are you doing anything exciting this weekend?'

'We've a theatre visit Saturday night that I'm really looking forward to. But it'll be gardening mostly. We try to get ahead of the weeds this time of year although I'm not sure it ever works.

13

Thank goodness we don't have quite the spread you've got to look after. And you?'

'The house is being taken over by my son and his family for a weekend visit, so no peace for the wicked there. But it'll be good fun with the kids. See you Monday then.'

When Lazio pulled into his drive, his son, Saxon, and family had already arrived for the weekend.

The crunch of car tyres on gravel brought the two children running round the end of the house.

'Quick, come and see what we've found, Grandpa,' said Hannah bouncing around him and pulling on his hand.

On the lawn, a trail of feathers led to a dead blackbird that had lost out to a cat.

'Can we have it stuffed?'

'No! No! We have to bury it properly,' said William.

'It should really go in the dustbin,' said Lazio, 'But don't touch it, get a spade from the shed.'

Whilst Lazio adored children, at that point he was more anxious to get his hands on something to drink. He had just invested in several cases of vintage Bordeaux that was exactly to his taste and Friday evening, after a long week, was the ideal time to get to know it better.

And he saw a glass coming towards him as he turned to the house.

Saxon's wife Katherine was everything her father-in-law was not. Tall, slim and elegantly clad she moved across the lawn like a deer.

Glass in hand she shouted 'Hiya! I bring sustenance for the mighty.'

Lazio kissed her and took the glass.

'How are you and what do you think of this latest stuff, then?' he asked, sniffing it appreciatively.

'I'm fine and I've also got the better body. But Bordeaux's men's stuff, it's German white for me however out of fashion it may be. Anyway, how are you and are you still holding that university together?'

'It would definitely fall apart without my deft touch on the tiller, but there's lots of things going on. I'm thinking of launching my own company to handle my latest ideas on steel hardening. That'll be a first.'

'Sounds good. But will you still teach?'

'Definitely. Can't retire just yet. But these spin-out companies are all the rage just now. I would really only act as an advisor and go in as and when needed. I'd also have a strong input on strategy as a major shareholder and director. It could also bring more research work into the Combined Engineering School. And, in time, it would go public or be bought out by a large company, then I could retire.'

A small handbell called them all in for dinner.

'Come on, kids,' shouted Katherine, suddenly concerned that the garden had gone quiet. 'Dinner's ready.'

She shrieked in horror as two dirt-streaked children burst out of the bushes.

'What ever on earth have you two been doing? Look at your shoes, and your knees, and your hands and what's on your face?' Katherine looked ready to faint with each succeeding discovery.

'We decided to bury the blackbird,' said William, 'but we haven't touched it.'

'But you seem to have touched everything else. You're both filthy.'

Lazio broke in.

'I think they've been in the far rose bed. The gardener's been clearing out the old bushes so the ground is very soft. But it's also been well layered with old horse manure,' he added with a broad grin.

Katherine, pristine in designer suit, could hardly believe these urchins were her precious children.

'Don't go in the house,' she shrieked. 'Take your shoes off here and don't move. We'll have to delay dinner for ages while we clean you up. And stop grinning, dad, you're no help.'

The commotion brought Helen to the kitchen door. She sized up the situation right away.

'Lazio, bring a bowl from the utility room while I run some hot water. Katherine, send Saxon for their dressing gowns then keep an eye on the vegetables on the Aga. William, sit down and don't move. Hannah stop crying, we'll soon sort out your new dress.'

The garden returned to peace.

'Right,' commanded Helen when her troops were in place, 'we'll just scrape off the mud so we can have dinner, then they're straight into a bath. Socks off, children, they're not coming near the house either.'

Gradually, order came out of chaos. William explained how he'd buried the dead bird and Hannah said she'd made a cross to mark the spot, her marked dress well out of mind. Lazio wanted to know if they'd found the shovel all right but Katherine was keen to turn the talk to less mournful matters.

'Dad says he's thinking of starting a company to sell one of his ideas,' she said to Saxon. 'Sounds exciting.'

'Let's hear more. I'm always looking for new ways to make money.'

'I'm afraid this is very mechanical,' said Lazio. 'No computers in there at all apart from a basic PC.'

Saxon had shown his father's engineering aptitude from early on but he had gone into electronic engineering and then onto computer systems. So he was always ragging his father that there was no future in getting his hands dirty on oily rags, while heaving great spanners about was hardly rocket science.

Lazio just kept quiet and bided his time. His latest idea would silence Saxon, if it were ever possible to stop the younger generation taking potshots at the older.

So the talk went round the table until it was decided to defer coffee until the children had been soaked in deep, hot baths.

While the ladies fussed off, Lazio caught up with his son's latest news. As IT manager for an international oil company, Saxon was always implementing the latest developments in computer systems, so Lazio was able to compare them with his department's systems.

But Saxon soon turned the conversation to William and how he was doing at school.

'He's still top of his class at most things and we'd really like to get him to public school in September. That would really develop him. The headmaster says there's a very good chance he'll get to our first choice, so we're both hopeful that happens.'

Lazio sensed what was coming.

'And the fees?'

'Ah!' Saxon shifted in his armchair, 'I'd like to talk to you about that. It's not that we can't afford the fees, but it's the length of time that we'd have to pay them. We'd hate to have to take him away after a few years and you know Katherine, she always wants the best so the extras could be heavy. We're OK for now but if things got tight in the future would you be able to help?'

'I don't know. Professorships never bring in the income you'd expect from the title. This house is hugely expensive to keep going and, as you're always saying, there's no future anyway in getting your hands dirty heaving great spanners around. So I might be coming to you for a handout.'

Lazio just about managed to keep a straight face as he watched his son's discomfort.

'Don't worry. I'm sure we'll be able to come up with something. I'll talk to your mother first but carry on with your plans for William.'

'Gee, thanks, dad. That's a great weight off my mind.'

'And, now, what are you and Katherine wanting to do over the weekend?'

* * * * * * * *

Chapter 2

The first port of call for Lazio on Monday morning was Jenny, the dean's secretary, where he left a written report on John Fleming's accident.

'How's things in the seat of power?' he asked.

'Oh, we're ticking over here quite nicely, thank you. But what's the gossip from the lower decks then?'

'Gossip!' spluttered Lazio in mock indignation, 'We don't have any of that in Combined Engineering thank you very much. We just like to keep our lines of communication open, that's all. But did you know that...'

The phone rang.

'I'll get it and come in right away,' said Jenny.

'Sorry,' she said to Lazio, 'got to go, the godfather calls. But keep your lines of communication open!'

'Godfather,' thought Lazio, 'This place gets more like the Mafia every day.'

On the way to his own office, he stuck his head round David Bearing's door.

'Morning. Good weekend?'

'Yes, fine, thanks and you?'

'Brilliant. Had Saxon and the kids over. Nothing like a couple of urchins to take your mind off things. Went to the theme park as expected and thoroughly enjoyed myself. And then there's the benefit that someone else takes them off your hands when the weekend's done.'

'Yes,' said David ruefully, 'we've still got that pleasure to come. But Andrew starts primary school in September so Madeleine will have a bit more time to herself.'

'At least that won't cost you. My grandson starts public school at the same time and no doubt grandparents will be expected to

18

contribute if tradition has any say in the matter. Anyway, it wasn't all pleasure as I had to take time out to knock off a written accident report for the dean. But that's done and delivered now, do you want a copy?'

'Yes, please. But no rush. What's more important is the Technology Transfer Day on Wednesday.'

'Good Lord. I'd forgotten all about that,' Lazio came into the office and sat down.

'It's OK, all the arrangements are made but I've only just finished our presentation,' David pushed a file across the desk.

Under Lazio's tuition, he had been visiting these events for many years and was well aware of their true purpose. He knew that, to outsiders, these days are arranged by the Government's Department of Trade and Industry as a showcase to sell British technology to the rest of the world.

Outwardly, they enable universities and companies to make money out of the research work they cannot use themselves. They promote the country as a leader in research and so encourage foreign companies and students to bring money into the UK.

But Bearing knew their deeper purpose was to enable observers in the UK to get an idea of what other countries were working on. What he didn't know was that MI5 agents circulated amongst the dark suited scientists and businessmen at these meetings, in their role as the country's eyes and ears.

'There's no mention of our latest work on hardening, as you asked,' he said, 'I've just stressed that our facilities have been recently upgraded and we're available for research projects on steel. I've also mentioned some of the work we've done since the last TTD as a fill in, but the emphasis this time is on departmental facilities and expertise.'

'Excellent. That will suit me just fine for this year. Don't forget that the key thing as ever is to find out what other people are up to.'

David nodded in agreement, inwardly thinking he could probably teach his professor more about the ways of the world than Lazio could teach him.

While Lazio rode along on top of the world, hardly noticing anything below, David Bearing was much more aware. He felt he was much more realistic about the world and events generally.

'I'll take the file and read it now,' said Lazio.

'OK, see you later. By the way, I hear down the grapevine that Smithson is about to publish his latest paper on steel hardening. That should be in time for the Technology Transfer Days. I'll see if I can get you a copy. It's just an extension of his work on chemical hardening so no major surprises.'

'David, you never fail to amaze me with your contacts. I'm sure I never pick up so many bits of news. But I hope your flow of information is all incoming, though.'

'Don't worry, our department's good and tight. No-one knows what we're doing and no-one will steal a march on us. See you later.'

But I do worry, thought Lazio. David Bearing may have been in steel research for the last ten years but he appeared to have an unusually large number of contacts willing to gossip. He hoped David was right about his own department not being leaky. Professor John Smithson was at a rival university and his research into steel was less developed, but if he heard of the latest Palfrey developments...

* * * * * * * *

The Technology Transfer Days were held, as usual, in a conference suite adjacent to the Department of Trade and Industry headquarters in Victoria Street, a busy London street with few shops but dominated by a constant flow of taxis, buses and cars converging on nearby Victoria Station.

The DTI building is off the beaten track for visitors to London, which helps maintain the anonymity beloved by civil servants. But it is within walking distance of their masters in the Houses of Parliament and, thanks to Eurostar and Victoria station, within a few hours of the political world of Brussels.

Inside the conference suite men and women in dark suits milled around while earnest huddles of threes and fours were dotted here and there. To one side, tables and chairs were cubicled off by partitions and other groups sat in discussions. It was a room full of company directors, inventors, academicians and providers of funding, all hoping to benefit from each other.

'Can I have your name please?' One of a bevy of young people riffled through the name badges laid in order on the baize-covered table and found David's. She also handed over a thick folder of times, events and attendees.

'There's been no last minute changes to the running order and coffee's round to the right.'

'Thanks.'

David Bearing, fitted up with coffee, mingled through the crowd to see who was there, chatting to familiar faces and ending up in the side room allocated to displays. Baize-covered tables supported odd pieces of equipment while uninspiring wall posters and piles of literature showed red-hot developments that would save the world if only the exhibitors were to be believed and if only sponsors could be found to put up the small fortune needed to fuel them.

These exhibitors had already applied for and been granted initial government funding for their research, now they had to find other financial support to move into production with their ideas. They served to demonstrate publicly how well the government was helping industry. But these bit players probably never realised that the major projects and the big money were dealt out elsewhere and at government level. Secrets that were worth knowing were soon snaffled by state organisations and taken out of general circulation.

'Hello! How's life in the sticks?' came a jovial voice from behind David. 'Have you come down here to learn how to do it properly, then?'

It was Dr John Smithson, Professor of Chemistry at London's premier engineering university. He had come into the science of steel hardening from the chemistry side and would argue for hours on the merits of using chemicals compared to other methods.

Lazio Palfrey dismissed Smithson's research as cookery.

'All he needs is a bloody great cauldron to boil up his concoctions. Anyone can do that. He probably has three witches living in the department disguised as lab technicians. That'll be his secret weapon.'

But Smithson worked to a different agenda. A couple of years nearer retirement than Lazio, Smithson was also taking a quieter route through life. His work was not in direct competition with Lazio's but there was still rivalry between the two to be top in their field.

His sponsors were the large chemical producers keen to find new ways to use their products. At Burnstone, Lazio's sponsors were the steel manufacturers and merchants, keen to develop new and improved features to keep customers buying.

'If you'd ever care to venture north of Watford, you might find that Leicestershire is way ahead of you,' replied David. But John Smithson didn't rise to the bait, perhaps to the relief of Lazio's blood pressure had he known. He just enquired at what time David would spill the beans in his presentation.

'I'm next but one after you, and what are you going to tell us in this paper of yours?'

'We're announcing a couple of patents on plasma deposition and hoping to get some takers while I'm here today. We can do so much more with chemistry today now that electronic control can run the processes. High voltage discharges in a vacuum are producing hard finishes on steel that nobody has ever seen before.'

You should just see what we're doing, thought David, but instead he said, 'Well you should be OK, there seems to be quite a few faces from eastern Europe, I should think the chemical industry over there will be pleased for any new ideas it can get.'

Before John Smithson could ask what David would be announcing, one of the organisers came up to say they'd located the person he'd been looking for and Bearing was left again to his own devices. He finished wandering round the exhibits, chatting to people on the way to pick up any snippets he could about the latest trends in technology and the way industries were developing.

He availed himself of the buffet lunch, which was always traditional with sandwiches, chicken legs and snacks on offer. Passably well cooked, it was the more attractive because one could pick and peck as one fancied. He dallied over coffee intentionally so that he was one of the last in to the main conference room where presentations were to be made.

Choosing a back row seat in the corner, he could see who was taking notes and who was paying more than average interest to each speaker. Those were the people he would contact later to push his own university's facilities.

Although the steel group in the Combined Engineering School had plenty of sponsors for its research work, it was always good to have a few names on ice ready for when projects came to an end. He was also able to pass on contacts to his colleagues in other groups ready for when he needed a favour in return.

When John Smithson stood up, David noticed a small group of sallow faced men sit up a little straighter. From his corner he could see the high cheekbones that suggested they were from eastern Europe.

This was an interesting time for east west relations. Trade was opening up following the fall of the Berlin Wall over a decade before and eastern economies were improving. Companies now had a little money to spend on buying ideas from the west and it was becoming more popular for western companies to set up factories and offices in the east, not only for the low wages and rents, but to establish a foothold ready for when business volumes would increase.

Both steel and chemical production were big business in eastern countries. The first used virtually slave labour to produce low cost steel in high volume and the second thrived because factories were not subjected to the safety and environmental legislation that raised manufacturing costs for their western equivalents.

The people showing interest in Smithson's presentation could have been from either the steel or chemical industry. David Bearing would shortly find out.

When he came to deliver his presentation, he had the double task of delivering what he had to say and remembering who looked interested. It helped that many of them asked questions afterwards. David took particular pains to write down their names and details so he could follow up as many as possible later.

At the end of the session, David moved towards the small group he'd first noticed to collect their business cards. He presented his and was surprised when one asked where Lazio was.

'I always notice him,' said Sergei Danelski. 'He is a lot more colourful than my countrymen and he does take up rather a lot of space.'

David burst out laughing at both the image and the simple naivety of the comment. 'He's very busy right now, we've a heavy workload on, and so I'm not here for the hard sell this year. But we've still room for any projects you may have in mind.'

Danelski took his elbow and moved over to the side of the room.

'Does that mean we can expect some new technology to appear before long, then?'

That took the wind out of David's sails. He quickly revised his opinion of the man's naivety.

'We're always working on new ideas, we have to; what have you got in mind?'

'Oh! Nothing, nothing. It's just unusual for Lazio to be away. One wonders if he might let something slip if he were here, he has a fine reputation to maintain, you know. But, seriously, when you do get something to offer, let me know first. You don't always have to go through the expected channels, you know, there's no point in people taking ten per cent off you when they haven't earned it.'

'Can't agree more, but are you looking for anything in particular? Your card says industrial consultant, does that mean you are a free agent?'

'Agent? Agent? I'm not an agent. I just have all sorts of contacts in eastern Europe who can pay good money nowadays for new technology. Now I must go, but keep in touch!'

Before David could explain that a free agent had nothing to do with secret police, not in Britain anyway, Danelski was lost in the throng that was leaving the conference room.

He moved through the thinning crowd, quickly caught up with another couple of contacts to exchange business cards and started his trek back to Leicestershire.

* * * * * * * *

24

Next morning, Lazio had a mid-morning appointment with the dean to go through the John Fleming accident report.

'Want a brandy to go with that coffee?' Alistair Wyatt asked Lazio. 'Nothing Italian, I'm afraid, but an excellent Armagnac,' Which he proved by pouring two doubles.

'So, what's the latest on Fleming - what's he going to cost us?'

Nice to know the priorities in this department, thought Lazio, but he said 'Nothing by the look of it. There seems to be no after effects of any sort whatsoever. He didn't damage himself when he fell and he's keen to continue working with the machine. We're working on a programme to keep the beam enclosed within the machine, we're measuring how far the radiation can travel and we've put some safety measures in place so it shouldn't happen again.'

'Has the word compensation been mentioned?'

'No.'

'Has he been to a solicitor?'

'Not that I know of, I think he would have mentioned it if he was thinking that way. We've known each other for a long time and I think he regards it as just a hazard of a job that is always ahead of known science.'

'Could his blackout have been caused by a medical condition that he didn't know he had and it was just coincidence that it showed up as he was loading the machine?'

Lazio warmed his brandy and considered the way the conversation was going.

'A possibility.'

'He's old enough to have medical problems that a young man might not have?'

'Yes.'

'And this work on testing and improving the machine that you mention in the report, you say you are looking at it now.

'Yes.'

'But I am sure it was thought about as part of the project before the Fleming thing?'

'Well, I suppose it would have been mentioned.'

'Yes, yes,' said Alistair testily, 'but it wasn't stimulated by the accident, was it?'

'Well...'

'Well nothing, I'm telling you it wasn't.'

'OK' said Lazio, 'It wasn't'

He shifted uneasily in his seat. Double brandies were fine at ten o'clock on a Sunday morning with the newspaper to hand and a little light gardening before lunch. But they dulled the reflexes for an intellectual duel.

'That's right. So can you send over some documentation that shows the work was being considered from very early on? A project schedule would do, or your preliminary notes on the machine's design. Take a few days to sort it out, but I would like some written documentation to show that we had all aspects covered well before the accident. You can't be too careful in these matters and I need that sort of documentation as insurance.'

'It shall be done,' said Lazio, not particularly comfortable with creating documents after an event. Drafting the document was no problem, it was sorting out the computer to change the dates on its internal records. That was something he couldn't ask just anyone to do under the circumstances.

'Well done,' said Alistair, 'Anything else to discuss?'

'I have to talk over with you my plans for launching the machine commercially. I think that will need a limited company setting up, but I'll sort out your documentation first.'

Alistair rose to indicate the end of the meeting.

'Good, I think this machine has some exciting possibilities,' he said, 'so keep it going,' And he guided Lazio to the door.

Turning back to his drinks cabinet, he took out a small funnel, poured his untouched brandy back into the decanter and pressed the intercom switch for his secretary.

'Jenny, will you send an email to Professor Palfrey, please. Confirm our meeting and say I look forward to his project documentation in the next few days as discussed. Thanks. Oh! By the way, don't send it right away, wait until about four o'clock and send me a copy. And could you bring me a fresh coffee, please'

Devious to the end, Wyatt wanted the email to emphasis what might have been diluted by the double brandy he'd fed Lazio. Until the effects wore off, he could imagine an email being accidentally deleted, filed or forgotten if it had been sent right away. He made a note in his diary for a few days forward to check that Palfrey had responded.

* * * * * * * *

'So how was London?' asked Lazio later as he sat with David Bearing in his office.

'Busy and grimy as ever. Madeleine says that if I worked there full time, I'd need twice the number of shirts I've got at the moment. Leicester may have its pollution problems but collars and cuffs stay clean for a lot longer, so I suppose that helps the lungs as well.

'On the technical front, there seems to be few really exciting developments at the moment. Unless the presenters have got secrets up their sleeves, their research is evolutionary rather than revolutionary.

'Smithson is still ploughing his chemical furrow. He's made some advances in plasma deposition but the technology needs vacuum chambers, very high voltages and virtually a laboratory environment and I can't see it becoming a main stream commercial technology. When you look at the simplicity of our set up, the two approaches to hardening just don't compare. By the way, I've got a copy of his latest paper for you.'

'Well done,' said Lazio, 'I shall enjoy reading that. Let's hope he doesn't have a sudden change of heart and try a new approach, though. We don't want any competition from his department. And what about the steel business in general, what did you pick up there?'

'Your old friend Sergei Danelski was there and asked after you. He seemed a bit keener than usual to see what new ideas we have coming forward. He seemed to think that if you were too busy to be there, then something big must be brewing. I hope I persuaded him otherwise.'

'He's a crafty bugger, one of those people you can never quite fathom out. He seems to have a finger in every pie that's going - provided some cash comes out of it. Did you get anything out of him?'

'He says that, in general, eastern European companies seem to have more money to spend than last year. A number of countries still depend heavily on steel production so it might be worth making some advances in that direction, if only to get a foothold at this stage.'

'The opportunities certainly seem better than here,' mused Lazio, 'perhaps it's an area of development we ought to give some thought to. Mull it over yourself and let's put some plans together. Do we want some formal market research, or could we build up a database of contacts ourselves? I'll have a look at our budget. With the western steel industry in its current state, just about any other market could prove more fruitful for research projects.

'But first, can we go back to Fleming's accident. I've just had a session with the dean, who seems to get more devious by the day. He wants some documentation to say that we had thought through the potential for accidents with the hardening machine and we had discussed safety with everyone who might come into contact with it right at the start of the project. He's shit scared that Fleming will want some horrendous amount of compensation because of this business.

'If you could change your report on the safety measures so it looks as though it was done very early on, that would be a start. The crucial thing is to make sure that the computerised date and time stamp shows an early date. That's something I can't do but it shouldn't be a problem for you.'

'I can do that OK,' said David, 'But we're starting to get into some murky waters if Fleming does take the huff. Just think it through. Alistair gets a report that carries your authority, so he's totally in the clear on the safety issue. But Fleming's never been warned at all about any possible hazards from the machine, and, if push comes to shove and his version is believed, where do you stand? And me for that matter? We could be finished just to protect the dean.'

'Oh Gawd!' said Lazio, twisting in his chair. 'Bloody machine. I told you it was going to give me nightmares.'

David ignored the outburst.

'Have you got any sort of record of the meeting with the dean?'

'No, I didn't take any notes. And the bastard fed me a double brandy, which doesn't help my recollections. Hang on though, he sent me an email afterwards to make sure I wouldn't forget to do the report. But I deleted that.'

'That's no problem, Deleted stuff is kept on the main computer for about a month before being archived for ever in a hard disk in some dank basement. I can soon pull it out, it could be useful evidence if things get nasty. But if we word our report carefully, we should be able to forestall any problems.'

'Great. Can I ask you to do that as a matter of urgency then?'

'Sure, if there's nothing else you want just now, I can do it this afternoon.'

'If you would, please, that'll be one less nightmare.'

After David had left his office, Lazio mulled over the conversation. Whilst he looked forward to reading Professor Smithson's paper, he wasn't totally happy that David Bearing had got hold of a copy so quickly. He knew that important technical papers are published sooner or later, either in a learned journal or at a conference, and the information then becomes public knowledge. But he couldn't understand why Smithson should have given David a copy right away.

Sometimes it happened if a professor wanted to dishearten other researchers by showing his lead publicly. But he knew Smithson of old, and he wouldn't play games like that.

And David showed perhaps a bit too much familiarity with the university's computer system. He was, after all a lecturer on steel and had no reason to get involved in the inner workings of unrelated departments such as admin and IT.

After a few more minutes' contemplation, he picked up the phone.

'Hallo, can I speak to Saxon Palfrey, please.'

* * * * * * * *

Chapter 3

After observing the Technology Transfer Days, Sergei Danelski and the group flew back to Khazatan. Avoiding their local airline, they opted for the greater comfort and safety of British Airways.

'You won't get me buying a ticket and then having to pay for fuel as well,' said Danelski, referring to the number of times that Aeroflot's planes ran short of fuel and had to break their journey to top up. Inevitably, that meant a whip-round amongst the passengers to buy the fuel.

'Anyway, you can't get that money back on expenses. Those admin types stuck in their offices don't believe it happens, so it's lost money.'

Danelski was one of those mysterious figures that eastern Europe seems to breed quite regularly. He probably did not appear so to those born to the culture but what he actually did for a living and to whom he reported could never be properly fathomed by anyone in the west. Appearances on this side by comparison are clearly defined - even though that appearance is a false front.

He had been employed as a manager in an engineering firm near Moscow but after the fall of communism had returned to his home country of Khazatan. The firm had produced components for the Russian army and had given Danelski an insight into government and military workings. The job also involved a lot of travel, visiting military sites to check on their needs for spare parts.

Danelski was astute enough to collect a file of names of people he visited and, now, his wealth of contacts and freelance status made him invaluable to western companies that wanted to gain a foothold in the country.

They were gearing up for the new opportunities they hoped to see in eastern Europe and needed all the help they could get to avoid being strangled by local red tape. Danelski eased the way for these companies, but at a price. Now he was well cushioned in life by the backhanders that resulted.

'I think I've seen more potential business on this trip than any other. What about you?' Sergei asked his travelling companion.

'Yes, but business for whom? Capitalist companies, Khazatan industry or ourselves?' He laughed heartily at his own joke, knowing full well that western businesses wouldn't stand a chance of getting into the country without substantial payments to people such as him and Danelski.

'Did I ever tell you how I helped an American engineering firm get settled into Dbrov, right down in the south?' said Sergei. 'It was beautiful. I was one step ahead of them all the way. I managed to hear about them right at the start when they were looking for a cheap factory, thanks to one of their loud mouthed directors.

'They were as naive as a bunch of new born babies. They thought they knew it all, but they didn't get very far. Every office they had to deal with, I had got there first. Everything would have been held up with some delay or other, but I was the big man when one word and a cash transaction got them the permissions they were wanting.

'And you should have seen the money they had to spend, and all in dollars as well, none of your rouble rubbish. Mind you it cost me dear to sort out the officials in all the offices. They're a switched on bunch and knew the financial score from the outset.

'Now, the firm can't help but do well. They're paying peanuts to our people. The factory came dead cheap and I got them some machinery for next to nothing as well. They ship the parts back to the States and sell them like they're home made. The customer's none the wiser and the profit is huge.

'But I have got something out of them in return. They're financing a new school and the regular wage packets are something the local workers haven't seen in decades. What the government boys will get from them is anyone's guess.'

'So what are you doing next?'

'Well, I can't retire on what I'm paid by the Khazatan Research Institute for this visit to London, that's for sure. But there's a fair few companies I need to talk to now. They'll pay for some market research, if it's only to impress their shareholders that they want to expand. And one or two could get serious - then I might be able to retire. I mean, look at the money floating about in London and just think how far it would go down there.'

Danelski indicated the villages they were flying over.

'What could you buy down there if you were paid fifty thousand pounds a year?'

'Just about the whole bloody lot.'

'Precisely. But that's because you're a local. If you were a westerner, the price would be way up and you'd hardly get anything. But you're stuck because you'll never earn that amount of money in fifty years. So the trick is to act as a local front for the incomers and get the best of both worlds.'

His companion reflected on that thought as the seat belt warning lights came on and the stewardess announced they were twenty minutes from touchdown.

Danelski's first job on landing was to report to his current master at the Research Institute, a technical organisation closely connected to the government. It included a large engineering complex and was able both to research and to manufacture goods for the army. It also serviced the secret service and any other outfit that required hardware being supplied discreetly.

One section was funded by the country's steel makers to search the world for innovations and to vet them for commercial use. With his knowledge of western business, a thick book of contacts, an engineering background and his freelance status, Sergei Danelski was the ideal go-between.

But the building did not start to compare with its western equivalents. It was bleak and uninspiring. It hadn't seen a coat of paint in years and the glass hadn't seen a window cleaner for the same length of time.

Rusting engineering parts lay around the yard at the back, with frayed and holed tarpaulins covering what had been the more valuable parts. Piles of old bricks and rubble showed that the building had been modified at some time way back when.

Many harsh winters had seen off the tarmac road through the compound. Although compound was now too grand a title for the site. The chain link fencing had been carted off where it had some scrap value; the rest hung, rust red, on drunkenly tilted posts. Deeply potholed, the road was now really no more than a cart track.

Danelski picked up his car from the parking lot for the few minutes drive to the Institute, carefully negotiating the potholed drive when he arrived. The main door clicked open just as his hand reached for the intercom button and a secretary was waiting by reception.

The building may have seen better days, but the surveillance system was definitely state of the art.

'Mr Krachov is awaiting you,' she said as she led him towards the offices. 'Did you have a good flight?'

'Excellent, thank you.'

'Good. But be careful and talk nicely to Mr Krachov. He has a habit of refusing to pay British Airways ticket prices when Aeroflot are so much cheaper.'

'Fine.'

Danelski accepted without question that his debriefer had been updated with his movements, probably on an hourly basis. The country's security service was obviously as good as the Institute's surveillance system, he thought. If he wasn't careful, he'd have to part with one of his bottles of twenty year old Islay malt whisky to keep precious Mr Krachov happy.

After an initial preamble Danelski listed the people he had spoken to in London and outlined his interest in them.

'Regarding the steel business, something is definitely going on at Burnstone University,' he said. 'The engineering department leader, Professor Palfrey, was not there, which was unusual, and his second in command didn't convince me why. Their presentation was surprisingly bland. Most times they like to drop some sort of bombshell, it's in Palfrey's flamboyant nature to make a splash, but not this time. Either he's ill, losing his touch, about to retire or is cooking up something really big.'

'I also spoke to Professor Smithson of Empire University. He's got a couple of new patents on plasma deposition that he's wanting to sell. He says they can do so much more with chemistry today now that electronic control can run the processes. That's maybe something we should be looking at. The whole report is on this disk, do you want to check it while I'm here.'

Krachov ran it up on his computer.

'Looks good,' he said, 'you've done well.'

'And here's my invoice.'

Krachov pursed his lips as his finger ran past the amount for air tickets. He went to his wall safe and was obviously counting out notes.

Do I bring out the whisky in my briefcase? thought Danelski, I can't come back later and offer it after I've been paid.

He decided to open the envelope that was now offered to him while he was still in the office.

'It's all there,' growled Krachov, 'including your British air fare - for this time.'

With a brief 'Thank you. Good to do business with you,' a relieved Danelski scarpered.

* * * * * * * *

Krachov circulated the Danelski report around the technical and economic committees at the Institute prior to the next monthly meeting. But he discussed it in detail with the organisation's main director. Khazatan was still learning its role in the wider world now it was no longer part of the Soviet Union and it had a long way to go before it could compete with the well-established western countries.

'We have so many opportunities and leads here that it will be difficult to prioritise our next action,' he told the director, Vladimir Arbatov. 'It's the usual problem: our engineers are very well trained and can match the ability of those in the west. But their employers never have enough money for them to implement their ideas. So we're still lagging because we can't get the experience of commercial development.'

'What do you suggest?' asked Arbatov.

'We've got to continue our policy of working with western companies so we can raise our income, expertise and confidence.

But we must still watch that we don't get tied in too tightly so we can't get out and go it alone when the time is right.'

They both knew that co-operation with Europe had plenty to offer: military protection through NATO and commercial protection through the European Union; money would become available to build new roads and to resurface existing ones; and, in their wake, would come the multinational companies building offices, factories and warehouses.

Expansion of the local gas, water and electricity utilities would all be financed by Europe to meet the new demands. In fact, outsiders would help supply all the ingredients to support the country's economic development.

But Khazatan was not totally dependent on this help. Its steel industry was a good source of income for the country. It may have been based on near-slave labour; it may have been using equipment that was prehistoric; and its health and safety considerations were minimal. But its contribution to the national economy was very important. It was looking for new products to increase its income. And that would mean more research work and more money for the Institute.

'We've still got to get the message across that we can't copy western ideas without regard for their patents and copyright laws. It's not that we could be prosecuted for pinching their ideas, we can soon screw out of any of that sort of thing, but we have got to trade with these people and their friends. We're on our own, commercially speaking, there's no mother Russia to support us now.'

Krachov was a realist.

Arbatov still harboured the hope that the Russian union could be rebuilt one day.

The two reflected the split in outlook that still existed throughout eastern Europe. While the public face of communism had been toppled, the private face still existed. Although those in power had been replaced, the old guard had not gone away, they had just gone underground. They were employed by companies and organisations that were faithful to the old way of life; or they were still in government, quietly working, quietly awaiting a new call to arms.

The west was trying to capitalise on the unsettled situation by offering aid. If it could capture the loyalty of eastern European countries, then Russia would have no chance of rebuilding its empire. Financially, that country could not match what was on offer from western companies.

Because the Khazatan steel industry was so important to the country, it had a strong say in many matters and was able to send a representative to the Institute's strategy meetings. He was first in when the cost of buying-in the ideas that had been on show in London came up on the agenda.

'Mr Chairman, do we know how much Professor Smithson wants for the patents he mentioned at the London meetings?' asked Alexander Kasvanov, the committee member for the steel producers association.

'Our contact reports that it's a case for negotiation. Smithson hopes that whoever buys the patent will give him the work to continue its development. He'll want to extract the maximum amount of income from it,' replied Vladimir Arbatov, chairman of the committee by virtue of his role as the chief director of the Institute.

'If we're interested, would it be possible to offer his department more research work? If we offer a package deal, it might cost less overall than just buying the patent rights,' said Kasvanov.

'Well, the British government has allowed universities to take some research commissions from Russia, so I don't think it could say no in principle to us. The cost of the patent rights will obviously be higher if that's all we take.

'In view of the huge market for hardened steel, there will be large profits from using the latest technology so I propose we ask for London station to get someone to visit the patent office and look at all the patent details. Then we can assess its value and work out our own figure. But stress that they must go in person and not request the details by post. Don't forget we've had doctored documents in the past when the patent people realised who was asking for information.

'And what about this paragraph on Professor Palfrey? There's a hint of something going on, should we investigate him a bit further as well?'

The steel industry representative was keen to extract the maximum from the meeting.

'Let's try,' said Arbatov. 'If anyone is doing anything revolutionary, it will be him. We can probably get someone with an engineering background in there so they understand what's going on. Perhaps someone posing as a technical journalist doing a piece on Palfrey. The report suggests his ego will love that and he'll give all sorts away. And, as a bonus, university security is non-existent as far as our boys are concerned. '

There seemed to be an air of general approval around the table.

'Will you propose that Smithson and Palfrey are investigated further, then?'

'Yes.'

'A seconder, please?'

A hand was raised.

'All those in favour?'

All hands went up.

'Thank you, where's our government liaison officer lurking?'

'Here, Mr Chairman,' said Leonid Lebdev from way down the table.

'Work for you then,' and he passed down the table a file.

'There's a copy of the report from our agent to give you the background on these two bods. The research director here will tell you later what information he wants and then it's the usual business of persuading your people to get some action going. Good luck and make sure you've something to report on at the next meeting.

'Next item?'

* * * * * * * *

While eastern European steel companies wanted to advance and were looking for new ideas to increase their markets and turnover, those in the west also wanted new ideas, but for a different reason - to pull them out of the state of recession that had beset the whole industry for a number of years.

New plastics, greater use of aluminium and more steel being recycled meant the market for new metal had shrunk dramatically.

Steel from Japan and eastern Europe, sometimes being dumped below cost price, had also helped depress the market.

Early in the year, while the Khazatan Research Institute had been planning its London visit, the economic situation had been discussed by a British company, Glen Parva Steel Producers. At the March board meeting, plans had been discussed ready for the annual general meeting in April.

'It is vital to show the shareholders that we are making efforts to get the most out of the existing situation,' said the chairman, Charles Thurmaston. 'With the government making no real efforts to intervene and stop the dumping of cheap steel, we are left on our own to stand or fall. If we sit still, our share price will fall through the floor.'

At the AGM, the shareholders had backed the board's strategy for the future and now, in mid-May, it had to start and put its ideas into practice.

Once the routine business of the board meeting was out of the way, Thurmaston asked the sales and marketing director to outline the plan to increase turnover.

'Firstly, the financial director and I have agreed a new pay structure with the sales team and this is stronger on incentive payments than before. It also extends to the office staff. If they can pull together as a team, they can make a great deal of money.

'They have already asked for some training courses to help them perform better, so that's a good sign. There's also been some suggestions about revising the admin side of sales so we can get quotes out faster and have a better mechanism for chasing them up later.

'The new sales brochure will be printed in the next couple of weeks and this highlights the bigger range of steels we're now offering plus the tailored blanks service. Now the laser welder and cutter have been installed, we can supply steel cut to size and with varying thickness.

'The car industry is using the technique in doors and body panels so they get the strength where they want it, but each piece is lighter than using the same thickness of steel across the whole panel. I'm very hopeful it will do well for us.

'We're working on these initiatives now and there are some others to come when these are established so I am hopeful for a good year.'

And Alan Birstall closed his folder to the sound of murmurs of approval around the table.

The chairman thanked him and turned to the next item on the agenda.

'This is where I get to sound off again, I'm afraid,' he said with a smile, 'but it's an idea I shall be handing over if it's agreed.

'As some of you know, I have been discussing a plan informally with a number of people and now I think it's time to move it forward. The principle is that while Alan is strengthening our position by the usual means of increasing market share and so on, we take other steps - ones that will weaken the competition.

'Investors in the steel business will then see that Glen Parva is the place for their money and shareholders in other steel firms will be tempted away from their present investment. That will put us in a very strong position to make a takeover bid for some of these other outfits. Their shareholders will force the directors to accept our bid, and our stronger share price means we can pay whatever is necessary.

'The way we weaken the competition is to buy up the places where research is being carried out. This will give us a monopoly of new ideas so the company becomes known for being first with the latest innovations.

'University departments are generating the greatest amount of new thinking just now because commercial companies have closed their research and development departments to cut costs. They are outsourcing the work and the universities have most of it. I'm not sure if they realise it, but, at the moment, the academics probably know more about steel science than we do. They've been able to expand their knowledge, buy a lot of new equipment and indulge in some futuristic research as their income has jumped in the last few years.

'If, by fair means or foul, and it may well have to be the latter, we can buy up a university department, then we will receive the benefit of its expertise, get our own research work done at a lower rate and, most importantly, deny the facilities to our competitors.

'That puts the ball in your court, Geoff, as technical director, to decide which university is right to go for. And in your court, Bill, to decide how much to pay, so would you like to continue first?'

'Yes, thank you, Charles,'

Bill Oadby was ideally placed for the sort of in-fighting that the chairman had in mind. After many years with a leading accountancy firm, where he had worked on many takeovers, mergers and buy outs, he had seen how companies worked at first hand. Eventually, he could sit on the sidelines no longer and moved into industry to try out his knowledge for himself.

Glen Parva Steel Producers seemed to have an aggressive set of directors and the company was moving ahead in what was a difficult industry, so when it advertised for a new financial director, Bill was very keen to get the job.

Having nursed the accounts for a couple of years, it seemed his time had now arrived.

'The beauty of this plan is that it does not affect profitability and will not weaken our balance sheet. Whatever we pay will show up as an asset and we can lose the actual amounts under the headings of goodwill, intellectual property rights and purchase of capital goods.

'These are areas where we already spend so it will not be possible for a shareholder to work out exactly what the plan will have cost. That will stop any hard questions from the awkward squad at the next AGM. But the plan will significantly boost our potential turnover and that will send the share price way up.

'In addition, we can apply for government and European funding for specific research projects once the plan is under way. There are a number of schemes where it will come in on a fifty fifty basis and that will make our own money go much further.

'Once we've introduced the plan to our stockbrokers and word gets around, the shareholders of other steel companies will want to come on board very fast. But, as you say, Mr Chairman, which university do we go for?'

40

'Would you like to come in on that one?' Charles asked Geoff Aylestone.

'Yes. Thank you. If we're aiming for top slot, then we've got to go for the top department and that's at Burnstone Uni. The professor in charge there, Lazio Palfrey, is a bit of a character but he's very forward thinking. He sits on all sorts of committees and has his ear very close to the ground.

'We've used the uni from time to time and the results have been very good but they've been pricey. I think that option will take us forward fastest and give us the greatest credibility in the steel business.

'But I'd also consider John Smithson at Empire Uni. We've used him most but his view is more conservative and he opts for development of traditional thinking. So while the research work is good and solid he doesn't quite have the pzazz of Palfrey.'

'I think it's the pzazz we've got to go for first,' said Charles Thurmaston. 'Does anyone else have a view?'

Bill Charnwood, a non-executive director, raised his hand.

'The stock market works more on sentiment than practicalities and that's where we want the results first. We can worry about producing the actual benefits after that. We could also investigate Smithson but I'm not sure if it would be wise to commit money in two different directions at once. There's also the problem of trying to manage several ideas at the same time and we don't want a management overload that means we don't succeed.

'I think we could finance two ventures,' replied Bill Oadby, 'But I agree with you that it would be more prudent to go step by step, on the management aspect as well. We don't want our stockbroker to think we're in a rush, that's fatal. He's got to see a planned strategy where we don't fully commit to step two until step one shows it is delivering.'

'Alan, putting on your marketing hat, what are your comments?'

'I'm all in favour of the plan, Charles, I'd like to be in on the early meetings to see what's on offer at Burnstone so I can see how the venture might develop. In the meantime, I'd like to change our PR agency to one that is stronger on the financial and political

41

side. Not that this plan will get political, at least I hope not, but the guys I'd like to use have the right mind set for pushing our case out to shareholders and financial institutions. Our present agency is fine on product launches but we need more than that now.'

'Fine,' said Charles, 'So how do we make the first move? Do you go in with the financial angle, Bill, or should Geoff make the first approach as this is a technical business?'

'I'd go for offering a financial package to the dean first,' said Bill Oadby. 'I think he'd be a softer touch when faced with a handout than the department would. At Palfrey's level they're always afraid of losing their independence. But if the dean is behind us, Palfrey really has no choice.'

'And you, Geoff?'

'I agree. But it would be difficult for me to go in first. Palfrey and I know each other pretty well, we're both on the Steel Industry Technical Committee and the government's think tank for the steel sector and we cross paths at association meetings and seminars. I wouldn't like him to think I've gone behind his back and so upset our relationship.

'I also have an understanding, shall I say, as some of you know, with his sidekick, a chap called David Bearing. He's a fund of useful information and I wouldn't want to antagonise him at all. But I'm happy to come in once negotiations are under way. We'll have to work together afterwards anyway.'

Bill Charnwood put his hand up. 'Can I propose, Mr Chairman, that you make the overture to the dean on a general, off the record, basis and we decide next action after that?'

'Yes, I'm happy to take that route. Any other ideas?'

A couple of shaken heads but no other response.

'Well, let's have a seconder and away we go.'

Bill Oadby duly obliged, all the directors were in favour, and the meeting moved on to the next item.

* * * * * * * *

Chapter 4

'Hallo, Saxon, Lazio here. Have you got a few minutes?'

'Sure,' came the reply. 'What can I do for you?'

'You know we were talking when you last visited about this new company I'd like to set up, well, things are moving forward and one thing I'd like to do soon is to improve the computer security system here. There will be a lot of confidential stuff moving about between me, the dean, the accounts department and the commercial manager because the uni has to be involved in new company start-ups.

'The problem is that there is very little security on the internal computer network. There's plenty between the uni and the outside world, but I'm more concerned about an insider hacking into my personal system. You know what these students are like, anything for devilment,' He lied.

'Well, that's solved quite simply,' said Saxon, 'just get your IT department to install a firewall around the terminals that you want protected. There's plenty of software that will do the job.'

'I thought there would be, but I'd want it installed by a completely independent person - would you do it for me?'

'I could, but it would mean getting into the main server and that would need the co-operation of your IT manager. And, generally, we don't like odd private systems cluttering up our servers. If your place is anything like mine, it's bad enough having to cope with the weird and wonderful alterations that management wants without having a mass of private systems to interface with.

'You could put what we call an intelligent node between your department and the rest of the university. I could probably do that without anyone knowing, although it might come to light sometime and that could be awkward for you.'

'But that still leaves a lot of computer terminals in the department that could be used for hacking,' said Lazio. 'I suppose I just want my own terminal, and my secretary, Ann's, to be really secure.'

'That simplifies the job. The two terminals are in adjoining rooms, aren't they?'

'Yes.'

'Right. What I could do is put a small server in your office, connect your two terminals to it and then plug it into the main network. The server would be what we call transparent, so there would be full communications between you two and the rest of the uni as you have at the moment. But when you wanted privacy, your work would be stored in the new server and not on the uni system.

'Only you and Ann could access those documents and databases. But you could still send them to whoever you wanted without the main system grabbing them and putting them into storage. It does mean you will have to back up your own system yourself because it is independent of the main system. And if a hacker knew where your emails had been sent, they could hack into the receiver's storage area and pick them up from that. But there again, you can't look after other people's security for them.'

'That sounds fair enough to me,' said Lazio.

'Would you like me to order some kit and come up one weekend when no-one's about if you'd like it to be that secret.'

'Yes, please. You'd get paid, of course. The department's got a decent budget and I authorise special payments. I'd need some sort of invoice but it can be made out for any sort of engineering equipment.'

'I'm sure I can fix that. But, first, can I get you to draw up a list of the things that you want the firewall in the server to keep out and what sort of communications you want to allow through. There's a lot to be considered and if you draft a proposal, it'll help you think things through. Email it to me at home, then it won't get lost at work.'

'Right. Thanks a lot, Saxon, that's a great relief. Talk to you later.'

Lazio was bouncing as he waltzed into Ann's office.

'Just off to see James Russell and then lunch. See you later.'

And he was gone.

He was about to steamroller into the commercial manager's office when Russell opened the door and was nearly flattened by Lazio's momentum.

'Whoa there!' he laughed, 'that could have been fatal!'

'Sorry,' said Lazio, 'Lot to do.'

'Well, I'm off to lunch so you can't do much here, are you coming down to the refectory?'

'Yes, it's on my list of things to do.'

'You put eating on a list, do you? I can't imagine you in particular would ever forget.'

Lazio sniffed obviously and disdainfully.

Gotcha, thought Russell. But he said 'Anyway what were you coming to see me about?'

'Setting up my new company. I have to talk to you and the dean about the scheme in principle before I can start spending money and getting things moving. He's free at ten on Thursday morning, how about you?'

Russell consulted his pocket book.

'Yes. I can be there.'

'Great. Thanks.'

Further conversation was halted as the two approached the refectory. A rush of students was building up and several obviously had designs on the Professor.

Lazio shouted over their heads. 'See you in the morning, then.'

And James left Lazio's grey head and flash of bow tie to cope with the students around him.

* * * * * * * *

Feeling somewhat like the pied piper of Hamelin, Lazio gradually freed himself from the crowd, picked and pecked at the buffet and took his tray to the comparative calm of top table.

At one end was a huddle of lecturers from the biology department. He saw an opportunity.

'Hi! Richard, mind if I join you?'

'Sure,' said Professor Richard Daly, head of the biology department, with some surprise. 'But I'm not sure if us biologists should be seen in the company of mere engineers, you know.'

'Cheeky beggar. It's you who should be honoured,' said Lazio. 'Anyway, I've come to see if you've any brains worth picking.'

'Oh, Oh. Fighting talk, eh? Just because you're bigger than us. No matter, we're a kindly bunch. Pull up a couple of chairs and sit down.'

Lazio pulled out his white handkerchief and waved it in the air. 'Truce, truce. I come on a serious matter,' he laughed.

'Do all Italians regularly carry a white flag?' asked one of the group with a big grin on his face.

'That's not funny.'

'Well you started it.'

'And I'm ending it, OK?'

The group fell into an embarrassed silence as Lazio's face flushed with anger.

Daly broke the awkwardness, 'To what do we owe this unexpected visit, then?'

'Well, if you can be serious for a moment, I'd like to know if any research has been carried out into the effects of very high frequency radio waves on the human body.'

'How high a frequency?'

'Well above the gigahertz microwave frequencies - into the quintahertz range.'

'I've not heard of anything like that,' said Daly after some thought. 'Anyone else know of anything?'

'Not at that frequency,' said one. 'We all know what happens when the human body is exposed to radar, it's the same as your Sunday joint in the microwave: the atoms become excited, move faster, generate heat and that cooks you.'

'But what happens when the atoms move many times faster?' asked Lazio. 'Could they become jammed together and turn flexible material into solid?'

The table was quiet with thought.

'And if that happened, would the material then be preserved rather than cooked?'

'That is a possibility,' said Daly. 'And when the radio waves were switched off, the material would immediately return to its original state without damage.'

'You could then preserve humans without freezing them,' came one suggestion.

'But what about the nervous system. We don't know how that would respond to such a high frequency,' said another.

'Anyway,' said Daly. 'What's this all about? Is Combined Engineering going to develop a death ray?'

'I don't think so,' said Lazio. 'We're a bit more realistic than that, thank you. I'm looking at using radiation to harden the surface of steel. We're succeeding, but I'm not totally sure why. Our chief theory is that the radiation compresses the orbit of the atoms, making the material harder because it is denser. It only works at quintahertz frequencies, though. But the material doesn't expand out again once the radiation is removed.

'I just wondered if there might be a common link between the behaviour of living and inorganic materials that you biologists might know about. We're also looking at safety of the technology. What happens if a human gets in the way of the radiation?'

'We could hazard a guess but, in all honesty, I don't think anyone will have an answer you could trust. The physicists are only just researching tera frequencies so anything higher is ten years away yet at least. But your technology certainly seems to be in the realms of the possible. Your best bet is to talk over the idea with someone at the American space agency, for example. They're always into weird and wonderful ideas that are light years away from reality.'

Lazio let the implied slur on his own research pass.

'OK. Well thanks for the input. Can I get anyone a coffee?'

'No, thanks,' said Daly. 'We're off to a departmental meeting now and there's percolated to be had there. It's somewhat hotter than you get here, and better flavour. But if I come across anything about very high frequency radiation I'll let you know.'

Lazio was tempted to say that it must be Italian coffee they were going to have, but he decided there had been enough inter-departmental rivalry and just thanked the group for their time.

Over his own coffee, he mulled over the conversation with the biologists. It was encouraging except for that sarcastic remark about a death ray. He'd been working on a very practical level with his steel hardening, but that comment brought in the realms of science fiction. But John Fleming? What had actually happened inside his body? Lazio was very pensive as he walked back to his office.

* * * * * * * *

In the dean's office on Thursday morning Lazio was sat with Alistair Wyatt and James Russell - but no brandy this time, he noted.

'Can we start from the top?' asked Alistair. 'James and I know that you want to start a spin out company to develop and sell your quintahertz machine. And James understands that it will need funding. But can we go back to the concept. How did that come about?'

'About three years ago, we were asked by the Ministry of Defence telecommunications section to find out the best way to machine a material called terratanium. It is hugely expensive and very hard. It conducts electricity but is an insulator at very high frequencies. The combination is unique. The nearest alternative is a light metal that has little mechanical strength.

'Terratanium has been known about for some twenty years, but no-one could think of an application for it. Today, as radio frequencies have risen, the metal is ideal for microwave antennae. I won't bore you with that side of things but when our client realised what he'd got hold of, he quickly took all the research back in-house and I heard no more of it. Obviously highly secret.

'Anyway, during our summer sort out in the lab, I found a couple of samples that had been forgotten. When I had some spare time, I put one on a milling machine to see how far the material could be worked before it became mechanically weak.

'I was able to go a long way and it set my mind thinking. It is well known that electronic radiation can harden up metals like steel. But with the microwave guide I had re-worked, I could produce radiation of a much higher frequency than ever before.

48

Well off the scale of the test meter we had used in the lab, in fact. So I called it quintahertz, as mega, giga and terahertz frequencies are already being used.

'In my spare time I built a radiation transmitter from what I had learned during the MoD project. It hardened a small sample of steel better than any other method I knew. So I machined the microwave guide a bit further, increased the power and now I can harden pieces of a commercial size.

'The results are many times better than any other method, and at much lower cost. The key benefit is that cheap steel can be made to appear like top quality stuff because the surface is so hard. There's less friction when parts rub together, they last longer and the idea will make millions of pounds for steel producers and engineering companies. With the steel industry in such a parlous state around the world, companies will be queuing up to buy the machine.

'So the question is: where do I go from here? The machine we have now has been built in my spare time and with my own money. Obtaining more terratanium cost me an arm and a leg, for example. So I'd like to maintain a financial and operational interest in its future.'

'That's all very well but you can't have control of a company and expect others to put in major funding,' said Alistair, 'There's always risks present. Look at safety, for example, what's the score there?'

He obviously still had John Fleming's accident in mind.

'We're taking a two-pronged approach right now before we do any more development. First is a redesign of the control system and the mechanical protection so any operator or bystander is fully protected because the machine can't run until all the safety measures are in place. Then we will run a series of tests to measure radiation leakage, if any, at a number of frequencies and at different distances from the machine. The difficulty is that no-one has yet designed any test equipment to cover what the machine does and we're having to modify what we've already got.'

'Is that an insuperable problem?'

'I don't think so. It should just be an extension of known theory.'

'But it might give you another product to sell in time if it results in new test equipment.'

'Indeed it might.'

'OK. Now what sort of resources do you want and how much money are you after?'

'Well, I've discussed this at length with James here, looking at time scales, cash requirements and resources such as new equipment. The bottom line is that the project needs half a million pounds over the next two years.

'That will enable me to develop a commercial design that is ready to put into production. Then we will need the resources to build and sell the machine and to continue development of the technology.'

'To be blunt, the university won't go all the way on that amount for the proposal you've outlined. It still strikes me as highly risky. What are your comments, James?' asked Alistair.

'Well, I think it's refreshing to find a proposal that isn't highly fanciful and that, potentially, has a very sound market to aim at. But, as you say, there's certainly risks when an idea is treading on such new ground.'

'So what's the immediate need?'

'To balance the department's books: fifty thousand pounds now. To finish development of the safety systems and tests is just a matter of taking Professor Palfrey's time. But then cash will be needed for outside specialists. Palfrey will need the services of a machine building company to produce a working prototype that will suit a factory rather than a laboratory; an electronics specialist will be needed to check the design of the radiation transmitter; and the result will have to be sent to a testing establishment for safety and performance certification to confirm it meets key industrial standards.

'We can go some way to helping Palfrey raise the required capital from the university development fund, but it is really down to him to convince outside investors to part with their cash.'

'That all seems a fairly heavy workload to manage, Lazio, how will Combined Engineering fare when your attention is directed elsewhere?'

'It shouldn't suffer at all. During term time the project would be slotted into the departmental research timetable just like any other. The next few weeks will take some time, though, but we are moving into exams and then the holidays, so there are no lectures to prepare. I can see where my summer will be spent.'

'Right. Now, what does the university get out of all this?'

'It fits into the usual arrangements we make for spin out companies,' said James. 'We'll put in the fifty thousand in return for an outline agreement. Depending on what finance Lazio can raise, the university would want a thirty per cent shareholding in the company and a fifty per cent share in the IP, the intellectual property. This means Professor Palfrey has control of the company for all aspects except major strategic changes, when he has to obtain agreement from those shareholders with over twenty four per cent of the company.

'I've explained to him that he can split his seventy per cent with others although we would want to know whom he had in mind before making any deal. Our share of the IP means that the university benefits from ongoing licence deals or patent sales. The limited status of the company means that either the university or Professor Palfrey could buy out the other and take total control if needs be.'

'And once the company has a machine it can unleash on the world?'

'Then we are talking serious money. The agreement will say that the company should move into premises on the Science Park and bring in-house the production, testing and further development of the quintahertz machine. That will mean technical and admin staff being appointed. But that can be gradually built up, perhaps using revenue from machine sales.

'But whatever is discussed, someone from my department will attend all board and executive meetings to ensure the university's interests are looked after.'

'Well, gentlemen,' said Alistair, spreading his hands on the desk expansively, 'I have reservations but I think I can recommend all this for approval as it stands to the business development committee. You'll have to produce an outline agreement so the university solicitor and accountant can check it out before the next meeting if you want an early decision. Remember, they're both slow readers.'

'Thank you very much,' said Lazio.

Alistair rose in his usual way to indicate the end of the meeting. Outside the dean's door. Lazio punched the air.

'Well done, James, thanks for everything, is that another notch on the bedpost for you?'

'Just keep the smart comments for the dean, he's the one you've got to watch. If you make a pig's ear of this deal he'll have the project off you in no time.'

But Lazio could only see a cheque for fifty thousand pounds.

* * * * * * * *

At home that evening Lazio was bouncing. He kissed Helen on the back of the neck as soon as he got in the kitchen, much to her surprise.

'That smells good,' he said lifting the lid off a pot cooking on the Aga. 'Do I detect lamb casserole?'

'You do indeed. The butcher says it comes from Newbold's farm over at Barsby. It's just about falling off the bone it's that tender. Anyway I would have bought it just to keep it in the family, so to speak.'

'What do you mean, family?'

'Well you could be teaching their daughter, Sarah, next September.'

'Pretty slim reason for buying his lamb. Any way it's David Bearing that looks after the first year engineers, thank God. I don't have to get near the spotty things till they're a bit more mature.'

'And what about the female students?'

'Ah!' Lazio sensed he was heading for deep water and changed course. 'I hope you haven't chucked my best Bordeaux in that pot.'

'That doesn't answer the question,' said Helen. 'It just changes the subject. And I don't chuck your best Bordeaux anywhere. Not at the price you pay for it.'

'It's very reasonably priced, thank you very much. Bill hasn't been supplying people round here with wine for the last ten years because he rips people off.'

'That's it. He doesn't rip people off. Just you.'

'Ouch,' Lazio was losing on all fronts. But he knew how to wind up his wife in return.

'So what's Newbold's daughter like?'

'She's very sensible. Her mother brought her to the last Women's Institute meeting. She sang Jerusalem beautifully.'

'No. I mean what's her figure like? She's not blonde is she? You know how I feel about blonde hair.'

Helen shook her own dark locks and stirred the casserole a little too vigorously. Lazio picked up the sign.

'Will she want a little private tuition after hours, do you think? I need to know because that's my specialist area. David doesn't get a look in there.'

'Lazio Palfrey! Do you want this wooden spoon clapped smartly round the back of your neck? Because that's the way it's going.'

'But then you'd have to come in the shower with me and wash the bits off my back where I can't reach.'

'Just go to that wine rack and get yourself a glass,' said Helen. 'You're as bouncing as this lamb was a wee while ago. Do I need to ask what sort of day you've had?'

'Pretty good actually. The dean's going to give me fifty thousand pounds.'

'Well don't tell Bill or your next Bordeaux will be even more expensive.'

'Thank you. Oh, I forgot to tell you the other day, we'll be seeing Saxon for a weekend in the near future. He's going to fit a gizmo to my computer system at the uni to make it more secure. And I was talking to some biologists about the quintahertz machine. They don't know of any work being done in the area I'm working on so we're obviously well ahead of any competition.

'I could have the new company up and running before too long. The uni money will pay back what I've put into the machine so far and if I get the rest of the funding right, I should be able to draw a salary from the company as well as what I'm getting from the university. This summer will be busy for me but we could have a good holiday next year. Something exotic. Where do you fancy?'

'Off you go again. The money's for your machine, not you, and don't forget you said you'd help Saxon with the fees for William in September. And if you don't put some aside, you'll be down again when things aren't going as well as today.'

Helen Palfrey was well into her role as balancing act to her husband's volatility.

'I suppose you're right. But there's no harm in dreaming.'

'I'm not so sure. Anyway, start dreaming about food instead. It'll be ready in about a quarter of an hour. Buzz off and change. I've got the table to lay.'

Lazio was just at the kitchen door when the telephone rang.

'Keep going,' said Helen, 'I'll take it.'

An unfamiliar voice asked for Professor Palfrey.

'Can I take a message? He's just changing for dinner.'

'Not really, I just wanted to talk to him about his project. I won't keep him long, it's just that I'm away for the next week.'

'Well, you've got about five minutes if his dinner's not to spoil. Lazio, someone from the uni. I said you've got just five minutes. Will you take it upstairs?'

An aria from Verdi's Rigoletto was cut off in mid flow and Helen heard the upstairs telephone lifted. She put her receiver down and went to move the casserole to the cool side of the Aga.

'Good evening, Professor Palfrey. My name is Mike Fleckney and I specialise in neurology at the university. My colleagues in the biology department tell me you're wanting to know how the human nervous system responds to very high frequency radiation. Is that right?'

'Well, sort of. But carry on.'

'It's just that I have been recently researching in that area. I've been looking at the effects of next generation mobile phones on the brain. As you probably know, frequencies are going up and up. That means handsets can be smaller and lighter, there is less power consumption so the batteries last longer, and less interference with other electronic equipment. We're well away from the region you are calling quintahertz but I think I'm starting to see how radiation can affect the human body at that level.'

'Right. I have to say that my interest is actually in inorganic materials, steel specifically. I just wanted to explore what happens in humans to see if there is any common behaviour.'

'When you get down to the basic chemistry, there is really no difference. Atoms spin round in orbits whether it's meat or steel. And once radiation resonates with the natural frequency of the atom, you do get this compression of the orbit. In steel, it will compress and harden the material. In animals, and humans, the flesh and muscle still compresses, but that stops circulation of the body fluids so the body simply ceases to function.

'If the radiation is removed within seconds, fluids move back into the body cells and they carry on functioning as though nothing has happened. If the radiation lasts longer, the cells dry out and lose the ability to expand. That effect is permanent.

'When I was in America last month I heard that their Defence Research Agency was looking at the technology as a weapon for the police. A sort of super stun gun. It could knock out a group of people, such as terrorists and their hostages, give the police time to sort the goodies from the baddies, and then everyone would recover with no after effects.

'Good American stuff if you ask me, probably no chance of it ever being developed, even if they were allowed to use it anyway, but you know what they're like over there.'

'I'm beginning to get an idea,' said Lazio.

'Would you like to see the paper I wrote on this mobile phone research?'

'Very much.'

'I can't let it out it openly just yet, it's still awaiting release approval from the client, but if you don't let it go any further, I'll email it over to you.'

'Thank you very much, I'd appreciate that. I'll delete it as soon as I've read it.'

That conversation had taken half an hour. The house had gone quiet and the smell of cooking had evaporated. Lazio felt hungry. He looked into the lounge, Helen had started to read the paper but it now lay in her lap as she dozed. Uncertain what to do, Lazio hovered - just as Helen opened her eyes.

'Have you finished talking?' she said.

'Yes, I'm afraid I got a bit carried away.'

'Why am I not surprised? Don't worry, casseroles are better for being warmed up and the wine has had plenty of time to breathe.'

* * * * * * * *

Chapter 5

'There's a call from Mr Charles Thurmaston. He says he is chairman of Glen Parva Steel Producers and has a business matter he would like to discuss with you.'

'Put him through, Jenny,' said Alistair Wyatt, pressing a switch under his desk to start the tape system that recorded his telephone calls and meetings.

'Good morning, Professor Wyatt,' said Thurmaston, 'I haven't had the pleasure of meeting you personally but my company uses the services of your steel research people in the Combined Engineering department. I have been asked by my board of directors to make an initial enquiry off the record to see if the university would be interested in principle in helping us with our development plans. Do you have a few moments so I could give you an outline of what we have in mind?'

'Yes, I do. But shouldn't you be talking to Professor Lazio Palfrey, the head of steel research? I've no doubt he is familiar with your company and its activities. I am afraid that steel is not my specialist area.'

'I appreciate that and we would of course discuss the projects we have in mind with Professor Palfrey in due course,' said Thurmaston. 'But our overall plan goes beyond the needs for research. To develop further, we need to enhance our total image in the market place, to show that, as men of steel, we are totally committed to the industry.

'We need to involve the university as a whole as a mark of our commitment. It comes down to share price. If that is strong, the company can move forward positively. But share prices are funny things, as you probably know. It's company potential that gets them up, not the results. So the more support we get from outside the company, the better we are regarded by stock market traders, the more deals we can cut and our balance sheet continues to improve.'

'So you are asking the university, in effect, to endorse the activities of Glen Parva Steel Producers.'

'Yes.'

'And you would use our reputation as a major university in the academic world to boost your company's image.'

'Not directly, or obviously, but yes.'

That is going to cost you handsomely, thought Wyatt. No doubt the mucky hand of commercialism conceals some mud ready to sling as always and we will want paying well to compensate for any that sticks to us.

'Well, we would need to know a great deal about Glen Parva first. How large is your company, for example?' asked Wyatt.

Thurmaston was immediately on his soap box.

'We are the largest steel producer that is wholly UK-owned. We contribute more to the country's economy than any other steel firm. We are a major employer and we intend to become an international player. We have assembled a world class board of directors to take the company forward.'

He didn't say that Glen Parva would become the largest benefactor of Burnstone University. Alistair Wyatt decided it for him.

'I'm sure Professor Palfrey will confirm all that. Perhaps you'd like to visit us for a few days to see round the company?' asked Thurmaston. 'Our headquarters in Birmingham are somewhat functional but we have sales offices around the world where you could get to meet some local customers at first hand. Bring your wife, of course.'

Wyatt did not respond. He did not want any sign of acceptance to appear on the tape relentlessly running in his desk cupboard. Instead he showed concern for his employer.

'Well, this certainly sounds a major project and no doubt Glen Parva could usefully help Burnstone University develop. But it could not give you blanket endorsement in return. We would have to take that step by step, although I am sure we would not refuse any reasonable suggestion. And what would you want from Professor Palfrey's department?'

'Lots of research work. We have many major ideas that need investigating. We would pay the department in the usual way but we have one stipulation, though. In return for funding a large number of projects we require agreement that the department will not take work from any other steel company.'

Wyatt's devious mind immediately clicked to the real reason behind Thurmaston's call. Glen Parva wasn't so interested in Palfrey's work, it just wanted to deny the facilities to its competitors.

Palfrey wouldn't want to commit his department to just one firm under those circumstances. None of the department heads ever wanted to. It was commercialising their academic reputation and debased then in the eyes of their peers. They couldn't do any work of their own because the client would claim it for themselves. It also cut their income when they were tied to just one client, who invariably used the agreement to keep prices down.

'That will be difficult to implement,' said Wyatt. 'Heads of departments value their independence very highly and money rarely convinces them otherwise.'

'Well there must be ways of persuading Professor Palfrey to agree,' said Thurmaston. 'We have a lot to offer the university.'

'In any case, I couldn't say yes to any sort of agreement that involved the whole university without consulting others.'

'I appreciate that but we do need to move fairly fast. Our shareholders are expecting action.'

'Can you leave it with me for a couple of days?' said Wyatt.

'Certainly. And I'll send you a copy of our latest chairman's report and company accounts in the meantime so you can see the full background to Glen Parva and where we sell around the world.'

'Thank you, that would be appreciated.'

Wyatt switched off his tape recorder.

'And to answer your initial enquiry, strictly off the record, I think we can do business. I have to stress that is my personal view at this stage.'

'Fair enough. Thank you for your time and I look forward to hearing from you.'

Alistair Wyatt put the telephone down and sat back in his chair. Two days ago, Palfrey was in his office wanting funding for a major new project, now someone comes along offering gifts. Coincidence or what?

* * * * * * * *

Alistair Wyatt didn't greatly believe in coincidence. As an arch planner he was used to events being linked by deviousness, not chance. But it had been coincidence that linked Palfrey's visit and Thurmaston's phone call. It was also coincidence that, about the same time, the strategy meeting at the Khazatan Research Institute decided to send someone to talk to John Smithson and to investigate Lazio Palfrey.

Leonid Lebdev had been filled in with all the background information that the research director had and was now briefing his contact in London.

So it was a couple of days later that Professor John Smithson's secretary told him that a technical officer from the Khazatan embassy was interested in the patents he had recently announced were available for transfer.

'Excellent,' he said when he came back from lecturing and heard the news. 'Fix up a meeting as soon as you can. Allocate about two hours, he may want to see round the workshops. Have a chat with him if you can to see what other information you can find out so I've got something to go on when he arrives. Ask if he's been here long and check he knows how to get here as well.'

Boris Pushtin was going to surprise Smithson. Slim built, with characteristic high cheekbones, he had a very easy going manner and spoke excellent English. He made full use of London social life and did not always use his spells of leave to go back home.

A young engineer, he was hoping to progress in the Khazatan diplomatic service. He had seen the frustrations that beset working engineers in his home country and decided that his technical ability would be best used in bringing new technology to the notice of his fellow engineers back home. As a technical officer in the London embassy, he could keep at the forefront of developments in the subject he loved and had a better future than in a Khazatan engineering works.

He had gone to study the patent details at the Patent Office in London as soon as he had been briefed. He familiarised himself with what Professor Smithson had developed and he then had to find out what the steel firms back home thought they would be worth.

Alexander Kasvanov, the representative of the steel manufacturers, was shown as the contact name in his file. He telephoned him from the office.

'Good afternoon,' he said after Kasvanov had announced himself, 'I'm calling from London with the results of some investigations I've been making and wanted to check that you are the person I need to talk to.'

'If you are Boris Pushtin and have been finding out about some new patents taken out by a Professor Smithson, then I'm your man all right.'

'Well, he's filed a couple of patents on plasma deposition. It looks as though it is just an extension of existing technology, not anything brand new. It uses a much higher level of electronic control than I've seen before so it's much more efficient. It will produce harder steel for less energy than before, but it's still a chemical system of hardening.'

'That's what I thought might be the case,' said Kasvanov. 'It's a development that the Research Institute people are working towards here. It would be quicker for us to buy the patent rights than to let our people potter on, but I'm not sure it's something we'd want to spend a great deal of money on. Anyway, I'll speak to some people here to see what they'd be willing to pay for the patents. When's your meeting with Smithson?'

'The day after tomorrow. Ten thirty. But I'll have to leave the office by ten. Have you got my mobile number?'

'Yes it's in the file. I'll call you later.'

Pushtin then had to come up with a plan that would get him in to see Lazio Palfrey. Lebdev had suggested the idea of him acting as a technical magazine journalist and he found that quite acceptable. It meant a visit to the overt surveillance department of the embassy to get fitted out with a story and the bits needed to play the part.

Overt operations meant going into a situation openly and contacting the target apparently in the normal course of events. It required quite different planning from covert operations where operators had to remain hidden and break in at night to collect information. There was to be no thud and blunder in this operation.

The overt surveillance group were delighted to see him.

'We've been waiting for you. First customer we've had in weeks,' said the manager. 'What's your brief exactly?'

Pushtin gave him the essentials.

'Hm, no changes there then. They might have given us an interesting one to work on. Anyway, let's start with you. Journalists are generally not the neatest dressers. You'll have to get rid of the silk tie. Have you anything that's a lot older?'

'Not really,' said Pushtin, somewhat mortified that he was expected to have old clothes.

'OK. We'll find something in the wardrobe. Have you a check shirt and a sports jacket instead of that smart suit?'

'I think I can do those OK.'

Pushtin was thinking of the country weekends he'd spent with people where brand new clothes were definitely out. It was rumoured that English gentlemen threw their new corduroy trousers and tweed jackets into their dog's basket for a day or so to knock out the newness.

'No coloured handkerchief in your top pocket, please, and don't polish your shoes before you go. What sort of briefcase have you got and does it look new?'

'It's maroon leather, slim line and not knocked about, if that's what you mean.'

'Yes, but is it fitted with a camera?'

'No.'

'Well, leave it behind then. We'll give you one for the job. It will have also seen some action. You can supply your own contents provided they're not too ostentatious and they don't have your initials on. That goes for your cuff links as well.'

'Do I get a new name as well, then?'

'Most certainly you do.'

'What will it be?'

'No idea just yet. But it's being attended to. Now, let's run over your background story. How did you get to be an engineering journalist in Britain?'

'I think I can use my real life story to answer that question. But instead of going into the diplomatic section, I'll say I went into journalism. I feed stories back to my editor in Khazatan and act as a technical advisor in the London embassy when firms want to export into Britain or UK firms want to export to Khazatan.'

'One aspect of that story won't work. There's no magazines worth reading in Khazatan. But I think here comes an answer.'

A member of the overt surveillance department came into the office with a large cardboard box that she dropped unceremoniously and noisily on the floor.

'The complete kit of parts for an engineering journalist,' she announced. 'And it's bloody heavy.'

'Well, you managed,' said the manager with a distinct lack of chivalry, 'Now, Boris, root around in that lot and pick out what you'd like for the trip,' He lifted out a pile of magazines and put them on his own desk.

Pushtin picked out some well-chewed pencils, a battered calculator and an English dictionary, holding them disdainfully between his fingertips.

The manager pushed a copy of the magazine European Engineering Times across to him.

'Right, you're going to be Mikhail Romanov, overseas reporter. There's proof of your cover, inside is your name, your editor's details and a contact point if anyone wants to check out the magazine. You'll have to learn all that by heart.'

Pushtin opened the front cover and slid off the paper clip holding a plastic bag of business cards inside. They were in his new name and the details matched the list of information in the editorial section of the magazine.

'Treat those carefully and don't leave the magazine behind. They'll be needed for someone else sometime and we don't want to keep on having to print new ones.'

'It says the office is in Brussels; what happens if someone calls that number and asks awkward questions?'

'If anyone tries that Brussels number, one of those telephones over there rings,' The manager pointed to a rack of phones.

'And how does the person sat there know what to say?'

'She has this to read off,' he held up a card covered in plastic to protect it. 'And if the caller is persistent, she calls me. I'm the editor,' he said importantly, 'so if you don't get this interview I can give you the sack.'

He laughed heartily at his own joke, which didn't help Boris Pushtin's discomfort one little bit.

'I just hope I turn out to be a good actor,' he said.

'Don't worry,' said the manager recovering his composure, 'Once you're wearing different clothes and have learnt all the detail in the magazine you'll automatically start to act the part.

'Remember, it's not what you are, it's what you appear to be that's important. The way to stop anyone having any suspicions is to appear exactly as your target expects you to be. The mind is a wonderful thing. And it's all in there. Start chewing a pencil now, that'll help.'

And he started laughing again as he saw Pushtin with his well-manicured hands and nails handling the pencils as though they'd come out of the less pleasant end of a dog.

'Thanks a bunch,' said Pushtin. 'Do I have to call Palfrey myself to set up the appointment?'

'Jeez, no. You've got an advertising department that has to go in first. Don't you know anything about publishing? The advertising boys heard that Palfrey's department wants to get some business out of eastern Europe so why doesn't it advertise in the magazine? In return, the mag will carry an article specifically about Palfrey and his work. Apparently he's so egotistical, he won't be able to refuse that sort of publicity.

'Now, you need to put together a list of questions to ask Palfrey so the interview seems genuine. Read the articles in the magazine, they'll tell you what you need to ask. But don't get too carried away. There's supposed to be something brewing and that's what you're really after.

'What I suggest is you get this interview with Smithson out of the way before filling your head with the main assignment. Then come and see us again, dressed and ready for the part. We'll check you out and look at the questions. We might also have some more information for you about Palfrey.'

'And where will that come from?'

'That's a question you don't ask,' Openness still did not come naturally to the older generation in eastern Europe.

'Sorry. You're right. Well, thanks for all your help. I'll drop by after the Smithson business is tied up.

'Don't forget your briefcase.'

* * * * * * * *

Alistair Wyatt sat thoughtfully with his chin in his hand. People didn't make overtures to him very often in the way that Charles Thurmaston had done. There was a lot to be considered.

Glen Parva Steel Producers obviously had money to burn. They'd pay for more research than most companies, they had extra to offer for the university generally, and it appeared as though they were also offering him and his wife a trip abroad just so they could get the opportunity to spend their money with Burnstone.

The company was obviously ambitious but what had it got to hide? Did it use sweatshop labour in far flung countries or was it an arch polluter of the environment? If it was simply ambitious and was going to gobble up smaller steel companies, there would be redundancies, bad press and perhaps government intervention. That would poke their share price in the eye right enough.

If Burnstone University became embroiled in any of that, it would land on his plate and leave a black mark that would affect his career for one thing. But if the university had made enough money out of the deal, that would prevent any back stabbing. Senior staff always appeared unworldly but they were aware of the

65

facts of life as well as any one. At the end of the day, they knew exactly who paid for their precious after-dinner port and brandy.

And for the deans of universities, where there was little scope for upward promotion, the rewards would come from government for services to education, to industry or for whatever reason that ended up with a visit to Buckingham Palace. For lesser mortals, there was well paid work on government committees and organisations. But all of that would be immediately cancelled out if the slightest whiff of impropriety surfaced.

But while the university had its good name to sell to Glen Parva, it also had Palfrey's latest idea as an additional bargaining chip. Wyatt had not the slightest compunction about taking that off Palfrey. Underneath their apparently mutual and sociable fraternisation in public lay a distinct frostiness.

Palfrey could not keep up with Wyatt's deviousness and wanted no part of it. Wyatt could not stand Palfrey's idiosyncrasies and on more than one occasion had referred to him as that Italian buffoon in a backwater. But Wyatt, as a biologist, had pretensions of his own and thought that his research into genes and DNA ranked above all else.

So he had no second thoughts about bringing the quintahertz machine into his scheme of things, whatever hopes Palfrey had for it and its future. He rang the Vice Chancellor's personal number to keep the call strictly between themselves.

'Good morning, Vice Chancellor, it's Alistair Wyatt here, have you got a few minutes to spare, please?'

'Yes, go ahead.'

'I've just had a business proposal from a company that could help the university raise its academic profile. It has used our steel research facilities before, so we do know of it. It is off the record at the moment, their chairman is just testing the water, but I wanted to discuss it with you as administrative head of the university before thinking about it further.'

'Hold on a minute.'

Wyatt heard the phone laid on the desk, and the sound of a door closing.

'Right. What are the details?'

'Glen Parva Steel Producers are the country's largest steel maker and they want to expand internationally. They are taking all the usual business steps but they also want to raise their public profile and use us as an example of the way they benefit society as a whole.'

'That all sounds very philanthropic, what do they really want?'

'They want to place a lot of research with the science faculty on the understanding that we won't work for any other steel company.'

'Right. And what does the university get?'

'A major donation.'

'How big?'

'Amounts weren't mentioned but I get the feeling that there will not be the millions needed to put up a new building or start a new department, for example. If it were a million or so, that would buy major new equipment for the genetic engineering lab, for example. Out of all the departments in the university, that one would attract greatest academic interest if we could develop it. Gene research is the headline topic just now.'

There was silence as the Vice Chancellor considered his options.

'Take the proposal forward,' he said. 'If the company is offering over two million, come back to me because that should go to the university as a whole. If it's under that amount then I'll leave you to handle the negotiations at faculty level. And if that's the case, two things: can you let me see the agreement before it is signed. I think the management committee should be advised not because it would be in their jurisdiction, but just as a courtesy as it is almost a university matter. Secondly, make sure we get the maximum amount of publicity for ourselves out of whatever the money goes towards.'

'Right, Vice Chancellor. Thank you very much. I'll keep you posted with developments.'

Wyatt could hardly stop rubbing his hands together with glee as he put the phone down. Glen Parva's deal wouldn't go over two million come hell or high water. And with biology as his specialist subject, boosting the genetic research facilities would enable him to head up some rewarding research. Rewarding in terms of his prestige and standing with government bodies, that is; his staff would have to work out the benefits to genetics.

It just left Palfrey to sort out. That was something he might enjoy.

* * * * * * * *

Boris Pushtin took a taxi to Empire University and was soon accepting the offer of coffee from Professor Smithson.

'So you're interested in acquiring my latest patents on steel hardening my secretary says.'

'Indirectly. I'm acting for an association of steel producers in Khazatan and they will have the final say on any deal. But I have to say at the outset that our steel industry is working towards the same objective. It will get there in the end under its own steam but any help it can get to move forward faster is always of interest. But such help would not command the same price as brand new technology.'

'I appreciate that. I am quite familiar with developments generally in eastern Europe. But I do think there is new technology in these latest patents. The electronic control side, for example, is very different.'

Smithson realised that Pushtin was talking down the price and he had to find out more about the man to see what level of negotiation was possible.

'Would you like to come and see the equipment in operation?'

'Yes. That would be good.'

'Are you involved yourself in the steel industry?' asked Smithson as they walked towards the laboratory.

'Not specifically. My background is in general mechanical engineering but you will know that involves a lot of theory on surface treatment of metals.'

'And would I be right in thinking that you were trained here in the UK?'

'No, not at all. It was all at the University of Khazatan.'

'Sorry. I assumed from your excellent English that you must have spent a lot of time here.'

'Just the reverse. It was my command of English that got me posted to London as a technical officer. I decided that life might be more enjoyable if I worked on my English rather than my engineering.'

'Well it seems you've got the best of both worlds.'

Smithson opened the door into the steel laboratory and walked over to a large stainless steel box that looked like a baking oven on legs, although the small porthole in the front was well bolted on and far more substantial than would be needed for inspecting loaves of bread.

'This is set up for a routine piece of research,' said Smithson as the lab assistant came over and switched it on. 'It doesn't have the latest system that is covered by my patents but it is only just behind that development.'

While they waited for the vacuum to build up inside, Pushtin looked around and admired the equipment on show. Somewhat different from our own set up back home, distinctly more professional, he thought.

A couple of cracks of high voltage discharge from the chamber indicated the end of the hardening sequence.

The lab assistant took out the sample of metal with a pair of tongs and laid it on a bench. Smithson pointed out the even finish and showed Pushtin a computer printout of an earlier set of tests on a hardened sample.

'Very impressive,' said Pushtin. 'But I suspect this work is of more value to you than to us. What's your figure for an outright transfer of the main patent?'

'Remember that the new technology will make you a lot of money,' said Smithson. 'And we both know that steel producers need all the help they can get. It also depends on whether your people in Khazatan want to take the technology forward or whether we can become involved with development,' said Smithson.

'Let's just talk about a straight transfer first,' said Pushtin. 'I have a figure from the representative of the Khazatan steel producers association for that and it will show if we're in the same ball park for a start.'

'What's that figure then?'

'Well, what's your figure?'

The two men smiled at each other enjoying the game of negotiation.

Pushtin pulled out an envelope from his inside pocket and laid it on the bench. He left his hand on top of it.

Smithson took the computer printout, wrote a figure on the back of it and folded it over.

'Host first?' said Pushtin.

Smithson showed his figure. £150,000.

Pushtin slid out a piece of paper from the envelope. £75,000.

'It was nice meeting you,' said Smithson, somewhat disgusted by the low offer.

'The UK steel industry won't pay your figure, that's for sure,' said Pushtin stiffly.

'The world's a large and hungry place,' replied Smithson leading the way to the door.

Pushtin put the envelope carefully back in his pocket. He didn't want the second piece of paper to fall out. £160,000 was written on that.

He rang Alexander Kasvanov as soon as he got back to the office.

'I've got your pictures of the set up at Empire University. The photographic department is taking the camera out of the briefcase as we speak and the prints should be in tonight's diplomatic bag. Smithson gave me a demo while I was in the lab so there will also be a picture of the sample if the gizmo worked properly.

'We were miles apart on price so the visit hasn't cost you anything. He only wanted £150K so I played the £75K card and that ended the negotiations there and then.'

'Well done,' said Kasvanov. 'I hope that amount didn't insult him too badly. Our boys will soon be up with Smithson's developments anyway. So now you're moving onto Palfrey. Good luck. I gather that will be a more difficult operation.'

'Yes. But also more interesting. It'll also take a week or so to complete. So I'll call you or Lebdev then.'

* * * * * * * *

'Good morning,' said a German sounding voice, 'Can I speak to the person who looks after your advertising, please.'

'We don't have anyone specifically for that,' said Ann Whittaker. 'In fact we do very little advertising. But I'd be the first point of contact anyway, so can you tell me a little more?'

'Indeed. The magazine European Engineering Times is preparing a special feature on the steel industry and as we circulate widely throughout Europe we thought it might benefit your department if you were mentioned.'

'Right. Firstly, we probably would not want to put out a general advertisement anyway. We are very busy just now and budgets are always tight. We'd only be interested if we had a specific reason for advertising and there's nothing I know of at the moment. What I suggest is that you send in your advertising rates plus a copy of the magazine and I'll pass it on to the head of the department. He would make the final decision anyway. But thank you for calling.'

Ann went to put the phone down but the caller was more persistent than most magazine types.

'Sorry to press you, but we would really like to include you in the magazine as Professor Palfrey is regarded as such a leading researcher in this industry. Say we offered to carry for free a feature article that profiled the Professor and highlighted his recent work?'

She knew immediately that Lazio could not even think of turning down such an offer.

The caller continued.

'It would help support your presentation that was made at the Technology Transfer Day a few weeks ago. Our reporter says you have a lot to offer and business may not always be so good. The steel business is always being set back by economic problems as you well know.'

'All right,' said Ann. 'I'll pass all that on to Professor Palfrey and he or I will get back to you. What's your phone number?'

The caller gave a Brussels number.

'That's the switchboard number. But I will be out of the office from this afternoon for a few days. Can I pencil in a date now when our reporter could come and see Professor Palfrey? Then we can tie the whole thing up here and now instead of it dragging on.'

Ann usually resisted such pressure but this caller was obviously going to be persistent.

'Professor Palfrey could possibly spare an hour and a half on Thursday morning at eleven. Can your reporter make that day and will it be enough time?'

'Yes. He's based in London at the moment and can get to Leicester for then without any trouble. It will be Mikhail Romanov. We could also do with some photographs to go with the article. Is it OK if he brings a camera?'

'That's a question for Professor Palfrey,' said Ann. 'If he says no, or if he doesn't want to be interviewed, I'll call you back. Who am I speaking to?'

'Oh just ask for Mikhail. It's simpler if you deal with him direct as I'm going to be away.'

'OK. What's his number in London?'

'Ah. Just use the Brussels number because we're never sure where he might be. But we can soon contact him.'

'Fine. See him on Thursday then.'

'Thank you.'

Phones were replaced.

Ann's caller let out a sharp breath. Whoops. We're not sure where he might be? More a case of not sure who he might be! He dialled Boris Pushtin's mobile phone.

'Hi! Is that Mikhail Romanov?'

'Er, yes,' said a very guarded voice.

'We've got you an appointment for Thursday morning with the good professor Palfrey. And you don't have to get up too early to get there either.'

'Great. Thanks.'

'Now. Will you drop in on Wednesday so we can have a dress rehearsal, and we'll check you out again on Thursday morning

72

before you go, just to make sure. It sounds as though you'll have to get a lot more used to being called Mikhail.'

'OK, I'm working on it. See you later.'

'By the way, you got some nice shots of Smithson's lab. Just make sure you do is the same thing in Professor Palfrey's department.'

* * * * * * * *

True to form, Lazio Palfrey's main concern on the morning of Boris Pushtin's visit was what he should wear.

'For goodness' sake,' said Helen, when she went into Lazio's dressing room to chase him on.

The table was covered in bow ties and three waistcoats were laid over a chair back.

'Well, I don't know whether to look businesslike or to show my character,' said Lazio.

'It might help if half this stuff went to the charity shop first,' said Helen holding up a luminous bow tie. 'You wouldn't have so much stuff to confuse you in the morning.'

'It doesn't confuse me,' said Lazio, holding up a mottled bow tie.

'Well, you can't have that one anyway, its pattern has come from the egg that's dried on it.'

Helen raked through the ties, looked at the waistcoats and picked up the bottom one.

'Right. Put these on.'

That was the voice that would stand no argument.

'There,' said Helen as though dressing her grandson, 'that strikes a nice balance between business and character.'

As Lazio turned to the mirror, Helen swept the ties into their drawer, shut it with a bang and put the unused waistcoats on hangers.

'Right,' Lazio knew when not to argue. 'That's perfect,' he said in a tone that suggested it was his idea all along. 'Thank you.'

So it was a match made in heaven when Palfrey and Pushtin met later that morning. While Pushtin could not show his peacock feathers openly, at least he could appreciate the other's efforts.

'Thank you very much for agreeing to do the article,' said Pushtin. 'We were very keen to get you into this issue as it is an important one for men of steel.'

'It's funny you've not been round before, then,' said Palfrey. 'How long has the magazine been going?'

'Quite a few years, although I've not been with it long.'

'Have you got a copy of the magazine I could see?'

Pushtin brought out his copy.

'I'm afraid I can't leave it with you. It's the only one I've got. There's always a great demand for them.'

Lazio flicked through the pages.

'That's curious, there's one or two articles I'm sure I've seen elsewhere,' said Palfrey. 'But it was quite some time ago. Do you often lift stuff from other magazines?'

Pushtin reddened. He hadn't expected such a direct barrage.

'Well, I can't say. I don't know where the editor gets all his material from.'

'And I don't see your name against any of the articles.'

Pushtin was struggling.

'There's a number of reasons we use so many different names. We can't have our readers thinking that the publishers are just a one man band. But I'm listed on the editorial page.'

Lazio handed back the magazine.

'Where would you like to start, then?'

'Could I have a look round the department first, to get an idea of what you can do in addition to your steel hardening activities, then I've got a list of questions I'd like to go through.'

'Right. We'll go to the laboratory first. This is where most of the students do their work. We have several other rooms but they're for routine testing and engineering work. You can leave your briefcase here, it'll be quite safe.'

'Thanks, but it'll be easier to take it as my notepad's in it. It's also got my camera. I was hoping to take a picture of you amongst your machines, if that's OK?'

'Sure.'

'What are some of the key pieces of equipment that you use?' asked Pushtin as they entered the lab.

Lazio took him around the latest additions to the department and was pleased to note that he appeared to understand steel and the way it was worked. He also appeared very keen on detail and looked into every corner, although he seemed singularly welded to his briefcase.

'Anything interesting under the dust sheet?' asked Pushtin, indicating the quintahertz machine.

'Not for you, I'm afraid,' said Palfrey. 'We can't have all our secrets on show.'

'OK. Can I take it that it's for hardening steel?'

'We don't do much else right now, so it might be.'

Pushtin laughed 'Well, can I have a picture of you before we leave. Stood against this machine over here would be good.'

'But that's probably the least interesting piece of equipment in the place.'

'Maybe, but its got colour and detail and will look good on the page.'

'Suit yourself but I'd rather you featured one or two other bits.'

'Yes, I can do that as well. We do need more than one pic.'

After Lazio's ego had been captured the two returned to his office to finish the interview.

At twelve thirty, Ann Whittaker came in to remind Lazio that he couldn't talk all day about his beloved steel research.

'You have confirmed that we need to see the article before it goes to print?' she asked Lazio.

'Yes. There's no problem with that,' answered Pushtin.

She handed him a business card.

'Use my email address when you send the text through. I can then contact Professor Palfrey wherever he is and make sure it is turned round quickly.

'Regarding the advertisement, we'll take a quarter page black and white at the price quoted on your list. I've an artwork here you can use, but I would like it back in due course.'

'Thank you. We'll take care of that. So thank you for arranging the interview and thank you Professor Palfrey for your time.'

Pushtin slid the artwork back in its envelope, closed his briefcase and was shown out by Ann's assistant.

'Now, now,' said Lazio Palfrey as Ann looked wistfully after the slim retreating figure. 'Remember you're a happily married woman.'

* * * * * * * *

Boris Pushtin dropped off his reporter's kit as soon as he reached the embassy.

'Thank God that's over. I don't think the life of a grubby reporter is quite for me,' he said to the manager of overt operations. 'I also forgot to ask you this morning if you'd got any extra information about Palfrey. You said you might trawl up something more when we first worked on the case.'

'Don't worry, we found some more stuff. But you don't need to bother you head about what it was. If you followed orders, you will have brought back what we wanted in your briefcase. Don't forget to come back in about two hours time to identify the pictures.'

Pushtin went off to update Leonid Lebdev.

'There is something under wraps in a corner of Palfrey's laboratory. I asked what it was but he wouldn't let on. He did say it was secret, though. But there should be some pictures of it if my briefcase camera worked OK.'

'Good. Now listen carefully. We need a map of the department. Can you draw one to scale and put as much information on it as you can. Put each machine on it with a description at the side. Include the machine you saw under wraps and show where Palfrey's office is. And make sure it comes with the photographs in the diplomatic bag tonight.'

Damn, thought Pushtin, I thought I was on an early finish. That means more trouble with the girlfriend.

* * * * * * * *

Chapter 6

Unaware of the plotting going on around them, David Bearing and John Fleming had continued to work on the safety of the quintahertz machine.

A month had elapsed since John Fleming had his accident and it was no longer a talking point. John made no reference to the incident at all and appeared to have no after effects either mentally or physically. His doctor had given him the all clear and life in the steel research laboratory went on as normal.

During that time, Bearing had extracted a favour from the electronics department and several students had produced some test equipment that was able to measure the strength of radiation from the machine. The students created a map of readings while the machine was running and Bearing was trying to decide what it meant.

'We're really quite in the dark about the meaning of this chart,' he had said to Professor Luke Verity, head of the electronics department. 'Your students have done a thorough job but how would you analyse the results.'

'Well, this chart shows how strong the radiation is at any point within a couple of hundred yards radius of the source, which is your quintahertz machine. The students took readings at many spots and the chart contour lines link up the radiation strength between the measuring points.

'What we can calculate is the power that is generated by your machine at any point in this area. Now, if it was a radio transmitter, for example, we could work out if the signal is strong enough to drive a receiver. That is a basic exercise in electronics.

'But what you need to know from the safety point of view is the effect on humans. This means how much heat the radiation would generate in human tissue and how much effect it would have on the nervous system, which is really a whole series of electrical circuits. Where you'd get that information from I've really no idea.

'You could try the makers of microwave cookers or radar scanners but as you're working at such a high frequency, I suspect that there are no relevant figures that you could use. One way would be to toast a steak from the butchers and get a food expert to analyse the result.

'You have got some sort of reference point through Fleming's accident because you know the radiation strength where he was standing and the apparent effect it had. Unfortunately, you can't check what went on inside him while he's alive.

'You could try the Ministry of Defence, perhaps. They're always working on weird and wonderful ideas. Perhaps they'd pay you to conduct some research. You're going to need some sort of official approval that the machine meets the usual safety standards before you can sell it anyway. Not an easy problem, I'm afraid, but good for character building.'

'Thanks very much but we've enough of a character in the department already.'

Verity smiled.

'Tell Palfrey he'll have to give his garden over to a herd of cows and sheep for testing purposes. That should make his bow tie waggle.'

'Do shut up, he might think it's a good idea.'

David Bearing had also spent an enjoyable afternoon extracting Alistair Wyatt's email to Lazio Palfrey from the depths of the university computer.

The archive files were held behind a computer firewall that prevented unauthorised people getting to them. Bearing relished the challenge of obtaining authorisation, illegal as it may have been.

He'd found that the managers of many computer systems never changed the security settings that were put on when the computer was being made. So once you'd found out the standard factory settings, it was easy to break into most computers from that manufacturer.

That didn't apply to the computer systems at Burnstone, but the network still had a weakness: its power. That meant the system could produce a million passwords a minute under the right programming. Few firewalls could withstand that sort of attack for very long before the right password was acknowledged and the wall opened.

Even if the firewall needed several passwords before it would allow anyone to access the computer it protected, a simple change to the hacker's program enabled it to eat away at the security protection, layer by layer.

Bearing sent the rescued email to Lazio's computer and ran off a hard copy for himself, just in case.

It was then just a few moments work to delete the date and time stamp on the quintahertz documentation and replace it with a much earlier date as Alistair Wyatt had demanded. Bearing then added some paragraphs about safety and sent the files on to Lazio with instructions to check the text and then to save the files as he would do normally.

That would place the files back in memory, but with a date stamp that showed they had been originated around the start of the quintahertz project. It would also keep the dean happy.

For his part, John Fleming had been fitting shielding panels to the machine and had installed several microswitches that meant the machine couldn't be operated until it was fully safeguarded.

He'd devised a fail-safe system for holding the radiation beam focussing device in place and a blanking plate that prevented the beam shooting off sideways.

So development of the quintahertz machine moved forward, as did the university timetable. Exams and holidays were at the front of everyone's minds and it promised to be a hot June.

* * * * * * * *

The first weekend of June started on the sixth and heralded a busy summer for the Palfrey household. Helen had been asked to judge at several country shows while Lazio was busy arranging his new business and keeping the developments moving on the quintahertz machine. The hot weather brought barbecues out of hibernation so many evenings would be spent visiting friends.

But this first weekend saw a houseful at the Palfrey manor. Saxon had collected together the equipment needed for the security improvements to his father's computer system and it had been decided to fit it on the Saturday afternoon when no-one else would be in the department. He'd brought Katherine and the children up, who were even now looking for more dead birds in the garden.

Helen Palfrey had also persuaded their daughter, Donnatella, and her partner, Simon, to come for the weekend.

'Simon can set up the barbecue because Lazio and Saxon could be all hours fixing whatever they're trying to do,' Helen had said. 'And we haven't seen you for ages anyway, so it should be a really good family weekend.'

'And when are you going to make me even more of a grandfather?' Lazio asked Donnatella almost as soon as she had arrived at the house.

'There's plenty of time yet. I'm still only twenty eight, remember, and life's very good. A few more years and I'll be ready to steady up and enjoy raising a family. Don't fret. You're in the twenty-first century remember, much as you may dislike it. And don't be greedy. You've already got two that get you into more trouble than you can handle.'

'Sounds as though you've heard about their last visit, then.'

'Along with most of England, yes. I gather Katherine's shrieks travelled the length of the village.'

'Well, you can't stop kids being kids.'

'And most men either.'

'Are you getting at me?'

'Yes.'

'Then I'll go away and dig out the bits for the barbecue. I know how to handle women like you.'

Donnatella shook her head at the retreating figure of her father and went to commiserate with her mother.

* * * * * * * *

Saxon Palfrey put down his coffee cup.

'That was an excellent lunch, mother. But how we're going to work this afternoon, I don't know. Are you fit?' he asked his father.

'Just about. Let's see how we get on with the first task, which is to carry all your stuff into the Maserati. I think we ought to take that instead of your car as it's known on campus and won't attract any unwelcome attention.'

'Let's go.'

* * * * * * * *

'First thing. Where do you want this box of tricks to sit?' asked Saxon indicating a largish cardboard box. 'It's the intelligent node that fits between you and your secretary and the rest of the world.'

'That's definitely got to go in my office,' said Lazio. 'And somewhere that Ann won't notice it.'

'How about under the table in the corner? You can put a chair or box in front of it if you want. I've brought a selection of cables from work so there's no problem connecting it up.'

'Go for it.'

Saxon cabled the unit to his father's computer and pushed another cable through the ducting into the next office.

'Which is Ann's computer?'

Lazio pointed it out, and that was connected to the node. Saxon took the cables that had connected the two to the outside world and plugged those into his box.

'That's it. Switch on and see how it goes.'

While the computers started up, Saxon explained the system.

'What you've got in that new box is a huge amount of memory that will store your output for the next ten years probably. The data in the store cannot be accessed from outside by any means, it can only be called up from your computer, or Ann's, and only if the right password is used. So any sensitive information is totally secure.

'You can choose whether to send data to your private store, or to the university system. But you will have to use the university system as often as possible because if the pattern of your usage suddenly changes, the uni system will flag up a warning for the IT manager.

'You can call up files from the intelligent node and send them to the uni archive or to anyone else, but then you are dependent on their security arrangements to fight off hackers. But the uni system does not realise this node has been fitted.'

A green light flashed on the unit.

'Right. The systems are all set. Here is a card with the operating details on, let's se how it goes.'

Lazio transferred some files to and from the uni archive and Ann's computer and declared the system to be pretty simple.

'Well you know where to find me if you get stuck,' said Saxon, echoing the confidence that everyone didn't feel about Lazio and computers.

'You have to remember that hackers who can get through the main university system firewall could read the titles of all the documents you've been working on and trace them to the place they're stored. But they won't be able to get to the locations in your private system.

'Now I'll tell you about a security measure I've built in. If a hacker has a go at the department, I'll know within a day. I've put in a program that will log all unsuccessful attempts to get into your private database. That includes the times when you mis-type your password. The data will be automatically emailed to my home computer once a day and I can tell you what has happened.

'Later on, once the system has settled into use, I'll send up a software patch to change the system. It will then update me weekly or monthly instead, although I can call up the information whenever you think there's anything suspicious going on.'

'That sounds excellent. Thank you very much.'

'No problem. Pleased to help. And here's my invoice.'

'That's my son. You always were keen on getting your pocket money on time. Not much changes.'

'You should know. Good teaching always lasts.'

'Come on. I'm sure I can smell food on a barbecue.'

* * * * * * * *

'So how's the new company coming on?' asked Saxon, on the drive home, hanging on like grim death to anything that came to hand in the Maserati.

'Well, I've got to go hunting for most of the funds I need to keep the thing going, but the uni will cough up fifty thousand pounds to keep it moving forward, so that's not so bad. The machine's just about fully developed and the results are unbelievable, even though I say it myself.

'I'm also going to get a mention in an engineering magazine. A reporter came a few days ago to interview me, so that could be good for business.

'Anyway how's yourself? Is William fixed up for school next term?'

'Yes. That's all booked up. Everything else at home is also fine. Work goes well. The world needs ever more oil so the future's bright there. But we'd still like to keep you in reserve for William's fees as I said last visit.'

'No problem there,' said Lazio with a confidence that he didn't entirely feel.

But he was right about the smell of food. It came in the smoke that had drifted across the drive and the two picked it up as soon as Lazio turned the Maserati in through the manor gates.

'That smells good,' Lazio said to Simon as he came round the end of the house. 'Just right for two guys who've been working their butts off all afternoon.'

'Thanks,' said Simon. 'When are these two turning up, then?'

'Just grab this glass of Bordeaux,' Donnatella said, coming up to her father. 'Ignore the comments however accurate they may be.'

'And whose side are you on?'

Donnatella slipped her arm through Lazio's.

'Come and show me round the garden. Mum and Katherine will be a few more minutes in the kitchen. It's been so long since I was last here, but it's good to be back.'

'We'd love to see you more often as well. I mean, you've not all that many ties in London, why don't you come up here more often?'

'It's practicalities, really. Life's so hectic that you really need all the weekend to get ready for Monday morning again. Simon and I can't get out of bed on a Saturday before about lunchtime and then there's always a party at night. You never know who you might meet there that's good for business so we don't like to miss too many.'

'Well, you bounce at your age. I'm sure your mother and I did, but we couldn't think of doing it now. Anyway what do you think of this new rose bed? We've had it completely dug out and replaced, it must have been nearly a hundred years old.'

'It seems a shame to have disturbed it, then,' said Donnatella.

'Oh, you've got too. Plants don't last for ever although they seem to. It's just that they last so much longer than we do. Less stress, perhaps. But we've plenty of stuff that was planted before the war, so we're not being too destructive.'

There was suddenly a great shout as Saxon's two children burst out of the kitchen door.

'Grandpa! Food's ready. You'd better come quick.'

Hannah was in the lead.

'Where's the cross that we put to mark our dead bird? William and I can't find it anywhere.'

'Perhaps it's gone up to heaven with the bird,' suggested Lazio.

Hannah gave him a withering look that would have done credit to an adult, let alone someone nine years old.

Donnatella burst out laughing.

'I think you've got your grandfather sized up pretty accurately,' she said. 'But always remember he's no different from any other man. They all need a withering look to keep them in their place.'

'I'm sure I don't,' said William. 'And I'm eleven now.'

'You've still got plenty of time to suffer and learn,' said Lazio. 'I'm hundreds of years old and I'm still suffering.'

'That's because you won't learn,' said Donnatella.

'Where's this magnificent food, then,' said Lazio, well used to ignoring barbed comments. 'I'm famished.'

* * * * * * * *

Alistair Wyatt read the annual report that Charles Thurmaston had sent him from Glen Parva Steel Producers to see what potential there might be for any dark secrets to come out of the woodwork.

He concluded that the risks appeared to be the same that any large company might be exposed to. Although the scenario of steel making, with its huge smelting furnaces turning out red hot material by the ton, was vastly different from his own laboratory-scale work, where DNA doses were measured in fractions of a gram, he felt he could assess the risks that came with Glen Parva's operations.

Underneath it all, Wyatt felt a thrusting company with strong aims that it was vigorously pursuing. Its balance sheet was strong, he noted with satisfaction, and that was where he had to do his planning.

The deal with the university would have to be long term for either side to gain measurable benefit, five years at least. And Glen Parva should be good for several millions over that time. So the deal would have to be staged so that no slice of funding went over the Vice Chancellor's two million pound stipulation, or the deal would largely be taken out of his hands.

And what about this visit to see the company at first hand? He would show the list of sales offices to his wife and let her decide where they should go. She would like that. He was well travelled and had no strong feelings on the subject.

Burnstone University had links with universities on most continents in common with the global outlook that all academics needed in the current environment. That meant overseas seminars, teach-ins and liaison visits which took Wyatt abroad most holidays. But he would have to do no work for the Glen Parva trip.

On the deal, though, Wyatt had plenty to think about. His main aim was to pull in as much as possible and to spend as little as he could. A nice little war chest of cash, tucked away, would enable him to initiate a major project in his specialist area of biological research just when he wanted to.

Some money would have to be allocated for public relations exercises. He couldn't see Thurmaston agreeing to foot the bill for every bit of publicity that was organised.

Then there was Palfrey. He would have to be bought off. Thurmaston and his team would soon spot the quintahertz machine and that would be brought into the equation a bit smartish.

So Palfrey's company would have to be stalled, but at least he could use the situation to keep the Glen Parva board on its toes so the agreement didn't hang fire for too long.

Palfrey's project wanted half a million just to get the machine into production. It could need much more after that to get the company up and running. That would make a hole in the deal.

So Palfrey would have to take his money in stages. And if the machine did not perform, Palfrey would suffer. Wyatt liked that idea. And if the stages ran over several years, the initial payment could be small, leaving more for Wyatt and still keeping the total deal under the Vice Chancellor's limit.

But he could say that Palfrey would be guaranteed an income from Glen Parva for the ongoing research in the department. So he wouldn't have to spend time chasing sponsors. He would be restricted in the research he could carry out, but that wouldn't go on for ever. Palfrey would just have to make the best of it for a while.

And then there was the terratanium material that Palfrey needed. Glen Parva might be able to use its purchasing power to buy the metal at a lower price than Palfrey could. That would be a bonus point for the deal. But by accepting material, not money, it would help Wyatt, to all intents and purposes, to keep the deal under the two million limit.

He ran over the total deal. A win situation for everyone he thought. Now he had to extract the maximum from Charles Thurmaston, pay the minimum to Lazio Palfrey, and put as little by as he could for the publicity stunts that Glen Parva was obviously going to set up to keep their name in lights.

* * * * * * * *

Alan Birstall had moved quickly after the May board meeting at Glen Parva. He had listed a number of measures at that meeting that would help drive the company forward and the rest of the board had approved them all. They would expect a report on positive action at the June board meeting and Birstall knew from experience that one month was no time at all to stir other people into action.

As sales and marketing director, he had the authority to lean on the people involved inside the company. But it had taken him some time to check out fully the public relations agency he wanted to move to. It was now early June and he had had some fun trying to fix up a meeting with the agency principals before the next board meeting. He just about made it.

'Hi!' said Kate Bellew to Alan. 'Come on in.'

They moved into Bellew's office with its view looking down the Thames towards Tower Bridge.

'Take a seat.'

'Thanks. What a view. How do you get any work done here?'

'Yes, it's difficult sometimes. Especially, on a clear morning when you can see across to Crystal Palace and the television mast. But the pollution soon rises and then you'd rather look at your paperwork than the grey mist.

'Anyway, first things first. Would you like some coffee?'

'Yes, please. White, no sugar.'

While Kate called a secretary, Alan took stock of the palatial office with its picture window, crushed leather seats and veneered desk. Totally different from his own functional office in the Smethwick factory, not one of the most desirable parts of Birmingham he thought. It smelt rather nicer as well. He was no expert on perfume but he could handle working with this public relations agency.

'Now, I must apologise for not being able to se you sooner but it's a particularly busy time for us just now. There's only a short while before Parliament rises and the MPs disappear off to far flung places. I didn't want to start you off with a junior exec.'

'Thanks, that's appreciated. I have to report some progress to the board this month, but we are looking at a long term relationship.'

'Good. We can always get better results as the partnership gels.'

Kate opened her file.

'I've gone through the introductory letter you sent me and the company's annual report, and I've got the notes from our first telephone call so can we go through these points in detail first.'

'Yes,' said Alan. 'But before that can I just confirm that you are not working for any other steel producer, or any associated company in the industry.'

'No. And I am the only director who deals with industrial clients. If we can agree terms, then we will not take on anyone who might create a conflict of interest.'

'Good. Now, what about routine matters such as product launches and company news announcements, would you want to take those on, or shall we continue to work with our present agency?'

'We need to take on all aspects of PR,' said Kate. 'It can easily create problems if two different teams are aiming at the same goal. But we have staff for that level of work. Their costs are no so great as for work done at a senior level, but they are still supervised by me, so you get the best of both worlds.'

A knock at the door announced coffee. Delicate bone china cups and small chocolate biscuits all marked with the Hoogen, Bellew, Cutler logo were perfectly in keeping with the office. And probably perfectly in keeping with their bill as well, thought Alan.

'Now, the company needs to boost its share price and you propose to expand internationally to consolidate your global position. That means we have to cultivate some government and City contacts who have mutual interests. It could mean you have to change your financial advisers but we'll check that out later. The government angle is important because, at your level, steel is a political issue rather than just a purely commercial venture.

'Taking over other companies could prove more of a PR and political exercise than simply making a bid for their shares. So we need to start by announcing your accounts for last year. We'll link that in with your strategic plans. We'll use interviews with financial journalists to start off with. There are several with international links, so that will take the message to the countries you want to target. Your financial advisers will also have to talk to the major journalists. Do you know what experience and contacts your brokers have in government circles?'

'I don't know in depth. But I can check them out.'

'Well, I'd like to be in on that. HBC will have to work closely with them so I would like to check our mutual rapport. I can then say whether you'd be better off changing. I don't mind with whom we work, but they have to be top hole. Our reputation depends the company we keep as well the results we create for you.

'Now, what was the first project you had in mind?'

Alan outlined the board's aim to tie up Burnstone University.

'That sounds eminently sensible. With ideas like that, I think we can work together very well. But I have to say that working at this level may appear expensive when we work out our fees. From your side, though, you will get results faster and better than you could do yourselves, and that means a better bottom line on the accounts.'

Alan suddenly pulled himself together from a reverie that had been induced by Kate's tailored suit, her black patent shoes, that perfume and the rich surroundings. Yes, he could definitely handle a better bottom line, however expensive.

Fortunately, he managed to stop himself saying so.

Instead he said, 'So we need some detailed work here. Where do we start?' He really meant 'When?' The steel business had suddenly taken a very attractive turn for the better.

'Signing a contract first, I'm afraid. Then I'll send you a checklist of objectives for the company and a timescale as we see things. Once you've agreed or amended that, there'll be meetings with your financial people and the university, and we move on from there.'

'Sounds good. I think this will turn out very beneficial.'

He decided to chance his luck.

'I was going to have some lunch and a bit of shopping before heading beck to Birmingham. Would you be able to show me a good place to eat.'

'Love to. But not today, I'm afraid. This desk may appear empty, but that's only an illusion. But you'll find something good within a few yards, whatever direction you take. Bad eateries don't last long in this neck of the woods.'

She stood up to stop any further bright ideas emerging.

'The contract will be through in a few days and I look forward to talking with you after that.'

'Fine. Goodbye for now and thanks,' Birmingham never seemed less inviting.

* * * * * * * *

'And now, Leonid Lebdev, how are things at the London station?'

Vladimir Arbatov had moved down the agenda as he chaired the June strategic committee meeting of the Khazatan Research Institute.

'Good results, Mr. Chairman. Firstly, an agent has visited Professor Smithson on the pretext of discussing some patents he wants to sell. It appears he is not so far ahead of us and so we won't be doing business with him this time. But we've got some good pictures of samples that have been hardened. We've also got pictures of their vacuum chamber and the controller. I've passed the file on to Alexander Kasvanov.'

'Yes, Mr. Chairman. The steel association technicians are analysing the pictures now and we'll get back to you if we need anything else,' said Kasvanov.

'Secondly, Mr. Chairman,' said Lebdev. 'We got a man in to see Professor Palfrey. This one is interesting. There is a large piece of equipment under wraps in the department. The dustsheet hasn't been casually thrown over it but has been well tied down. No chance of getting in to it easily as you can see from the photograph. Palfrey is quoted as saying 'We can't have all our secrets on show.'

Lebdev passed a picture up to Arbatov.

'How do you know it's not just an old piece of kit that's stored there?'

'I asked that question myself. But our man says there isn't room in the laboratory to store stuff that is not actually used for research. There's a pile of metalwork outside that it would have joined if it wasn't being used. But more important, there was no dust on the covering sheet. That's unusual in a metal working room where fine dust is regularly kicked up and where the cleaners don't often come in. Our man estimates the sheet had probably been put on that day.

'He was also surprised by the small amount of research projects going on. So our estimation is that something is going on that Palfrey doesn't want anyone to know about. It's going to be under that dust sheet and it's taking up a lot of research time.'

'That fits in with what Danelski said after his London visit,' said Arbatov. 'What do you recommend we do next?'

'Well, I've mulled this over and suggest two ideas although if anyone has any others, let's know. The first has already been initiated by London station of their own accord, so they're obviously short of work these days. They're hacking into the computer system at Burnstone University and are tunnelling towards Palfrey's department. They say there's a complex firewall system and huge numbers of files to wade through so it won't be a quick result.

'I suggest we encourage them to continue to see what information they can trawl up.

'Secondly, we break into the department and steal the machine.'

That cheered up the assembled committee.

'Great,' said one member. 'We haven't seen any action like that for a long while. Can I volunteer my services?'

Arbatov shot him a withering look.

'Well, there's two quite different approaches to the problem, anyone else any other ideas?' he said.

'Our technicians would love to get their hands on whatever's under that dust sheet if all our suspicions are right, but what if it turns out to be just a pile of junk?' said Kasvanov.

'That's a chance we'd have to take.'

'I propose we break in,' said the member who had already volunteered his services.

'OK,' said Kasvanov, after a pause, 'I'll second that.'

'All in favour?'

All hands went up.

Arbatov smiled to himself, this was getting to be like the old days.

'Lebdev. More work for you. But I'd like you to take one precaution. Float all the plans past our covert operations people here in Khazatan before London is authorised to go ahead. I know you keep them in touch as a matter of course but I'd like you to use their experience on this one.

'London might just be a bit rusty on these sort of operations nowadays and I class it as a delicate project. Not many people would want to steal a piece of what could be junk from a specialised university laboratory and the finger could soon point at us.'

'Fair enough,' said Lebdev. 'I appreciate your concern.'

'Good luck.'

* * * * * * * *

Chapter 7

'Well, I really love having the whole family together but the peace and quiet when they've gone is also very enjoyable.'

Helen and Lazio Palfrey were walking arm in arm through the manor garden on the Sunday evening after Saxon and Donnatella had collected together their respective families and partner and started back home.

Lazio agreed. 'It's like the uni in the holidays. Pressure's off and it gives you time to think and appreciate. Is that why we live in the village and not London?'

'One of many reasons really. Including our honeysuckle. Have you caught that aroma?'

The evening air was suddenly thick with rich, heavy perfume. The honeysuckle had spread along a fence for several yards and had taken over a dead beech tree that had been split and felled by lightning many years before. It now provided shelter to aconites and daffodils that came up earlier than those in the rest of the garden because of the protection.

'And have you seen the buds on the new roses? Massed they are.'

The two carried on their inspection until Helen shivered.

'Ooh. Can you feel the dew rising? Are we going to turn for home?' More a statement than a question. 'By the way, Jim said on Friday that the lawnmower was ready for servicing. Sounds like more expense.'

'Well it wasn't done last back end so he'll be right. I'll ask him if he can arrange to get it sorted. Can't have a disgruntled gardener.'

'Now. I was just going to do sandwiches tonight as there's only the two of us, if that's all right with you. There's still some clearing up to do after the barbecue and you've eaten too well all weekend anyway. Will you butter the bread?' Again more a statement than a question.

'Might just about manage that. Then I've got some reading to do before morning.'

'That reminds me. Did Saxon get the computer bits sorted all right for your office? I clean forgot to ask him.'

'Yes, I had a play with it all. Seems to be a good system. He can also watch it from home.'

'Just be careful what sites you visit on the internet, then.'

'Thank you very much,' said Lazio in mock indignation. 'I'm above that sort of thing.'

'Except where blondes are concerned.'

'Ouch.'

'Anyway you might give Saxon ideas.'

'Chance would be a fine thing with these youngsters today.'

* * * * * * * *

After they'd eaten, Lazio brought his reading into the lounge on the understanding the television wouldn't be on. Helen was quite happy with that. The television was on less and less nowadays. Between the radio, the Sunday Times and their increasing collection of compact discs, there was more than sufficient entertainment worth catching on a Sunday evening.

He still had the paper to read from Mike Fleckney. Neurology was probably as good a place as any to start with to try to understand quintahertz theory. Apparently, mobile phone frequencies were rising all the time but no one had fully worked out the effect of holding a radio transmitter so close to the brain.

Fleckney felt his research was moving towards the frequencies that Lazio's quintahertz machine was generating. And the phone business was pushing hard to raise its frequencies ever further.

Lazio thought that if he could increase his understanding of the reactions inside organic materials such as human tissue, then he might gain an understanding into the way the phenomenon worked on the inorganic metals such as steel. At least there was research into the human angle. The effect on steel had never ever been considered.

Lazio was also naturally curious about the effect on his lab assistant, John Fleming. He ran up his laptop computer and got into the paper. It all seemed to come down to the basic chemistry where atoms spin round in orbits whether in meat or steel. And once radiation resonated with the natural frequency of the atom, orbits would be compressed. That happened in both hardened steel and dead meat.

Lazio's mind went back to the phone call with Fleckney.

'When I was in America last month,' he'd said, 'I heard that their Defence Research Agency was looking at the technology as a weapon for the police. A sort of super stun gun. It could knock out a group of people, such as terrorists and their hostages, give the police time to sort the goodies from the baddies, and then everyone would recover with no after effects.'

But Fleckney had been dismissive of the idea. Although today's battlefield was full of high tech gizmos, the idea of the death ray hadn't been seriously mooted since it had been the central feature of comic strips in the 1950s.

His paper said the human nervous system was not a continuous run of nerve fibres There were breaks every so often but it was not fully understood how nerve impulses were transmitted across the gaps.

The impulses were electric in nature and could be disturbed by the presence of strong electric fields. One test showed that people felt a tingling sensation when a very strong source of electric energy was brought near to them.

Fleckney proposed that, at very high frequencies, the nervous impulses would resonate with the transmitter. They would either rapidly increase in the same way as feedback that occurs in public address systems when the microphone picks up the loudspeaker output and causes a deafening howl; or the pulses would be paralysed. Both results would probably cause unconsciousness. In the first case, through an overload in the brain; and in the second, because the paralysis would close down the brain's system.

Lazio was both fascinated and repelled.

In either case, the body's systems would take time to recover once the transmitter power had been taken away. The chemical composition of the nervous fibre and its links would take time to return to normal and the person would be incapacitated during this time.

Fleckney concluded that this resonance happened with every mobile phone call but the power and duration of the call did not combine into a sufficiently powerful force that could be considered as hazardous. But would the effect accumulate over time or would the body repair itself between calls? That's where further research was needed.

Provided the subjects had not been cooked in the meantime, thought Lazio.

He sat back and considered what he had read. Fleckney's paper covered exactly the effect that the quintahertz machine had had on John Fleming. Could the machine act as some sort of anti-personnel weapon? It had done so quite effectively on his lab technician. But it seemed like taking a sledgehammer to crack a nut. Unless the effect could be created over a wider area.

Lazio pictured whole armies falling down at the press of a button. He then pictured the size of machine that would be needed. A factory building came to mind. Not quite the ideal battle weapon. But the natural inquisitiveness that was part of the dedicated academic would not go away.

How would one start to find out if such a machine was feasible?

'I'm going to brew up some coffee, do you want a cup?' Helen broke into his reverie.

'Yes. Yes, please. Are you going to percolate some?'

'Yes, if you like. You seemed miles away, is it a good paper.'

'Stimulating,' said Lazio, 'very stimulating.'

He settled himself again in the armchair and disappeared into his reverie. How to find out?

He pictured students and lecturers lying unconscious in corridors and classrooms around the laboratory. Not quite on. It needed some non-human targets and a test range. But how big?

He went to the lounge window and looked the length of the garden. Touch and go.

When Helen came in with the coffee, the lounge was empty, the laptop quietly buzzing besides Lazio's chair. She brought up a side table and put the coffee on it with a couple of chocolate biscuits. She stood listening quizzically to the empty house.

'Where's he gone now?'

Helen moved to the door in time to hear Lazio coming down the stairs.

'You didn't pull the chain,' she said accusingly. Then she saw the binoculars. 'Couldn't you find it when you got there?'

'What are you talking about?'

'Toilet, binoculars. What do you think?'

Lazio was obviously still miles away.

'I've been up in the garret, not the toilet.'

Helen knew when not to pursue a conversation that was obviously way beyond her understanding.

'Oh,' She took up the paper again.

'I wanted to see how far you could go in a straight line from our garden before you came to any buildings or livestock.'

A flood of questions came into Helen's mind but she decided to repeat the 'Oh.'

'Don't let your coffee get cold,' she added.

Lazio went off into a world of his own again.

There's a corridor perhaps two miles long before the ground starts to rise up by about a hundred feet, he thought to himself. If the beam of the quintahertz machine is focussed into to a really narrow angle, it could be aimed down the corridor without hitting anybody and the high ground would stop the beam if it really went wild.

'There are plenty of hedges in the way, though, but you could see if any birds or squirrels fell out of them. There'd be no need to change the frequency. There is probably very little difference between human and animal tissue anyway.'

Lazio began to get very keen on the idea and started writing down copious notes. He got out of the chair and started pacing around the lounge, chin in hand.

He'd have to keep very quiet about this. If word got out he'd be a laughing stock. A steel researcher building a death ray machine, whatever next.

'How well do you know the Newbolds?' he asked Helen.

'Well, more in passing I suppose. Why?'

'Would they have a big trailer I could borrow?'

'Well they have plenty of livestock to transport about and most farmers have some sort of trailer anyway. How big do you want it?'

'I don't know at the moment, it's just an idea I'm mulling over.'

'Well don't wear out the carpet while you walk about. Is it anything I can help with, you've obviously got some idea that's stirring you up.'

'No. No yet anyway. I've just got to think something through a bit. I'll be in the study if you want me.'

Helen looked at his hardly touched coffee and sighed. We're in inventive mood, she thought. That means I'll have to repeat every question twice for the next three days to get any sort of a sensible answer.

* * * * * * * *

Alistair Wyatt took a few days to think over how he should handle the offer from Glen Parva Steel Producers. He also wanted to give his wife the chance to decide on where they would like to visit. She loved surprises.

'I've always wanted to go to Bombay, you know. It's built on seven islands and after we'd been to Rome on its seven hills, it became something I felt I had to do. Silly, really, but do you know, in all our travels, we've never been to India,' she said.

'Only because you've been worried about the temperature and the water. Otherwise we could have gone. I've wanted to go for years. The company's got an office and an arrangement with a firm out there, but the area's called Mumbai now, they changed the name a few years ago. Anyway, we can justify the free trip now if anyone asks by taking some time to look round the university there. We don't have any departmental links with it. Perhaps we ought, if only to keep tabs on what they're doing.'

That was Alistair Wyatt, ever the devious.

And that was reflected in his response to Glen Parva, as Charles Thurmaston reported to the June board meeting.

'This business with Burnstone University is going well. I had to trim some of their demands, but that was only to be expected. Anyway, what we've agreed in principle is that we'll donate £750,000 to their gene research department, £500,000 to their steel research department and £50,000 to strengthen their PR operation.

'As a separate issue, we also have to make good the loss of revenue as the steel research department can't go elsewhere for business or sponsorship. Currently, they pull in two million a year as research revenue. Nice business if you can get it.

'There's also the matter of a sweetener to the Dean, Alistair Wyatt. He says he will have some trouble in selling the deal to the steel department but it looks as though the problem could be solved if we show him round the Mumbai operation.'

There was a snort of derision from down the table.

'What's Mumbai got to do with it?' asked Bill Oadby. 'That's going to be a bloody expensive sweetener.'

'Perhaps he's such hot stuff he needs the curry,' suggested Alan Birstall. 'Anyway, Mumbai is only a sales office, and somebody else's at that.'

'Perhaps we ought to send you out there to make it something better as you're the sales and marketing director,' said Thurmaston.

Alan grimaced.

'Thank you, Mr Chairman. But I'll have to go out there when we tweak up the joint venture with Sandrapoor Steel Mills. That'll be enough punishment thank you.'

Charles Thurmaston didn't share his sales and marketing director's facetious outlook on life.

'Wyatt suggested Mumbai because it's a developing area and he could then judge how Glen Parva might progress there. He also asked if he could have time to visit Mumbai University. Burnstone doesn't have any links with an Indian university and if anyone questioned his taking a freebie, he could say he was also working for his university to develop its links. I thought that was a good idea.'

'I agree,' said Alan Birstall by way of apology.

'Why are we as a steel company putting money into gene research?' asked Bill Charnwood. 'Or have I missed something?'

'No,' said Charles Thurmaston. 'It's to show that we have a caring face and are aware of our social responsibilities. We put some of our profits into areas that will benefit humanity instead of hogging them all for ourselves. Shareholders love that sort of thing nowadays. It also helps when we accidentally dump ten tons of pollution into the river.

'Now, before we go into details of how this deal will work, can I ask for a proposal from the board that these heads of agreement are acceptable in principle?'

He had no need to ask. Any rebuttal of a chairman's suggestion was bad news for both chairman and the board that had elected him. Effectively, it verged on a vote of no confidence. Today, the board was in total agreement.

'Thank you,' said Thurmaston. 'Now let's look at the detail. Firstly, Alan, where are you at with the new public relations agency?'

'Well, having spent most of the past month trying to pin it down, we've had our initial meeting and it looks as though we may have to change our financial adviser for a start. They're very keen to cultivate government and city contacts for us, and that means our stockbrokers must be top hole at taking to financial journalists and people like that. I don't think our present people fit that brief all that well.

'They're also keen to present our latest accounts with a bit of a splash. They think they are very good and see an organised presentation as part of the ongoing PR process.

'But first they'd like to meet the people at Burnstone with a view to putting out a press release to the local papers and to the relevant scientific journals. That would announce the link up between us and them and start putting out the message that the university is helping the country's steel industry in its time of need while Burnstone is helping push forward the boundaries of science and providing a better understanding of how humans and their genes work.'

'Plenty to be going on with there,' said Thurmaston. 'Now, Geoff, on the technical side, are you set to go and see Professor Palfrey once the deal has been agreed.'

'Yes. No problem there.'

'Well, there's a little surprise for you when you do go. Palfrey has just let it be known that he's working on a new way to harden steel. It uses very high frequency radiation and the first results are excellent. The prototype machine is just about ready to go into production. The dean says Palfrey hasn't assessed its potential yet so it can come into the deal at a knockdown price.'

Geoff Aylestone raised his eyebrows.

'Cunning old fox. He's never let on about that. But what do you mean about it coming cheap, that's not like Palfrey.'

'Apparently, Palfrey is thinking of setting up his own company to finish development of the machine and then to market commercial versions. But he's short of money and needs more funds to do that. He's just been to see the dean to see what the uni could put in and to clear the way to start up his company.

'The inference is that we provide the necessary finance and then sell the machines either through Glen Parva or through a new subsidiary.'

'And what does Palfrey get out of it?'

'That's yet to be decided.'

'I'd better find out for myself then what the potential might be for the machine,' said Aylestone. 'What sort of timescale are we working to?'

'I think the first thing now is to arrange a meeting face to face. So you've got a few days. If we all go to Leicester, you can meet with Palfrey; Alan can talk to their PR department; and both Bills and I can discuss financial details with the dean. If necessary, we can have a meeting with us all there at the same time.

'I'd like you to come, Bill,' Thurmaston indicated Bill Charnwood, 'because you get to see more boardrooms as an executive director than we do. You can then check how we're doing against other firms.'

'No problem.'

'Right. If everyone's in agreement, I'll set up a mutually acceptable meeting date.'

Nods all round.

He turned to his agenda.

'Next item.'

* * * * * * * *

Alistair Wyatt decided he would have to sort out Lazio Palfrey before the meeting with the people from Glen Parva.

It wouldn't be easy, but there was a lot at stake. Not only for now but for the future as well. So he had put in a lot of thinking before asking Palfrey to drop in. He opted for the morning meeting and the large brandy with coffee routine.

Lazio couldn't refuse the offer, there was no changing the habit of a lifetime, but he still smarted from the last visit when brandy had been offered.

'Would you like to try this one?' Wyatt asked. 'My wife bought it from her delicatessen when we had a pasta evening a little while ago.'

He proffered a bottle of Italian brandy that immediately split Lazio's loyalties. Italian, yes; brandy, oh dear. Not really one of Italy's strengths. The words paper and sand sprang to mind. But he couldn't play the traitor on this occasion.

Lazio looked at the label. Forty five per cent proof. Jesus Christ. Power without intelligence.

'That looks very good,' he lied. 'But just a small one, please, I'm lecturing in an hour.'

'I'll come to the point right away, then,' said Wyatt. 'The business development committee hasn't yet given the OK to your fifty thousand pounds. We are also concerned at the total amount of capital needed for the venture. It looks as though you'll have to put your plans on hold for a bit. We think the whole scheme is a bit too big for the university to handle internally.'

Lazio saw himself having to put up with the leaks in the manor roof and the gardener griping about the lawn mower for some time to come.

'Perhaps I could wait until the committee actually tells me its decision before I change any of my plans.'

'If you wait until then, and the verdict goes against you, then you are stuck. There's no appeal and you are out on your own. Finito'

Lazio took a swig of his brandy. It seemed the only thing of comfort just now.

Alistair didn't tell him he hadn't even started to put a proposal to the committee.

'Look. Don't take it too hard. The committee is inundated with requests for money. They can't meet all of them.'

'Yes. But this idea is very strong commercially and should bring a good deal of kudos to the university. Especially when I've put so much of my own money into it.'

Lazio had slumped, deflated, into his chair.

Alistair almost felt sorry for him.

'I'll tell you the real reason I've called you in. You could wait until the committee makes a final decision as you suggest, but an alternative may have just cropped up.'

Lazio pricked up his ears.

'Well, I can't let my own staff down. A couple of weeks ago, a company offered us some money in return for help with its business strategy. I think it would fit in with their plans if some of the funds went to your department as a leading part of the university.

'I'd have to sort out the details, of course, but they could possibly fund the whole of the quintahertz project and then market the machines as well.'

'That sounds a possibility,' said Lazio. 'Who is the company?'

'I'd rather not say just now. But if you're broadly in agreement, I can channel the discussions that way. I mean, it doesn't greatly matter to me where the money goes as long as the university benefits as a whole.

'What do you think?'

'Please go for it. It sounds the best possibility just now, and I can always say no if the detail doesn't suit.'

'That may not be possible,' said Wyatt quietly.

103

The remark may not have been picked up by Palfrey, but it was certainly caught on Wyatt's recording system.

'The company is also somewhat hard nosed,' said Wyatt. 'More than we are used to here. So you may not get everything you want. They may want to pay you only out of the sales they make. They may not want to put too much money up front.'

'I'm sure they'll be reasonable,' said Palfrey, totally inexperienced in the dirty tricks that companies with power can play on the weak.

'Indeed,' said Wyatt. 'I'm sure they'll be very reasonable'

But he didn't say with whom. Neither had Palfrey spotted the silvered forked tongue that had convinced him to take the path Wyatt suggested without questioning it.

* * * * * * * *

Two days later, Lazio Palfrey was again summoned to the dean's office.

'You're seeing a lot of him lately,' said Ann Whittaker when she passed on the message. 'Have you two got something going?'

'Not me. But he's up to something yet again and I bet it doesn't do me any good.'

So it was a somewhat prickly Palfrey that told Wyatt's secretary, Jenny, that he wouldn't be requiring coffee as he wasn't staying that long.

'Right, Lazio,' said Alistair Wyatt as soon as the door was shut, 'How would half a million pounds suit your department?'

That took the wind out of Palfrey's sails completely and utterly.

Wyatt may have been a microbiologist but it was psychology that got him the deanship.

'That would be most useful I do have to say. Thank you very much.'

'I thought you'd like the sound of that,' said Wyatt. 'Should enable you implement one or two projects.'

'Indeed. That is good news.'

Wyatt reclined in his chair. He loved having his ego massaged.

'Any projects in particular come to mind?'

'Well, yes. I was talking to David Bearing just the other day about some new equipment we could do with.'

But Wyatt, having established the feeling of the meeting, wasn't interested in details. He nodded in response.

'It doesn't come without some caveats, though.'

'Don't worry, these things never do.'

'They would want to include the quintahertz machine.'

That was a bucket of cold water after the warm shower.

'What. You can't agree to that. You know exactly my position. The hours I've put into it, and the money I've spent getting it to where it is now, you can't do that to me.'

'Don't worry. We're not giving the machine away. What about the huge numbers you were going to sell, you'll get something out of that.'

'Like what?'

'You can discuss the details with them yourself. They're visiting in the next few days or two, so you can hammer out the fine detail then. They will also be putting a lot of work your way. Possibly two million a year, so don't be too hard on them.'

'That's sounds good on paper, but that's the department's annual turnover anyway. We won't be able to do any other work at that rate. We'll end up employees. That will do my reputation no good whatsoever. You must have realised that. What about academic integrity? Where will our innovative research fit in? We'll just be some company's tame research department.'

That's an accurate assessment, thought Wyatt.

'Look, it won't be forever,' he said. 'Just look at the short term benefits.'

Palfrey looked as though he might erupt.

'Anyway, who is this marvellous company that's going to do all these wonderful things?'

'Glen Parva Steel Producers.'

'What. That load of commercial money grabbing shysters. You expect me to be their employee. Right. You have my resignation as of now.'

Palfrey stormed out of his chair.

'Lazio, Lazio. That won't do you any good at all. You will throw everything away if you're not careful. You just can't walk away from Burnstone, think of your future.'

Palfrey paused at the door.

'This deal isn't just about you. It's about the whole university. The deal isn't really for Combined Engineering, that's just a spin off I've been able to negotiate to help you with your machine. With the steel industry in such disarray what other options do you have just now?

'Look. Don't go steaming off. Give the whole thing some thought. It's not the end of the world. You have to think of the whole university and the total benefits. Don't make it awkward for everyone.'

But Lazio wasn't prepared to be that generous.

'What happens if the work they offer isn't suitable.'

'Lazio. Use your intelligence. You're all men of steel. You can work something out. You've already had good dealings with them, and they think the world of you. Look. I don't want to pull rank but I have to think of the greater good for the whole university.'

Lazio felt sewn up into the tightest straitjacket imaginable. He was really more cross with Wyatt's deviousness than he was with the deal.

'OK. I'll think it over.'

'Thank you.'

That was a bit livelier than I'd expected, thought Wyatt as the door closed behind Palfrey, I think I deserve a brandy.

* * * * * * * *

Lazio went steaming straight into David Bearing's office.

'You're the man with all the information. What's going on at Glen Parva Steel Producers, then?'

'I've no idea. We haven't dealt with them for ages.'

'Well, they're bloody well going to take us over, lock stock and barrel.'

'What are you talking about?'

'That bloody worm Wyatt has given them the quintahertz machine and said they can have all our research time. Just so he can get some money out of them for the university. And I bet most of it goes into his bloody pocket.'

'Sit down,' said Bearing, fearful for his boss's blood pressure. 'It can't be that bad.'

'It's a bloody sight worse. If I don't agree, Wyatt says he'll pull rank and force me to accept.'

'Yes, but come on. There must be a bit more to it than that. They just can't have all that for nothing.'

'Well, they're going to give us half a million pounds.'

Bearing laughed out loud. 'What's wrong with that?'

'Don't laugh. What about our academic integrity? We'll just be puppets for them to play with. And what about all the time and money I've put into the quintahertz machine?'

'Ah. Now we're getting to it. But you've been paid a salary for your time, most of the bits came out of the department's budget and you're getting a pile of cash to benefit from. And I'm quite sure it won't go on for ever. Glen Parva must have more things to think about than one university department.

'Anyway, you work with their Geoff Aylestone on a number of committees, why not talk to him?'

'I can't go and admit I don't know what's going on under my nose in my own department, can I? Would you have a word?'

'I hardly know the man,' lied Bearing.

'Well, we've not much time to spare. Wyatt says they're all coming up here in a few days to sign the agreement.'

'Alright, I'll cook up some excuse to give him a call and see what's to do.'

'Great. Thanks a lot.'

David Bearing finished off the research paper he was writing, checked his emails and then typed in the password for Alistair Wyatt's email archive.

Calling up the search function, he typed in ''Glen Parva'' and found two incoming and three outgoing emails. They didn't say anything incriminating, they just confirmed what had obviously been a number of detailed telephone calls between the dean and the company's chairman. Typical, he thought, it had never ever been possible to tie down Wyatt but one day he'd be too clever for his own good.

That thought made him think further. What had the dean actually been saying to Lazio?

He typed in the password for Lazio's email archive. Strange. Lazio hadn't sent or received an email for the last week. That was impossible. David checked his own archive. There were two from his boss in that time. He hacked again into Lazio's archive. Same result - and no sign of the emails he'd sent David.

What is going on, he thought.

He hacked into the university's main archive. No emails recorded there for the last week. If there had been some system crash, it would have affected his computer as well. But it hadn't.

There was a mystery that he couldn't resolve.

Both Bearing and Palfrey went home with furrowed brows.

Bearing kept quiet about his. Madeleine wasn't into computers one little bit.

Palfrey opened his heart to Helen, who listened sympathetically.

'You mustn't let this get to you. It won't do your blood pressure any good. You're working all hours and I don't know the last time we went for a decent walk. We're not getting any younger you know. You have to look after yourself more.'

The lecture was interrupted by the telephone.

'It's Saxon for you.'

'Hiya! How's things?' said Lazio.

'Fine. You all OK your end?'

'Yes. Fine. Why?'

'Anything of interest going on just now?'

'Well, lots as it happens. But it's all work. I was just telling your mother.'

'That's a coincidence. Someone's just tried to hack into your computer. First time since I installed the intelligent node.'

A cold hand clutched Lazio's heart.

'Any idea who or why?'

'The name David Bearing ring a bell?'

'Oh my god. How did you find that out?'

'Just a hunch really. His initials appeared in the routing details. Normally, you couldn't find out any more than that but I ran up the list of email addresses for the university staff and found his initials there. I mean, they could be the initials of someone else, there's no being absolutely sure, but it just seems a coincidence that he's in your department.'

'I didn't say anything at the time, but he's the reason I got you to install that intelligent node in my office,' said Lazio.

'Well, he tried at four thirty two and four thirty eight. And there's something else. When an amateur goes hacking, they leave fingerprints all over the internet. You can't trace them directly, but if you go to the service provider they'll tell you who it is, provided you're in some position of authority. But this guy is professional. If I hadn't stumbled on that coincidence, there would have been no way of finding out who it was.'

Lazio felt physically sick.

'Thanks for that, Saxon. The times you mention were just a few minutes after I'd left his office. It just adds to what has been a bit of a bloody day.'

'Sorry.'

'No. It's not your fault. I suppose it's good to have one's suspicions confirmed. I'll just have to mull over how I handle it.'

Lazio thought through the snippets of information that David Bearing had come up with recently. That paper he'd got from John Smithson. He'd been suspicious about that from the start, and it was that which prompted him to strengthen his computer system. He decided to ring Smithson.

'John, it's Lazio Palfrey, Burnstone.'

'Hi. Long time no see, where have you been hiding?'

'That's the question I was going to ask you. Haven't seen you at any of the committee meetings for a long while, are you in retirement?'

'No, more's the pity. Just the opposite in fact. More work than I can handle.'

'I gathered that might be the case. My man, David Bearing, was at the last Technology Transfer Day and says you had quite a lot to report on.'

'Yes. There's a few patents that have gone through the process and are now on the market. Are you interested in any?'

'No, thanks. Not quite my scene. But I was interested to read the paper you gave David. I wouldn't ever go along that line of research but it made me think about my own work.'

John Smithson sounded puzzled.

'What paper was that? I don't think I've ever given a research paper to any of your staff. You're the competition. You have to get your own.'

Lazio's heart sank.

'I think David did just that.'

'What do you mean?'

'I think David might be a large scale computer hacker.'

'Oh dear. That's not good news.'

'I've no confirmation you understand and I've yet to talk to him about it but I think it might be an idea for you to check your firewall. Maybe change the password or whatever you do to these things.'

'I'll do that first thing in the morning,' said Smithson. 'Thanks for letting me know, that's appreciated. Will you let me know if anything else crops up and I'll keep you in touch if there's any developments this end.'

'That's spoiled my evening,' Smithson said to his wife. 'Looks like someone's been hacking into my computer system. All that research is so highly confidential. If any of the information gets out, my sponsors will crucify me. The results are absolutely vital to these companies. They're so twitchy about losing out to the competition. I think I'll try and get hold of the IT manager now.'

While he went off to get some contact numbers, David Bearing was being rung at home.

'Hi. It's Geoff Aylestone here, how's things?'

'Interesting,' said David. 'Were your ears burning this afternoon?'

'Not so I noticed, why?'

'Glen Parva was being discussed in some depth. I gather you're coming up here in the next few days with all sorts of goodies for us.'

'Yes, that's right. I was hoping to get to you before the news broke but I'm obviously late. I couldn't tell you before the deal was decided and then it happened quite quickly. It's all been going on above my head so I'm not fully in the picture myself but I didn't want to spoil our relationship because you have helped so much in the past with snippets of information. You may know more than me yet again.'

'I've only got what Lazio Palfrey has told me,' lied Bearing. 'But it seems a fairly comprehensive takeover of the department by Glen Parva. What's behind it?'

Geoff outlined the company's strategy and where the university fitted in.

'But what I need to know is a bit of background about the quintahertz machine. You've never mentioned that but it seems important. Have you anything written up about it?'

'Well it's something we've only just got going properly. There is an outline document but it's top secret as far as Lazio is concerned. I'll email it to you if you like but don't let it get out. Lazio is staking his future on it and it is very important to him. It'll also be worth a mint to the steel industry and I think Lazio is hoping to retire handsomely on the profits.'

'We were told the opposite and that we'll get it at a knockdown price.

Bearing immediately sensed the hand of Alistair Wyatt hovering over the deal.

'I think you'd better talk to Lazio when you come up. I'm hearing two different stories so I'd really rather not comment. I've only just heard about the deal myself.'

'OK. Well make sure you're around when we come up. It'll be good to have a pint together. Oh and don't let Lazio know I called, don't want to complicate things.'

* * * * * * * *

111

Lazio Palfrey was in the department next morning earlier than usual, much to Ann Whittaker's surprise.

'Can you find David and get him into my office before he starts lecturing, I need a word a bit sharpish.'

Ann scuttled off. That wasn't Lazio. Are we in for a bad day, she thought.

David appeared a few minutes later.

'Sorry to bring you in such a rush,' said Lazio, 'I just wanted a bit of advice before I go off lecturing.'

'No problem. How can I help?'

'I needed to get a bit of background on the internet. Is it true that people leave tracks when they go surfing?'

'Absolutely. Why, what have you been up to?' David had a broad grin on his face.

Lazio evaded the question.

'How difficult is it to conceal those tracks, so no-one can trace you?'

'It's not easy, you have to know what you're doing. You'd have to find a professional hacker and download some special software from their site.'

Lazio pushed a wedge of stapled pages across the desk to David. It was the research paper from John Smithson.

'Don't rush to answer, but did Professor Smithson hand you this personally, did he post it to you or did you get it over the internet?'

David Bearing felt an immediate need to sit down.

'I see,' said Lazio. 'Just don't say anything.'

Lazio looked down thoughtfully at his desk.

'All these snippets of information you come up with from time to time, do you get those the same way?'

David nodded.

'That's why you were able to retrieve my email from the dean so easily?'

David nodded again.

'So what is on your computer just now that shouldn't be there?'

'Nothing.'

'Well, as soon as you've finished lecturing, you will make absolutely certain that is the case. Both here and at home.'

'OK. I'm sorry. What is Smithson going to do?'

'I can't answer for him at all. What he'll do, I've no idea. How could you be such a bloody idiot? If this comes out that you're a common hacker, that's your academic career ruined. You've two young kids and a good wife to think of. Just go and pray for their sakes that this doesn't leak out. And lay off your computers until you're absolutely sure that nothing else comes out of the woodwork.'

* * * * * * * *

Chapter 8

David Bearing was going to find it hard to refrain from hacking as his boss had ordered. But Lazio obviously knew more than he was admitting. There had to be a reason why David couldn't see any of his recent emails that was for sure.

But he loved pitting his hacking skills against the world in the same way that others love crosswords, competitions and similar challenges. Unfortunately, what had started out as fun turned into a dark, addictive and serious business.

The slide had been helped by Glen Parva Steel Producers. Geoff Aylestone had got on well with David when they had met at a steel seminar several years before. David liked the company's thrusting attitude to life and passed on any snippets of information that he thought would help the company progress.

That was borne out of friendship. But when Aylestone gave David two air tickets to Hong Kong, his hacking became serious.

'A couple of us are not going to the next steel trade conference,' he said. 'But no-one need know. Take Madeleine and have a few days holiday. You can even go to the conference if you want. It's just a small thank you.'

Aylestone knew that, on his lecturer's salary, and with two small children, a holiday in Hong Kong was totally out of the question for David Bearing.

Later, when David wanted to upgrade his computer, Aylestone supplied a complete system.

'This is on Glen Parva's books,' he had said. 'but it's supposed to be in some remote sales office. It'll be written off in two years, well before any auditors go poking about, and no-one will ever enquire after it.'

So David hacked into other company websites and read their internal emails and technical papers. He loved the ease with which information could be sent about. No spy cameras or photographic dark rooms, all his visiting was done from home whenever he wanted. And documents and drawings could be sent through to Geoff Aylestone in a matter of minutes. That kept Glen Parva well clear of any suspicious activities.

After Palfrey's warning, David decided to immerse himself in academic work for a few weeks. But first he had to send the email to Aylestone giving him the background on the quintahertz machine. Emails weren't covered by the warning, especially from his home computer. No problems there.

Or were there?

As David clicked on the Send icon to connect his computer to the telephone line and the internet beyond, a computerised box across the road from his house woke up. It read the email as it passed. And, periodically, it put out a signal to hold up the transmission while it read the memory in David's computer.

That email took a long time to send, thought David afterwards. I suppose there were a lot of big diagrams to go through. Could have been a busy night on the internet as well, slowing down all the systems.

About eleven o'clock, a car stopped a quarter of a mile from the end of David's road. A figure with a dog got out, quietly closed the car door and walked away, apparently taking the night air before bed.

Opposite the Bearing house, the figure bent down by a telephone junction box as if attending to the dog. But, instead, it undid the door on the box, reached in and lifted out a small cassette. It put back the cassette that was already in its hand, closed the door, stood up and carried on walking. In the dark no-one would have realised what it had done. Ten minutes later the figure and the dog returned, continued on to the car and drove off.

All David's computer secrets were on their way to London.

* * * * * * * *

'Now we're getting somewhere. Look at that.'

The manager of covert operations at the Khazatan embassy in London was watching a computer screen with several of his

115

technical team as the cassette revealed all David Bearing's computer secrets. One find was a number of computer passwords for the university.

'No wonder we couldn't get close to Palfrey's department, just look at those passwords you need.'

'These autohacker machines are brilliant, aren't they?'

The attempts by the team to hack into the computer system at Burnstone University had not proved profitable. But it had yielded a list of staff and their home contact details. So several autohacker boxes had been strategically placed in telephone junction boxes around Leicester.

'But look at this,' said the team leader, reading off the screen. 'This software is licensed to Geoffrey Aylestone, Glen Parva Steel Producers Ltd. It's not David Bearing's computer anyway.'

'Do a quick search on the words Glen Parva,' said the manager. That brought up the email that Bearing had sent to Aylestone with the background to the quintahertz machine.

'Wow,' said the manager. 'Quickly run me off a copy of that then I must go to my admin meeting. What the hell's quintahertz when it's at home? Go on, search on the word, then I've really got to rush.'

That brought up the email Lazio Palfrey had been ordered to send to Alistair Wyatt and the details he had sent to James Russell of the company he was wanting to start. Ninety per cent of the secrets of quintahertz and what it could do were now in the manager's hands.

He grabbed the printouts almost before the last sheet had finished printing.

'I'll read these during my meeting,' he said. 'See you later. And if anyone asks, we've definitely got enough material to justify going further into this whole thing.'

* * * * * * * *

'Another little trip up to Leicester for you,' said the manager of overt operations to Boris Pushtin. 'This time, we're after plenty of pictures, a layout map and lots of information from where you're going.'

He slid a large photograph and a magnifying glass across the desk.

Pushtin recognised one of the photographs he'd taken of Lazio Palfrey. It was of him beside a machine that he'd said wasn't particularly important but which Pushtin said was colourful and would look good in the magazine. Palfrey hadn't realised that, on the wall behind him, was a burglar alarm control box with a phone number to call in case of problems.

'That's the phone number for the place you're going to: Premier Security Systems. You're going to see how secure they are. We will be visiting them out of hours in a few days, so we need to know how to get in without waking anybody up.

'Act as a possible customer. Here's your business card. Tell them they can't keep it as it's the only one you've got. More important, it's the only one we've got. Our lords and masters will have to top up our supplies soon that's for sure.

'Anyway, use your imagination to get shown round their place, you need to be convinced that they've got security right for themselves, for example. But keep your eyes peeled for where their archives might be. There could be a room full of filing cabinets, for example. That's the real target.'

'Here's a map of the industrial estate they're on. Method of transport is train and taxi. You ask to be dropped off at this factory here,' The manager indicated with his finger.

'It's out of range of any security cameras the target might have, but it's not too far to walk. You then come back here afterwards and call a taxi on your mobile phone. Here's your faithful briefcase. Any questions?'

'No. Seems straightforward enough. I'll check train times but I could probably go now and be there for mid afternoon. Is that OK?'

'Yes, no point in hanging around.'

So it was about half past two when Boris Pushtin pushed open the front door of Premier Security Systems. A loud chime advertised his action and showed him where the main burglar alarm control box was sited.

'Could you give me some brochures on your security systems, please,' he asked the receptionist.

'Certainly. Is it for a house or something larger?'

'A factory. It's not yet built but it will be like the others already on this estate.'

'So it will be quite a big system?'

'Yes. We want maximum security.'

'I'd better get the manager in that case. Would you like to take a seat for a moment.'

She rang the sales manager while Boris took a few photographs with his briefcase camera as he looked around the reception area.

The manager came through with a pile of leaflets which he set down on the table.

'Would you like a coffee while I go through our products?'

'I'm fine thanks, I've only just had lunch,' Boris didn't intend to spend the rest of the day in the building however important a customer he might have appeared. Girlfriends and evenings ranked higher.

He managed to sit through the manager's spiel without twitching until asked for specific details of the proposed factory.

'That's for someone else to decide, I'm afraid, I'm just here on a fact finding mission.'

He smiled inwardly at the double meaning.

'But I would like to see some of the sensors in the flesh, so to speak, so I can talk about them when I get back.'

'Come and have a look round then. We've fitted top of the range systems throughout. You can't see behind the scenes, of course. The software and the back up systems, that sort of thing. But they're all the latest technology.'

The manager took Boris through the building, his camera silently recording every office area and security gizmo.

Back in reception, Boris thanked him.

'Very impressed. I think we can do business. One of our people will be in touch within the next few weeks.'

'Just before you go, can I take a few details for our records. What did you say the company name was?'

Boris produced his business card.

'I can't leave that with you, I'm afraid, it's my last one and I'm not sure if I'll get any more before we open our Midlands office. But everyone can be contacted through the Brussels number.'

On the train Pushtin drew a map of Premier's building layout. Just one floor, fortunately. All the office doors had been open and he'd been round the workshop. He counted the number of offices on his map and realised he was a door short. Between the toilets. The only door that had been shut.

And he hadn't seen the rows of filing cabinets that were supposed to contain the details of all the company's installations. So that was where the archive must be. Crafty move. The room was insulated on either side from any office fire by toilets with their abundance of water. There was probably no window to the outside. People would expect the toilets to be in one block and if there were a door in between, it would just be a cupboard for the cleaners and their materials. Full marks for security.

It was gone six when Pushtin arrived back at the Khazatan embassy. Most staff had gone home so he deposited the briefcase, brochures and map with the night duty officer and escaped to the pleasures of a London evening.

* * * * * * * *

Two days later, about four thirty in the morning, an estate car stopped outside the same factory where Boris Pushtin had been dropped off. A man in factory overalls pulled a bicycle from the back, threw a haversack over his shoulder and cycled off towards Premier Security Systems.

Five minutes later an alarm sounded beside the bed of the firm's managing director. Fighting free of the duvet, he leant over and switched it off.

'That bloody thing'll give me a heart attack one of these days,' he said to his wife who had sat up beside him.

He dialled 999 on the bedside phone.

'Police, please.'

'Morning. The burglar alarm has just gone off at Premier Security Systems,' he said. 'Could you please attend?' He gave the address and his own telephone number.

He then rang another number.

'Hi. Have you picked up the PSS alarm?'

'Yes,' said a voice at the other end. 'A security vehicle is on its way. There was one quite close. We've also rung the police.'

'Whoops. So did I. That should get two vehicles there. I'm going there now myself. It'll take me about twenty minutes.'

The man on the bicycle left the Premier building, cycled two hundred yards down the road and hid the machine in a stack of containers on a lorry park. He watched through a gap in the stack as the alarm siren wow, wowed into the brightening day.

A security van appeared after a couple of minutes. The driver took an Alsatian out of the back and went into the building. The siren stopped as a police car pulled up.

The driver went into the building. After about ten minutes the two emerged, chatted on the forecourt and the police car left. The security guard let his dog off the lead for a run.

Then a Jaguar appeared and an overweight man got out, shirt hanging out of the back of his trousers.

'Hi. What's the damage?'

'Opportunist break in by the look of it. The front door's been jemmied and the burglar alarm control unit smashed. The siren was still going when I got here so whoever did it probably just ran when they couldn't stop the thing. I've looked around and there seems to be no damage and no drawers opened. Do you want to check the petty cash?'

'Yeah. I'll take a look inside.'

After a few minutes, the front door was pushed shut. Then the managing director appeared from round the back of the building.

'Right, I've secured the front door with a couple of chairs and I've told the office manager. He'll be round in an hour or so. No-ones going to try again in broad daylight so I'm off for some breakfast. The engineers will sort out the control panel when they come in. Oh, and the petty cash tin hasn't been touched'

The police car pulled up again.

'I've driven round the estate and can't see any obvious suspects. It was probably someone trying their luck on their way to work.

It's happened before. They're either on shift now or they're halfway up the motorway in a lorry from the park there.'

The constable indicated the pile of containers that still hid the man on the bicycle.

'Tell the boss to send round the tape from the security camera to the police station and we'll see if we recognise anyone.'

The man on the bicycle waited until five thirty and cycled slowly round to the back of Premier Security Systems. He hid the machine and applied a credit card sized piece of plastic to the back door lock.

His foot allowed the door to open about a tenth of an inch. He checked his escape route through a gap in the back fence, ready to run if the siren went off again.

With his adrenalin running on maximum, he opened the door fully.

Silence. Relief.

Ten seconds later, the door between the toilets yielded to the plastic card. This firm was rapidly losing the marks for performance that Boris Pushtin had given it.

He switched on the light in the windowless room and pulled on the filing cabinet drawer marked B. It opened immediately. Lose more points, he thought.

Then he saw the several inches thick file marked Burnstone University. This promised to be a long job. But Premier Security Systems came to his help again. The drawings were in order and cross-referenced.

He followed the drawings from the Science Faculty down to the Combined Engineering laboratory. They showed room layouts, windows, doors and, in heavier ink, the cabling and sensors for the burglar alarm system. Beautiful.

He drew out of his haversack a long white plastic tube, folded a drawing so it fit the width of the slot on the side, put it into the device and pressed a button on the end.

The drawing was drawn through the device and out the other side accompanied by the low whirring of an electric motor. Several other drawings were given the same treatment.

The drawings went back into the filing cabinet, the plastic tube went back into the haversack and the man went for his bicycle. He phoned his car driver as he cycled back to the rendezvous. A couple of minutes later they were on their way back to London.

'There's no fun in this business anymore,' he said to the driver. 'I remember when we used to bug and burgle our way across London in the old days. I can tell you some stories there. But this job, it was easier than taking sweets off a kid. And then, with all this technical stuff, all these drawings could be in Khazatan within minutes of our getting back, courtesy of the internet. But amateurs could do this job nowadays.'

And that was the assessment of the Premier Security Systems staff as they came into work. Opportunistic. Nothing stolen. Petty cash all intact. Just brute force on the door and the control panel. No skill. Amateurs.

But that was the talk of innocents. The prize had been lifted and they would never know.

* * * * * * * *

'Whom have we got left to send?'

There was a crisis meeting at the Khazatan embassy. Project Burnstone had been given a higher status after the data on David Bearing's computer had been assessed. Vladimir Arbatov and his colleagues at the Khazatan Research Institute agreed to upgrade the investigation. Now the project was in the last stage, the lifting of the quintahertz machine from the Combined Engineering laboratory.

But the number of embassy staff had been reduced in recent years and, as policy was to use different people for each stage of a project, Burnstone was proving expensive on resources.

'We're going to need three men,' said the manager of covert operations. 'And if this thing is two metres all round, we'll never get it in a car and I think it's pushing it to take a lorry in there without arousing suspicion. We've no idea how much it could weigh. So we'll probably have to dismantle it. We could be there all night.'

122

'We also need a specialist to get the team into the uni in the first place. We've already used the two we have here on station, one for the security firm break in and one to look after the autohackers around Leicester.

'We could take a chance and use one of them again, but if the plod catch anyone and then get really heavy, the links might come to light.'

'Why not send Boris Pushtin back in? If he's caught, he can always say he'd gone back to finish off his visit as a journalist. That should stop any deeper investigation and we can soon extract him from the hands of the police, if it came to that. He's into engineering things anyway, so he should know what to strip off the machine.'

'Well, if head office want to stick by their policy to use different guys for each part of a project, they'll have to send someone over. If there's Pushtin to show everyone the way round, any expert can be used to get in. And we can take one of our drivers for the third person. All he'll have to do is to heave stuff around as the other two tell him. And one of the duty drivers can take them up there. Problem solved.'

The Khazatan break-in specialist arrived on the Friday evening Eurostar. It was packed with businessmen and politicians on their way home for the weekend from Brussels and Strasbourg and the customs check was cursory.

She had flown into Paris in the morning, dropped into the Louvre art gallery for a while and visited several shops to ensure a clean break in her trip. The Cold War and Russian communism may now be well in the past but her lords and masters still insisted on old-style anti-surveillance tactics.

She turned left out of Waterloo station, round into Lower Marsh Street and right into Frazier Street. At the far end of the street, the driver of a black Mercedes watched the slight figure walking towards him. No-one followed her. She got in the car without a word and the car took her by a roundabout route to the embassy in Kensington.

The manager of covert operations met her and introduced her to the driver turned helper, who looked at her with obvious disdain;

and to Boris Pushtin, who was obviously delighted to have her on the team.

They went over the plan and then down to the garage to check out the equipment. Anouska seemed well pleased.

'It all seems straightforward enough. The target looks as soft as one would expect. Let's go for it.'

'We've decided to do the job on Sunday evening towards midnight,' said the manager. 'The university campus is at its quietest then. These places often put extra staff on for Saturday night, because there's so many people floating about rather the worse for wear. Then they run light on Sunday night when the students have spent their money and realise they haven't done their work for Monday morning.'

'So what are you planning to do tomorrow?' asked Boris.

'Do a few sights, perhaps. It's been three years since I was last in London and I've got to go on the London Eye if nothing else.'

'Do you want some company, I'm at a loose end this weekend.'

Anouska saw the manager of covert operations roll his eyes with an oh-my-god look of there-he-goes-again. He picked up his papers and excused himself.

'See you Sunday afternoon. Enjoy yourself in the meantime.'

But whether that was directed at Boris or Anouska, neither could tell.

'This job does bugger you about something rotten,' Boris said to his girlfriend later in the privacy of his office. 'Can't tell you about it but I can't see you on Saturday either. Sorry. I'll ring you on Monday. Love you lots.'

Of course Boris couldn't tell his girlfriend about it.

They both slept late on Sunday morning. It was going to be a long day.

Anouska woke first.

She rolled over and looked at Boris.

'Look at the angel,' she said out loud. Boris stirred. Anouska pulled one of the hairs on his chest.

'Ow.'

'So you are awake.'

'I am now. No need to do it again.'

'Shame,' said Anouska.

She climbed on top of him.

'You ready for tonight then?' she said rubbing herself against him. 'Don't these jobs turn you on? They do me.'

Boris was helpless. She made love to him. It was good.

'And now you can bring me champagne.'

Boris rang room service.

'And bring a breakfast menu as well, please,' he asked.

It had been a demanding night, even by his standards.

He looked at the two empty bottles of champagne on the side table.

'I wish I was on your sort of expenses.'

'Oh. My boss won't pay for this sort of thing. The hotel will have to do two bills, one for you and one for me. But you don't mind do you?' she said, sliding her hand up his leg and moving against him again.

He came just as room service knocked at the door.

* * * * * * * *

After checking their equipment and going through the plan again during the afternoon, the team set off for Leicester and Burnstone University. Arriving about eleven thirty, the driver went straight to the playing fields on the edge of the campus. Driving on to the grass, he doused the lights and was just about able to fit the four by four between the cricket pavilion and the tall hedge behind.

Anouska had taken the lead in an unspoken agreement. She pulled up the tailgate, heaved out the fold-up ladder in its nylon bag and gave it to the driver that was to accompany Boris and her. She handed Boris the bag of tools to dismantle the quintahertz machine, and took her own bag.

'Communications check.'

She pressed the button on her pager once and those in the pockets of the other three vibrated silently for a few seconds.

'All get that?' Three affirmatives.

Boris gave two presses on his pager, the helper gave three and the duty driver, four. All working.

125

'OK. Off you go,' The helper moved into the moonless night. Anouska counted twenty paces to give a safe distance between them. The driver was expendable. If he were intercepted, she and Boris would have time to move back into the darkness ready to try later.

'OK. Boris. Unto the breach we go.'

On the edge of the car park outside the Combined Engineering building the trio halted. Anouska drew out from her bag several lengths of rubber-covered tubing and screwed them into a pole about twenty feet long. She fastened a cutter on the top and uncoiled a pull-wire with a handgrip on the end.

'Now, remember,' she said to the helper, 'Don't cut the camera cable where it hangs loose or someone could see the end hanging down.'

He nodded. Disapprovingly, he hadn't said a word to Anouska since they'd been introduced. Obviously a man of the old school.

He moved round the edge of the car park until he was behind the security camera and then moved towards the mast. About four feet from it he switched on his laser torch and a brilliant spot of light two inches across shone on the camera at the top. He traced the loop of cable that gave the camera enough cable to pan round and saw that, where it went into the housing, it was fastened by several clips.

Aiming the lofting pole between two of the clips, he placed the cutter jaws against the cable and heaved on the pull-wire. The protective sheath round the cable didn't give way and the cutter slid off the cable.

He got it back into position and tried again. He felt something give but the cutter again slid off. His arms were tiring under the weight of the pole, which started waving around, and there were several muffled clangs as the pole hit the camera. The third attempt was successful and he felt the cutter jaws close fully.

Quickly, he rejoined the other two in the bushes on the edge of the car park. Anouska unscrewed the pole, stowed it in her bag and the trio moved back about twenty yards.

It was some twenty minutes before the night security guard came round to see why one of his television screens had gone blank. He shone his torch briefly up at the camera, and the fact that it was still there seemed to reassure him. He shone his torch round the car park but the black overalls and balaclavas reflected nothing back. He went off to enter a camera failure in his log.

'We'll hang on for a bit just to see if anything else happens,' said Anouska. But the campus was quiet.

After a while, she prodded the helper.

'OK, ladder man, do your stuff, and don't leave the bag lying around. One flash when it's in position'

He went over to the building and unfolded the ladder. Made from plastic covered aluminium reinforced with titanium, it opened out from a package about the size of a man's arm. It nicely reached the first floor window that had been targeted and could take the weight of several men. He flashed his torch.

Anouska gave her bag to Boris and walked off with her window opener. It was a conventional, battery operated drill but was fitted with a saucer instead of the usual type of drill bit. At the top of the ladder she pressed the saucer against the glass and pressed the trigger.

The outer saucer sealed itself against the glass, catching the drillings and keeping in the noise. The drill was a circular plate edged with diamonds that cut a circle five inches across. A rubber sucker prevented the glass circle from falling inside the building. Thirty seconds whirring was all that was needed.

Great, thought Anouska, no double glazing. She reached through the hole, opened the window and climbed inside. She called to the helper and flashed her torch towards Boris.

The ladder was pulled up and the three sat on the floor with their backs against the wall.

'Right. Let's take stock. It's one fifteen so we've got three hours until it starts to get light. Let's check the map.'

The upper floors of the Science Faculty and the internal corridors and rooms were not fitted with any alarm system so the three were able to move freely along the corridor and down the stairs to the ground floor. The sensors were all in the outer rooms so they had twenty seconds from opening the door into the

Combined Engineering lab to switching off the alarm system before the alarm would sound.

But as soon as they pushed open the doors into the lower corridor an unseen hand switched on the lights.

'Shit,' said Anouska and tried to dive back through the doors. Boris and the driver tried to follow but as the doors only opened one way they just piled up in a heap. They turned to face their fate.

But no-one was there.

Hearts pounding, they waited, but no sound came. The lights burned on, spoiling their night vision. Anouska opened the door and went back through followed by the other two. She pressed her finger against her lips to silence Boris and the helper. After a couple of minutes the lights went off.

'Bloody hell,' said Boris. 'I'm not built for this. What do we do now? The map's quite clear that there's no alarm system in the corridor. But there could be a system from another security firm, of course.'

'Try again,' said Anouska.

The driver went through the door by himself and on came the lights again.

'I've got it,' said Boris. 'It's a gimmick to save electricity. There's personnel sensors in the lights and they switch off when the corridor is empty. Let's just get into the lab as fast as we can.'

Fortunately, none of the other cameras on the campus could see the building with its lights going on and off.

Inside the lab, Boris went over to the security alarm panel and punched in the disarming code. An obliging green light came on.

'Just wait till our night vision comes back a bit,' said Anouska.

The moon had risen while the three were going about their business but it was in a cloudy sky and the light was coming and going. After a while Boris saw the benches stand out in the darkness of the laboratory.

'It's over here,' he said moving towards the corner where he'd last seen the covered up quintahertz machine.

But it wasn't.

'It's been moved,' he said rather pointlessly. 'Look. Here's the cover that was on it. His torch picked up a neatly folded dust sheet on a nearby bench. He shone his torch round the lab.

'Oh, jesus, I can't see anything like it at all.'

'That's bright. That's bloody bright,' said Anouska. 'All this frigging effort and the bloody thing's not here.'

The driver smiled broadly into the darkness.

'Right. We can't leave it at that. Lay the map out on one of these benches. Now, what's the alarm system like in the adjoining rooms,' Anouska was cross.

'They both come back to this one box,' said Boris after a while. 'So we can look in to the rooms either side, but I wouldn't go any further.'

'What about Palfrey's office? How far away is that?'

'It's at the other end of this corridor and it's on the inside of the building, so it shouldn't be alarmed if their system runs true to form. They seem to be concerned only with people breaking into the building. Once you're in they don't seem to bother.'

'Right,' Anouska said to the helper. 'You stay here with the bags until we get back. We'll check out some other rooms as far as we dare before we go to Palfrey's office. Find a dark corner that will hide the three of us if we have to come back a bit sharpish.'

They checked the adjoining rooms but Boris couldn't see anything that resembled the quintahertz machine in size or shape.

The doors to both Lazio Palfrey's office and the adjoining admin office were locked. Anouska pulled out a keyring of wires and started on Palfrey's lock. After a few minutes she could turn the handle.

'We're in,' she said to Boris. 'But before I open this door let's agree a plan. You go down the corridor and hold open the lab door. If an alarm goes off, I'm going to leave here a bit sharpish and we'll all hide in the lab.'

She waited for Boris to do his bit, then she flung open the door, switched on her torch and rapidly examined the door, the frame and the ceiling. There was no sound and no sign of any sensors or cameras.

She went over to the filing cabinet, which also yielded to her bunch of wires. With Boris looking over her shoulder, she went through the files.

'God. You smell gorgeous,' he said with his nose an inch or so from the nape of her neck. 'What's the perfume?'

'Concentrate on these files, please.'

The second drawer down yielded the quintahertz file. Anouska pulled it out.

'It's thin,' said Boris. 'I would have expected it to be a couple of inches thick. Do you want to go and get the copier while I look through the papers.'

Anouska disappeared.

When she came back, she was carrying the long white plastic tube that had been used to copy the drawings at Premier Security Systems a few days before.

Boris started feeding papers through the slot.

'This is a brainwave of an idea,' he said. 'It's just the copying part of a standard photocopier put into a plastic housing. You could almost slide it up the sleeve of your jacket and no-one would notice. The battery only lasts about thirty minutes but you can put a lot of drawings through in that time.

'The rest of the electronics is back at the office. You just plug this in and out come printed copies. Or you can plug it into a computer, see the drawings on screen and send them over the internet. Makes the security forces tear their hair out because you can send stuff about the world so quickly that they can't catch up.'

Anouska was putting the drawings back into the file as Boris copied them.

'Right. That's the last. What do you want to do now,' he asked.

'Go home fast,' said Anouska. 'I'm buggered.'

She pushed the lock shut on the filing cabinet, pulled the office door closed and applied her lock picking wires. A clunk marked her success.

Back in the lab, they collected all the gear together.

'Leave the burglar alarm, we'll go out of the lab door into the car park,' said Anouska. 'I'm past going upstairs just to go down the ladder.'

Behind the cricket pavilion, they wearily loaded up the four by four.

'Home, James, and don't spare the horses.'

As they drove out, the eastern horizon was just blushing into a new day.

'With a bit of luck, they'll all blame each other for leaving doors open and not setting the burglar alarm,' said Boris. 'They might never suspect a thing.'

'Until security go looking for a bloody great woodpecker.'

'What do you mean?'

'Well, what else could cut a camera cable twenty feet up in the air, peck a five inch hole in a window and not pinch anything? Give us your shoulder, I can't keep my eyes open,' said Anouska.

As the car warmed up, Anouska's perfume rose up under Boris' nose and he drifted off dreaming of a certain hotel bedroom.

* * * * * * * *

Chapter 9

Lazio was still fuming over the idea that Glen Parva could get involved in running his department. He decided that positive action was the only response to Alistair Wyatt's devious dealings. If the uni was going to play fast and loose with him, he would make life difficult for them. No-one knew much about the detail of the quintahertz machine, so he would take it home for some out of hours testing and keep the key paperwork in his safe so it wasn't easily accessible to all and sundry.

As far as the hardening of steel went, he was happy that Wyatt knew of the machine's potential, and that would keep the value of quintahertz high. But he decided it would be a damn sight more expensive for anyone to get hold of the technical detail.

He was also keen to try out this idea of knocking things out with the machine. He hadn't started to think about a use for such a capability but the natural inquisitiveness that made him a researcher drove him on.

So he'd asked Helen to contact Mrs Newbold at Barsby to see what the chances were of borrowing a trailer and a couple of bodies. The answer was positive and Lazio drove over to check out the possibilities.

'The thing's not that heavy,' he told Tim Newbold, 'but it's delicate and it's a couple of metres in all directions. And I can only move it on a Saturday afternoon.'

Tim took him round to the machine shed.

'This Ifor Williams trailer is the cleanest thing we've got. It's Sarah's double pony trailer so it should be wide enough.'

Lazio checked with his tape measure.

'That's ideal. Thanks very much. Now I could do with a waterproof tarpaulin. The machine will have to stand outside for a while and I'd like something that comes well down to the ground all round. I've only got a light dust sheet at the uni.'

'Tim went to a pile of covers in the corner of the shed. This blue one will cover it twice, probably, but we'll have to have it back to cover our machines once ploughing's done at back end.'

'No problem. Now what about manpower? I could get our gardener to come and help.'

'No, we'd rather do it ourselves. I mean my son and one of his friends will do it but you'll have to work round their cricket fixture list. And they might appreciate a bob or two for their efforts.'

'Yes, that'll be OK,' said Lazio. 'Now, will it take a tractor to tow the trailer?'

'No. No,' laughed Tim. 'We use the Range Rover for that one. We do like a bit of comfort for ourselves, you know. It'll be a smart enough rig to go into your university, don't you worry about that.'

So while the Khazatani professionals had been working to lift the quintahertz machine, two amateur removal men spirited it away from virtually under their noses.

It now sat behind the Palfrey potting shed.

In the meantime, Lazio had been busy working the last block of terratanium on the milling machine in his department's workshop. The design would force the energy from the machine into a much narrower beam and extend its range. Driven by his stomach again, Lazio was thinking more of a silent way to knock down game birds from a distance rather than any other use.

And so, on a still and mild June evening, Lazio put his plan into action. Half past six found him grilling bacon in the manor kitchen. As the appetising smell permeated through the house he checked a pile of plastic bags: lawn seed, bread crumbs, porridge oats, diced carrot and turnip. Plenty there. He checked his camera. Fifteen shots left. That should be enough.

The Palfrey cats stalked around the kitchen, tails up and expectant.Helen came in.

'Just about ready,' said Lazio. 'You OK with what you've got to do?'

133

'I think so,' said Helen. 'You have told me about a hundred times, remember. I check the line between here and the hill to make sure no-one is walking near. When it's all clear, I'll drape this tea towel out of the window. I then watch what happens.'

'Right,' said Lazio. 'Don't forget that I have to lay out this bait first and then we'll have to wait about ten or fifteen minutes for something to come out and investigate it.'

'I do hope it will be all right,' said Helen. 'You're sure it won't make a great noise or go out of control?'

'Just get on up to the garret with those binoculars or it might get you instead.'

Lazio burnt his fingers trying to cut up the hot bacon rashers. Hope it doesn't melt the plastic bag, he thought as it went into his game bag with the rest of the bait. He managed to get out and shut the kitchen door with the cats frustrated inside.

Leaving his camera by the quintahertz machine he walked through the gate onto the footpath behind the manor and then out into the field behind. The sheep moved obligingly out of his way. At the far hedge, he started laying a trail of seeds and crumbs back towards the house. The carrot and turnip was left in the middle of the field and the bacon was spread just inside the gate.

Lazio plugged the quintahertz machine into the extension lead coming out of the potting shed. He watched the computer set itself up, checked the readings and then went and stood behind the machine, his hand on the radiation switch. He could just see the all-clear sign of the tea towel draped over the garret window ledge.

He'd timed the operation just right. The sun wasn't too far down on the horizon and the birds were looking for the last meal of the day but people had finished working outside. The less watchers about, the better.

A village cat, outstanding white in the lowering light, stalked down the hedge towards the bacon. As it turned to the smell, a competitor slid under the gate and the two had a stand off across the rashers. Lazio thought about aiming a stone at one, but the two had come to an agreement and slowly moved towards each other and the bacon.

Lazio knew that the first to get there would grab a piece and run fast. He couldn't wait for that, so he pressed the switch.

Both cats went down in a heap without a sound. Quite the weirdest sight Lazio had ever seen. But there was a clatter as something fell down through the hedge next to them.

He threw the game bag over his shoulder, picked up the camera and took pictures of the two cats. He went through the gate to see all the sheep standing and then went to investigate the clatter. A squirrel lay stretched out in the hedge bottom. That was another picture.

He went back along the trail he'd laid. All the sheep moved away, so no effect there. A brace of pigeon lay on the porridge oats. Lazio pulled their necks and had them stowed in his bag in seconds. By the far hedge, three sparrows lay on the grass. More pictures.

He found an open spot in the hedge but couldn't see anything laid about in the next field.

Lazio felt very pleased with himself. Birds knocked out at a hundred yards. Three time the range of a twelve bore and none of the noise. Pity there hadn't been any partridge or pheasant around.

Back in the house he met Helen in the kitchen. She looked shaken.

'That was the strangest sight I have ever seen,' she said.

'Don't dwell on it,' said Lazio, 'Have a look at this instead.'

He pulled out the brace of very plump pigeon.

'Supper. And no pellets to get stuck between your teeth.'

Helen didn't seem wildly impressed.

'I'd better look inside them right away,' said Lazio. 'D'ye fancy pouring us a couple of large ones while I do it. The J&B Rare will do fine for me.'

When Helen came back with two tumblers, Lazio had, fairly expertly, spatchcocked the two birds.

'What do you see in there that's different?' he asked.

Helen turned on the light.

'All looks perfectly normal,' she said. She poked the birds with the knife. 'They feel just like they ought. I'll hang them for a couple of days and we'll see what they're like then, but I reckon they will be just fine.'

'That's what I thought. So what did you see from upstairs, then?'

'I saw those cats go down. Almost in slow motion, no noise, no kicking,' she shuddered and tried her whisky.

'I heard the noise in the hedge that you went to investigate, but I couldn't see what happened there. Now the sheep, that was interesting. There was a line of them across the beam, tucking into whatever you had left. Two or three in the middle jumped as though they'd been poked in the rear. You know how animals react when they touch an electric fence, or cattle get prodded. They moved away but went straight back to eating. So the beam was probably only three or four feet across and that would have been, what, sixty or seventy yards away from your machine.'

'It didn't leave a great burn mark on the side of the hill, then?'

'Not that I could see, but that might take a day or so to show up.'

'What have I bred?' said Lazio almost to himself. 'I'd better go back now and see if anything is still laid out there.'

'Oh, I hope not,' said Helen. 'I'm quite fond of that white cat and ours don't seem to object to it either.'

Lazio retraced his steps in the gathering dark, getting wet feet from the rising dew for his trouble. The cats had gone, so had the squirrel, and the sparrows, and his carrots and turnip. The sheep had gone back to grazing and just stared at him as he walked through. The world appeared unchanged.

Back indoors, Lazio wrote up a detailed report on the evening's work. He was able to assess roughly the shape and range of the beam but he felt disappointed that the sheep were unaffected while pigeons and sparrows beyond had been knocked cold.

'So where do I go from here?' he mused.

* * * * * * * *

'Did anything go missing from your department over the weekend?'

It was the security officer for Burnstone University.

136

'Well, I haven't noticed anything myself and no-one else has said anything so probably not. But what might have gone missing?' asked Ann Whittaker.

'I don't know. It's just that, last night, someone cut the cable to the security camera that watches your workshops and a hole's been cut in a window not far away. We've told the police but I doubt they'll find anything to go on.'

'So you think it's more than students larking about, then?'

'Oh, definitely. Firstly they would have had to shin up the camera mast about twenty feet to cut the cable. I know some of them are monkeys but that sort of climb is going some. Secondly, the window wasn't smashed but a neat five inch hole was cut in it. You can't get that sort of cutter from Black and Decker. They also tidied up after them. There's no sign of the piece of glass that was cut out and there's no dust on the floor.'

'Sounds very strange. I'll tell Professor Palfrey when he comes in.'

'Thanks. And you might be extra careful over the next few days with anything that's valuable or confidential, they could be back.'

'Did you hear that?' Ann said to John Fleming, who had come in just as the security man left. 'It appears things have been going bump in the night. Have you noticed anything missing or moved in the laboratory or any of the workshops?'

'Not so I noticed. But I can go back and check for certain. What's up, then.'

Ann recounted the conversation.

'These engineering students get up to all sorts, half of which I don't mention. But Sunday night's a funny time. I'll go and have a good look round. But can I have a quick word with the boss first?'

'You could if he were in, but he's not here yet.'

'You sure?'

'Most definitely. I had to unlock both our doors and he couldn't sneak in if he tried.'

'Was he in earlier then, do you think?'

Ann gave him a look.

'Leopards don't change their spots.'

'Well someone was in bright and early because the lab door was open and the burglar alarm switched off when I arrived. Dr Bearing says it wasn't him and Professor Palfrey is the only other one with a key.'

'Perhaps security were poking around to see what they could find.'

'Possibly. But they of all people ought to know not to leave places open without telling somebody. All sorts of stuff could walk.'

'I'll tell the prof when he gets in.'

'OK. And can you tell him that the electronics department have dropped in a test meter for his quintahertz machine.'

So the place was well abuzz when Lazio finally arrived.

He went through his desk and filing cabinet and reported to Ann that all was well.

'I'll go down and see John Fleming and see what's to do there.'

'Just before you go,' said Ann, 'have you heard from that reporter who came from European Engineering Times to interview you?'

'Not me. Wasn't he going to send through his article for me to clear before it went to print?'

'And he was also going to return the artwork for the advert. I'll give him a quick call.'

'And remember you're not free for dinner with him,' said Lazio as he went off.

When the Brussels telephone number was answered, Ann asked for Mikhail Romanov.

'I'm sorry I don't know the name at all. Have you got the right number?'

Ann repeated the number.

'Are you the offices of European Engineering Times, then?' she asked.

'I'm afraid I'm not that either. This has been a private apartment for years. I've lived here five years myself.'

'Well, I'm sorry to have troubled you.'

'Don't worry, I get odd calls from time to time. Maybe it's our duff telephone system.'

So Ann had another tale to relate to Lazio when he came back from the workshop.

'Well, there's something funny going on,' he said. 'Security swear they haven't been into the workshop, so who switched off the burglar alarm and unlocked the door is a mystery.

'Can you get the burglar alarm people to come over and change the security code. That should stop any more unknown tourists going round. You'd also better tell security about our Mr Mikhail Romanov.'

'It's all a bit creepy, isn't it?' said Ann.

'It'll turn out to be a combination of spotty students and end of term. Always a bad time. Just forget about it. And as for journalists, well, what can I say?' Lazio was totally unconvinced by his own show of confidence but he wasn't going to let it show. He went on to other things.

'Can you ring James Russell and see if he's got a few minutes for me, please, I'd like to get an update on the bit of business we were discussing a while back. I'm just going to park this bit of test kit in my office.'

* * * * * * * *

'James, I'm worried that this Glen Parva deal is going to take the quintahertz machine out of my hands without my getting much back,' said Lazio Palfrey in the business manager's office.

'It's not only the cash, it's what they'll do with my idea. What would happen if I sign it all over to another company now, without involving the university so they couldn't get near it?'

'That's a situation I've never heard happening before. I would think that if a professor goes off on a venture that doesn't suit the university, the two won't be together for very long. Deans can make life very uncomfortable for their staff if they want. But I think that would be more of a restraining force than any legal angle.

'You'd have to study your contract of employment very carefully. In industry, there would definitely be a clause to say that all your ideas belong to your employer, full stop. There may be nothing like that here.

139

'If there's no contractual arrangement between you and the uni then I suppose you can do what you like. But if you had used uni time and resources, they would have to be refunded. But that could be spread over any time scale that you could negotiate.

'Then there could be a catch-all clause that says if you do anything of detriment to the uni as a whole, that could be grounds for dismissal. So if you sell the quintahertz machine and Wyatt doesn't get his deal with Glen Parva as a direct result, then you're in the oggin.'

'Bugger,' said Lazio.

'Look,' said James Russell, 'Don't get stewed up over it. One-sided contracts don't work in the long run, and they can't be upheld legally anyway. The other side wants something out of the deal as well as you, so you've all got to work together. Just don't do anything rash.'

'OK,' said Lazio. 'Thanks for the pow wow.'

After leaving James Russell's office, Lazio dropped in to the office of Professor Luke Verity, his opposite number in Electronics.

'Thanks for sending round the test meter. It looks a smart piece of kit.'

'No problem. Once we'd found a decent sized shoehorn, it all went in the box quite nicely. Don't take the back off though! Do you understand how to use it?'

'Yes. My lab technician gave me a quick run down. It all seems quite straightforward.'

Lazio refrained from asking Verity what he wanted for making the meter but it didn't matter, the electronics man had already set out his stall.

'I'd like to talk to you sometime about making it into a commercial piece of kit so you could sell it with your machine. At the moment I've charged it to the electronic department's development account so there's no rush. Let's know how you get on with testing it.'

'I may try it this evening if I've time. I'll call you later.'

140

Next stop was his own workshop. John Fleming was hovering, dying to know what his boss was doing at home with the machine. Lazio stayed tight lipped.

'How are you getting on with sorting out the standards that the machine needs to meet,' he asked Fleming.

'I'm awaiting two quotes from test houses that will test it to the existing industrial standards. I've classed it as an engineering production machine because everyone understands what's required for that. If we call it something fancy, we might have to go into how it works and the test house might find some other, more complicated standards that it ought to meet. That'll put up the price and it could take ages to get certification.'

'Well done. I'd like to get this thing moving now as quickly as we can. Don't want anyone else to beat us to it.'

Whether Fleming knew about the impending Glen Parva deal or not, it didn't show.

Back in his office he asked Ann to brew up a coffee and to keep all callers at bay for an hour or so.

'I'm well behind with my report for the government think tank and I've got to give it a kick in the pants if its to be finished.'

But he was more concerned with his quintahertz machine, which he could see disappearing over the horizon and out of both sight and reach.

There was no one he could talk it over with. He couldn't expose his ideas and plans to anyone at the university for fear it leaked out. Friends in the steel business would have their own agenda and probably give him the answer that suited them.

When he'd chatted to his bank manager about his work in the past, the poor man's eyes had glazed over in the same way that happened to people at parties. He needed someone with a technical mind and a bit of business know how.

'Hi, Saxon, it's dad. Have you a few minutes to spare just now?'

'I've got a meeting in about twenty minutes but go ahead. We can always finish talking later.'

'It's about this quintahertz machine. You know I wanted it to be the basis of my company, well, it's turning out to be more of an albatross about my neck and I'm not sure what to do with it just now.

'The prototype is ready to be demonstrated publicly. The idea works beautifully and the machine is safe and ready for use, we're just about to get it certified to industrial standards and then we're there. The first prob is a lack of the readies to market the machine and to set up production facilities.

'The uni was prepared to go part of the way on funding but, suddenly, a steel firm comes out of the woodwork and sets the cat amongst the pigeons. It has grand ideas and that includes virtually taking over my department, and the machine.

'In the meantime, I've discovered another use for the machine. Nothing got do with steel hardening, the idea came out of the accident that John Fleming, one of the lab technicians, had a couple of months ago.

'I'm sure the idea's got potential, but where I go with it, I don't know just now. And I don't know how to keep it out of the hands of this company that's just popped up.'

Lazio recounted the test in his garden and outlined the offer that Glen Parva had made to the university.

'You've got some heavy stuff going down there,' said Saxon. 'I need some time to think that all through. Can I call you back later? It may be tonight.'

'That's no problem,' said Lazio. 'I perhaps need some time to think things through as well. I can't wait too long, though. I'll hear from you later, then.'

* * * * * * * *

As soon as Lazio Palfrey had finished his tutorials, he tucked the quintahertz test meter under his arm, grabbed his briefcase, wheedled his fifteen stone into the Maserati and headed for home.

When Saxon phoned later, his father had paced the garden many times, fuelled by his favourite Bordeaux.

'Hi. Sorry I couldn't get back earlier but I'm OK now. You're not in the middle of dinner, are you?'

'No. No. That pleasure's still to come. So what are your thoughts?'

'Well, I hate to lecture you but I do think you're overrating the importance of the quintahertz machine to the Glen Parva deal. Just think of it from their point of view. Where are they coming from? They didn't choose Burnstone because of your machine, they didn't know about it at the beginning, anyway.

'They probably came because of your reputation in the steel business. That makes your department the most important one to be taken out of the commercial equation if they want to deny your expertise to their competitors. Provided you don't work for any other company for a while, that's all they're really interested in.

'I think you are going to have to negotiate with them at some point, but keep pushing the machine down the agenda. Tie up all their time on other issues. They just want to get on with their business, this deal is costing them money and they'll want a return on it. Quintahertz is just icing on the cake for them. They're into bigger things like major acquisitions. That's where they want the university to boost their standing in the commercial world.

'They won't be around for ever. Pretend the machine isn't as ready as they think. Keep all the technical knowledge out of the way and don't make it sound so interesting. At the end of the day you'll have to strike some deal - but you'd have to do that with your own company anyway.

'First thing I'd do is to float your employment contract past a solicitor, just for confirmation if anything. He'll say whether the uni owns your ideas and if there's a catch-all clause about not acting to the detriment of the uni.'

Where have I heard that before, thought Lazio.

'Now, regarding this other idea for the quintahertz machine. This is serious stuff. It's arms, defence, weapons. That sort of thing, isn't it?'

'I suppose so. I can't think of another use, apart from making it easier than a twelve bore to pull down game.'

'And that's probably illegal anyway. You are limited in the ways you can kill game birds I think.'

'Yes, you're right. There used to be something about not being able to pick 'em off from a moving car, for example. I think that was classed as unfair.'

'Anyway, you need to be talking to someone who makes guns, rockets and those sort of weapons if you want to sell that idea. I think in all honesty that if the idea turns out to be feasible, you'd never be allowed to make it anyway.

'But the problem with selling ideas to companies is the deal you can strike. They're very fond of offering huge amounts of money, but in stages. A bit up front and the rest as they sell whatever it is. Sounds good, but if they put the idea in their safe and don't use it, then they don't have to pay you more than the up-front cash, and that may not be much, relatively speaking. Then, if they use your idea but claim it as their own, the big companies have so much legal capability, it would cost you more than it's worth in time, effort and money to take them to court to get justice.

'I think I'd go to the Ministry of Defence. You must have some contacts from your think tank committee work.'

'Yes, I can go that route without any problem. I've done work for their telecoms people in the past.'

'But remember, they can be bastards as well. They can get away with murder under their secrets acts and things. You're a very small fish in that sort of world.'

'Right, Saxon. I take your point. You've certainly given me some stuff to think about there. Thanks a lot, that is really helpful.'

'Well, take it a bit further then give me another call.'

'OK. Talk to you later.'

* * * * * * * *

Whatever plans and hopes that Lazio had for his machine and his new company were put on hold when he was told that a contingent of directors from Glen Parva Steel Producers would be visiting two days forward.

When they were brought into Alistair Wyatt's study, Charles Thurmaston introduced Alan Birstall, as sales and marketing director, and Geoff Aylestone as technical director.

'We also have two other directors who would like to visit at some time, but we will have to arrange that later,' said Thurmaston to Alistair Wyatt and the Vice Chancellor once they were seated.

144

The talk and the sherry went round on matters of no great consequence as the two sides summed each other up. Wyatt was wary that Thurmaston would leap on his corporate soap box again and bore everyone with how brilliant the company was.

When he felt that stage was imminent he reached for the phone and called Lazio Palfrey to join them. He would have preferred to negotiate on Lazio's behalf and then present him with the decided package, but, remembering the professor's outburst, decide to include him early on.

He wanted to see Palfrey's reaction. If he's confrontational from the start, then he's for the chop without any question, thought Wyatt. But if he's amenable then he can't go back on that and play awkward later on. The last thing he's going to do is to upset my applecart.

But lunch went very well. Leicester's finest restaurant came up trumps and set the tone for a pleasant afternoon.

Palfrey was more jovial at lunch than Wyatt expected. That unnerved him a little. Had the old fox concocted some plan of his own? But there was no finding out just yet.

Once back at Burnstone University, Alistair Wyatt took Thurmaston off to see the biology laboratories; Alan Birstall went with the public relations officer to discuss tactics and Lazio took Geoff Aylestone to Combined Engineering.

'This is a change,' said Lazio. 'Last time you were here you were a client, now you're my boss.'

'Look, Lazio, I'm not totally happy with this situation myself and I suspect you aren't either.'

'To put it mildly.'

'The situation won't go away, we've just got to make it work. If we don't, we're just going to make each other miserable. We've known each other for a long time. We've just got to work together. Glen Parva is on a roll and it's bigger than both of us. If we can't make it work, the rest of the directors will make it work for us.'

'An irresistible force meets an immovable object, eh?'

'Only if you want a fight. But let me outline our position. The bottom line is that the company is very ambitious and intends to be the top steel producer in the world, given time. Amongst other issues, that means we have to offer the latest products and the latest technology to support our claim.

'Now, we have some ideas we'd like you to look at, but we're really looking to you to come up with the exciting stuff. So you can have a pretty free hand. In the main, you can research what you like and we'll pay. The only stricture is that it is exciting and it boosts Glen Parva's image as a mover and shaker.

'Now isn't that a more interesting proposition than being given a series of mundane research projects where you probably already know the answer but have to go through the routine to earn your fee? And it should appeal to your students as well.'

Palfrey was somewhat taken aback by Aylestone's comments. He hadn't envisaged such a positive picture. Life, perhaps, might not be so bad under that brief. But what about his quintahertz machine and his own company? He could see that hope, and the money, disappearing over the horizon.

So the tour around the department went on until Lazio suggested they retired to his office to decide where to start.

'But what about the quintahertz machine?' said Aylestone. 'I haven't seen that.'

'Well, it's at home while I run some higher power tests on the radiation beam. I felt there wasn't the room here to test it fully but with all the fields behind my house, nothing would come to harm. You heard about the accident, I suppose. I didn't want to cause any more mayhem here.'

'I hadn't heard about the accident. What happened?'

Lazio gave him the works about John Fleming's incident and was secretly delighted to see that Geoff Aylestone was somewhat set back.

'Well, we'll have to get that sorted,' Geoff said, 'because I think the machine has a tremendous future.'

'No doubt about that,' said Lazio. 'But it has taken a huge amount of money and effort to get it this far and it's all been my own money. I should be able to make quite a lot out of it if I had my own company to develop and sell it. But if it's a case of Glen Parva taking it over, then I'm inclined to leave it where it is for now and work on other things instead. It'll keep.'

Geoff wasn't going to let that jewel disappear.

'Look. Make Glen Parva work for you. Just now it's flush with money. Take the opportunity to work out a good deal for yourself. To be straight with you, the company will probably want to take it over, it represents a hell of an opportunity for us to lead the field. But if you set up your own company, it still wouldn't be yours personally. And look at all the risks of doing that. Are you sure it will sell as well as you need? And it'll cost you an arm and a leg to set up the production side, that's for sure.

'And say someone out there comes up with a better idea that beats yours. Or say the Americans just rip you off and make a straight copy. You'd never find the money to fight that and you'd be sunk. If you use your intelligence, you can make money out of this thing and let Glen Parva carry the risks. But, for heaven's sake, don't say that to anyone or I'll be out on my ear.'

Lazio seemed mollified by that speech and settled back in his chair obviously thinking hard.

Geoff Aylestone also sat back in his chair, but with a sense of relief. He'd seen Palfrey in full sail in committee meetings when he wasn't getting his own way and hadn't relished dealing with him on a one-to-one basis. Especially when he would be telling Palfrey what he could and could not do. But his careful preplanning had paid off.

'OK,' said Lazio. 'Let's give it a whirl.'

'Great,' said Aylestone. 'Shake on it.'

'So where do we start?' said Lazio.

'Let's have a copy of your business plan for quintahertz. If I think it's fundable, then I'll see you get your money. For the rest of the projects, can you draw up a list of research that you consider will help Glen Parva reach its objective. You've heard more than enough about that today from Charles Thurmaston.

'However, there is one area I'd like you to include. That's a project on tailored blanks. We'd like to break further into the car market and if we can come up with some good research on the benefits of tailored blanks as opposed to a blank of plain sheet steel, that would help us no end. And don't forget that the research will do you some good personally. If you're seen to be doing all this leading edge stuff, it'll boost your own standing no end.'

Lazio certainly couldn't disagree with any of that.

So when the two went back to Alistair Wyatt's study, Geoff was able to signal a good result to Charles Thurmaston.

'Well, gentlemen,' said Wyatt. 'I think I can predict a good future for both the university and Glen Parva Steel Producers with this arrangement we've decided. There's just the formality of signing the final contract but I think we can celebrate while we're all together.'

He opened a bottle of Bollinger with a flourish.

Charles Thurmaston raised his glass.

'A toast, gentlemen, to the continued success of Burnstone University and Glen Parva Steel Producers.

* * * * * * * *

Chapter 10

'It can't have been taken away much before we got there,' said Anouska at the debriefing after the abortive break-in at Burnstone University to steal the quintahertz machine.

'You could see its outline in the dust on the floor. We did check other rooms as far as we could using the map and the security information.'

'I can't see why it should have been moved,' added Boris Pushtin. 'If the thing is that secret, the less it is moved about the better. It only stirs up interest if there's a fuss round it. The other curious thing was the small amount of paperwork in Professor Palfrey's filing cabinet. I'd like some time to study the copies we brought away, but there doesn't seem to be much technical detail there.'

'Well, we're going to have to locate the machine,' said the manager of covert operations. 'Our lords and masters have got the bit between their teeth and they won't let go now we've put this much effort into the project. I won't send the drawings through to them for a day or so and perhaps something will crop up in the meantime. We're still digging into the uni computer system.

'Can you two mull over events so far to see if you can think where we might go looking for the machine? When do you go back to Khazatan, Anouska?'

'I'm booked on the five o'clock flight out of Heathrow but I've nothing scheduled for this afternoon. If you want my view now, Palfrey has had some inside information and had the thing moved. Though why anyone here should tip him off, I just cannot think. I'll talk it through with Boris to see what motives we can come up with.'

The manager went off to his hacking team to see if anything fresh had come up from the autohacker data collected from David Bearing's computer.

'Good news and bad news. We've found the passwords to the Combined Engineering department computer and got in so far, but Palfrey hasn't sent anything out for a week or so. The only traffic out of the department is low level admin stuff. Palfrey's obviously active because we can see incoming emails to him and he must be responding because there's no emails chasing him for an answer.

'There could be yet another firewall around the old boy, or someone's tipped him off about something and he's deleting all his stuff. But he's got to keep copies of some things, that just stands to reason. And if he is deleting stuff, he knows what to do in detail because our forensic software cannot pick up anything on his hard drive.

'When a file is deleted, it's only the header address that is erased. The body of the file stays on disk. The computer doesn't realise the data is still there and so nothing shows up. In the end, when the disk gets full, the data gets overridden and then it is lost. But with huge amounts of storage capacity on these disks, it would take years to fill up completely. In the meantime, a forensic program can read all the disk whether there are headers in place or not.'

'There's also this email to a Geoff Aylestone at Glen Parva on Bearing's computer. It gives some pretty hot detail about the quintahertz machine, including some drawings, but I don't know if it's enough information to build one.

'It's obvious that the company and the university are going to work together but I'd say it was early days for them to take the machine away. Wouldn't they leave it for Palfrey to work on? It sounds as though there's still some development needed for the safety angle and to get it certificated for commercial use.

'Oh, by the way, the autohacker tapes on Palfrey's home telephone line are all empty. He doesn't seem to send out or receive emails there at all, or to use the internet either.'

'Well, thanks for all that. All this stuff is going into your report, isn't it?'

'Yes, except that every time I finish it, something else crops up. We're having a go at the Glen Parva computer system just now, so I'm waiting for the outcome for that.

'The other two autohackers we've installed aren't showing any of the keywords we're searching for. It seems that Palfrey and Bearing run the department by themselves.'

'OK. Can you let me know as soon as you get anything more. Things are hotting up and I need all the info I can get as soon as it's ready.'

The manager took lunch by himself. There was plenty of thinking to do. If all the documentation that had been copied from Palfrey's office and that had been lifted from David Bearing's computer were good quality, then his boss in London and the Khazatan Research Institute would be happy. But it might not prove to be sufficient.

The costs of the operation were also mounting. Bringing in a special agent for an abortive operation didn't look good on anyone's cv.

That gave him an idea.

He rang Boris.

'Hi! Is Anouska still with you?'

'Yes.'

'Right. Can you both be in my office in about fifteen minutes?'

'Sure, what's up?'

'You'll soon find out.'

He took his plate to the counter and carried on eating while the waiter calculated his bill. Why do they always take so long when you're in a hurry? he thought.

'I've got an operation for you both tonight,' he announced back in his office.

'It's back up to Leicester, with welly boots - you're going on a midnight walk in the country.'

'Don't worry,' he said to Anouska. 'I'll let your head of section know I've changed your itinerary.'

'I don't think that's my main problem,' she said, glancing at Boris.

'Once head office knows that we haven't got a quintahertz machine for them, there will be an area of high pressure suddenly emerge right over my desk. I can do without that anyway but right now I've no answers for them. If we have to mount a search and rescue operation to find the bloody thing, they'll go hairless. So let's eliminate two options ASAP. That's Palfrey and Bearing.

'I'd like you to look around their houses tonight. You say, Boris, that the machine is about a two-metre cube in size. If either of them have taken the machine I think it's a dead cert that they won't have taken the frame inside the house. The computer and control panel, yes. But they're not going to take a pile of old iron into their best living room, that's for sure.

'It's a long shot but it might just save my bacon. Bearing's house is in a fairly built up area, so you'll maybe have to drive round until you can see into his garden. Palfrey's manor backs onto a public footpath so it should be easy enough to see into his back garden and get to his garage, but that's where you'll need the wellies.

'I suggest you go and get some kip for a few hours. I'll sort out street maps, night glasses, some warm gear and a driver. If you want anything else you'll have to arrange that yourselves. If you're back here by nine, leave at half past and in Leicester for twelve, that'll give you about five hours before sun up.'

'Look,' said Boris. 'Why don't we take things a stage further while we're going all that way. If we see the thing, why don't we try to bring some of it back?

'We don't need the frame, there's nothing special about that I'm quite sure. But if we can get the computer off it and anything else that looks interesting, that's all we need.'

'Yes, but say they've taken part of it away; you get some, which won't be the important bits, but it will alert them that something's going on.'

'But that could still be the case if you arrange to have the thing lifted as a whole. And think of carrying this ruddy great frame, awkward and heavy, out of someone's back yard in the dead of night without waking the dog. You'll never do it.'

'OK. But remember, you're our resident engineering expert. If you cock it up and we don't get anything worth having, it'll be round your neck.'

'I can handle that.'

'I'll organise a bag of spanners with all the other stuff then.'

'And put in some bolt croppers and heavy cutters, I'm not spending all night undoing bolts. Oh. And don't bother sending the cutters we had for the camera cable last time, they were worse than useless and nearly kiboshed the whole operation.'

'Message received and understood. Any questions?'

'Not from me,' said Boris with an expectant grin on his face, 'I think I might cope, if I can stand the excitement.'

'I have no idea what you mean at all,' said the manager.

'And neither have I,' said Anouska.

Outside the office, she said, 'I've packed and moved out of my hotel so I've got to go and look for a warm park bench.'

'And what then?' said Boris. 'Your place or mine?'

'Does yours have any champagne?'

'More than yours will.'

'Prove it.'

About three thirty the following morning, the manager's phone rang. He just about managed to wake up and get to the receiver before the answering service cut in.

'We've got you an early Christmas present,' said Boris. 'It's the complete system, plus.'

'Plus what?'

'Plus great dollops of mud.'

'Thanks a bunch, that'll give me something to dream about. Bloody well done, and don't drop it on the way in.'

'What are you going to dream about?' asked his wife as he rolled back into bed.

'Dollops of mud... just don't ask!'

* * * * * * * *

It was a few days before Lazio could generate enough enthusiasm to try out the test meter that the electronics department had built for him. And it was only after the Glen Parva meeting,

153

when he was feeling slightly better about the deal, that he decided to run a test.

He untied the rope holding the Newbold's tarpaulin around the quintahertz machine, pulled it off and just about collapsed as he saw the empty frame.

Brackets were twisted where heavy cutters had cut away the computer housing and the terratanium block. The sample shelf had been cut off, no attempt made to undo any of the bolts, and all the cabling had been cut away, just the cable ties hanging loose or on the floor.

Lazio ran hot and cold. As shock set in, he half ran, half stumbled back into the kitchen.

'What's wrong?' said Helen, as he just about fell through the door.

'I've got to call the police. Someone's taken the quintahertz machine.'

Helen took one look at the grey face.

'I'll do it, you come and sit down.'

Helen guided him into an armchair in the lounge, his chest heaving as he struggled for breath.'

She poured him a quick brandy.

'Sit there, drink that slowly and don't move.'

She went to the phone in the hall.

'Is that Doctor Simpson? It's Helen Palfrey, Lazio's not very well, could you come quickly, please?'

* * * * * * * *

Kate Bellew had suggested that the Café Royal would be a good place to announce the annual accounts for Glen Parva Steel Producers.

'It's traditional,' she told Alan Birstall. 'And while I wouldn't suggest it as a venue for some companies, it represents solid British tradition and that is a good message for your company right now.

'There's a very good set of accounts to announce and some interesting points of strategy to add so we want a large audience.

You always get more people when they know where they are coming to.

'Fortunately, Glen Parva hasn't had too much exposure in the press, so the financial pundits haven't talked up the share price in advance of the announcement. I always think it's a shame when a company has good figures to announce and the share price immediately drops.

'While I'm on that point, do your financial advisers and brokers know they will be dropped in due course?'

'No. That is still confidential. We have to be very careful about a crisis of confidence when changing people like that as you will be aware. We'll give them a month or two and then do the deed. There's always less interest in a company at the start of its financial year, so it should go unnoticed. Then they will be well cemented in place for the AGM next year. But we've got a positive reason for changing, so there's not much to worry about anyway.'

'Now, what about the deal you're proposing for Sandrapoor Steel Mills, will you be ready to comment on that at the announcement?'

'No, we'd like that kept in reserve for a bit, but we do want to milk the agreement with Burnstone University. The angle there is that Glen Parva is big enough to support both the steel industry in the UK, by sponsoring research, and the UK economy by helping the country keep its leading place in the field of biological research. Something that benefits mankind as well as the country.'

'That sounds good, we'll put that bit in just as it stands. Any other points to put in the launch announcement?'

'I don't think so. We want to keep some powder dry for later in the year.'

'Good. I'll finish drafting the announcement and send it up to you. And then I'll see you at the meeting in, what, ten days?'

'That's right. I look forward to it.'

Hmm, thought Kate, I think I could look forward to that as well.

* * * * * * * *

While Alan Birstall was pushing the company forward, Geoff Aylestone was hearing about the setback from Lazio Palfrey.

'I'm sorry about this,' said Lazio. 'It doesn't get us off to a good start.'

'These things happen. What exactly was taken?'

'The whole shooting match apart from the welded frame. Computer, control panel, terratanium block.'

'And any paperwork?'

'No. There's no paperwork missing at all. That's one thing I've always liked about the machine. If you don't know how it works, you won't be able to find out just by looking at it.'

'Well that's something, at least. How did they get round the university's security, then?'

'Ah, it wasn't at the university, it was in my garden, they just took the bits out of the back gate. I'd been running some tests that I thought were a bit dodgy to run at the uni.'

'So it could just be local opportunists seeing what they could nick.'

'Unfortunately, I don't think so. They'd come prepared. They just sliced through the steel brackets, probably with bolt croppers, and they also took all the wiring. Then they wrapped the frame back in its cover, just as I'd left it, so I've only just noticed that the bits had gone.'

'Any idea when they went?'

'Well, it's been a dry summer here so there's not much to show on the ground. The garden gate area gets really muddy in winter but now it's just a dust bowl. There seems to be more footprints than usual, but they're not recent. The police say there's really nothing to go on.

'There's also a bit more to the jigsaw. Last Sunday night we think we were broken into. There could be a link.'

'What do you mean 'you think you were broken into', don't you know for sure?'

'No.'

Lazio recounted the cut camera cable, the large hole in the window, the switched off burglar alarm and the open door to the lab.

'That adds up to a serious mess,' said Geoff. 'There's some planning gone into that operation, for sure. But by whom? I get a feeling that they knew the value of what they were after, and they were professionals.

'If another steel company gets the quintahertz machine, that could lead to just the sort of competition that we are trying to avoid at Glen Parva. And if they can get in and out of your department just like that, then what about your other research projects? You can't rely on anything being confidential any more.

'And who knew about the machine?'

'Only a few people inside the university. Definitely no-one outside.'

'So could it be a put-up job to scupper the deal we've set up?'

'I can't see why. I don't know who'd benefit from that.'

'Well, let's see what the police come up with. In the meantime I'll have to discuss the whole thing with the other directors. I'm afraid this puts a whole new light on the agreement. We can't be expected to pay for something we're not going to get and we have to think about the research programme we discussed as well. Leave it with me for a bit.'

The conversation with Geoff Aylestone just about finished Palfrey. He was still feeling somewhat groggy from the shock of finding that the quintahertz machine had gone missing.

On the one hand, the incident might turn off Glen Parva so he could carry on running the department as he wanted. But no Glen Parva meant no money for a new quintahertz machine. And he certainly couldn't afford to buy any more terratanium out of his own pocket.

The next telephone call didn't help either. Helen had taken it and he heard her say that he was out and wouldn't be back for a bit. The person at the other end seemed to do all the talking so Lazio was hopping up and down with curiosity until she finished.

'That was Saxon.'

'Why did you say I was out? I rather wanted to talk to him.'

'Sorry, but you could have done without his news just now. He says there's been a couple of heavy hacking attacks on the department's firewall and it looks more determined than an amateur having fun. He advises changing the passwords on the main system. Whatever all that gobbledegook means.'

157

'I'm going to have to get a tin hat,' said Lazio. 'I seem to be under attack from all directions. I just wonder what the devil is going on. I think I'd better go off to the uni early and talk to one or two people to see what we should do.'

'Have a spot of lunch first,' said Helen. 'It's ready now. It'll only take a couple of minutes.'

'But it's only just gone eleven, what are you doing cooking lunch this early?'

Helen led him into the kitchen and took the clingfilm off a plate of ham and lettuce.

'Bloody hell,' said Lazio. 'What's this?'

'This is your first step towards losing two stone. Doctor's orders.'

'Oh, god. Misery upon misery. What have I done to deserve all this?'

'You've had too many second helpings, that's what. You've also had too big a first helping and you don't take any exercise these days. Your blood pressure was right up when the doctor came and you terrified us both. You're a mess and I'm your wife so sit down and be told.'

Lazio did so.

'And you've got to promise not to have lunch when you get to the uni. You might be a pain in the butt from time to time but I don't want to lose you just yet.'

'About two o'clock I'm going to faint.'

'Well I hope Ann Whittaker has the good sense to tip a large bucket of cold water right over you. That might make you see sense. I think I'll ring her now and get it organised.'

'I feel like a rabbit eating this stuff.'

'You, a rabbit, give me strength.'

* * * * * * * *

'Right,' said Detective Inspector Wigston to his sergeant in Leicester's police headquarters. 'This business at Burnstone University. These are the incidents I've taken from the crime log over the last month that seem to stand out from the usual stuff and could be linked to it.

'First we have a break in on June twenty-seventh at Premier Security Systems that seems highly odd. Nothing taken, but there's not much to take anyway. They don't sell things over the counter, so there's only a small amount of petty cash laid about; they don't sell items that can be sold in a pub like videos and mobile phones; and they of all people are going to have a good burglar system.

The video camera shows a bloke making off on a bike, so he didn't expect to carry much away on that. We can't see his face as he goes away but we can guess at his height and weight. It's a shame the camera only runs when the alarm is triggered otherwise we'd see him coming towards the building. So what was he after?

'Next, a break in at Burnstone University on July second. Or was it a break out? Again nothing taken. They walked past sellable stuff including several computers in the laboratory and didn't touch one.

'But on the sixth, or a few days before, someone lifts a piece of research equipment that had been in the laboratory but had been moved to the professor's back garden.

'Then he reports some serious hacking attempts on his computer system.

'Now we've just got this report from the telephone company about these autohackers. They've found four around Leicester. Very sophisticated bits of kit apparently. The engineers have been told to leave them in place but to drive past more often than usual in case someone's acting strangely in the area. They want us to put them under twenty-four hour surveillance but we just haven't the bodies to spare for that.

'I've spoken to the managing director at Premier and to the professor at the university, Lazio Palfrey's his name, and here's the report on those interviews. But that was before I thought there could be a link.

Before we start looking for any evidence to link the two, can you go through the crime log for the last couple of weeks to see if you can pick up anything else that's out of the usual run of petty theft. I think I've got it all but I'd appreciate your checking as well.

'Then I think it's a case of going back to the two reports and looking at them to see if there's any common points. We've only looked at them so far from the break-in angle. It could be worth checking with the two guys to see if there were any odd incidents before the break-ins. And we need to know who placed these autohacker machines and who they were aimed at.

'That little lot should keep you out of mischief for a while.'

* * * * * * * *

On the day that Lazio Palfrey discovered the theft of his quintahertz machine, the parts were being connected together by engineers in the Khazatan Research Institute. They still carried the marks of the mud picked up in Lazio's garden although most had dried into dust while the parts had been padlocked into the white canvas diplomatic bags that, by international consent, were never opened by customs as they passed from one country to another.

The quintahertz machine had taken three of these bags that, on other occasions, had contained terrorist weapons, highly secret papers and dead bodies.

Vladimir Arbatov hovered anxiously around the engineers as the cabling was connected to the various parts. As the main director of the Institute, it was his authority that had started the investigation and he was anxious for a good result.

'You can tell your people they have done very well,' the chief scientist said to him. 'We appear to have the complete system. The cable wiring harness was intact and, apart from having to dig some mud out of the connectors, it has all gone together perfectly and there are no cables or connectors left over. I'm just waiting for the documentation to be translated before we go any further. I'd love to switch it on now but we'd better wait.'

'Yes, you're right. I'll go and ring Alexander Kasvanov with the commercial information while you're waiting. But don't start without me. That's an order.'

The papers that Lazio had left behind in his office file contained some marketing assessments of the commercial value that the quintahertz machine would bring to its users. Arbatov had immediately seen its importance but he would not tell anyone until the document had been translated into Khazatani.

Old habits die hard and Arbatov continued to cover his back on every occasion. When people had to make their own analysis, it was advisable that all foreign documents were first translated into Khazatani by accredited translators. If his version of events were misunderstood, it would do his career no good. Better to have the interpreters to blame any problems on.

Alexander Kasvanov was also waiting anxiously for the results. If the rumours were correct, the Khazatan steel association that he represented would be well pleased with this new machine. It would greatly help their push into western Europe, where customers paid much higher prices for steel than in eastern markets, and where customers paid in money rather than goods, a double benefit.

Over the years, he had been given a car instead of a salary on several occasions. He generally kept the new one and would call Sergei Danelski to take the old one and sell it abroad. That cost an arm and a leg by the time Danelski had driven it to France, Germany and even Spain on one occasion, and then had to fly back home. But, as Kasvanov received two or three times the amount he would have got in his own country, he was still in pocket - eventually.

Now he was receiving a different sort of bonus as Arbatov faxed through the translated documentation from Palfrey's file. The package included the transcript of several emails sent round Glen Parva Steel Producers.

Alerted by the information lifted off David Bearing's computer, the London hackers had tried the Glen Parva system and got in almost immediately. Now, Arbatov was reading their plans to expand globally and their plans for Burnstone University. They also placed a high value on the quintahertz machine.

This was all highly valuable stuff and the Institute would probably extract a high price for its services. He decided to call an immediate meeting of members of the steel association.

Before he could start ringing round, Arbatov was back on the telephone.

'We've just fired up the machine at a couple of samples. It's literally the first run so we've no idea what the results will be. Sod's law says they'll be crap at this stage, but if you want a sample for yourselves, I'll keep you one.'

'Yes, please. I'll come over as soon as I've fixed up this members meeting.

* * * * * * * *

Chapter 11

Lazio was somewhat rebuffed by Geoff's reaction to his phone call about the missing quintahertz machine. But he suddenly saw a chink of light.

If he's thinking about renegotiating the deal, I could maybe set up something in the meantime with the machine using its human effects. That has nothing to do with steel, so he can't complain.

If the uni or Glen Parva don't like that, there's not much they can do because they must be too far involved now to back out from the sponsorship deal. With the machine gone, I'm the only person with any information about it. So, if they don't look after me, there's no quintahertz machine.

He accessed the address book on his laptop and dialled a number.

'Hi, James. This is Lazio Palfrey, Burnstone University, how are you doing?'

'Fine, fine. Good to hear from you after all this time. I'm still at the same desk, soldiering on; but what about you?'

'Same thing really, but I've got a little development going that I was hoping you might be able to help me with. Do you remember that telecoms project we worked on where we machined some blocks of terratanium for you?'

'Yes, we're still carrying out research into its potential as it happens.'

'Is there any chance of obtaining a plain block of it from your goodselves by fair means or foul?'

'There's a question. I'm not sure if we're allowed to sell material just like that. And every bit of scrap probably has to be accounted for because it's so bloody expensive. I'll have to look into it and see what we've got. Are you still on the same Leicester number?'

'Yes. Not much changes here. But, before you go, I could do with a contact name. I've got an idea that needs developing and I'd like to talk to someone about it. It's for an anti-personnel gadget.'

'Hang on, I'll run up our directory... How about Roger Wishart, Business Development Manager for Light Weapons? He's actually in DARE, the Defence Agency for Research and Evaluation, but they're on the same site here.'

'Sounds fine.'

James gave him the number and email address.

'Let him know how you came by his details and by the way, if the idea needs some terratanium, there probably wouldn't be a problem about transferring some stock internally from one department to another, if we can agree a price.'

'Thanks for that, I'll look forward to hearing what material you can find. Talk to you later.'

Lazio rang the Wishart number and got through straight away. He explained his idea for the quintahertz machine.

'I've called it Stop, which stands for Suspends Total Operations of Personnel. It's been tried on a human body, albeit accidentally, and I've got photographs of its effect on animals out in the open.'

'Sounds a bit potent,' said Wishart. 'I'd be inclined to keep it under wraps, I'm not sure how legal it all is.'

'That had started to concern me,' said Lazio. 'That's why I'm looking for someone with a safe area such as a proper firing range to try it out on. I could also do with someone with ideas on how to increase its power and how to test it properly.'

'And what sort of application had you in mind for the weapon.'

'Well, I was looking at some soldiers in Northern Ireland a while ago while they were hunting a sniper. Two got picked off while they were going through the streets. I thought that a more powerful version of Stop would lay out everyone for fifty or a hundred yards in front of the soldiers, who could then go in and haul off the terrorists, leaving the rest to recover.'

'And you say it has laid out small animals a hundred yards away?'

'Yes.'

'Well, could you bring it down here and give us a demonstration?'

'That wouldn't be easy,' said Lazio, who did not want to admit that there wasn't anything to see right now.

'If I brought down the drawings and diagrams, could we do a deal whereby you build a machine to test?'

'Our engineers would rather see the machine in operation, could they come up to see you?'

'The problem is that the machine has been converted back to its original purpose and will shortly have a new owner. I'd rather not get them involved in any other use - they might take the new idea for themselves.

'If you think that you're really not interested in it, don't worry. I've a number of contacts overseas I can talk to. I haven't the time or facilities to develop the machine further myself, so it's just a case of finding a partner.'

'Well, there's a bit more to it than finding the time and facilities to build the machines,' said Wishart. 'There's no end of legislation you'd have to fight through first with an invention such as that. You cannot manufacture or supply a weapon in the UK without a licence. Even the biggest companies sometimes have difficulty in renewing their licences and they've got special factories, experienced engineers and good track records.

'I am afraid that UK law doesn't allow anyone to make weapons in a back room, even if it is in a major university. Your place would have to be to be totally secure and where do you test it legally? And who will buy it? Your customers also need licences. And when it's a completely new type of weapon, the Health and Safety Executive has to be involved. You'd be years getting it to market.

'There could also be a problem selling the idea to another country. You can't sell an idea abroad if it could be used against this country in a time of war or if it represented a threat to our national security. You first have to offer it to a government appointed agency such as ours.'

'And if you don't want to develop the idea, what then?'

'We give you a certificate to say you can dispose of the idea yourself.'

'And if I offer it secretly to another government without telling you?'

'That would be breaking the law. And few countries would accept the idea under those circumstances anyway. I suppose some people get away with it, but it would come to light at some stage and, unfortunately for you, Professor Palfrey, we now know of your idea.'

If Palfrey had thought that talking to a government department would cheer him up and give him some hope for the future after his weeks of setbacks, shocks and disappointments, then he was mistaken.

'Before we go any further,' said Wishart, 'come and see us. Let me set up a meeting with an engineer and one of our marketing specialists. You'll find we're very reasonable people to work with for all that our hands are tied by weapons legislation and national security rulings. Do you want to give me a couple of dates that would suit you and I'll see what I can arrange?'

* * * * * * * *

Geoff Aylestone read over the notes he'd been taking while Lazio Palfrey had recounted the loss of the quintahertz machine. Then went along to Charles Thurmaston's office.

'Have you got a few minutes?' he asked.

'Yes, come on in.'

Geoff shut the door behind him.

'We've got a problem with Palfrey. His department seems to have very poor security. He's had his quintahertz machine stolen and it seems much more than a casual job.'

'What makes you think that?'

Geoff recounted the details of the break-in at the university and the steal from Palfrey's garden.

'Whoever took the machine was very determined to get it and set up a very professional operation. Neither the police nor Palfrey has any clue as to who might have done it.

'Palfrey says he hasn't told anyone outside the university about it. None of his research has been published, and the machine's only been finished in the last few weeks. They're still waiting for some of the formal certification to arrive. The police say they can't find any clues whatsoever. No fingerprints, no footprints, no eyewitnesses and no trace of a getaway vehicle.'

'Well somebody knew about it whatever Palfrey says,' said Thurmaston. 'Perhaps there's a mole in his department that's leaked the information. You don't think he's sold it to spite us and is covering it up. He wasn't too happy with our virtual takeover of his department, was he?'

'That's true. But he's gone to extreme lengths to cover any trails if he has sold it. Why didn't he leave it in the laboratory for them to take? And why go to all this business of cutting a camera cable twenty feet up in the air, that can't have been easy and was dead risky anyway. And this five inch hole in the glass.'

'I went to see the latest James Bond film over the weekend,' said Thurmaston. 'I'm not so sure it is as good as the others, as it happens, but this incident at Burnstone could have come straight out of it.

'I mean, I can't see another steel company taking it. It's not a standard piece of kit, it needs someone like Palfrey to get it going properly. So they'll have to come out in the open to access some research facilities. Look at us. Glen Parva's amongst the biggest steel producers yet we couldn't take over the quintahertz machine just like that. And I don't know any other company that could. Do you?'

'No. I have to agree with you there,' said Aylestone. 'Let's look at the James Bond angle, why would Blofeld want quintahertz?'

'Well, he wouldn't. If he were making some super gun or bomb, for example, he'd use existing technology to harden the steel. There's plenty of cheaper ways than quintahertz, and they're tried and tested. Quintahertz is only of value to someone who has lots of high quality work to put through the machine.'

'So who, then?'

'I've really no idea. Why don't you ask Palfrey to put the word around his fellow professors? I think they'll be the first to know if someone wants some work doing on the machine. And what about your David Bearing? Find out what he has to say.'

'Good idea. I'll do that. But what about our agreement with Burnstone, where do we stand with that?'

'Well, the lack of security is a concern because that could affect all our research projects. And that is for the university to sort out. I think we should put a hold on that part of the deal until their burglar alarm system is upgraded.

'But we mustn't forget that we didn't know about quintahertz when we first thought of this deal so it shouldn't figure too prominently now. If it's not available, we don't pay for it and we put in some contingency planning in case some other company comes up with the machine or something similar and starts competing with us.

'We mustn't lose sight of the tailored blanks project, that is really important to the company and we have put a lot of work in there, researching the market and selling the idea to the car companies.

'If Burnstone plays difficult over upgrading the security in Palfrey's department, we just threaten to pull out altogether. That'll put the wind up Professor Wyatt, he's dying for the cash to extend his precious biology department. And don't forget Professor Smithson at Empire University, he was in the frame along with Palfrey at the start. If Burnstone does not co-operate, we'll go there.

'Thinking about it, that could be a smart move. We sign up Empire, so that takes them out of the equation as far as our competitors go, then we let it be known that Burnstone is no good for research. Things get stolen, there's no security, that sort of thing. So that's them taken out of the reckoning as well. Two for the price of one, although our expansion programme would be set back by a good few months.

'Would you mention Palfrey's call to the other directors and tell them what I'm thinking we should do. Then we'll either have a meeting to discuss other ideas or I'll give Professor Wyatt a ring.'

* * * * * * * *

168

Sergeant Gaulby re-checked the list of jobs he'd been given to investigate by Detective Inspector Wigston and typed up his report.

'There's some interesting stuff here,' he said to his boss as he handed it over. 'Not your usual Leicester felons at work, that's for sure.'

'Why do you say that?'

'It looks like there's several links with a degree of planning and intelligence behind them that I haven't seen before. I reckon it was the same person that surveyed the burglar alarm place and the university for a start. And these so-called autohacking devices are all on uni staff telephone lines.'

'I've not heard of these autohackers before, obviously some sort of bugging device, do you think we should get the telephone company to come in and give us the low down on them?'

'I'm sure the computer fraud squad would benefit from that. They seem dead simple to use and they're highly sophisticated. I reckon we'll see more of them as time goes by.

'Basically, you dump them in a roadside telephone box and that's it. Anyone can get a key to these boxes, you only need a length of metal with a triangular cutout in the end.

'The autohacker is battery powered and has an internal aerial so it can listen to everything than goes on in the box. You programme it with the telephone number you want to listen to and when it hears that, and the computer signing on, it switches on and records emails and web addresses.

'It can also hold up an email while it looks inside your computer's memory. You never know. You just think that the system is running a bit slow, that's all. It's frightening stuff really. Then you take out the memory cassette, which is about the size of a credit card, put in a new one and the machine carries on listening while you read all the stuff on the card.

'The phone company spotted them during their routine line checks. The autohacker draws some energy from the signal on the line and the engineers see a drop in the signal on their test equipment. They checked all the lines it happened on and found it came down to four roadside boxes. They ran tests on those lines and saw a bigger dip on one number on each box.

'When I saw Professor Palfrey's name against one of the numbers, I asked him if he knew the other numbers. They turn out to be his number two, Dr David Bearing, and two other members of staff. I wouldn't tell him how we'd come by the numbers.

'Both Palfrey and the manager of the burglar alarm place have had visitors they remember in particular, and they both say the person was a while male, mid-twenties, slim build and high cheekbones. He spoke good English but seemed more eastern European. He had a business suit on at Premier Security Systems and a sports jacket at the uni.

'The manager at Premier remembers him because he doesn't normally deal with casual callers, but this seemed to be a big job so he was called in. The chap said he was getting quotes for a new factory, similar to others on the estate, but the manager didn't remember until later that the council had said it wouldn't extend that estate because it was developing another elsewhere.

'Palfrey's visitor said he was a reporter and promised to write an article in a magazine about him. The prof hadn't heard of his magazine and thought the articles in the one that he was shown were old ones anyway. That was back in early June. After about four weeks, Palfrey's secretary thought they ought to chase up this guy but the break-in happened first. When she tried his number it turned out to be a private line.

'There's two other links: Premier Security Systems put the burglar system in at the University; and the manager was given the same telephone number in Brussels as Palfrey, although the visitor's name was different.

'The uni's visitor took several photographs of Palfrey in the laboratory, one was beside a machine that Palfrey said wasn't all that important. When I went to have a look at it, I realised that the burglar alarm control system would have been in the background complete with phone number. That led the visitor to PSS.'

'It all sounds very deep to me,' said Wigston. 'It's going to take a lot of police resources to get to the bottom of it. And what are we going to get out of it? We're looking at two break-ins, four unauthorised telephone taps, one theft of electronic equipment and possible fraudulent misrepresentation. That's eight cases on the books at the moment. We've few clues to go on, more incidents might come out of the woodwork, and I think there's only a slim chance of any convictions coming out of the whole thing.'

'Won't do much for the crime figures,' said Gaulby.

'Just what I was thinking. We need international help to checkout the Brussels phone number and our pseudo visitor could be out of the country by now anyway. Say we said the whole thing could be a security matter, we'd have to hand it over to MI5. That would be the last we'd hear of it but it would be eight crimes solved at a stroke.'

Sergeant Gaulby immediately realised what his boss was thinking.

'Well, sir, if I reviewed my investigation in the light of it being a possible security matter and said as much in the report, you'd definitely have to send it upstairs to the Chief Constable, wouldn't you?'

'Definitely.'

Gaulby picked up his report.

'You'll have this back shortly.'

'Good man.'

Good man indeed, thought Gaulby, it will take work off my desk as well as his.

* * * * * * * *

For all his years in the police force, DI Wigston was surprisingly excited about his trip to MI5 headquarters in London. There must be a bit of James Bond in us all really, he thought.

But he was a disappointed man as he drove away from Vauxhall to pick up the M1 back to Leicester.

It had taken longer to have the vehicle checked by security on the forecourt than to hand over the four autohackers and the written report to the preliminary case officer who came out to meet him.

He had been taken to a small, bare room just inside the side door of the building while the PCO scanned his report and checked the contact details at the end.

'Very good' said the PCO, rising from his chair. 'Thanks very much for your efforts.'

'Don't I get a receipt for that little lot?' asked Wigston, indicating the autohackers.

'Afraid not.'

'And might I enquire your contact details?'

The PCO stretched out his arm to guide Wigston to the door.

'That's not necessary. As long as we know where to contact you, that's all that's needed.'

And Wigston was back in the July sunshine before he realised it.

* * * * * * * *

After Alexander Kasvanov had organised the meeting of his steel association members, he reported back to Vladimir Arbatov at the Khazatan Research Institute.

'The association would like to set up a package deal with the institute so we can both get the most out of the quintahertz machine.

'We are offering to buy the rights to the machine so the association can arrange to manufacture it and sell it to its members. We are also considering the idea of licensing the technology so steel firms outside Khazatan can buy a machine but under a strictly controlled contract that means we receive a good income from the agreement but do not suffer from any competition.

'We would also like the institute to continue to refine the machine as part of the deal. That should ensure a good return for the institute for its work in obtaining the machine and also increase the income for our association members.'

He passed over a set of stapled sheets.

'This outlines our offer.'

'Very good,' said Arbatov. 'I'll pass it on to our economic and strategic committees for a rapid decision. I'll tell them time is of the essence and it can't wait for a scheduled session. That will stop it being discussed in an open meeting. Once that happens, objections may be raised and the matter will go on for ever.

'That brings me to a point I was going to discuss with you and Leonid Lebdev. What happens when the machine comes on to the market and people find out where it was invented?'

'Arbatov and I have already discussed that,' said Leonid Lebdev. 'and the external affairs minister of the government is also aware of the way that we have obtained the machine. Several points apply. Firstly, the design has to be changed so there are some obvious differences between ours and the original. That will deflect most of any criticism. Secondly, it is only Professor Palfrey who can legitimately take action against us and he won't have a tenth of the money that would take, so a problem there is highly unlikely. He can always be bought off anyway.

'If the UK government comes over all protective and wants to make an international incident of it, that will be because they have a hidden agenda and that would have to be dealt with at the time. But, at the end of the day, as soon as Palfrey delivers the first commercial quintahertz machine, all sorts of people will be inside it and making their own developments. Your association just has to make sure that, if the shit hits the fan, you've made your money out of the thing.

'I can't disagree with that,' said Kasvanov. 'My members are already making plans to produce some new products with the technology. And that brings me onto my next point: Glen Parva Steel Producers. If they continue to expand, they will become serious competition to our own steel producers. They may have lost the quintahertz machine for now but it will only be a matter of time before they and the good professor make another.'

'Glen Parva also concerns me,' said Arbatov. 'From the emails that have been intercepted and from what London station picked off their computer, they appear to be an aggressive company. How would the association cope with the competition?'

'By thwarting their attempts to grow. We'll never beat them in a head-on open competition but there are other ways and we've already made a move. The emails show that their next target for acquisition is Sandrapoor Steel Mills. This is a clever move. India's economy is quietly strengthening and Glen Parva obviously hopes to gain a strong foothold in the country before anyone else discovers the opportunity.

'But perhaps more important is that India would provide a good launchpad into Japan and China. The trading links between the three are probably stronger than with western countries so it would be easier to jump off from India than Britain.

'So the association has commissioned our old friend Sergei Danelski to see what Sandrapoor thinks about it all. He has found an intermediary who knows the managing director and the first feedback is that the company doesn't want to be taken over by anyone. It has a joint venture agreement with Glen Parva and it doesn't want the relationship to go any further. But it realises that Glen Parva could put up a stronger case to shareholders and financiers than it could by itself and so the board is worried about the future.

'One answer is to offer Sandrapoor a deal that is better than Glen Parva can make. We could offer them quintahertz technology at a knock down price by charging the loss to our national development account. That would give them a chance to offer really high quality steels at competitive prices.

'Then they have some spare capacity in their low cost, high volume mills. We could offer to take it off them to balance out the rest of the quintahertz cost. The machinery is much newer than ours, so one of our members would get an upgraded facility at well below cost.'

'Glen Parva can't offer quintahertz cheaply, their shareholders would go up the wall if they tried, and I'm sure it wouldn't want to buy a steel mill than is older than anything they have already, so that rules them out of acquiring Sandrapoor because the shareholders would see our offer as a much better option.

'In our overall plan, Sandrapoor will be a proving ground that will provide valuable information for our push into western Europe which, let's face it, is the key market of the world nowadays.

Vladimir Arbatov sat back with a satisfied smile on his face.

'It's no wonder we produce so many chess masters in eastern Europe,' he said. 'Your quintahertz strategy can only checkmate Glen Parva. I'm glad we're on this side of the chessboard.'

* * * * * * * *

Alan Birstall had been delegated to go down to London on the day before Glen Parva's results were publicly announced at the Café Royal to discuss with Hoogen, Bellew, Cutler how best to present the deal with Burnstone University. The break-in and the police investigation were also on the agenda.

'From the announcement point of view I don't see a problem with the burglary,' said Kate Bellew. 'It's a nuisance, agreed, but we don't have to say anything about it. It doesn't really matter that signing the agreement has been delayed. The company doesn't have a high profile at the moment so no-one outside needs to know about the hiccup. We can still get plenty of mileage out of the deal.'

'But if the burglary comes out later, the stock market won't like that. They don't like nasty surprises, do they?' asked Alan.

'That is true, but we can distance ourselves from the event. It all happened before the agreement was signed. Nothing to do with us. Remember that you didn't know about it before drafting the agreement so it's obviously not a major consideration. But if the machine fulfils its promise, then we can soon turn it to our advantage in public relations terms.

'Don't forget that there's plenty of positive stuff in the announcement. Concentrate on that. Journalists can only absorb so much and there's only an hour to fill. Provided there are plenty of presentations from the other directors, the time will fly by. And the questions will soon dry up once food is announced.'

Alan read through the press release that Kate passed to him and decided that he couldn't improve on it. He also checked the press pack with its reams of dry figures, the chairman's reports and photographs of the directors.

'Right. That looks very good. So we all meet at the Café Royal at nine thirty, run over the fine detail, finish by ten thirty, have coffee till the start at eleven and lunch at twelve.'

'That's it,' said Kate. 'There's several interviews requested by journos and those are booked during the buffet. I'll give you a rundown on the angle they'll probably take when we're all together tomorrow. There's nothing after one o'clock as they all have to rush off to get their stories in that night's print run. Should be a good day.'

'Well, thank you for all your efforts,' said Alan as he rose to leave. 'By the way, last time we met you said you'd love to show me a good place to eat sometime. How are you fixed for tonight.'

Kate demurred.

'Well, I had got some things to do,' she lied. 'But it looks as though it will be too warm an evening to work inside anyway. Do you fancy one of the restaurant boats on the river?'

'Sounds good to me.'

'I'll get my secretary to ring round and book something. Where are you staying?'

'The Rathbone Hotel, just off Oxford Street, it's an easy walk to the Café Royal. Do you know it?'

'Yes, one of my favourite watering holes is in the same street. The Eagle Bar Diner. Why don't we meet there and have a drink first, then if I'm held up, at least you've somewhere buzzing to sit. About seven?'

'Yes, go for it.'

* * * * * * * *

Kate made sure she was a tantalising few minutes late. Alan had his nose in the Evening Standard but he noticed her as soon as she walked in.

She was no sooner seated than the bar manager came over with menus.

'Hi! Lovely to see you. How's things?'

'Very good,' said Kate. She turned to Alan 'Let me introduce Peter Groom, shaker of the meanest cocktails in London. We're just in for drinks,' said Kate, turning back to Peter as Alan studied the menu.

'Hey!' said Alan. 'Got to try the Men of Steel cocktail. What's in it?'

Peter gave him some of the ingredients. 'Dark undercurrents. Intrigue. That's the theme.'

'That'll do for me.'

'Sounds worrying,' said Kate with a laugh.

Later, they took a taxi down to the cool and quiet of the river restaurant.

About nine the mist started to rise off the river and the waiters came round closing the windows.

'Another coffee?' asked Alan.

'No that's fine,' said Kate. 'I hope the place met your expectations.'

'It exceeded them, or was that due to the company? And I don't often get introduced to the manager of the places I frequent either, that was a bonus.'

'Oh. That's my security system. Peter looks after me, a single girl can't be too careful nowadays.'

'Well how do you feel about sharing a taxi back, then?'

'I think that might be in order,' said Kate.

When the taxi pulled up at the entrance to the suite of flats above the Barbican, Alan stayed seated as Kate got out.

But as she turned to say good night he asked 'Any chance of coffee?'

Kate smiled.

'Just a small one.'

Alan paid the driver and followed Kate. As she opened the door, the lights turned up and the curtains closed.

'All mod cons,' she pointed out.

But, judging by the spacious apartment and the furnishings, it was just par for the course.

While Kate was in the kitchen, Alan noticed silk scarves laid over the chair backs and arms.

Idly, he picked one up and ran it through his hands.

'Do you like that?' she asked as she came back into the room. She came and stood closer to him than he expected, her hands behind her. Alan automatically took a pace towards her but she didn't move. He put his arms round her waist and pulled the scarf tight behind her.

'So how does Peter help you now?' Alan teased.

'I pull my hands free and telephone him,' said Kate breathing fast.

Alan released the scarf and wrapped it round her wrists.

'Perhaps I don't pull my hands free,' said Kate, pressing herself against him.

Alan knotted the scarf.

'And coffee will have to wait,' he said.

Kate pushed against him and he moved backwards into the bedroom. He sat down on the bed as it pressed against the backs of his knees. Kate fell on him and rolled over sideways.

'Help,' she whispered. 'Help.'

'I don't think you'll need any help at all,' said Alan.

As he reached for the buttons on her blouse he noticed the silk scarves fastened to the four corners of the bed.

'I think coffee will have to wait for quite a while.'

* * * * * * * *

Chapter 12

'What a day,' Said Lazio, drawing the cork from a bottle of his precious Bordeaux. 'I feel absolutely wrung out. Having that rabbit fodder at lunchtime hasn't helped either. How long will I have to put up with that sort of thing?'

'That's up to you,' said Helen. 'You've got two stone to lose, remember. The doctor did say there's an alternative though.'

'Thank god. What's that?'

'You put on ten inches in height.'

Helen stirred her saucepan a bit harder and kept her back towards Lazio to hide her smile.

'What a bloody stupid thing to say. What does the man think he's up to. He wants to retire now if that's the only advice he's got.'

'Come on, ratbag,' said Helen. 'You know what you say: if you can't take it, don't hand it out.'

'Thank you very much. I'm going down to the pub if that's the only sympathy I'm going to get.'

'Do you want to eat first?'

'Ah. Alright then,' Lazio softened his tone.

What are we having?'

'Vegetarian hotpot.'

'Vegetarian hotpot! When have we ever been vegetarian for heaven's sake.'

'It's a very low calorie recipe, just what you need. Get out two plates. And get the middle size plates, not the biggest.'

'Why that size?'

'Because you can fill them up and think you've had a lot when you have actually had less than normal.'

'From which handbook on torture do you get all these ideas?'

'Just get the plates out. Sometimes you drive me to distraction. Tell me what happened at the university this afternoon for goodness' sake.'

'Well, after this morning's call to Geoff Aylestone at Glen Parva, I decided I was going to keep this idea of Stop for myself. What is going to happen on the hardening side of things if we don't get the machine back I've no idea. Geoff is also concerned about security generally in the department and doesn't know if the company wants to build another machine. So I'm in limbo, not sure what to do for the best.

'And the phone call from Saxon about the hacking didn't help. When you think about what has gone on in the last few days it's all so worrying. Not knowing what's behind it doesn't help.'

'You mustn't let it get to you,' said Helen. 'It's a one-off, I'm sure. You've never had anything like this happen before and it can't keep going on anyway. Just think of yourself. You can do without the extra stress, that's for sure.

'You'd know what I mean if you had seen yourself when you found the machine had gone. I don't know if you realised, but I called the doctor before bothering with the police. I think as people get older, they can't handle stress as well as they could when they were young. Neither of us bounces back so easily nowadays. Perhaps we've seen so much more than the young that we are more afraid of what might happen.

'Anyway, bring your plate into the dining room while we're talking, the table's laid. What else happened this afternoon?'

'Well, having decided to act independently on the Stop idea while Glen Parva decides what it's going to do, I called an old contact in the Ministry of Defence. He put me onto a chap in the Defence Agency for Research and Evaluation. Business Development Manager for Light Weapons I think he was called.

'Anyway, he frightened me to death with talk about legislation, health and safety and whether I could legally build a machine like Stop. He's going to fix up a meeting as soon as he can with some of their experts. So I'm stuck until he gets back to me.

'He really wanted to see the machine but I couldn't tell him it had been pinched. I said it was under new ownership and had been converted back to hardening steel so there wasn't much point. But he still seemed a bit persistent so I don't know what will happen there.'

'Well, I think you're getting out of your depth with all this,' said Helen. 'You're not in the business of killing things and you don't understand what's happening with the biological effects. If the ministry is interested in the idea, sell it to them. Forget this business of starting your own company and making the machines yourself. Think of the risks of developing and manufacturing the machines. And where would you start to get the money? It would probably need millions.'

'Saxon said as much to me a few days ago.'

'And he's right. I know we're short of money and the house needs work doing to it, but we'll survive. We always have done. Look after yourself first. If you go down, everything will be lost.'

'OK,' said Lazio. 'You're right and I can't fight you all. Let's sit back and see what Glen Parva and this defence bod come up with. Is there any more of this hotpot going?'

'How can you dare say that? You don't like vegetarian and you're only putting up with it from the way you went on before. Anyway, you're not allowed seconds. But there's plenty of fresh fruit in the bowl.'

Lazio groaned.

* * * * * * * *

With the university year just about ended, Lazio had to evaluate his last year's teaching and update his department's curricula for the new year. There would also be department and faculty meetings to ensure that Burnstone maintained its high place in the university education ratings.

As he and Helen had not planned a summer break, there was some spare time during the holiday and, with no quintahertz machine to work on, Lazio spent some days producing detailed drawings and sketches ready for the meeting with the Defence Agency.

In one of his pictures of the unconscious animals in his garden, the machine could be seen in the background. So Lazio was confident he could gloss over its theft.

When Roger Wishart rang to set up the Agency meeting, Lazio was able to take the first day that was offered.

'I'll drive down,' he said to Helen. 'I know it'll be about a three hour trip but the place is well off the beaten track and it will take much longer to go into London and then take a suburban line and a bus or taxi.

'The meeting's at two, so the M1 and M25 motorways should be relatively quiet, then Farnborough's just a few miles down the M3. Even if the meeting takes a couple of hours, I should be home for dinner by seven.'

'Well, concentrate on your driving, not your dinner.'

Roger Wishart collected Lazio from the Agency's reception area and took him a short distance to the usual type of interview room reserved for unknown quantities who visit defence establishments: breeze block walls, painted, not plastered; basic chairs; and a single, simple desk.

Most noticeable was the complete lack of the usual decorations found in offices: no calendars, no posters or notices and bare window ledges. There was no way to guess what the people who used the room might be like.

He introduced Lazio to Liz Ewshot from the marketing department and Rod Lightwater from the engineering side.

'Nowadays, DARE is an independent body and has to stand on its own two feet. We can't rely solely on the UK military to keep us going as we did in the past. We have to sell ideas and pull in research work from around the world, so marketing has a say in most things we do.

'Rod here has a lifetime's experience evaluating the weird and wonderful from the technical angle and my role as Business Development Manager is to ensure the business as a whole moves forward, stays competitive and maintains its profitability. Every country has its own defence research and evaluation organisation, so there's plenty of competition out there.

'Can we start by going over what you have already told me about the Stop machine? Then Liz and Rod will no doubt have some questions to fill in the gaps.'

'That's fine by me,' said Lazio.

Wishart ran through the history of Lazio's development, starting with the Ministry of Defence work on telecommunications and ending with the results of the tests in the manor garden.

That's our telephone conversation just about word for word, thought Lazio. Obviously that had been tape recorded. He pulled out his photographs and drawings as Wishart came to the end and spread them out on the desk.

'This shows what happened to the small animals and birds but it doesn't show the sheep which appeared to be stung and jumped out of the way of the beam. They were about sixty or seventy yards away from the machine. The beam would have to be more powerful to affect humans at that range.'

'Do you think the machine could be made more powerful without any major problems?' asked Rod Lightwater.

'Yes. At the moment, it's only fitted with a small, general purpose power supply that's delivering a couple of hundred watts. Nothing is overheating, including the terratanium focusing device, so all the components can obviously handle a lot more power. I'd go up a factor of five as the next step.'

'And you see one application as a close combat weapon. Why is that?' asked Liz Ewshot.

'If it only knocks out people for a quarter of an hour or so, your troops have to be pretty close to get to the enemy before they recover.'

'So why would you want to make the machine more powerful?'

'That would be to increase the spread of the beam so it covered a wider front. There's no point in making the beam go further if you can't get to the target in time as I said.

'But I don't think the machine can be infinitely extended. From the experiences I have had in scaling up laboratory-sized pieces of equipment to create commercially-sized units, there always seems to be a practical limit to how big any one device can be made.

'My guesstimate is that it could be made powerful enough to lay out an average-sized human on a fifty yard front at a distance of two to three hundred yards.'

Liz looked thoughtful as she made notes.

'So if Stop was built into a fast jet, it could come in at low level, knock out an enemy gun emplacement and give the forward troops time to move up and take out the gun crew permanently,' said Wishart.

'Yes,' said Lazio. 'That's a distinct possibility. But I was thinking more of fighting urban terrorism. You could spray the beam around without worrying about catching civilians because they would recover without any after effects.'

'That's a good thought,' said Ewshot. 'But we could never sell it for that very reason. People in general wouldn't allow its use anywhere near civilians on principle. You also have to think of people who are in the bath, cooking or holding children. What happens if they suddenly go unconscious?'

'I take your point,' said Lazio. 'That does limit its potential.'

'There again, we have no suitable weapon to incapacitate hostage takers for example. If Stop could be focussed tightly onto a flat, for example, and the other residents evacuated, it could bring police sieges to an end very quickly. And with no noise or flash of light, it could be used without the public at large being aware. Now that is interesting,' said Ewshot.

'It could fill in the shortcomings of nerve gases and biological gas clouds that cannot be accurately directed and can be blown off target by wind, for example,' she added. 'But I think it still has the potential of being classed as an undesirable weapon and that would limit its marketability.'

'And you had planned to set up your own company to develop and build Stop machines?' said Roger Wishart.

'That's right.'

'And there is an operational quintahertz machine in existence at the moment?'

'Yes. But only for hardening steel.'

'But, on your own admission, it can be easily converted to a Stop machine.'

'Yes.'

Where the hell is this line of questioning going, thought Lazio, suddenly feeling somewhat uncomfortable.

'Well,' said Roger Wishart, 'Before this meeting I discussed the device and its implications with several colleagues. We felt there was only one course of action we could take and what I have heard during this meeting confirms that feeling. Does that go for you two?'

He looked at his colleagues who both nodded assent.

'Professor Lazio Palfrey, as an authorised representative of DARE, the Defence Agency for Research and Evaluation, itself an authorised body of Her Majesty's government, I have to tell you that I am requisitioning the Stop machine and placing it under the jurisdiction of the Official Secrets Act 1992.

'You must now deposit with me the photographs and documents you have shown us, plus any more you may have about your person. Other documents pertaining to the Stop machine must be delivered to us by an approved method within forty eight hours. We also require access to view, and remove if we think fit, the existing Stop machine and any associated components or devices.

'If you retain any documentation, or copies thereof, or any material parts of the Stop machine you personally will be in breach of the Act and subject to whatever penalties that may be deemed appropriate by a properly constituted court of law. You may not discuss the machine with any other person and you may not disclose any information about the machine and its potential either verbally, electronically or in writing, unless the recipient is authorised to receive such information under the Official Secrets Act.'

Lazio's jaw sagged as though he had been sandbagged. That speech was even more unexpected that when Alistair Wyatt had told him that Glen Parva wanted the quintahertz machine for themselves.

Roger Wishart took advantage of Lazio's inability to speak and slid two pages of headed notepaper across the desk to him.

'These two letters are written versions of what I have just told you. Please sign them both. One is for you to keep, the other for us.'

Lazio signed without looking. He couldn't take his eyes off Wishart's face.

'You bastard,' he said.

Wishart laughed awkwardly.

'Just doing my job,' he said. 'But you can appeal. It's all in here.'

He passed across a slim booklet with the portcullis and chains symbol of government printed above the title ''What the Official Secrets Act Means To You.''

Palfrey said nothing. He threw the booklet to the floor.

'That's what it means to me,' he said, walking across it as he went to the door.

'Where do we come to see the Stop machine, then?' asked Wishart.

'I am highly delighted to say that you can't see the machine,' said Lazio, his hand on the door handle. 'It has been stolen and I haven't a clue where it might be.'

He was halfway through the door when Wishart called him.

'Professor, security won't let you out of this corridor without me. Please come back. When was it taken?'

Lazio gave him the bare details.

'So who in Leicester police is on the case?'

'I've absolutely no idea.'

'Professor Palfrey, I don't know what dealings you have had with government representatives but if you are going to be difficult with us, you will find that we can make life infinitely more difficult for you. You may be a man of steel, but our mettle is a great deal stronger.'

'I'm sorry, I can't remember the name of the policeman who interviewed me and that has been the only contact I've had with the police. My secretary might have the name somewhere.'

Lazio was becoming somewhat chastened to find himself out of the seat of power for once. At least he could get back at his dean Alistair Wyatt one way or another but these people were different.

'We'll have to make enquiries of our own,' said Wishart. 'Remember this is now a matter of state.'

Could I forget, thought Lazio.

Wishart rose and led Palfrey down the corridor to reception.

'Goodbye, but just for now anyway. We may need you later on to help us build a Stop machine from scratch. Sorry this hasn't been the happiest of visits.'

'I'll say,' said Lazio. 'What about all the money I've put into the thing, and the money it was going to make for me? Plus all the hours I've put into designing and developing it.'

'The booklet covers all that,' said Wishart, remembering where the first one lay. 'I'll send you on a fresh copy.'

'Thanks. That would be appreciated.'

'I can't comment officially on our action but you seem to have devised a potent device that could also be of great interest to a foreign power. We have no option but to take it into our care. It's a compliment to you and you should do well out of it in due course. It's for the greater good.'

'Well, bugger that.'

With a heavy heart, Lazio turned his back on Farnborough and gunned the Maserati up the motorway. First the hardening machine given to Glen Parva and now Stop has been stolen off me in broad daylight, he thought. Is there no end to it?

Unfortunately, there wasn't.

Lazio's singular manner of driving took a toll of his cars at some time or other and now it was the turn of this one.

About forty miles short of the Leicester turn-off the engine lost power leaving Lazio in a fast lane of continuous cars but with suddenly falling speed.

He managed to heave the car over to the slow lane amidst flashing headlights and blasting horns. The Maserati seemed to settle down at about fifty five miles an hour although the engine was running roughly. Lazio checked the gauges. Everything seemed OK except that the water temperature gauge had stopped working.

After about ten miles Lazio noticed an increasing smell of hot metal from the engine. The oil pressure gauge was slightly down on what he expected. After the day I've had I'm going to run for home, he decided. I'm in no mood to sit on the hard shoulder at this time of night.

The Maserati disagreed.

A tapping noise told him the big end bearings were being knocked out as the low oil pressure cut the lubrication they needed.

The engine lost more power and Lazio couldn't stand ill-treating his favourite metal any longer.

As he stopped on the hard shoulder, steam, hot oil fumes and smoke poured from under the bonnet and he could hear the cracking sounds of overheated metal as it cooled.

* * * * * * * *

Wishart lost no time in reporting to his officer.

'We've a piece of potent kit here in this Stop machine,' he said. 'No-one has seen anything like it before. Rod Lightwater says he has read something about the possibilities of extremely high frequency radiation but that was in the USA and was highly speculative.

'This Professor Palfrey could be the first to make the idea work. If so, it could be the first practical use of terratanium. The MoD telecoms people have been investigating the material for several years but it's low key research as there doesn't seem to be a great future for it - until now.

'Rod says the machine is so simple it's bordering on genius. But there are two problems.

'First, someone has pinched the prototype. Second, Palfrey is an extremely disgruntled gent now we've requisitioned the machine. I think he could go and do something silly because he seems very short of cash just now. He says he's put a lot of money into the project.'

The officer looked thoughtful.

'What do you suggest we do next, then?'

'I think we should contact the Leicester police a bit sharpish. We may need to take the case out of their hands and give it to our investigative brethren at MI5. That will cover our backs if any nasty surprises come out of all this. If we tell the police the parts are now covered by the Official Secrets Act they'll probably want to ditch the case very rapidly anyway. They won't want to do any work if the glory is likely to go to a government department at the end of the day.

'And I think it might be an idea to put a tap on the Professor's home phone just in case he has any unwise ideas. If he was behind the steal of the machine, I shouldn't think he'd make any calls from work though.

'In the meantime, Rod has got some engineers analysing the paperwork we've taken from the Professor and the rest should be with us within forty eight hours. I've told Palfrey we may need him to come down and help us build a new Stop machine.'

'Right,' said the officer. 'I'll allocate a project manager to get all that organised and to act as the first point of contact. I think we should also collect the frame of the machine from Palfrey's garden to tidy things up. We can't expect him to put that in the post. And if Rod and perhaps yourself go up with the van, on the pretext of clearing up some technical queries, you can have a look round his place. If he's still upset and you think he could be a risk, I could authorise an advance to tide him over and quieten him down.

'I'll also authorise a Highest Priority notice so there's no delays in any department. We'll review the status of that in ten days. I'll let you know who will manage the case just for your own information.'

'Thank you,' said Wishart. 'Good luck with it all.'

* * * * * * * *

'In a few hours time, we should know for certain where your Stop machine is.'

The Director of IS5, the industrial surveillance section of MI5, was sat in the office of Grant Hawley, Director of DARE.

'That's good news. Can you give me any idea where that might be?'

'We think it will be in Khazatan, one of the breakaway states of the USSR as was. The Leicester police alerted us the day before you did. One of the suspects in the theft left a telephone number with your Professor Palfrey and the same one with someone else he came in contact with. Although it was a Brussels number, it actually connects to the Khazatan embassy in London.

'But while we're following up that lead, I need you to explain the link between what seems to be two quite different machines. This Professor Palfrey is trying to sell it to a steel firm as a steel hardening machine while he's flogging it to you as a potential weapon. Does it work both ways?'

'Yes. It all stems from the effects of very high frequency electromagnetic radiations. Palfrey reckons to be able to generate radiation in the quintahertz region. No-one has worked at that level before. Basically, the radiation stops electrons whizzing round molecules of matter so the material collapses and becomes harder as a result of the compression.

'In steel, the metal becomes very hard at the surface so it doesn't wear so easily. Obtaining a high quality hard surface at a commercially acceptable cost is the holy grail for men of steel. That's the probable reason your Khazatanis are interested. Palfrey discovered the technology after working with some MoD bods on a material known as terratanium.

'What he discovered by accident was the effect on humans. The radiation has the same effect on living cells. When they collapse, the body's functions stop and unconsciousness follows. The body can recover from a short dose but the cells would be permanently damaged under prolonged radiation and death would follow. The human angle is where we will be researching.'

'So how did he find out about this effect?' asked the IS5 director.

'It sounds as though you haven't heard about the accident to his lab technician.'

'I haven't.'

'The poor fellow got in the way of the beam during some tests and was knocked out for a bit. He's fully fit now but that set Palfrey thinking and when he discussed the effect with the biology department at the university, realised he had developed a potential weapon.'

'So whoever has the machine now could go through the same loop and come to the same conclusion?'

'Exactly.'

'I think that raises the priority of our investigation without any doubt.'

'Well, we've already put it on the highest priority rating here at DARE so queries and decisions are taken before any other project in the department. So what do you do next?'

'The staff list of the embassy shows only one person with any engineering qualifications and we're watching his flat now. As soon as he comes home, we'll have a quiet word with him. He fits the description that the Leicester police were given and we've sent them a photograph to take round to the Professor and several other people who saw him. That should confirm the Khazatanis as the perpetrators.'

'So has Palfrey been broadcasting to all and sundry his development of the Stop machine?'

'No. He maintains he hasn't told anyone outside the department. So we don't know how the Khazatanis latched on to the machine. But we feel they don't know its potential as a weapon. They would just know of it as a steel hardening machine.

'Our economics department says Khazatan has a strong steel industry and the country's economy is pretty dependent on it. So any new idea such as this hardening machine could help their steel industry quite considerably. That would explain why they were so persistent in stealing it. They also bugged some telephones, probably to get more background information.'

'Palfrey mentioned its steel hardening function,' said the DARE director, 'but he glossed over it and the department he met with can only see things as weapons, so they would not have picked up on its significance to men of steel. So I suppose you want the machine back before the Khazatanis discover what Palfrey found out, that it could be a potent weapon.'

'Absolutely. It's not that the Khazatanis would use it against us, they're too small to wage war on any developed country, but they could sell it for a large amount of money to a country that is big enough to make a significant threat out of it.'

'You've got some job on, then.'

'Not really. Apart from the time pressure, it's routine stuff. We can always find some means to lean on tiddlers like Khazatan. They'll end up being pleased to give the machine back to us when we've finished with them.'

'We might be able to help you there,' said the director of DARE. 'If we do decide to go ahead and build a more powerful version of the machine, we've got to test it. Our people in nerve warfare at Porton Down can set up trials on drugged sheep and cattle but we really need humans who can give us some feedback on its effects.

'Unfortunately, the supply of willing jailbirds and servicemen is drying up. They're all so aware of effects that can surface many years after they undergo these sort of tests that they're just not interested. And life in prisons and the services is so soft nowadays, they're not greatly bothered about early release as an incentive.

'But if we could find a country miles from anywhere where no-one is interested in the peasants, that could be a good test bed for Stop. Perhaps you could build that info into your dealings with the Khazatanis.'

'Food for thought indeed. So keep me in touch with developments. Any snippets that may mean nothing to you could help us a great deal with this lot.

'And while I'm here, would your electronics people like the four autohackers that were found in Leicester to play with? We think they're built in Israel and these are the first we've seen in the UK. We've lifted all the data off the memory cassettes so they're clean from the security angle. They're in my car boot if you've got someone who can heave them out.'

* * * * * * * *

Chapter 13

'How's things with our arch wheeler dealer, then.'

'Can't complain, plenty going on I'm pleased to say.'

Sergei Danelski was in a meeting with Krachov, his contact at the Khazatan Research Institute.

'We hear news of you popping up all over the place nowadays. You'll be expanding and starting your own company before long.'

'No chance. That's strictly not on the cards. My business is personal. Never trust anyone, not even a work colleague. When I retire, that's it, unless you cross my palm with plenty of silver on special occasions. But I might sell you all my contact secrets - the more work I do, the more contacts I get. The list just builds up and up. What would it be worth to the Institute do you think?'

'Oh no. I'm not being drawn into that one, thank you very much, you keep me out of your wheeler dealing. I'm no match for your deviousness. I want to die an honest man with a clear conscience.'

'Some hope in this place!'

'Thank you! Now, down to business. India. Mumbai. A little business negotiation on behalf of one of our steel companies. Fancy it?' said Krachov.

'Always in for a curry, especially when they're authentic, what's the detail?'

'Well, I gather you've already done some initial work on this one. It's Sandrapoor Steel Mills.'

'Right,' said Danelski. 'I haven't done anything direct with the company but one of my contacts says the managing director, Vishay Bhopari, is trying to fend off a possible bid from a British company, Glen Parva Steel Producers.'

'And that's where we need some more information and where we'd like to float a deal to help him. The Institute will handle the arrangements for all this to start off with, which is why I've called you in. We'd like you to make the direct approach to Sandrapoor.'

'I have no problem with that. Sounds good basic stuff. What's the offer?'

'It's in two parts. Firstly, we have developed a new method of hardening steel. Sounds pretty ordinary but it has a huge potential. Briefly, we can take the cheapest steel, harden the outside and make it perform like the highest quality steel.

'As you'll know from your engineering background, components made from hard steel wear longer, need less lubrication and maintenance, and the lower friction means that machines use less power. The surfaces will also withstand a higher level of mistreatment. And if the core of the component is a dead cheap steel, you've got a first rate component at a really low cost. Our steel people expect to make millions out of it.

'If Sandrapoor agree to cancel their joint venture with Glen Parva and set up one with our Babrusk Steel Mill, we'll arrange for Babrusk to licence out this latest technology at a knockdown price. The new technology will make Sandrapoor a leader in India, whose economy is developing strongly, and throughout Asia generally.'

Krachov did not admit to Danelski that it was the latter's visit to the UK's Technology Transfer Day that had started this rabbit running. Better that he thought it had come exclusively from the Institute.

'The reason we can offer it at a knockdown price is because the deal would be financed by the Khazatan National Development Fund.

'But if the company is not that well off, we have a second part to the deal. We know that Sandrapoor has excess capacity in its high volume, low cost mill. Another of our steel companies, Stavrol Rolling Mills, would buy the machinery off the company. It will upgrade Stavrol's capability, give Sandrapoor extra cash to finance the hardening machine and take a loss making venture off its books. Their shareholders should love all that. If they come over to us, it pokes Glen Parva's expansion in the eye and benefits our own people no end.'

'Well I can handle that without any problem. What's in it for me?'

'We're offering you a three part deal: one percent of the total deal cost if Sandrapoor signs up to take our hardening technology under a joint venture; three per cent of the sale price of every hardening machine for the next five years; and a negative fee of one half per cent if Stavrol has to buy the Sandrapoor mill to clinch the deal.

'Fifty per cent payable when they agree to come to the negotiating table, the balance when the agreement is signed and commission on machine sales payable monthly.'

'No deal. That's flat.'

Good, thought Krachov, I was expecting that.

'What's the problem?'

'I'm not interested in ongoing deals, never have been. It's got to be clear cut: one event, one payment.'

'I'll take two per cent if Sandrapoor signs up, full stop. If you sell hundreds of machines, than that's your good luck. And you know there's always good luck around when you deal with Sergei Danelski.'

Krachov roared with laughter.

'What a load of balls you people always come out with. One and a half per cent for a signed joint venture, not a rouble more.'

'One and three quarters.'

'OK but a negative fee of three quarters if we have to buy up Sandrapoor's excess capacity.'

'Blow that. I know where you're coming from. Sandrapoor would love to sell its mill and it will be newer than anything that Stavrol has, so there's no way a deal can be cut without that bit of it being included. So I'm going to lose money without any doubt,' Danelski looked very pained at the thought.

'My heart bleeds for you. OK, one and three quarters of the total deal value.'

'No. That's the same deal but put differently.'

'Well we've got to bring something into the deal as a disincentive. We don't really want Sandrapoor's excess capacity. But you'll offer it just to make your bargaining easier, won't you.'

'Of course.'

'OK. One point nine per cent of the total deal.

'Nope. Two per cent.'

'No deal.'

'OK. One point nine it is.'

The two shook hands on the outcome that they expected from the outset.

* * * * * * * *

'Hi! It's Geoff Aylestone here. How's things with yourself?'

'Fine. Fine,' said Lazio Palfrey, who promptly gave a series of sneezes. 'Apart from some damned summer cold I've picked up. Excuse me a minute.'

Geoff heard a series of explosions as Lazio blew his nose.

'Sorry about that. I'm as bunged up as they come.'

'Sounds as though you spent last evening in a damp field with a young lady. I used to end up like that afterwards.'

'Chance would be a fine thing,' said Lazio. 'But that's another matter. What can I do for you?'

'This business of the quintahertz machine. We've discussed it, the directors that is, and we'd really like to see the security beefed up a bit around your department. It may sound like shutting the stable door after the horse has bolted, but we're thinking of the future. There will be a lot of research work going on and we think that the world is getting so competitive that there will be more break-ins by companies wanting to find out what their competitors are doing.

'I don't mean more break-ins at your university in particular, but all over the country. I think everyone should increase their security generally. Would you give it some thought and let me know what you propose? It will have to be good but I'm afraid it will have to be at your expense. But it should be to your benefit as well.'

'OK. I'll get some quotes in.'

'Thanks. Now, regarding the lost quintahertz machine. We've mulled over two options. One is to wait until it surfaces and then go in with the legal beagles and get it back; the other is to crack on, build a new machine and aim to beat the competition, whoever they are, to the market place.

'I mean, the machine or the technology has to come out into the open at some time. It's a commercial project and you only get business by going out to people and selling the idea. It can't stay under wraps for ever but it might take a long time to come out or it might emerge in China or some other rare place where we haven't a hope in hell of getting it back or stopping their people using it.

'What do you rate the chances of building another machine? Have you got everything that's needed and could you do it?'

'Yes. I could get a working model up and running in a couple of weeks or so.'

'Really?'

'Only through a stroke of luck. I've got a spare terratanium resonating antenna here. It's a wide angle unit but that's fine for hardening steel. We can use a standard computer as the controller, I've got the master disk of software in my safe, and the intermediate components can be bought off the shelf from the appropriate electronic distributors.

'What will take time is building a new frame, fabricating the shielding panels and setting up an interlocking system so there's no chance of another accident.'

'I thought you said they'd left the frame behind.'

'Er, yes, but it was such a mess I cut it up and got my wife to speak nicely to the dustmen when they came. I was so upset I couldn't let it lie around home.'

Geoff Aylestone was quiet for a minute. Lazio knew his lie had been spotted. But he couldn't say that the dustmen had come all the way up from Farnborough.

'Well, if we know the risks we can work round them. But we'd like the next machine to be built here in our Birmingham factory. That will give our sales and technical bods a chance to get to know the machine.'

Now Lazio knew that Geoff was lying but he couldn't say anything against the idea.

'We've also got the chance to try it on some jet engine turbine blades so we need to get your input on that. The application is very interesting. It's for aircraft that are used on Middle East routes. There's always sand flying about their airports and it wears away the turbine blade edges so they don't work so efficiently.

'They're already hardened, but if quintahertz can improve on the current quality, it should prove a lucrative market.'

'There's only one thing,' said Lazio. 'Money. I can't do anything myself and the department budget is fully committed. It always is at this time of year to make sure we get our full budget for the next academic year.'

'Well, we'll pay and offset it against the sponsorship money. If you can send me a list of what's needed as soon as poss, I'll get our purchasing department to do the necessary. And you'll be able to come across to Birmingham to oversee the project, won't you?'

'Yes. There's no problem during the summer holiday except that my car's blown up handsomely and I'll have to use my wife's. But that shouldn't be a problem.'

'OK. I'll get some space cleared in our lab. Talk to you later, then.'

* * * * * * * *

Charles Thurmaston was in good form on the morning of the financials announcement at the Café Royal. All chairman like a good set of figures to present and this time was no exception.

He was also able to elaborate on the sponsorship deal with Burnstone University, the move into the car manufacturing market with the new tailored blanks project and the reorganisation of the sales departments to cope with the expected increase in business.

After the other directors had said their pieces, the first question from the assembled journalists struck right at the subject Thurmaston wanted to avoid. Global expansion. The Financial Times always was on the ball.

'Mr Chairman, you and your sales and marketing director have said very little about global expansion. Can you tell us something more about your plans?' asked the FT's man.

'Not at this stage, I'm afraid. But, in general, we have plans to expand globally, as one would expect from a company with the size and ambition of Glen Parva.'

'What countries have you in mind?'

'If I told you that, you would know the companies we are targeting and, as you well know, surprise is vital when stalking another company.'

'Well, you must have some major plans in store if you have started working with Hoogen, Bellew, Cutler to handle your PR. We all know their lobbying capability when big mergers are in the offing.'

'And who says we're working with them?' asked Thurmaston.

'Nobody. But when your sales and marketing director was seen dining out with one of HBC's directors last evening, it's not going to be purely for pleasure.'

Alan Birstall raised his eyes to the ceiling. Charles Thurmaston leaned round behind Bill Oadby.

'Does he mean you?' he hissed at Alan.

'Yes.'

'No comment. Next question.'

But the FT journalist was persistent.

'But shouldn't you be worried about your shareholders who could be concerned that you are trying to expand when the steel business is under heavy pressure? If your finances are committed to expansion, there will be few reserves to draw on if there is a market downturn or global unrest generally.'

'You can assure your readers that these points have been fully discussed by the board. Our strategy is to use our expertise to maximise the local assets of any company we take over. We do not envisage putting in capital as the main plank of any acquisition.

'Our concern is to reduce the risk of expansion by limiting the cost. Acquisitions will be expected to grow organically, so shareholders should see a steady rise in share price and dividends over the next few years. Now can we have a question from someone else, please.'

After several less demanding questions, lunch was announced and the journalists moved very quickly from their seats.

'He must have seen Kate and I at dinner last night,' Alan said to Charles. 'I should have perhaps told you before.'

'Don't worry,' said Charles. 'But I've a feeling that FT guy will be a bit persistent now he's got whiff of a story. Have a word with Kate and see what she suggests we do with him. Anyway, you struck lucky. Was she good company?'

'Very good. She needed restraining, though.'

'Boasting again!'

'You'll never know.'

* * * * * * * *

As Boris Pushtin went up the steps to the front door of the large house that was now a series of flats, a car quietly slid to a halt at the kerbside.

'Mr Pushtin?'

A figure emerged from the front passenger seat.

'Security service. Industrial surveillance section. We'd like to ask you a few questions.'

Pushtin had a warrant card pushed in front of him.

'Would you come and sit in the car, please, it's a little more private than out here.'

Pushtin looked up and down the street. A dark figure was stood on the far side of the car while a second car had pulled up behind the first.

'Do I have an option?'

'No.'

In the car, Pushtin asked the name, rank and number of his questioner.

'I'll ask the questions, thank you. What were you doing in Leicester on the fourth and the twenty-fifth of June.'

'No comment.'

'Two people in Leicester have picked out your photograph from a series we showed them. There's no doubt you were there. What were you doing?'

'No comment.'

'Well, I am arresting you on suspicion of being an accessory to theft and criminal damage in that city. I will caution you and then take you to Cannon Row police station for further questioning.'

His questioner showed him a search warrant made out for the address of his flat.

'First, please give me the keys to your flat.'

Pushtin handed them over.

'Anything in there we should know about before we go in? Burglar alarm set?'

'No comment. I claim diplomatic immunity and will not answer any more questions until I have seen someone from my embassy. But the alarm code is 1990.'

'OK,' The keys were handed out of the car window to someone from the car behind. And then to the driver, 'Off we go.'

* * * * * * * *

At Cannon Row, Pushtin was held in a cell until a representative arrived from the Khazatan embassy. The two were left for a few minutes and then the man from IS5 entered. He explained the reason for the arrest.

'Where is the missing property now?' he asked.

'It's not in the embassy, so there's no need to go storming in there.'

'So where is it?'

'It was taken from us and we haven't a clue where it went.'

'Look,' said the man from IS5 testily, 'We want the property back. It's not so much the value of the goods themselves but what they mean to people in industry.'

'I'm sorry I can't help you.'

'Let me spell it out for you. There's a bit too much industrial espionage going on just now. The loss of inventions and prototypes hurts our industries and our economy and the number of incidents is escalating. We're looking for the slightest opportunity to make an example of an eastern European embassy and close it down. Yours could well be the first.

'It doesn't matter if you stop trading with us in retaliation, that will hurt your country much more than ours. But remember that the problem of industrial espionage applies to the whole of Europe. If we close your London station, then the French and the Germans will jump at the chance of closing down your embassies there for the same reason.

'Where does that leave your head of embassy? When your people read the report we will feed to the newspapers, what happens to you all? Executed, I shouldn't wonder. It's a good story, the papers will give it a big headline. And none of your mates will come across to check that it's accurate, will they? It's not the truth that's important, it's what people think.

'So let's be sensible about this, shall we?'

'Look. We're both men of the same world,' said the Khazatan representative. 'You know how much I cannot say. We all dance to the tune of our superiors. I can tell you that what you seek is not in Britain but neither Mr Pushtin nor I will answer any more questions until our station head has discussed the matter with your Home Office.

'Just think on this. If you rush in you may get the machine back, but we will have the secrets. Where does that get you? Remember that our two countries need each other for a number of reasons that are slightly more important than a piece of engineering equipment. OK, we need European funding; but you need to keep us on your side.

'Now, Mr Pushtin could have been in Leicester for a number of innocent reasons. His business is to collect information as you well know. Unless you have a further charge you will now release Mr Pushtin'

The IS5 man stood up and knocked on the cell door.

'Mr Pushtin is free to go.'

Outside in the night air Pushtin said 'I suppose I'd better say goodbye to my girlfriend as soon as possible?'

'Oh, I don't know. I don't think this is serious enough for you to be taking the first plane out tomorrow. I think tonight was just a convenient excuse for them to take your flat apart and see what you've been up to. If you've been a good boy and they didn't find anything, then don't worry.

'But if you want an excuse for a last goodnight with your girlfriend. It's as good as any.'

* * * * * * * *

Chapter 14

'Nice to get the place back to ourselves now the customers have gone,' said Lazio Palfrey to his lab assistant, John Fleming, as they surveyed the piles of equipment that marked the students' rapidly discarded research projects.

'Indeed,' said John. 'But I find it's never for long enough, Christmas term seems to come round too soon.'

'Well, don't wish your life away, make the most of it while it's here. Anyway, we've some planning to do before next term now that Glen Parva Steel Producers are calling the shots for the next couple of years.'

'Will they be the only sponsor we have for that time, then?'

'From the steel industry, yes. We could take on projects for other companies, provided Glen Parva agree that there's no conflict of interest, but there's nothing in the wind at the moment apart from the projects that we already have on hand. We have to finish those, of course.

'But we've a lot of learning to do with these tailored blanks that the company wants us to investigate. I've got to bring the subject into the students' curriculum and you will have to check out some machinery that we haven't used for some time.

'I'm thinking of our welding and cutting machines in particular. We will also need gear to test flexing, joint strength and impact resistance. You'll have to lay in some steel sheets as our raw material as well.

'It might also be worth my talking to Glen Parva about getting some new machinery. They might be able to persuade a manufacturer to sell us something at a discount. We're also going to need some car doors and other panels so we can see what the car makers are doing just now. We'll have to test those to destruction to see what they can withstand at the moment.'

'So how will tailored blanks be used?'

'The idea is that a door panel, for example, is cut out of a single piece of steel that is relatively thin across most of the panel, but is thicker where there is stress, and where bits have to be fixed on, such as window winders, locks and mirrors. So the blank piece of metal is tailored in strength to suit the demands placed on it. But that makes it more difficult to analyse the mechanical strength of the panel, and that has to be done before the design can be accepted for a car.

'The target is to cut weight. Previously, a panel was the same thickness across the whole door although it didn't have to be that thick everywhere. Every kilogram you take off a car means less fuel is used, so the earth's oil reserves will last longer, and there is less pollution to come out of the exhaust.

'But the car makers are fighting a losing battle really because cars get heavier every year anyway. We all want bigger and better stereo systems, more electric windows, automatic seat adjusters and things like that, so the mechanics get lighter but all the extra electronic components just add more weight.'

'Well, it looks as though there's plenty to keep us occupied in that area alone,' said Fleming.

'We'll also be having some days out at Glen Parva's factory in Birmingham. They're going to build a new quintahertz machine but they want to do it over there because they don't trust our security system, unsurprisingly enough. Can you dig out all your notes on the safety systems we put on the last one and the test documentation and certificates?'

Fleming added more notes to his increasing list of things to do.

'Yes. Sure. So is the machine theirs now?'

'Not exactly. I still hold all the design rights and Glen Parva can't regularly use the machine once it's built and they can't sell any either. But it's their money that's going into the project so I suppose it will go to them eventually, I'm afraid.

'At the moment I've agreed to let them build the machine and try it on a single project. They want to use it to harden the fan blades in jet turbine engines.'

'I know it's none of my business really, but what about all the effort you've put into the machine? Don't you get anything back for that?' asked Fleming.

'I certainly hope so. What will probably happen is that they give me a lump sum for the rights to the machine and then I get a percentage of every one they sell.'

'So what happens if they don't do a good job at selling it?'

'Well, they'll have to make an attempt if only to get their own investment back, and the lump sum they give me. But if they fail, than that's my bad luck.'

'But that would have been a risk if you had started your own company and sold the machines yourself, wouldn't it?'

'Oh, yes. And plenty of people have told me that's just what would have happened. So maybe it's for the best. But it's still a bit of a bugger.'

'These things are sent to try us.'

And how, thought Lazio.

'So is there anything else you'd like me to put on this list?' asked Fleming.

'Did I mention the security system?'

'Only that Glen whatnot don't like it.'

'Right. Well, they say we've got to get it beefed up before we can start any of their research work. Could you take a walk round the place and see what you would recommend. I'll do the same then we'll compare notes and get some quotes in. I think we'll have to include my office and Ann's as well just to be on the safe side. Err on the side of caution, we might as well do a good job while we're on.

'And I think that's it for now. We'll get things moving and then discuss progress as we usually do.'

Or don't, thought Fleming as he compared his two pages of notes with Lazio's total absence of paperwork.

'I think I might go down and take an early lunch now,' said Fleming 'and build myself up.'

He glanced at his boss but the irony was lost.

'OK,' said Lazio. 'I'm having mine in my office. Helen's given me a salad,' It sounded as though Lazio was saying it out loud as though the action might transform the snack into a more acceptable meal. 'See you later.'

'Sure,' said Fleming. 'If you survive.'

He knew Lazio's lust for several courses as well as anyone.

My exact sentiment, thought Palfrey.

Ann Whittaker fussed around him with coffee while he sat at his desk. More out of respect for Helen, Ann felt she had to do as much as she could to keep Lazio on the straight and narrow with his dieting.

Lazio sensed her concern and felt he was being mollycoddled. That made him bristle. Ann picked up the signals and became even more twitchy.

The tenseness was broken by Luke Verity poking his head round the door.

'What's this?' he said, looking from Lazio to his salad.

'Don't you start.'

'Would you like coffee, Professor Verity?' asked Ann, 'I'm just brewing.'

She prayed that he'd stay and break the iciness in the room.

'Yes. Thank you.'

'Sit down if you have to watch, don't stand over me. It's only salad.'

'I can see that. It's just you and salad together that I can't get my head round.'

'Just watch out. One day you'll be in the same boat and I shall come and gloat over you.'

Ann came in with his coffee.

'Isn't he prickly?' teased Verity.

Ann put her finger against her lips.

Verity acknowledged the sign.

'Sorry. Can we talk about the test meter we made for the quintahertz machine? Did it do its stuff?'

'Yes. It was fine, thanks.'

'So how many do you want?'

'Hang on, it's early days yet. I've not sold a machine yet.'

Lazio updated his counterpart in the electronics department with the events leading up to Glen Parva's offer.

'It depends whether you want to make the test meters yourself and supply Glen Parva whenever they want one, or whether you want to sell them the design and let them get on with it. Personally, I don't think they'd want to make a decision until they've studied the market and taken the project a bit further. Do you want me to negotiate for you, or do you want to deal with Glen Parva directly? It's little matter to me either way.'

'I'd rather sell the design,' said Verity. 'I've got a company that could make the things but it's not really my area and it could lead to other work that I wouldn't want the company to get involved in. You can soon get spread very wide and lose direction in the electronics business if you take every project that's offered.'

'Well, I'm dealing with their technical director, Geoff Aylestone. He's probably the best person to contact first. I've got to call him a bit later so I'll mention the meter if you like and then you two can handle it whichever way you want.'

'OK. That sounds fair enough. Thanks.'

* * * * * * * *

''The Prime Minister has asked me to inform you, in strict confidence, that he has it in mind to submit your name to the Queen for ...''

That was the dream of Professor Alistair Wyatt: the letter bearing the government logo that signified his work for the country had been recognised with a Royal decoration. But he had never felt quite close enough to the establishment that such a letter would become reality.

Perhaps the relationship with Glen Parva Steel Producers might bridge that gap. The directors of the company were already close to those in government and their new PR agency promised to strengthen the links.

For all hopefuls, gaining public recognition was the ultimate in frustrating exercises. If Wyatt gave the slightest inclination that he had ambitions, the door would be firmly closed. Any obvious moves on his part would also bring down the shutters. It was back to the basic principle of advancement: pull is infinitely more powerful than push. But how to find someone willing to pull.

Wyatt may have been stuck on that point for the moment and his devious brain may have appeared to fail for once. But it was only short of stimulation and that was always available somewhere.

He reached for the phone.

Professor Grover Wisden was the typical government-linked academic. Three-piece suited, unadventurous, cautious to a fault, he had survived decades in the Scientific Research Council. In the last few years he had been moving through its many committees as chairman in a move that was as much pension-enhancing as strengthening his reputation as a professor.

The SRC was the link between government and the rest of the world. It negotiated a chunk of Treasury money each year for research of national importance and then vetted the thousands of applications for funding from universities, research organisations and commercial companies.

Each application for funding had to meet a number of criteria. Its ability to do the work and to produce results had to be proven; its research project had to fit in with government thinking of the day; and the results would have to attract the type of positive publicity that the government wanted.

But, in reality, the decisions were politically based. The unspoken question was 'Does the face fit?'

So Wisden's job was to balance his masters' desires for positive national publicity against the real worth of the research to both community and business. The relationship couldn't be calculated. It was based on the opinions of men and women in close council.

So if an applicant kicked up a fuss, or a huge amount of money was found to have been well wasted, the council was there to protect the government against the fallout. If it didn't manage to contain the flying mud, changes to its membership were very quietly arranged.

But the system could never be described as devious in the way that Wyatt's dealings in life tended to be. Perhaps that would prove to be the barrier between him and public fame. He had never thought along those lines but, in due course, the faceless ones might.

'Hallo, Alistair, how's things up in Leicester, then?'

Wisden was in cheerful mood today.

'Fine,' said Wyatt, 'Both the weather and the university. How's yourself?'

'Mustn't grumble. We manage to keep the wheels of research turning. Perhaps that's the best one can hope for these days in this economic climate.'

'Well you've got to have something to look forward to if you want to survive, that's for sure. I thought we'd see your name in the birthday honours list last month, that's obviously something to look forward to.'

'Ooh, mustn't comment on that sort of thing,' said Wisden. 'Don't want any gossip on those lines. Got to keep your head down on the job, that's the thing, what comes out of it is not for us mere mortals to divine.'

Wyatt accepted the rebuke but hoped that his message had been received. He knew that the subject always brought that sort of response but he felt the outcome from mentioning it would be more beneficial than harmful.

'Yes, of course. It was about the job that I rang you. We're talking to a pretty useful sponsor here at Burnstone at the moment. They're wanting us to beef up our biology research and I'd one or two ideas for projects but I thought I'd give you a bell first just to see where government thinking is heading as far as microbiology is concerned.'

'Well, the public line is that the PM is keen for Britain to develop a high-tech reputation. He wants lots of research to be carried out here, but of a sort that will encourage business to develop commercial projects fairly quickly. So he's not interested in blue-sky research that could expand our theoretical knowledge but would probably not be used by industry. He wants to see projects that he calls close to production: where there is a very high chance that the results will be taken up by industry.'

'That stands to reason,' said Wyatt. 'It's a great shame that there is so little money available for pure research. But that may change one day.'

'Now,' said Wisden. 'Someone is waiting to see me, can I call you back a little later?'

'Yes. I'm around all day. Have you got my number?'

'Yes, it comes up on a little screen here. Talk to you later.

Telephones were put down.

Wyatt sat back in his chair. Nothing much seemed to be forthcoming from Wisden. That seemed a bit odd. Their two academics paths had crossed for the last thirty years and they had regularly been able to help each other with snippets of information from time to time. But not now, it seemed.

His phone rang.

'Hi. Grover here.'

'Hi,' Wyatt sounded puzzled. 'That was a short meeting, wish mine were like that.'

'Yes, well don't worry about that. I'm on my mobile now so I can give you a bit more information than on my office phone.'

Aha, thought Wyatt. That's more like it.

'The inside line at the moment is that the PM wants us to favour research that leads to products that can be manufactured by our partners in Europe. It's highly confidential, but the PM wants to knock virtually all our manufacturing industries on the head. Clothing, cars, shipbuilding, farming and now electronics: it's all going.

'He's decided that we can make more money here as a service country than as a manufacturing base. So we become the generating house of the world for new ideas and products. The rest of the world makes them.'

Wyatt was taken aback that official thinking had progressed so far so rapidly.

'Now you don't need me to tell you that the unions would go clean up the wall if that government policy was to leak out. So do you see where your efforts should be directed?' asked Wisden.

'I need to think it through but I get the drift.'

'Good. Now, if you want a specific line to think over, look at this: hundreds of research projects have been carried out into genetic modification. But they're all at laboratory scale. Very few projects are being taken forward into commercial production. And if there's no commercial results, then research funding will dry up and the work will be wasted.

211

'Now, could the principles be applied to finding a cure for AIDS as just one example? So, if someone starts to work with an overseas manufacturer to develop a commercial result from existing research, that would be very acceptable. It means that we get inward investment for research but some other poor sod gets the unenviable task of selling the product to the rest of the world and its protest groups if they don't like the way it was made, for example.'

Wyatt smiled inwardly. That was the type of thinking he liked.

'I think we're pretty well set up here to work along those lines,' said Wyatt. 'You don't happen to know any likely suspects I could contact to get the ball rolling?'

'We might have one or two, you know we can't recommend or suggest anyone really, but leave it with me for a day or so.'

'Thank you very much,' said Wyatt. 'We'll have to meet up for lunch some time when I'm in London.'

'Yes, I'd like that. But, in the meantime, this telephone conversation never took place.'

'As ever. Bye for now.'

* * * * * * * *

'These test results look very impressive,' said Vladimir Arbatov to his chief metallurgist at the Khazatan Research Institute. 'What's your view?'

'I agree. Once we'd optimised the quintahertz link between the antenna and the rest of the circuit, the results went up compared to the very first run. But we think that the machine needs further improving before we can make a commercial version.'

'In what way?'

'First, there are a number of occasions where someone might want to harden a piece of steel deeper than the machine can go at the moment. I'm thinking of a component that has to carry a large load, so the wear rate is very high; or where a surface has to withstand an impact from another component.

'We should also be able to harden over a wider area for components that are larger than normal. That means a wider beam and more power being generated. We could scan a long component from end to end with the beam we've got but we can't work out how to make it sweep across. Moving the antenna from side to side would serve the purpose, but that needs a flexible link to the generator and that would lose too much power, especially as the angle of sweep increased.'

'Why not simply boost the power to the machine?'

'Overheating. The antenna and the generator would need a re-design and we haven't got the key pieces of information to do that. We've checked the information that was copied from Professor Palfrey's filing cabinet and gone through the documents that were on Dr Bearing's computer. There's nothing that helps us there.'

'Damn,' said Arbatov. 'It's a pity we can't send someone over to extract the good professor's brain from its holder.'

'I think there must be more documentation floating about somewhere,' said the chief metallurgist. 'How did the professor design the antenna in the first place? There must be some sketches. He'd keep them out of habit. When you're always coming up with things to patent, you know you have to keep the original paperwork to show to the patent people. And what about Glen Parva Steel Producers? From what we've intercepted, they will need to know all about quintahertz. In time, they'll also realise that the extra documentation is needed.'

'Let me think this through,' said Arbatov. 'Let me know if you or your boys come up with an idea but I don't want you to go outside the Institute looking for an answer. Not yet anyway.'

'There's also another problem, I'm afraid. We've only the one block of terratanium to play with and we can only machine that one so far. We need it chemically analysing and then we need a supply of the same, or better, quality. The metal has been produced in the past in experimental quantities but that was years ago and no-one has heard of it since.'

'That's a problem for our man of steel, Kasvanov. I'll give him a call.'

When the scientist had left his office, Arbatov picked up the phone to Kasvanov and explained the problem.

He then called the Institute's government liaison officer, Leonid Lebdev.

'Leonid, old friend, can I borrow that grey head of yours to help us with a little problem? It's this quintahertz machine. Our technical bods need more information. I thought we'd got everything but they say they need some engineering details about the antenna. You're up to speed on events and you probably know more than me about what's going on, what do you suggest we do?'

'Hang on a minute while I look at the file.'

Arbatov heard the rustle of pages being turned.

'Well, there's one obvious answer I can see straight away. There's a comment that the computer boffins in London couldn't access Palfrey's computer, so we don't know what's on it. That's probably where the information is.'

'So what does that mean, another raid?'

Arbatov heard more pages being turned.

'That's one answer,' said Lebdev, 'But there might be an easier way. There's a name here that's highlighted as a soft target if we need more help. It appears that a Dr David Bearing has been a very naughty boy. That means we must have some material on him that can be used as a persuader to get him to co-operate with us.'

More pages being turned.

'Hmmm. Yes. Some high quality material.'

Arbatov was consumed with curiosity. But he didn't dare ask what that material was.

'Right,' said Lebdev. 'Can you send me a write up on exactly what information you want as soon as possible. I'll let you know as soon as I've got an answer.'

'Great. Thanks very much. Look forward to hearing from you.'

* * * * * * * *

David Bearing had hardly got into his office and shut the door when it opened again and a young girl, twenty five or so, slipped in, shut the door and stood with her back to it.

'A knock would be appreciated,' he said with some surprise. He was sure the corridor had been empty when he came through. Totally unable to place the face, her air of purpose concerned him.

She ignored the remark.

'We have a job for you.'

David laughed at her apparent cheek.

'You've got a job for me?'

'Yes. We'd like you to provide us with a copy of some information.'

'What!'

The girl passed him a folded sheet of paper.

David read it.

'Are you out of your mind? I can't possibly do that. Who are you anyway?'

David's hand was shaking.

'You don't need to know that. Just do what the paper says.

'I think I shall call security first,' He moved to the telephone.

The girl's voice hardened.

'That would be unwise.'

'Why?'

'They might find out that you have been a naughty boy with your computer and they might make some enquiries and you might have the police breathing down your neck with some unfortunate consequences.'

David's mind flashed back to his interview with Lazio Palfrey about his hacking activities.

His heart ran cold and he sat down suddenly.

'What are you talking about?'

'Isn't computer hacking illegal? Especially when you get secrets from other universities and pass them on to commercial companies?'

'What makes you think I've ever done anything like that?'

'How about it's not your computer anyway and the software is licensed to someone else and doesn't the name Glen Parva ring any bells?' she asked.

'Oh! My god.'

'Precisely. Now you can stop any of your misdeeds from leaking out very simply,' she indicated the sheet of paper.

'But I don't know where the information is, I would get caught copying it, I just can't do that sort of thing,' David was falling apart.

'Read the last paragraph. The instructions on delivering the documents. You have a whole forty eight hours. We do have some compassion, you see. But not if you fail to deliver. And if you get someone to watch the delivery point, we'll find out and you'll be sunk.'

'At least tell me who this is for.'

But she turned and was gone.

David slowly took off his coat. For all of the cool July morning he was sweating.

A quick knock and Ann Whittaker popped her head round the door.

'Morning. Here's your mail. You have attractive company to start the day off, don't you?'

'Oh. That was nothing,' David mumbled.

'Are you OK. You don't look well at all.'

David stared at her distractedly.

'Oh. Someone jumped the traffic lights on the way in. Nearly cleaned me up. Bit of a shock. I'll be alright in a minute.'

'I'll bring you in a coffee. That might help.'

'Thanks. That would be good.'

David took himself off to the toilet. Anything to get away from people for a few minutes. He had to think and there was not much time to do it.

First, where would the papers be. He didn't dare access Lazio's computer until he could set up a different computer to do it from. The stuff could still be at Lazio's house. That would mean breaking in. It might already be at Glen Parva's offices. That put the papers right out of his reach. The only chance in the time he had was to go through Lazio's office.

With Ann sat next door most of the day, that was highly risky, even if he knew that Lazio was tied up lecturing. And then he couldn't use the photocopier. Wild thoughts raged through his mind. If he hit the fire alarm while Lazio was away, he could legitimately claim to be protecting key documents by taking them out of Lazio's filing cabinet while everyone else was rushing out of the building. That might make him a hero. Or not.

David drifted through the day while his body cleared away the vast amounts of adrenalin that had resulted from his early visitor. By late afternoon he had decided his plan.

First he rang Madeleine to say he wouldn't be home till half past six or so. Some research to finish off but it would only take an hour or so. Then he cleared his paperwork as usual, put on his coat, said goodnight to Ann Whittaker, and headed off as though for home. On the corner of his desk, clearly visible, he'd left a thick volume ''Classic Chess Strategies''.

He drove out of the university and away from Leicester until ''The Ploughshare'' announced its bar meals and happy hour to passing travellers. He parked up behind the pub at the far end of the cars already there, went in, ordered an orange juice and sat with a magazine in the corner furthest from the door.

After about three quarters of an hour, he left the pub and drove back to the university car park. He went in through the lab door and was pleased to hear the burglar alarm beep at him. That meant everyone had gone home. He switched off the alarm, went to his office and tucked the chess book prominently under his arm.

'Silly me, forgetting this book and having to come back for it,' he said out loud as if practising his alibi.

He used his access key to get into Ann's office, grabbed the keys that lay at the back of her desk drawer, opened Lazio's office door, then his filing cabinet.

His mouth was dry and he felt himself panting as he worked his way through to the quintahertz file.

Thank god. Thank god.

There was a sheaf of papers with ''Ministry of Defence - Secret'' stamped on the top. There lay the secret of the terratanium antenna and the final piece of the quintahertz jigsaw.

He pulled them out with shaking hands and stood sweating as the photocopier warmed up.

Jesus, why do these things take so long?

The sheets of paper went through agonisingly slowly. Shit. What to do with them? He couldn't go past the security cameras with a pile of glaringly white paper in his hand. He undid three shirt buttons and stuffed the wad inside. The originals went back into Lazio's file.

Right. Double check. Filing cabinet checked and closed, nothing disturbed. Door locked. Back into Ann's office, keys back in the drawer. Photocopier off. All as it looked when he came in. Good.

David Bearing set the burglar alarm and walked confidently out of the building, the 'forgotten' chess book prominent in his hand. He climbed into his car, where he'd left it to be easily noticed by security, and drove off. Elated, he'd managed to get the required goods without being discovered.

Unfortunately, that would be but a temporary situation. He had left behind a clear pointer to his evening's work.

* * * * * * * *

The following day, David checked out his camcorder, made sure the battery was well charged and a new cassette was in place. He took it into the office and stowed it in his desk drawer ready for the next morning when his 48-hour deadline expired. He would show whoever was giving him grief that he could fight back.

But he was to lose the next round as well.

Just before he pulled out of his drive ready to make the delivery as instructed, he checked the package of drawings. It fitted loosely in his inside jacket pocket. That was order number one. Then he was to pull into his usual place in the university car park, lock up the car, go to the front tyre that was away from the security camera, bend down to check it and slide the package onto the top of the tyre.

The next bit was his own plan. He would sprint into his office, collect the camera and sit by the workshop window, well back out of sight. Whoever came to pick up the package would be on tape, in close up, in colour, for all time. He felt sure he would not have long to wait.

He didn't.

He pulled out of the drive, moved off down the road between the parked cars and had to brake sharply as a car drove out in front of him. It stopped, blocking his way. Before he could sound his

218

horn a girl jumped out and ran towards him. It was his visitor from forty eight hours before.

'The package, please.'

Dumbstruck, David passed it over.

'Now, off to work and don't tell a soul.'

She ran back to the car, pulled over and waved him on.

He was almost at the university before he got his brain into gear. Damn, I never even got the car number.

* * * * * * * *

A few days after the meeting between the head of IS5 and the head of DARE, Grant Hawley got a phone call from his counterpart.

'I just thought I'd let you know that the stolen quintahertz machine is most certainly in Khazatan as we thought. There has been a high level meeting at diplomatic level and the Khazatanis made no denials. There was no confirmation either, but that's to be expected with this sort of thing.

'Apparently, our side said the British government was considering the matter but they could expect a major and serious response. What they've done could possibly happen to you at DARE as well as to any company because there's a lot of industrial espionage going on just now. Companies don't like to admit publicly that their computer systems have been hacked into and they've lost trade secrets, so not much is known about it. But when all the little incidents are added up, the total loss of inventions and prototypes is major.

'All the western countries are looking for the slightest opportunity to make an example of an eastern European embassy and close it down. So it's all on a knife edge. And it's the domino effect, as soon as one country takes action, the rest will follow quick as anything.

'Anyway, nobody expects them to give back the machine, but at least it should make them think carefully about what they do with it. If push came to shove, we'd tell our industrial attaches in the key embassies to let steel companies know they and their governments would face sanctions if they bought a quintahertz machine from Khazatan and not from the UK.

'So, on the hardening side, quintahertz is an international bargaining counter. But that's politics. Bugger the individual, just keep the country's scoreboard clean.

'As far as you're concerned, though, do you still need the test facilities we were talking about for Stop?'

'Most certainly,' said Hawley. We're increasing the power output from the machine and full testing is now even more important. Our project leader, Ben Blackwater, has organised several terratanium blocks from the MoD telecomms people and it's all go.'

'So there's room for negotiation with the Khazatanis, then? If they give us some testing facilities, we forget what they've stolen?'

'That's OK by us here. In all reality, they'll have worked out the inner secrets of the machine anyway so it's all a bit pointless now. But get as much leverage from it as you can. I don't know what Palfrey or anyone else would say, but there's nothing crucial they could do, so go ahead.'

'Right. I'll report back on that. So what I need to know now is the sort of test facilities you'll need.'

'That's the million dollar question. We've a shopping list and a half but from our past experience in this sort of thing, it will be a job for the military. We'll need some of their equipment anyway but then there's the problem of liaison inside Khazatan. You find the military take this sort of exercise over completely in the end,' said Hawley. 'We have had a planning meeting with the logistics department in DARE. Do you want to hear the outline?'

'Sure.'

'Right. We need two long-range Chinook helicopters and one ten ton lorry or three heavyweight Land Rovers with operational and support staff; a contingent of SAS as protection, a film crew, a stills photographer, operational facilities in Germany and short stay facilities in Khazatan.'

'Bloody hell. Have you any idea what that is going to cost?'

'More than we shall earn in our lifetimes, that's for sure.'

'I should think so.'

'Yes, but you're looking at it from an industrial viewpoint. Something like this becomes a military exercise and when the country is training its troops for anti-terrorist activities, money's no object. It would make your industrial budgets pale into insignificance.'

'Obviously. What's it all going to be used for then?'

'We need to run two tests. The first is a single shot, distance test where we fire the machine at some unsuspecting poor sod about a mile or two away, depending on what Porton Down suggests would be a good range for humans. We then move in closer until we see a reaction. Hopefully the target will first of all jump as though it's been stung by a wasp. That gives us a good idea of the range of Stop. Then we go closer.'

'OK. Don't go on. I get the point,' said the IS5 director.

'The next test is a fly-over to see the reaction from an airborne run on a mass of people. So we need Land Rovers to carry the gear on the distance test and a load carrier like the Chinook for the fly-over. And after the fly-over, we've only about a quarter of an hour to check out the village. So Chinook number two brings in the transport to carry our inspection team into the village.

'But we must forestall any funny business by the Khazatanis. So the SAS will provide a deterrent while we're in the country. We'll also use a military base outside the country, probably in Germany, as an assembly point where we set up the equipment. The Chinooks will fly the whole shooting match into Khazatan for the shortest possible time, so we may not have to spend a night in the country if we're lucky.'

'Gee, I'd love to be there. It sounds as though it'd be some show.'

'See if you can book yourself a ticket,' said Hawley. 'But we don't yet know who'll take overall responsibility. There's national security involved here, so the security services will want to run the show. But the military, as always, will want it for themselves so there will be some fireworks before we even start.'

'Well, let's keep in touch. I think it's obvious this thing will be taken away from us at IS5, but I'd love to know how you get on. Good luck.'

'Thanks,' said Hawley. 'I'll keep you in mind.'

* * * * * * * *

Chapter 15

'Damn this cold. Nothing seems to be shifting it. I've got a sore chest from coughing, a sore nose and a bloody headache.'

And don't we know it, thought Helen Palfrey as she glanced up at her husband.

'It seems to have turned into summer flu,' she said. 'Are you sure you're taking everything the doctor has given you.'

'Of course I am. What do you think I'm doing with all those bloody little bottles?'

'You forget we've been married thirty two years. I know you.'
Lazio sniffed.

'Try and look on the bright side, it has helped you lose a few pounds without much effort.'

'It's probably that pesky diet that's brought on this cold in the first place. You don't know how miserable it is eating salad.'

'And I suppose we women never suffer for you men. Your lot would never survive if you had to wear high heels, corsets and have babies.'

'Yes, but what about all the stress we have at work. Look at this business with Glen Parva and those bloody people at Farnborough pinching my idea. I see money running away in all directions and fat chance of any extra coming in.

'Look what we've got to sort out in the next few months. This roof has got to be done before winter. That's two thousand pounds. And the grass looks a mess for want of a decent lawnmower. The cheapest ride-on is another two thousand pounds. And then the bloody car. Three thousand pounds says the man who can, and without blinking an eyelid. We've also got to think of William starting school in September.'

'Look, you can't have your cake and eat it. Tell me what other professor has got an old manor house to live in, a huge garden and an expensive car like a Maserati to drive about in. And you don't want me to work. Just what do you expect?

'Anyway, you seem to have handsomely wrecked the Maserati for someone who's supposed to be an engineer. What work did the garage say the engine needed?'

Helen picked up the garage's estimate.

'Re-valve and grind down the cylinder head; replace the cylinder liners and fit oversize pistons; renew all conrods; re-grind the main crankshaft; re-grind the overhead camshaft; re-balance the flywheel; fit new seals and gaskets all round. They say the car had been driven far too long after the water had leaked through the blown head gasket.

'I don't know what half that means but there can't be much of the engine that survived.'

'Well I was fed up and I wanted to get home. And I thought the water temperature gauge had packed up. How was I to know there was no water for it to measure?'

'I'm gratified to hear that you like to get home so much but please take a taxi next time, it'll be about a tenth of the cost. In fact, with the cost of servicing that thing and keeping it on the road, you'd probably be better off selling it and taking taxis everywhere. The rest of the world would be a safer place, that's for sure.'

'Oh don't get at me. I feel awful.'

Helen went to the drinks cabinet and poured him a large brandy.

'Here, I'll brew you a coffee to go with that. A couple of those and these demands on your money won't bother you half so much. We've survived worse before. We'll get this sorted.

'Why don't you take tomorrow off and just potter about here. Tell Glen Parva they'll have to wait another day for your presence. The world won't stop because of that.'

'You're right' said Lazio. 'I'll do that. Did you say there was another brandy on the way?'

'Only if it'll stop you whinging.'

'It'll definitely do that.'

'Right. I'll put the kettle on first.'

* * * * * * * *

Lazio felt marginally better after his day off although the doctor hadn't been much help when he'd called in.

'I'd like to see a bit more weight coming off,' he said 'You're not in very good shape at all, I'm afraid, and all these extra pounds are putting more stress on the old ticker. Blood pressure's still high and you're not shifting this cold. You must try to regain a bit of your old form or your arteries will clog up and you'll then have to live with angina, which is a painful condition everyone could do without, or something worse. If you don't fancy walking, get a bike.'

That made Lazio splutter.

'Well you can ride it after dark if you don't want anyone to see. Or get an exercise bike.'

Lazio pointed out that it would have to be on prescription with the state of his finances but the doctor just said if that was the case, he'd obviously have to get his own bill in a bit sharpish.

With sympathy non-existent on all sides, Lazio put on a brave face when he went into Burnstone on his way to Glen Parva. He wasn't going to try for anything from Ann Whittaker.

'Have you heard anything from the police about the quintahertz machine?' he asked.

'Not a dicky bird.'

'Would you give them a quick call just to get an update and then could you ring admin to see how we're covered for insurance. I've no idea how much the machine would be worth or how much we could claim for but we ought to find out.'

'Sure thing. Will you be back after your trip to Glen Parva?'

'I doubt it. It's early to bed until I get rid of this cold.'

In his office, Lazio cleared the quintahertz file of papers, put them in a folder and stowed them in the boot of Helen's Peugeot alongside his last block of terratanium.

I'd grown quite fond of that machine, he thought to himself, as the Peugeot pottered over to Birmingham. Moving back to less exotic research while others played with his best ideas didn't go down too well either.

But it helped when he was treated royally when he finally arrived at the Glen Parva offices. His name and title were up in

225

lights on the welcome board in reception and the receptionist virtually carried him to a chair while asking if wanted tea or coffee. Being chatted up by a young lady was always very welcome.

So he was somewhat more cheerful when a virtual welcoming party emerged from the lift. Chairman Charles Thurmaston led the way out with Bill Charnwood and Geoff Aylestone shepherding up from the rear.

Charles greeted Lazio warmly.

'May I introduce Bill Charnwood as our non-executive director. He wasn't able to come with us to Burnstone but he was hoping to have a few minutes with you today. He keeps an eye on the outside world for us while we've got our heads stuck into the company and he'd like to discuss the general economic scene and what you feel about matters outside the steel business. You're our secret weapon.'

Ouch, thought Lazio, I don't want to talk about secret weapons, thank you. Might get stolen by some government department.

'But do you want to have a look round and sort out the technical side with Geoff first?'

'OK. I've got the rest of the paperwork here,' Lazio indicated his briefcase. 'But there's a great block of terratanium to come out of the boot.'

'Give me the keys and I'll get that sorted,' said Thurmaston.

'I'll see you later, then,' said Bill Charnwood.

Geoff Aylestone had certainly laid on the red carpet treatment.

After a tour of the Glen Parva factory, the two went to the laboratory where the frame of the new quintahertz machine was being assembled. Lazio looked with approval over the drawings that had been produced from his own basic sketches. They then moved onto Geoff's office where a group of turbine blades were laid out on the desk.

'These are some of the more exotic items our metals go into. As I mentioned before, this will be our first project with you. They have already been hardened by a standard plasma deposition process but we'd like to find out if quintahertz can improve on that either by itself or in conjunction with plasma technology.'

'Well, if it's Smithson-type technology, we'll beat the pants off it,' said Lazio, relishing the thought of getting one up on his competitor.

'At the moment, we don't know what the treatment is and we haven't pressed the point with the blade manufacturer,' said Aylestone. 'We'd like to go a bit further before we show our hand. So can you first devise a set of tests that maybe tells us whose treatment has been used to harden the blades. Secondly, we need a set of reference parameters so when we try other hardening methods, we have a base set of figures to compare when they're being tested. By then, we should have a quintahertz machine up and running.

'The whole point is to produce a design for turbine blades for use by Middle East airlines. They always lose their edge far faster than blades on jet engines that only fly around Europe. There's always sand particles about, sometimes up to several thousand feet, and, as you know, they're highly abrasive.

'With the blades spinning at several thousand revs, they hit a large number of particles at high speed, so it's a pretty tough environment. And operators are so sensitive about efficiency nowadays. As soon as the edge goes off the blades, fuel consumption rises and there's a great wringing of hands from the accountants as they worry about profit margins. So we've got a lot to go for.'

'I like the sound of that project,' said Lazio. 'I have some time to spare before the students come back for next term so I can make an early start. I the meantime, here's the rest of the paperwork for the quintahertz machine.'

He pulled out the folder from his briefcase.

'How's your purchasing department doing with getting all the components together?'

'Some bits are already here and the rest are ordered. I'm told all the parts are ex-stock so there shouldn't be any problems with long delivery. When I take you to see Bill Charnwood, we'll go via the stores and you can see what's come in.'

Geoff Aylestone looked through the sheaf of papers in the folder.

'There's quite a lot here. I'll study them a bit later on if that's all right. I can always give you a call or pop over if there's something that needs explaining.'

He was laying out the sheaf of MoD papers on his desk.

Lazio realised that they were in the wrong order.

'Sorry about that, I'm sure they were they right way round before.'

'Don't worry, they're just back to front. It always happens to me when I've done some photocopying. Right, there we are. Shall we go and look at some components in the stores, then?'

After approving what had been bought, Geoff Aylestone took Lazio up to Bill Charnwood's office.

'Look,' said Charnwood. ' Time's getting on, do you fancy chatting over lunch instead of in here?'

'That's fine by me,' said Lazio 'Got to keep body and soul together,' By which he meant that, as a guest of Glen Parva, he naturally couldn't embarrass his host by eating just one lettuce sandwich.

So the rest of the visit passed very pleasantly, but Lazio couldn't get out of the back of his mind the incident with the MoD papers being in the wrong order. That made him look inefficient.

* * * * * * * *

The following morning, Lazio was still troubled by Geoff Aylestone's suggestion that he couldn't photocopy a sheaf of papers without getting them in the wrong order. He was doing it all the time, for heaven's sake.

His peace of mind was further disturbed by Ann's report on her call to the Leicester police.

'They haven't any local suspects,' she said when he went into her office. 'And they think there's an international involvement. There was mention of higher authority. But who has more authority than the police?'

Lazio laughed at her innocence.

'Just about everybody nowadays, according to the newspapers, authority's a thing of the past, isn't it? The only reason we seem to have any authority here is because the students want to learn.

228

Well, most of them anyway. They don't have to be here, so they toe the line. But in schools, where they're forced to attend, the staff have very little authority, so I hear. The kids suit themselves and the parents seem to support them however illegal or undesirable their behaviour is.

'But if you want a serious answer, I would think the security services have more clout. They can go international without any problems, whereas the police can't. They'd have to use Interpol or something like that. But who really knows? And what if the matter becomes political? I'm sure all sorts of murky deeds go on without being reported. With government and people like that all the papers are locked away for fifty years or so. But the police don't have that protection.'

'Well, whatever is going on, they said they would let us know if there were any developments,' said Ann.

'Hmm,' said Lazio, 'It's a shame you didn't invite that young man, Boris Pushtin, out to dinner when he came to interview me. He's behind it all, I'm quite sure. We might now know what's going on and you could have made a million if you'd sold the story to the News of the World.'

'Professor Palfrey. Which file would you like me to throw at you?'

Lazio retired to his office. He may have been smiling but Ann's report had decided him that matters were getting out of control. He would have to update the dean, as his boss, but he half suspected that would be a most uncomfortable session.

It was.

'If you're not careful,' said Alistair Wyatt, 'you and your department will become a laughing stock. I don't mind that, but it would reflect on the university as a whole. We'd lose valuable sponsors, and that does concern me.

'First of all you half kill one of your staff and I have to take measures to cover up for you. Then the department has a break in and there are all the signs that it was either very carefully planned or it was an inside job. You have university property stolen from your back garden. Who, in heaven's name, knew that was there? Then half the staff have their phones tapped illegally.

'Now, you tell me you've been shielding a computer hacker with a strong possibility that he tipped off some foreign johnny about your quintahertz machine at a Technology Transfer Day and then photocopied documents from your office filing cabinet.

'You're not just here to lecture, you know, you've a department to manage and that just isn't happening.'

'It's a bit of a mess, I agree,' said Lazio. 'Which is why I was hoping for your help.'

'Well, you obviously need some help, that's for sure. I can't put someone else in to head up the department just now. But we've got to do something. Give me a while to think all this through.

* * * * * * * *

While Leonid Lebdev had been organising London station to lift the remaining quintahertz documents, Alexander Kasvanov was trying to hunt down some terratanium. After talking to several old hands in a number of steel companies, the general opinion was that he would not find any in Khazatan.

'The stuff was widely talked about probably twenty years ago now,' said his last port of call. 'But not even our fantastic communist scientists could find a use for it. If there's any paperwork describing it, it will most likely be in Moscow. And since the wall came down, there is probably no-one who would have half a clue as to its whereabouts.'

He reported back to Lebdev who well knew the score nowadays. You didn't get anything for nothing out of Moscow any more. And simple bribery was out - the deals were now calculated in telephone numbers.

But Palfrey must have had access to the metal. Lebdev went to see the scientists working on the quintahertz machine and sat with the file of papers. The clue lay in the Ministry of Defence papers that held the secrets of the terratanium antenna. They were dated three years earlier and referred to applications in the telecommunications field. So it must have been the MoD that sparked the quintahertz idea and they probably still had stocks of the material.

Lebdev reported back to his superior officer in government liaison.

'What about the element of surprise? Why don't we just put through a purchase order for some?'

'That might have been possible some time ago, but events have moved on,' he was told. 'The British security services now know we have a quintahertz machine and the government is in discussion with the British about it. But we may still be able to fit in a request for some terratanium in the negotiations.'

'Anything you can tell me about the negotiations?' asked Lebdev. 'Do they involve us in the Research Institute?'

'I suppose they will. I haven't heard anything definite, you understand, but we could need some of your scientific wizards as observers. The British want to organise a military exercise in Khazatan and we suspect it involves the testing of some new weaponry. They won't tell us exactly, so we'll need some technical help to analyse exactly what they are trying to do if they get here.

'It's pretty heavy stuff I gather, so we should be able to get anything we want in return, but they are playing a strong hand. They and their allies are getting fed up with the amount of industrial espionage going on at the moment in all the developed countries. So they want to set us up and make a public example of us to the rest of the world.

'With the way we've handled the quintahertz machine, they've got a lot of ammunition. So we have got to tread very carefully. But, on the other hand, there are very few countries that would be willing to offer them the facilities they want.

'I'll feed your request into the machine so keep your fingers crossed.'

'I will,' said Lebdev. 'But it might be worth telling whoever that if there is no more terratanium to be had, we can't develop the quintahertz machine and everyone's efforts so far will go straight down the pan.'

* * * * * * * *

Whether that would be the case or not, the plan to send Sergei Danelski to Mumbai was still live.

But he had some fast talking to do before he could get Vishay Bhopari, the managing director of Sandrapoor Steel Mills, to agree to see him.

'I'm not so sure a meeting would achieve anything,' said Bhopari. 'I think your principals are only interested in Sandrapoor for the short term. That does not interest either us or our shareholders.'

'I appreciate that,' said Danelski. 'And I would feel the same way. But my principals do have a long term contract to offer you, and I think you would find the specifics very attractive.'

'That may be, but you have suddenly come out of the woodwork and that smells very much like opportunism. We may not want to work any closer than we already do with Glen Parva, but they at least show steadfastness of purpose. They have been on the international expansion trail for a long time and continue to show progress in their aim. Our shareholders are also in for the long term and they like steadfastness of purpose.'

'Yes. But they also want a rising share price and bigger dividends, don't they. Our proposal has several strands that will definitely boost your share price and dividends for some time to come.'

Bhopari demurred for a while.

'Well, come in and see us then. I'm not convinced, but you can try your luck with the other directors.'

* * * * * * * *

Two days later, Danelski flew into Sahar International Airport in Mumbai. With the flight being on schedule, he had plenty of time to check into his hotel first and run over his approach to the Sandrapoor directors. The Hotel Kings International was rated three star and it provided the right match of comfort and cost that suited Danelski.

Later, in Bhopari's office, Danelski was introduced to the technical and financial directors and Vishay Bhopari outlined the conversation he'd had with Danelski earlier.

'I've explained that we are only interested in long term ventures with other companies and then only if we are forced into that situation. Danelski was already aware of our joint venture with Glen Parva steel producers and that they want to develop the relationship further. I have to say that I think that whichever of the Khazatan steel companies is allocated to deal with us, their aim will be to obstruct Glen Parva rather than to consider our wellbeing. As such I would suggest that the board does not recommend Mr Danelski's approach to shareholders.'

Danelski let Bhopari have his say. He felt that the managing director's tirade was because he was under more pressure than he could handle. He was right to some extent, but his own people were starting to get their act together and merited a hearing in their own right.

'I understand your concerns,' said Danelski. 'but our own steel industry is a major force and while we may be only at the start of our commercial journey, I can assure you our aims are as long term as anyone's.

'There is also the inescapable fact that, while Sandrapoor is a large and well-run company, its strategy only covers India at the moment. Your shareholders will soon want to see an international strategy. I feel you may not have the resources to support such an approach and your major shareholders will desert the company for others such as Glen Parva.'

Vishay Bhopari shifted uncomfortably in his chair. Danelski, the arch negotiator, picked up the sign immediately.

'I dispute that analysis totally,' said Bhopari.

Danelski was unconvinced.

'Let's look at some practical points then. There are a number of companies that work together in Khazatan and that are supported by a national research institute. So we can offer new products and enable you to keep up with the latest global technical develop-ments. These facilities far exceed those that are available either to you or to Glen Parva and, as you all will be aware of, it is technical excellence that gets you the sales orders in this business.

The technical director nodded approval.

'So I can reveal that we will make available to you our latest development - a brand new steel hardening process that no-one else in the world can offer. Initially, it would be at a very low cost because our National Development Fund is prepared to subsidise the first few machines.'

He outlined the quintahertz machine and what it would mean in terms of enhancing Sandrapoor's reputation and sales.

'Yes. But that is just one technical process. Surely the greater sales network of an established company would benefit us more?'

'On the surface, yes,' said Danelski. 'But have you the production capability to meet the new opportunities?'

He turned to the financial director.

'You will know the cost of funding increased sales. They can often sink a company that grows too fast, can't they?'

'Undoubtedly, but have no fears for us on that score.'

Danelski felt the managing director was out on a limb by himself. Reading between the lines, the other two directors appeared to have much more practical views on the company's future. But he decided he would have to play the second card to fully convince them all.

'We also have another proposal that no-one else will match. We are prepared to buy your high volume steel mill.'

That touched a nerve.

The financial director made a note on his pad and turned it towards Bhopari.

'And why would you want to do that?'

'The machinery would upgrade our Stavrol rolling mill and help us meet the rising level of orders we are receiving for low cost, basic steels.'

The directors hadn't expected that answer. But Danelski knew why they would appreciate the proposal. He didn't have to embarrass them further by stating openly the losses they were suffering at the mill.

The directors relaxed in the way that negotiators do when the key decision is made. Negotiating the fine detail is generally a mechanical process once the major outcome has been decided and it doesn't require the same degree of intense concentration and battle of mental wills needed in the first stages of discussion.

'And our approach is based on strict commercial considerations. We will not be aggressive for the sake of it. Aggression always leads to strong reactions and, in business, we do not think that is a wise policy.'

Danelski made no mention of Glen Parva's acknowledged aggressive tactics. The board was as aware as anyone of the company's reputation.

'In conclusion, I would like to say that if you really want to fend off Glen Parva, then we are a far better option. And you have to look at our proposal from the shareholders' point of view. Is it not better to anticipate them rather than to wait for them to take the decision for you?'

The directors' body language gave him the answer that he had come for.

'Well, Mr Danelski, we will give your proposal serious consideration. You appreciate we cannot do that without a full board meeting, but that is not too far off. We'll let you know the outcome as soon as we can.'

So Sergei was able go hunting for the real curry he had promised himself. It was a shame he had to play all the cards he had been given, but that had been pretty much expected. It reduced his take, but he would still do well enough. Now it was a case of waiting.

* * * * * * * *

Alan Birstall hadn't seen Kate Bellew for a week. He was beginning to get withdrawal symptoms. He paced up and down Birmingham's New Street station trying not to watch the arrival indicator as the delay time steadily increased.

Kate, at twenty nine, was the age at which he had got married. But that was five years ago. It had lasted about two years and he had been divorced for about two years. He could never say when the marriage had started to fall apart but he was away a lot, driving an ambitious career. By the time the divorce proceedings had concluded he was deeply involved in Glen Parva.

The divorce left him with the bitter, facetious sense of humour that was not often appreciated by the company's chairman. But he produced increasing sales and Charles Thurmaston couldn't deny the value of those.

Now Kate had reminded him of his pre-celibate years and he was more than ready to leave his desk for the sensual pleasures of a social life.

Finally, she was there. Thanks to the inventor of mobile phones he was pre-warned and ready at the carriage door as the mass of humanity emptied itself, and its chattels, on to the platform. Suddenly, there were those patent shoes, the slim legs, the tailored suit and the perfume that hit him as they air-kissed.

He took her Vuiton suitcase and laptop computer and led her out into the warm sunshine of the July morning.

'How was the trip?'

'Not so bad, although we seemed to stop for longer than we moved. Maybe it's me but I never notice when the train's moving, but as soon as it stops, the time seems to pass so slowly it's frustrating. It's better than coming here by car so you've got to be grateful for small mercies, I suppose.'

As Alan headed the car towards the Glen Parva factory he felt obliged to mention again that the firm's china didn't carry the company logo and would be somewhat heavier than that at Hoogen, Bellew, Cutler.

'I think I might manage to lift it,' laughed Kate. 'Remember, I am used to visiting industrial premises.'

'It's just that steel making tends to be the dirtiest and most fundamental industry going. Not like the PR business in any way, shape or form.'

'I might just cope. Didn't you notice I've put my hair up so a hard hat will fit properly?'

Alan muttered some mumbled apology. He couldn't admit that his attention hadn't really risen above the hem of her skirt. The peril of being a leg man was that one never noticed a lady's hair. Unfortunately, ladies lavished more attention on their hair than their legs, so the leg man was always at a disadvantage where women were concerned.

But he thought she would look very fetching in a hard hat. That slim, vulnerable figure topped off with the hallmark of the macho manual worker. That was some image.

236

An image that was roughly dispelled when the car behind sounded its horn angrily as Alan continued to dream while the lights changed to green.

'Sorry,' he said. 'Just thinking through what we've got to do today.'

'Don't worry,' said Kate, arching one eyebrow and quietly smiling to show that she didn't believe him.

By the time they reached the factory, Alan had regained his professional manner. He apologised for his office.

'Totally functional,' he explained.

'That's how it should be,' said Kate. 'You're here to produce three dimensional solid objects that people can pick up and physically assess for quality and all that. That's where you differ from the PR business. We're all about image. The goods we have to deliver are far less tangible and quite different from those that are in your delivery yard just now.'

He waited while she changed her shoes for a low heeled sturdy pair more suited to a factory floor and handed her a hard hat. She expertly tightened the harness by three holes.

'Always have to do that,' she said. 'No-one told me the first time I wore one that men's heads are bigger than women's. It fell over my eyes and I think they were all peeing themselves at the sight. Bloody chauvinists.'

Alan began to see why Kate was twenty nine and still unattached. There were obviously few men she respected sufficiently. But she had taken his offer to stay overnight at the flat without much persuasion. She was well aware it had only one bedroom. That quietly boosted his morale. She was also well unaware it contained a surprise.

After touring the factory, Alan deposited her in the boardroom to prepare her presentation while he went to round up the directors.

He smiled broadly as he came back in to find that one of the tea ladies had just poured coffee for Kate and was asking if he would like a cup. The contrast between this boardroom in Birmingham and Kate's office in London was such a contrast that he could have laughed out loud instead.

Apart from the fact that one had been designed and furnished by a horny handed son of toil thirty years ago and HBC's suite was hardly thirty months old, and the result of a handbag-carrying arty designer, he saw the starkly contrasting images of a highly beddable, business suited lady surrounded by bone china pouring coffee and a woman in an overall and apron performing the same operation but with considerably less panache and with somewhat more substantial crockery.

The tea lady decided that she was not going to be included in his joke and scarpered.

But Kate noticed.

'What's funny?'

'Nothing. Nothing at all. Have you got your stuff sorted?'

'Yup. Ready to roll.'

Once the directors were seated, Kate presented the newspaper cuttings resulting from the public announcement of Glen Parva's annual figures.

'They are all positive,' said Kate. 'And underline the story we are trying to push for the company. There has been a small rise in the company's share price since then so I feel we have got off to a very good start.'

The directors agreed.

'And now we move onto the next project: announcing the link up with Burnstone University. This will be in two stages. First we announce it from the steel industry point of view. This will highlight the technical and commercial benefits that Glen Parva will receive from its increased level of technical research.

'I am drafting a strategy document and first press release in conjunction with Geoff Aylestone and Alan Birstall and this will shortly be presented to the board for discussion.

'Then we have the more general contribution to company strategy: the public-spirited help we are giving to the micro-biology department for their research. We are agreed on the general results that we want from this investment and Alan and I are going to see their Professor Wyatt this afternoon to discuss specific topics that we can announce. Are there any comments on the operation so far?'

'I think I can speak for the board in saying that your work so far has been very beneficial to the company,' said Charles Thurmaston. 'I have heard a number of favourable comments about our decision to raise our profile. And I think the timing is spot on so we can properly benefit from these activities. But it is early days yet and continuing good results will be the real test.'

'I agree with all that,' said Bill Charnwood. 'But I would add, from what I see outside the company, that we need to start looking at our global expansion plans. It needs to be only superficial just now but we do need to get on and gather our thoughts.

'Remember that journalists have to fill space in their papers whether they have a story or not. On a slow day, they will put in their own speculations and we want to keep them on track if they decide to focus on us. But as Miss Bellew will be well aware, a steady drip feed will achieve that and save us having to rush out announcements to counteract anything that is printed that is non-productive.'

'Very true,' said Kate. 'The key to getting it right is for us always to be accessible to journalists and to have an answer to their questions. We do need help from all of you on that score. No-one should talk to journalists without our knowing. It's so easy to say something that can be misinterpreted and needs a correction later. The switchboard should have our name and number in large letters on it, so any caller that means publicity is put on to us first.'

'I'll check on that,' said Charles. 'Does anyone have any further points for Miss Bellew?'

A shaking of heads.

'Well, thank you for coming to update us and have a good trip over to Burnstone.'

After the directors had left, Alan complimented Kate on the presentation.

'Lunch,' he said. 'You deserve a good one after that.'

'Thanks, but I could do with a wash and brush up first. I've been on the go since six. And I'm not too bothered about a sit-down lunch, a sandwich would be fine. But I'd enjoy something more substantial once we've finished at the university.'

'We can easily drop into the flat on the way over. I'll knock up some grub while you do the necessary, if you like.'

239

'Sounds good to me.'

'It will be somewhat smaller than you're used to,' said Alan as they drove out of Birmingham. 'The divorce cost me dear and this was all I could rent afterwards. I could buy a house now, it's just that I've never got around to it. Work seems to get in the way of most of my plans.'

As the houses gave way to open country, Alan turned off the main road towards the village where a house had been converted into two self-contained flats. It was within easy distance of the pub that constituted the village centre, although the edge of the old village was being blurred by the addition of new houses that would make it a town before long.

Alan had redecorated the flat only a few months before as his tenancy agreement demanded, but he had bought several items to soften the bareness of the flat when he knew that Kate would be staying over. He'd replaced an aged divan base with a smart, traditionally-styled bedstead that had brass-railed head and foot boards.

'It may be smaller than at the Barbican but what a super view,' said Kate. 'And I bet the air's much cleaner as well. I think I could handle this.'

Alan showed her the bathroom, gave her some coat hangers, and disappeared into the kitchen to make the sandwiches.

He heard the shower go on and imagined that body, wet and in the buff. That did him no good at all. He adjusted his clothing to hide the obvious reaction.

'We can't be too long,' he shouted. 'With the amount of traffic about, we could be held up getting in to Leicester.'

* * * * * * * *

Alistair Wyatt greeted Kate warmly. This had to be handled carefully, it could be his passport to fame.

They toured the microbiology department and Wyatt pointed out where he would like to place new equipment.

'Of course, as Dean of the Science Faculty, I don't have all that much time to get into research myself. But we have some excellent staff who do nothing else. My role is to set strategy and then ensure that the staff carry it out. I'd like to do more but it's the same old story, the further up the ladder one rises, the further one gets away from the laboratory bench.'

'Do you find that frustrating?' asked Kate.

'A little. But my other responsibilities more than make up for it. You see, we have so many areas we could investigate that one has to be very careful which projects one chooses. The department could easily lose focus and become just a general research facility. You can't make a high profile out of that and so you don't attract either the best staff or the best students.

'But I try to keep close to government and meet their needs. You mix with the top companies then and get the maximum funding. But that's between ourselves.'

Kate diplomatically ignored Wyatt's self-congratulatory remarks which were no more than condescending to someone whose business was to cultivate government contacts.

He ran through a number of companies that Grover Wisden had identified for him and their ideas for research.

'My government contact tells me these projects would be in line with government thinking, so I have to assess them for profitability both in monetary terms and in reputation.'

'And in their impact on the public at large,' added Kate.

'Why that?'

'Because we will have to make some of your work public knowledge in order to boost Glen Parva's plans and reputation. The FT and the business pages of the Times and Telegraph, for example, handle gene research and that sort of thing intelligently, but you've no idea what the tabloids will make of it.

'You could be labelled as Frankenstein and the department as a local Transylvania. They'll find pictures of two-headed animals to head up their stories.'

'Oh my god,' said Wyatt. 'That would finish me.'

'That's why we're retained by Glen Parva. It's a very specialised business raising a client's profile. Once a company raises its head above the battlements, there's a ninety per cent chance their efforts will be misconstrued and they'll lose more than they gain because of the negative publicity. And it's very

241

costly to overcome mistakes. You just have to get it right first time.'

Kate was laying it on a bit thick but she had spotted Wyatt's penchant for deviousness. If he went off like a loose cannon, that would not help Glen Parva at all. It wouldn't do Wyatt any good either, but that was no concern of hers. She was pleased to note that she had somewhat deflated the dean.

'If you could let me know through Alan what projects you take on that involve Glen Parva's sponsorship of the department, then we can take each case as it comes,' Kate was getting the upper hand.

Wyatt agreed with that.

'And if you come across any high level contacts that might benefit us, perhaps you'd let me know in return,' he said.

'Now, if you'd like to come back to my office we can have a coffee and I'll call in James Russell, who looks after business development for the university; our PR people; and Professor Palfrey, who's our steel expert and who heads up the Combined Engineering. Then you will have met everyone who's involved.'

'I'd also like to discuss our plans to go to Mumbai,' added Alan Birstall. 'We're starting to think about our global expansion plans and it's highly secret but India is where we'd like to start.'

So Kate ended the visit with a notebook full of comments. This was going to be a busy commission, and good for income for the agency. Very satisfying.

On the way back to Alan's flat Kate said she would have to start typing up her report as soon as they arrived and it would take all evening at least.

Alan's face dropped.

'You can't do that, you'll be dead beat,' he said. 'Especially after getting up so early. Can't you do it on the train in the morning?'

Kate laughed at being taken so seriously.

'You ought to see your little-boy-lost look,' she said. 'It doesn't give me any option. Maybe I can manage to type the report on the train tomorrow after all.'

Somewhat relieved, Alan pulled in to a service station to fill up with petrol.

'That's what your flat needs,' said Kate, pointing to the rack of flowers outside the shop. 'I'll get you some.'

'Oh, no you won't. Leave it to me.'

'There,' said Kate, when Alan got back in. 'You need to think about your quality of life. Everyone should have flowers around the place, including the office.'

Alan considered the reaction of his staff if they found his office submerged in flowers. No thanks.

Then there was a hunt around the flat for jugs and tall glasses.

'No point in asking if you've any vases,' said Kate. 'Typical bachelor pad.'

'I could see if downstairs has got any.'

'Don't worry. I can see a vase right up the back of this cupboard, can you reach it?'

After a couple of deep fruit bowls had also been found, Kate said there were enough containers for the armful of flowers that Alan had come back with.

'I'm going to change into something a bit more comfortable before I practice my flower arranging,' she said. 'Any chance of a gin and tonic?'

'Coming up.'

He made two and knocked on the bedroom door before sticking his head round and delivering Kate's.

'Oh. Very proper,' said Kate.

She was sat on the bed wrapped in a large white bath towel that was one of the many purchases Alan had made to ensure the flat was more comfortable than usual.

She took the glass while Alan opened the drawer of the bedside cabinet.

'I brought you a small present,' he said. 'I hope they're the right size and colour.'

She opened the tissue wrapping to reveal four long silk scarves.

'I really can't do any work tonight then, can I?' she said.

* * * * * * * *

Chapter 16

The atmosphere was tense as the three Khazatan embassy officials faced three civil servants across a polished table in the Home Office building in Whitehall.

There were always equal numbers at such government-level meetings in order to maintain the diplomatic balance. That was just one of the rules of diplomatic engagement. But three on three meant serious matters were to be discussed. Quite different from the one on one meetings that never officially happened and where warnings or advice were given off the record.

Three civil servants meant the involvement of three government departments or organisations. That trebled the chance of the minutes being leaked to the press. This meeting would be as public as they get.

The British government had a lot at stake. The most important aim was to get agreement so DARE could test Stop in Khazatan.

'Khazatan is really the only country where we can run the tests on Stop,' said Grant Hawley as he briefed the chief of diplomatic negotiation. 'The concept is so unique and the fact that it has to be tested on live people makes it as sensitive an operation as we're likely to get. Nothing must leak out at all.

'The location has to be miles away from a major centre of civilisation in a country where communications are poor and where there are no organised political pressure groups. We must also have some hold over the country so if anything goes wrong we can oblige the government there to cover it up. If the talks fail to reach agreement with the Khazatanis, we at DARE are going to be somewhat stuck.

The chief negotiator took that message to the strategy meeting before the Khazatani delegation arrived.

'We've three holds on them if they play difficult over the testing request. Firstly, they will need some more terratanium for their hardening machine and we're pretty sure there is none in Khazatan. There may be some in Moscow, we don't know, but that will be inaccessible to them. They could make it, but that would probably take two years and give our steel firm time to clean up the main markets. But our MoD has some they could have tomorrow.

'Secondly, we can close down their London embassy on account of their industrial espionage. That will have a chain effect across western Europe as you can guess in the current economic climate. They won't want that. If it leaks out that we are considering such action, they'll be done for just on the strength of that.

'Thirdly, we tell them that if their hardening machine is touted around the open market, we will fully support any company or person that complains with sanctions of our own.'

He turned to the eastern European diplomatic expert.

'What are they going to threaten us with in retaliation, then?'

'Not a lot really. Like all eastern European countries their economy is in a very weak state. So they can't afford to be nasty to us. They need our companies to employ their inhabitants and give them some spending power. And they also need a contribution from those companies for schools and roads, for example.

'There will be some posturing, but that's to be expected. They could make it difficult for companies that are now set up in the country, and for those that are wanting to move in and take advantage of the low labour rates, low cost of land and the European grants that are keeping these ex-Russian satellite countries on-side with the West. But the answer to that is for the companies to look elsewhere. There's probably better options available in other countries. Remind them of that. There are competitors to Khazatan.

'They could claim support from neighbouring countries and so lever up their threat. But the essence of the matter doesn't warrant others getting involved. This is hardly a hanging matter at the end of the day.

'What really has to be considered is the strategy of the allied western powers. We must forestall any attempt for the old Russian satellites to join up with Russia again. We've got to keep them on our side, that must be the overriding consideration. But remember that they will do well out of the exercise. Just tweak up the money that is available for individuals to get their mucky hands on. That will still get action faster than any amount of words for all they say they've given up the old way of doing business.'

'Oh god. It's always money, isn't it?' said the chief negotiator. 'We sit for days round tables arguing the toss with every country and its neighbour on just about every issue under the sun - all the moral issues, all the national interest stuff, all the social responsibility cock, and then what? It's all converted into money and if the bottom line looks good, then everything's agreed. But if someone isn't making as much money as they think they ought, away we go for another session. As a negotiator it's just totally depressing.'

'Like when you're negotiating for promotion, eh?' said the third member of the team.

'Don't be facetious. Anyway, we've got a union to do that for us.'

He rang his secretary.

'Has the tribe of camel herders arrived?' he asked, knowing that his Oxford accent would contrast noticeably with the lack of English that he obviously expected from his visitors.

'OK. Show them in. Coffee will not be required.'

When the Khazatanis had sat down, he opened the batting.

'We three represent Her Majesty's Britannic Government, which has commanded us to lodge with yourselves a complaint of blatant theft, to whit: one steel hardening machine using quintahertz technology.

'This is extremely serious. You know full well how competitive the steel industry is just now. Steel is a major contributor to your own economy in Khazatan so you cannot deny that. We are all in a global arena today, and that includes yourselves. This machine, due to its unique capability, will give you a distinct advantage over our domestic steel producers. We will not allow that to happen.'

The Khazatanis responded exactly as had been predicted at the strategy meeting earlier. That gave the UK team confirmation of its high level of confidence about the outcome.

The negotiations ran on. Every so often the chief negotiator checked his notes. Or so it appeared. The Times crossword had proved particularly difficult that morning and it now rested part way down his notepad. Occasionally he made notes. He had done that four times during the main part of the meeting. That was four more clues completed.

He turned from it when he felt the negotiations were coming to their close.

This was getting to be a mechanical business, he thought, perhaps I'm ready for the promotion that cheeky beggar mentioned earlier.

He had been surprised, though, when one of the Khazatani team accused him of being un-British. He had just pointed out the harm that could come from any leaks to the press.

'It doesn't matter to us one jot whether the leaks are accurate or completely made up. We're only interested in making an example of you. What you should be concerned about is what your masters will do to you if the London embassy is closed down; and what they will then do if other countries follow our example. Do they still shoot traitors? Our hands would be clean, we have tabloid newspapers that do our dirty work.'

'That's hardly British,' said one Khazatani. 'It's blatantly unfair.'

'It's new British, old son. We can only be pushed so far. But let's move on to the core of this business. What do you want from us for this exercise we'd like to run? It's only for two or three days and about twenty men. You know the United Nations rate for this sort of exercise, so don't go too wild.'

So the negotiations moved to their conclusion with the Khazatanis promised one small block of terratanium within a few days and more to be taken to the country directly by the weapon testing team.

After they had left the meeting, the chief negotiator reminded his two colleagues that no leaks would be required.

'This is a finely balanced exercise,' he said. 'It could still go wrong. The deal has to stay totally secret because I don't think any of us could work out what the result might be from any sort of publicity. Tell your moles to stay underground until another story crops up. But we'll give them a field day if these camel herders play silly buggers.'

* * * * * * * *

'We've just got to hang him out to dry,' said Alistair Wyatt to Lazio Palfrey a few days after Lazio had asked for the Dean's help in bringing some sort of order back to his department.

'I know most of the evidence against Dr Bearing is circumstantial but there is so much of it that some must stick. I've been making some enquiries myself although I suspect the police aren't telling me the whole story. The security services have been involved in the investigation, I gather, so it has been taken out of police hands for the moment.

'There are two other points to consider. First, we have to be seen to be taking some action. There's all sorts of rumours going round at the moment and people are looking to me to quash them. Secondly, we've got to stop anyone else having bright ideas so we've got to come down hard on Bearing to set an example.'

'Can't disagree with all that,' said Lazio.

'Good. Well, let's get him in here from wherever he's lurking and sort it out. It has to be put to rest before the students come back next term and, frankly, I'd like to see him out of the door today.'

David Bearing felt uncomfortable as soon as Jenny, the Dean's secretary offered him a seat. She gave him the sort of sympathetic look for someone on the way to the gallows.

And he sensed the heavy atmosphere as soon as he entered the Dean's study. He hadn't been on this hallowed carpet since the day he joined the university and was welcomed in six years before.

'Sit down,' said Wyatt.

'I'm afraid we've a problem here and you seem to be at the centre of it. That makes it the second time in a month I gather from Professor Palfrey.'

David said nothing.

'A week ago a security camera recorded you coming back to the university one evening after everyone had left. Why was that?'

'I'd left a book on my desk accidentally and went in to collect it on the way to my chess club.'

'What else did you do while you were collecting the book?'

'Nothing.'

But you were in the building for just over twenty minutes, that's a long time to pick up one book, isn't it.'

'It can't have been that long,' said David, his face reddening. 'I might have just checked some chess openings in it before I went off. I can't remember.'

'Two days later, Professor Palfrey took a file from his filing cabinet and later found that a sheaf of papers in it had been unstapled and the sheets were in the wrong order. They were back to front. That happens when you photocopy papers in a hurry or are flustered and turn them over when they have been copied, doesn't it?'

'It can happen.'

'Professor Palfrey has timed the photocopier in Ann Whittaker's office. To copy the sheaf of papers in question would have taken about fifteen minutes with two minutes for the machine to warm up. Do you see a coincidence emerging?'

David's face had gone from red to white and his throat had dried up.

'No. Just speculation.'

'Ann Whittaker says that, several weeks ago, you were asking how many emails Professor Palfrey sent each day. Why did you want to know that?'

'I don't remember asking her anything like that. Why would I want to know something like that?'

'How about you had been unable to hack into his computer and wanted to know what was going on. And that was because, a short while before, Professor Palfrey had taken certain measures to protect his system. Measures that identified your efforts to access his system without authorisation.'

David now knew what had triggered his meeting with Lazio a month before.

'And our problem deepens when we find out certain things about the disappearance of the quintahertz machine,' Wyatt continued.

'We understand it has turned up in the east European country of Khazatan, once a Russian soviet republic. That is not nice, especially when we have independent confirmation of your admission that you spoke to a person from that country, namely Sergei Danelski, at a Technology Transfer Day. And how did anyone know it was in Palfrey's garden when he had told no-one and had moved it on a Saturday afternoon when no-one was around to see the move?'

'Look. You can't pin that one on me,' said David. 'I swear I never said anything to Danelski and I had no idea the machine had been taken out of the workshop. Why would I want to get mixed up in anything like that?'

'You tell me,' said Palfrey, who had sat silent throughout Wyatt's inquisition.

'So where do we go from here?' asked Wyatt. 'Do we go looking for more incidents, do we look for more proof or do we suspend you and hand the whole file over to the police?

'Or are we kind to you, fools to ourselves and accept your immediate resignation?'

Wyatt sat back in his chair, fingertips together as though in prayer, looked at David with one eyebrow raised questioningly and waited.

'This is all unfair,' David Bearing blurted out. 'It's all supposition.'

'Correction,' said Wyatt. 'Only some of it is. Would you like us to hand over your computer to the IT department with their forensic software that will lift everything off your hard disc whether it has been erased or not. And I'm sure you wouldn't mind them checking your home computer as well. If you feel you've nothing to hide, that is.'

'I don't seem to have much option, do I?' said David. 'But I still think it's grossly unfair.'

'It's not unfair, it's a case of integrity. We are interested in the university's reputation, not in retribution. And, as you will find out, reputation is not always founded on fact, but is very easily destroyed. That's why we have a duty of care to the university.

'Right, Lazio, take Dr Bearing to clear his desk. Ann will know what to say in the letter of resignation. Security will want his pass back, can you see to that as well, please.'

Outside the Deans' study, David cursed his luck.

'What am I going to tell Madeleine?' he asked.

'Maybe you should have thought about that earlier. Maybe I let you off too lightly a month ago. Think about the mess you're leaving behind. The Dean's always been a thorn in my side, this business will just make it worse,' said Lazio.

'Look,' said David, 'Couldn't we work together on this one. We know how devious Wyatt can be. Can't we put a case together now to sort him out? We might also get a better deal from Glen Parva.'

'Not now, that's for sure.'

After David Bearing had been escorted off the premises by security, Lazio updated the Dean.

'You know, I'm thinking we should still send a file on all this to the police. If only to scupper Bearing well and truly in the future,' said Wyatt.

Vindictive sod, thought Lazio, and after what he said to David face to face.

Instead he said, 'It's a thought. But if there's a leak and the business becomes public, would we want that? Would we want to go into court anyway if it went that far? He's still got to come back to us for a reference as we're his last employer, we can sort him out through that.'

'Good point' said Wyatt. 'We'll let it be then.'

Or not, thought Lazio, knowing the Dean's devious capability.

'Thank God for Saxon's box of tricks,' he said to Helen at home that evening. 'Without that I reckon David Bearing would have been all over my computer. As it is, the Dean doesn't know anything about my going to DARE with Stop so I've still got that card up my sleeve. I'm sure we'll get something out of that. You know, I'm sure David still knows more than me about the Glen Parva deal.'

251

'Yes,' said Helen, 'But at least you can sleep at night and you have a job to go to in the morning.'

'Ever wise,' said Lazio. 'Where's my Bordeaux?'

* * * * * * * *

It was mid-morning. David Bearing was driving out of Burnstone University feeling as though he had just come off a white-knuckle ride. The situation where you need to feel steady ground under your feet before you can start to think what you will try next.

He turned out of Leicester without any idea of where to go. The natural reaction of one who has to escape blindly without thinking.

You just can't go home unexpectedly in the middle of the day, he thought, so what the hell do you do?

He was able to drive without any problem. So let's just do that for a bit. Then the roadside sign for The Ploughshare came up. He'd pull in there and just collect all his thoughts. So, nine days after the photocopying episode had sparked his downfall, he was back at the scene of the crime. Well sort of anyway.

He asked for an orange juice again. It was as though his life was being re-run for him by outside powers.

His first thought was for Madeleine. How to tell her. Her first thought would be the welfare of the four of them. Money to buy food. He would get paid until the end of July, could he expect an August payout? He'd have to check his contract. Where the hell was that after six years?

Let's summarise the situation, he thought. There was a student in front of him with his project in a mess and the marking deadline coming up. What to advise?

Let's assess the material we have in front of us.

What conclusion does it point to?

How can we get to that conclusion fastest so the project shows some sort of result before the crunch arrives for having it assessed and marked?

He ran over his career in the same way. Now thirty five, he'd got his PhD and no-one could take that away from him. He'd had two years in industry. That was worth some bonus points. And ten years in academia, six under the world's leading expert on steel.

But his predilection for computer hacking had cocked that all up. So how did you make money out of computer hacking? He'd be brilliant at attacking people's systems, but everyone said people just didn't want to know where their weak spots were. Everyone had got some sort of protective system but no-one wanted their confidence denting by some whiz kid showing them how it could be breached.

It would take some time to find people who did want those sort of services and then where were his credentials?

'Can we talk to Professors Palfrey and Wyatt about how you tested their systems?'

Definitely not!

He'd have to tell Geoff Aylestone what had happened. Would he want Glen Parva's computer back? That would be a blow. What would anyone else do in this situation? The questions flowed fast - the answers didn't.

Palfrey? He'd never get into such a spot. Wyatt. That devious old bugger. What would he do? Power. That was his weapon of choice. He'd get you into a corner that you couldn't get out of without doing it his way

He let his mind roam over the problem in the type of brain storming session that was needed whenever an area of research was facing a brick wall.

All those snippets of information he'd fed Geoff Aylestone over the years. Would he want the world to know how he'd learned about John Smithson's latest research; which steel companies were using which universities for research; and how had he got the inside track on quintahertz?

Would someone at Glen Parva want to know the real location of the computer that he had given David to use at home and who had really used those air tickets supposedly meant for conferences in Hong Kong and other exotic places. He was sure Geoff would want all that kept quiet.

He reached for his mobile phone. A message had come in while he had been out of the car. It was from Madeleine. She sounded upset.

He thought for a moment then rang her back.

'What's going on?' she asked immediately. 'I rang you a while ago and everyone was out or unavailable. I went back to the main switchboard and they said you didn't work there. What's happened?'

'I'm afraid they're right. I don't work at the university anymore. They've sacked me.'

Madeleine started to cry.

'Look, I'm just getting something else fixed up. Give me a while. I'll be home by about six thirty or seven.'

He tried to give her some hope.

'Get out your cook book and do something really special and either open a bottle of red now or put a bottle of white in to chill. If we don't have something to celebrate it will still be very welcome. Get the kids off to bed early. By the way, what did you ring for?'

'Nothing really. I just got this feeling that I ought to phone you right away. Telepathy, I suppose.'

'It'll be all right, you see. Get cooking. I'll be in as soon as I can.'

'OK. Love you lots. Take care.'

'Love you too.'

David dialled up the Glen Parva number.

'Geoff,' he said when he got through, 'I'm in a bit of a spot. Can I drop in for a few minutes this afternoon and see you, please?'

'That's going to be difficult. We've some overseas visitors here all day and I've really got to be with them. They should go before finishing time but I can't say for certain. Can you call back about four or half past. I should know their plans by then.'

So he had a good few hours to kill. It would just be his luck to run into someone he knew if he stayed around Leicester so he decided to head towards Glen Parva's factory, pick up a paper or a magazine on the way, and hang around in a lay-by.

He managed to survive until a quarter past four.

'They will probably go about half past,' said Geoff Aylestone. 'I think they're just saying goodbye to the chairman now. But I was hoping to get away a bit sharpish tonight and it could take you an hour from Leicester now the traffic's building up, couldn't it?'

'I'm a bit closer than that, I'm only two minutes down the road.'

'Well, drop in when you pass, explain to the receptionist what the score is and I'll come down as soon as I can. You may have to wait a bit, though.'

'No problem. See you later.'

That all sounds very curious, thought Geoff.

It was a quarter to five when a group of smartly suited Germans were shown out through reception by three Glen Parva directors. Geoff Aylestone briefly acknowledged David Bearing as he brought up the rear of the entourage. When he realised the directors were going to follow the visitors out to the car park he stayed behind and motioned David over to a secluded corner of reception that was tucked away behind several large pot plants.

'Bit tough if they miss me now,' he laughed, indicating the main door. 'So what can we do for you?'

'I was hoping you might be able to give me a job.'

Geoff looked blank.

'Doing what?'

'Research in your lab, inspecting your partner's laboratories, quality control, advising customers. Anything like that.'

'What, full time?'

'Yes.'

'But what about the university, isn't that full time?'

'Not any longer.'

'Oh, what's happened?'

'They're blaming me for the loss of the quintahertz machine.'

'You?'

'Yes.'

Geoff leaned forward and rubbed his forehead in exasperation.

'I be damned,' he said. 'We thought Lazio Palfrey was behind it. We've been keeping him at arm's length in case he did anything else stupid,' He laughed.

'And did you have a hand in it?'

'Not at all. I don't know what they thought I'd get out of it. And Lazio certainly didn't have anything to do with it either. He's as choked off as anyone.'

'Well, they can't just sack you on those grounds, can they?'

'Well, there's a bit more to it. They've caught me hacking into the boss's computer files.'

'Anything else?'

'They know I've hacked in to other university computers.'

'Oh god,' said Geoff. 'I should think that's the last thing you want from someone in an area as sensitive as research.'

'They made me write a letter of immediate resignation.'

'So it's intensive gardening for the next few weeks?'

'Grave digging more like when my wife finds out,' David laughed ruefully.

'Well, how we're fixed for taking on new staff I've absolutely no idea. It's not my area at all. I'll have to give it some thought and talk to the lab people in the morning.'

'I'd appreciate that.'

'But I can't promise anything.'

'Well I think you ought,' said David, his face hardening.

That put Geoff's back up.

'And for why?'

'I've done you no end of favours over the last few years. The company has probably made millions out of my bits of information.'

'But you've been paid. You've had holidays, a computer.'

'Yes, but you wouldn't want any of that to come out, would you. It wouldn't help you or the company one little bit.'

'You are treading on very dangerous ground, David,' said Geoff, almost spelling out the words to get his message across. 'No-one holds Glen Parva to ransom. Dirty tricks work both ways and you wouldn't stand a chance, believe me.

'Don't say any more. Leave it with me. I'll call you as soon as I can.'

'Thanks,' said David. 'I'll appreciate anything you can do for me.'

Geoff sat for a moment after David had gone and then took the lift up to the third floor. He went through the chairman's empty outer office and knocked on the half-open inner door.

'Come in.'

Charles Thurmaston was standing by his desk putting papers into his briefcase.

'I think we had a good day with those Germans, didn't you?'

'Yes, there should be some good business to come out of it. But could I just take thirty seconds on another matter?'

'Go on,' said Charles, shutting his briefcase and reaching for his coat.

'I've just had David Bearing in from Burnstone University asking for a job. I think we need to give some thought to his request.'

Charles perched on the corner of his desk. 'But we've no vacancies at the moment as far as I'm aware anyway. What's happened and why should we take him on out of the blue just like that?'

Geoff ran over his conversation with David in the interview area of reception.

'Bugger,' said Charles. 'That could spoil what has been a good day up to now. We could find some job for him, I suppose, but we need to talk through how much damage he could cause the company if we don't. There must be some way to keep him quiet permanently. Oh, christ, what about Professor Palfrey? If he strolls in to find Bearing working away here, he'll go clean up the wall.

'Look, there's no immediate rush to sort this one out. Let's sleep on it. Come and see me in the morning, maybe we'll get the other directors in as well. Spread the shit around as far as we can, eh? That thins it out at least.'

* * * * * * * *

'Let's hope that puts an end to all the funny goings on we've had over the last few months.'

Lazio Palfrey was talking to Ann Whittaker as they checked out David Bearing's old office.

'You can have all the spare pens and pencils,' he said. 'And the next bod can have the reference books. I don't think I want any of his stuff. Got to make a fresh start and all that. Do you want a new chair?'

Ann tried David's old chair for size.

'Ooh, it's got a bit more padding than mine. I'll do a swap.'

'Can you call IT and get them to check out this computer and clear David's space on the mainframe. It might be good sense to change some of the passwords. And can you get John Fleming to change the code number on the burglar alarm, just in case. Then we've just got to look forward and thank heavens for that. This business has really worn me to a frazzle.'

'You want to take a few days off,' said Ann. 'You don't look well and I don't really like to say anything but you have been a bit sharp with the staff the last few weeks. It doesn't bother me, we've worked together too long.'

'Tell them I'm sorry,' said Lazio. 'This business with the doctor and this bloody diet haven't helped, and wedging myself into that soppy little Peugeot doesn't help either.'

'So what about Helen?' Ann asked in mock indignation. 'She has no choice but to use it. And you haven't taken her on holiday this summer. Maybe you ought.'

'Are you trying to get rid of me? But you're right. Once I get my Maserati back and paid for we'll take it for a test drive to Scotland or somewhere else quiet and peaceful. Paying for that's been a pain and getting the roof done hasn't been cheap either.

'I think I'll lose myself in the lab for a few days and start on this Glen Parva project. I'd enjoy that. I'm dying to see if these turbine blades have been hardened by a Smithson special. Tell you what, if anyone calls for me in the next couple of days, tell them I've died and gone to heaven.'

Anne laughed. 'They won't believe me. Not the heaven bit anyway.'

'Aha,' said Lazio. 'But few will have the qualifications to come there and check up.'

'I don't want to anticipate events so soon but what about a replacement for David? Do I need to do anything there?'

'No,' said Lazio,' It's a funny time to advertise. If anyone is still free to come at this time of the year, they've obviously not been able to get a job anywhere else for the Christmas term. That suggests they're not top rate material.

'And if anyone sees an advert going in now, they'll know something unusual has happened here. But if we advertise in October as normal, we could get someone for the Easter term. In the meantime you can bet your bottom dollar that word will get around and someone will come sidling up to us. We'll wait and see for a bit.'

'That'll put up your work load in the meantime, though.'

'Yes. I can't avoid that, but there's ways and means to get round it. Right, I think we're finished here. I'm going to work in my office for a bit and then I shall be found in the lab.'

'Enjoy yourself.'

* * * * * * * *

Chapter 17

'Hello. It's Alistair Wyatt here, Burnstone University. Did you have a good trip back to London last week?'

'Yes, thank you,' said Kate Bellew. 'You looked after us very well.'

'We try, we try. Now, if you have a few minutes, could I run past you the idea I would most like to research using the Glen Parva sponsorship?'

'Yes you can, but have you mentioned it to anyone there yet?'

'No. I wanted your opinion first because you're the PR expert. There are a number of ideas I could consider, as I mentioned when we last met, but I wanted to see if you thought my key idea would fit in with the company's strategy. I shan't mention that I have spoken to you but you can say something if you want. If Charles Thurmaston doesn't like it, I've others to look at.'

'Right. What's the idea, then?'

'It's to use novel research to look for an antidote for AIDS based on gene research. There still is no universal solution but the problem is growing globally. And it is particularly endemic in emerging nations, countries where Glen Parva could set up factories.

'If Glen Parva is seen to be actively helping to find a solution to this global social need, it would provide the boost to the company's reputation that I think it is looking for. I hope it would also avoid any problems with the press and their ideas of two-headed monstrosities.'

Kate laughed.

'I think it would certainly avoid that. It sounds an excellent idea all round to me. Put it to Charles.'

'Right, I'll do that. Thank you for your time.'

Wyatt decided there was no point in delaying so he called Charles Thurmaston right away.

'Hello. It's Alistair Wyatt here, Burnstone University. How's things with yourself.'

'Fine,' said Charles. 'Busy, but one copes.'

'Well, if you've got a minute, can I tell you where I'd like to start researching with your sponsorship?'

'Sure. Go ahead.'

Wyatt gave him the same story as he'd give to Kate Bellew and received the same enthusiastic response. He added that he had spoken to her earlier just to mull over ideas off the record.

'There's only one thing,' said Charles. 'As far as I understand it, you scientists are still miles away from finding a solution. Might people ridicule your efforts because you're not a medical man? Especially if you have the bad luck not to find an answer.'

'I think your first point is one of our strengths. As microbiologists we are more concerned with the mechanics of cells rather than the wellbeing of people. So we would come to the problem from a different viewpoint. And, as the medicos haven't had any success so far, our approach could be seen as the better one.

'But it doesn't matter if we don't find an answer, we will at least have eliminated some research dead ends and our methodology will be open for the academic world to learn from. That means we have advanced the world's knowledge and that really is the rationale for carrying out research.'

Wyatt was warming to his subject.

'I'd envisaged a three-pronged approach. Firstly, one student would investigate a piece of work that was carried out about five years ago but which wasn't viable for commercial production at the time. It's been lying idle since then, but there might have been some developments that mean the concept could now go into production. Basically, the Human Immunodeficiency Virus, HIV, would be isolated and genetically modified so it attacked or neutralised a live virus.

'Secondly, we would set a student to investigate the problem with a completely fresh look from the purely biological point of view. Looking at immune-boosting vaccines, for example.

'The third part of the research would be to analyse the current research efforts around the world and review the papers that have been recently published.

'This work would culminate in a brainstorming session with all the students, perhaps as a closed seminar with some outside researchers involved.'

'That seems a well detailed approach, I'd like us to go for it,' said Charles. 'But are you well enough equipped for that amount of research?'

'We are fine for the early stages but we will need some new equipment later on such as nanopositioners and perhaps an atomic force microscope would be nice. That can measure in fractions of a micron. When you want to move an atom the width of a molecule, you need some pretty specialised gear.

'But the extent of this project could attract a useful amount of funding from one of the European Union development organisations. That would make our money go probably twice as far.'

'That sounds good,' said Charles. 'And perhaps your visit to Mumbai University might prove timely. India has a major AIDS problem, I believe. It looks as though the visit might be arranged for early September, which would mean the temperature is starting to drop while you should not be too tied up in the new term.'

'Thank you. That sounds good and we look forward to it. I'll keep you in touch with developments in the meantime.'

* * * * * * * *

Neither man had mentioned the David Bearing episode. If Alistair Wyatt had thought that Bearing would head straight off to Glen Parva, he was admitting nothing.

And if he thought that talking to Charles Thurmaston would provide a clue, he was wrong. The chairman had been made fully aware of the situation by Geoff Aylestone the night before but he was keeping his own counsel until the matter had been resolved one way or another. And that was next on his agenda.

'So what have you come up with overnight?' asked Thurmaston when Geoff Aylestone came in to his office.

'The first thing is, if neither Lazio Palfrey nor David Bearing had anything to do with the disappearance of the quintahertz machine, who did? Have we got a mole in the company here?'

'That's a thought,' said Charles. 'But who would want to sabotage their own company?'

'Someone who's not paid very much?'

'But wouldn't there have been other incidents that we'd have noticed? If you want to make money you don't do one thing, do you? I mean, once you've supplied some information then whoever you supplied it to has got a lever on you to supply more, so it becomes an ongoing thing.'

'Perhaps this was the first and we've got some more surprises to come.'

'OK, but we haven't that many secrets that are worth pinching, have we? We're just a simple steel producer trying to make our way in the world.'

'Along with quite a few others, remember. And what we think is not important might be quite vital to some other firm.'

'So what next, do we look for a private detective to poke about amongst the workforce? I don't much fancy that.'

'Let's see what the others have got to say. Are they all able to come to the meeting?'

'Yes,' said Thurmaston. 'I asked them to be here for eleven.'

'Well, one thought occurs to me,' said Geoff. 'Let's see if David Bearing can be turned from poacher to gamekeeper. Set him up as a stool pigeon, put out some rumour and see if he picks it up without our telling him what we're up to. We might then be able to track the route of the rumour.'

'You're a devious so and so. But we're getting ahead of ourselves. How to handle the man to start with. I don't like the way he's thinking. If he does have information that wouldn't do us any good and if he tries blackmail I'd be inclined to cast him loose and be damned. But I had thought of a way we could shut him up for good.

'We employ him as a market research and intelligence consultant, but at arm's length. He has to set up a limited company of his own and we give that a contract for six months, say. To get that contract he has to sign an agreement that indemnifies us against anyone who thinks he has acted illegally on our behalf.

'In other words, the agreement is that all the information he supplies to us has been obtained legally. Then it's nothing to do with us if he hacks into someone else's computer. If we find out he has broken into someone's system, or their office, for example, we can cut the contract immediately to keep our hands clean. We would also hand over all his work to the police and they should be able to hang him out to dry.

'If that should happen, Glen Parva can wash its hands of the arrangement on the basis that we acted in good faith, protected ourselves and then got out as soon as we found something amiss.

'Now for the best bit. To get the contract, he has to sign a disclaimer that all the information he has supplied to us in the past has been supplied on the same understanding. That's just part of our due diligence to cover ourselves against any accusation that we employed a known crook. Whatever went on between him and his university is nothing to do with us and he was punished for that by getting sacked, so that's over and done with.

'But what it means is that if he tries to blackmail us, he shoots himself in the foot. We're in the clear. He will have signed to say that all his work for us was above board. So if it turns out that wasn't the case, that's nothing to do with us. He's the crook and we hand over all the information to the police as a responsible company should do.'

'That's brilliant,' said Geoff Aylestone. 'But I'd add two provisos. One, that he works from home and doesn't come in here without our knowing beforehand; and, two, that his name does not appear on any documentation, just his company name. As you said last night, if Palfrey finds out what's happening, all hell will break loose and we're dependent on keeping him sweet as part of our growth strategy.'

'That sets me thinking,' said Thurmaston. 'It could be useful to keep Bearing out of the way for a couple of weeks. Why don't we send him off to the Mumbai office ostensibly to assess their laboratory facilities and their technical capability? He might be able to find out some information as to why the joint venture isn't going as smoothly as it ought. That might help Alan Birstall when he goes out in September with Alistair Wyatt.'

'Sounds a good idea to me. If we tell them that this is happening to all our joint ventures, they can't argue. I think the plan should appeal to the rest of the directors and it should tie up what could have been a messy business. Fortunately, Bearing has a lot to lose if he doesn't co-operate.'

'Right,' said Thurmaston. 'Let's get some more chairs in and get this meeting sorted.'

* * * * * * * *

Unaware of the machinations at Glen Parva, Lazio Palfrey allowed himself to become totally absorbed in their turbine blade project.

This meant setting up a whole range of instruments in the workshop to measure how hard the surface of the blades was after their standard hardening treatment. Lazio had been lucky over the years with the amount of sponsorship he'd pulled in for the department and this showed in its sophisticated range of test equipment.

Before Lazio could start his measurements, the equipment had to be checked to ensure it was measuring accurately and John Fleming had got stuck into the calibration routines.

The department owned a set of calibration samples that had been precisely analysed beforehand and had cost a huge amount of money. But they improved the accuracy of measurement by a noticeable factor and so the research results were more accurate and thereby more valuable.

Lazio first ran the turbine blade samples through an X-ray machine and an ultrasonic scanner to gain pictures of the internal structure of the blades. He was looking for the minute cracks that indicated the first signs of fatigue caused by stress.

If there were any cracks, they would distort the next set of measurements and produce a wildly differing set of results. But these blades were good.

'How are we going, John?' Lazio asked his lab assistant after a couple of hours analysis.

'I've now got the hardness measurer, impact resistance and scratch resistance testers calibrated. Then I was going to set up the bending machine and the vibration displacement tester.'

'Good,' said Lazio. 'I'll go into the laboratory and run some chemical tests on these blades while you do that, then I won't be banging about while you're trying to calibrate the gear.'

'Thanks,' said John, remembering past occasions when his test meter needles would jump about as Lazio banged some piece of metal or other with one of his mechanical tests.

Lazio was feeling his old self. He had shaken off his summer cold and had finally got his precious Maserati back on the road, increasing the hazards to all and sundry roundabout.

'We're definitely not going to be able to afford a holiday now,' he said to Helen. 'Especially as we're going to get the house roof done as well.'

'Don't worry on my part. It's you that needs the break. There's been so much going on this year I'm not greatly bothered. But I wouldn't mind going to stay with Saxon and Katherine for a few days, look around the shops in London and perhaps do a show or something. I might be able to take the children off her hands for a wee while, especially if this warm summer continues.'

'Why not?' said Lazio. 'I've plenty to be getting on with here and the thought of traipsing around London doesn't fill me with any great enthusiasm at all. Just leave half a ton of rabbit food in the fridge and phone every couple of hours to check I haven't faded away to nothing.'

'I think I'm more inclined to get a babysitter in,' Helen said. And seeing her husband brighten up, she quickly added, 'And not the Newbold's daughter either.'

'Shame.'

'I was thinking more of Mrs Appleyard, you know, the chairman of the Women's Institute.'

'You wicked woman,' said Lazio. 'Setting me up with that old battleaxe. You can go off people you know - and very quickly sometimes.'

'Rubbish. And she might get you sorted out better than I can. You'd soon give up some of your bad habits.'

Lazio muttered under his breath about substituting one battleaxe for another.

'What was that?' said Helen.

'I said I'm off to start work on testing these turbine blades.'

'Liar.'

Perhaps it was the banter that acted as a relief valve between Lazio and his wife because they had not had an argument for as long as they could remember. Perhaps it was the mutual respect they had for each other. Both led independent and active lives but each made sure they had time together in the evening.

So August promised to become a month of consolidation. At the university, the burglar alarm system around the engineering department had been extended and upgraded; Ann Whittaker was busy preparing the introductory folders for the new intake of students; and Lazio told Saxon that he would leave his intelligent node in place in the office just in case.

The workshop started to fill up with sheets of steel for the tailored blanks project and it promised to be a busy year.

* * * * * * * *

A week after Sergei Danelski had discussed the possibility of a joint venture between Sandrapoor and Khazatan steel companies, Vishay Bhopari rang him.

'Hi. How's things?'

'Fine. Fine,' said Danelski. 'And your end?'

'Hot, very hot. We'd all like to be up country in the mountains in this weather.'

'Is the deal hot as well?'

'For all my reservations, yes. Now that we've got outside shareholders on board, life isn't what it used to be. They're more worried about share price and dividend than the quality of the company and its steel.

'I spoke to our two institutional investors, who hold the majority of our issued shares, and they say they will increase their pressure on us to do better if we don't take action ourselves.

'Basically, they want us to go more global and that will take more resources than we've got in house. So we've got to team up with someone. Glen Parva isn't right for us, all the board is agreed on that, but, until you came along, there wasn't any other option. We're not throwing ourselves on the open market and going cheaply to just anyone, we intend to control our future.'

'Well,' said Danelski, 'as I've already mentioned, we're looking to Asia and China for our expansion and India is a logical place to jump from, so you'll be pulled along on our coat tails. That should keep your shareholders happy.'

'Indeed. But the deal also has to include your taking our high volume steel mill off our hands. That will give us a nice boost to the accounts and we can put up the dividend to please the shareholders. It looks as though we need to meet and get some heads of agreement in place.'

'Great,' said Danelski. 'Would you and some other directors like to come over and see what we're doing here in Khazatan? You can see round the research institute; meet the steel association people; and go round Babrusk Steel Mill, that will be the company to partner you in the joint venture; and Stavrol Rolling Mill, who will be buying your high volume facility.'

'That sounds good. What time scale do you envisage?'

'With Glen Parva huffing and puffing on the horizon, the sooner the better. I'll talk to my people here now and get back to you as soon as I can.'

'OK. Look forward to hearing from you.'

But Danelski's first call was to his stockbroker.

'Can you buy a large tranche of stock in Sandrapoor Steel Mills, Mumbai, for me please. Don't go more than two per cent over last night's closing price. When you've done that, deal yourself in for the best you can get but don't go over three per cent. Can you call me as soon as the bargain is closed.'

He went and poured himself a celebratory vodka.

Forty minutes later the phone rang and his broker gave him the contract number for the deal.

'There was a half per cent rise in the share price after your deal went through. It looks as though you are not the only buyer today.'

'I'm not surprised,' said Danelski. 'There will be a few friends of Sandrapoor who think now is a good time to invest. Did you deal yourself in?'

'Oh, yes. It only takes one word from you for us to do something like that.'

'Thanks for the compliment,' said Danelski, who had no doubt that a duff piece of advice from him would be the last piece of advice he'd give - a bullet in the back of the head would see to that.

'Now don't hold on to them too long. When you've seen a good rise, cash in. Don't get greedy. I shall be out of the rest of the deal so I can't give you any warning but once details get out, it might not sound so attractive and the price could dive. You know how it can go.'

Danelski then rang round a few friends to return a few favours and to ensure he received some in return.

Lastly, he put Krachov in the picture at the Research Institute.

'Thanks for that,' said Krachov. 'I'll get a few shares myself and then pass the word round when I fix up a date for the Sandrapoor meeting.'

'Good luck, hope it goes well. I'll bang in my invoice for the first part of the deal in the next day or so.'

As the arch fixer of eastern Europe, he had to be seen to be on the ball where his personal finances were concerned.

* * * * * * * *

'Good morning, gentlemen, and welcome to Operation Lay-about.'

Major Alan Stenhouse, Royal Engineers, laid his papers on the reading desk in front of him and surveyed the group of people before him. Some casually dressed, some smartly suited, some in military uniform.

'And good morning, lady,' he added, with a grin, unexpectedly spying a female in RAF uniform and immediately displaying his many years of traditional military background totally dominated by males.

'Operation Layabout,' he clicked on the first slide of his PowerPoint presentation. 'In Khazatani, layabout is translated as idle. That suits us because it smokescreens that fact that we will be far from idle. We will also be laying about us with a weapon that I will come to later. The double meaning will be lost on most Khazatanis.

'The objective of Layabout is to deploy a new weapon against a target in Khazatan. It employs disabling technology for use against civilians as well as military personnel. People will be completely disabled for about twenty minutes and will suffer no after effects.

'During this time, ground forces would move in to separate and restrain the military targets. So the support teams have to be deployed very close to the target as they have only this short time span to move in to the target area and work.

'The operation has been classed top secret because the weapon will be deployed against civilians without their permission. That makes it a highly political hot potato. The test is being carried out on a remote village in Khazatan to keep publicity to the minimum. No details of the weapon itself are being released, so there should be no leaks of a technical nature.

'The weapon will be deployed in two modes. As a single shot from a static Land Rover and in fly-over mode from a helicopter. The first test will be on a single individual, the second will sweep a whole village.

'Now let's look at the sequence of events and individual responsibilities. Operation Layabout will assemble at RAF Lyneham on day one. During the day all gear will be loaded on to a Hercules aircraft for late afternoon departure to an undisclosed military base in Germany. This will be the main base for the operation and temporary accommodation will be provided for all personnel.

'Squadron Leader Jane Cannon is in charge of logistics,' said Stenhouse, indicating the female he had nearly overlooked earlier. 'Her staff will control the loading of the Hercules and deployment of the facilities in Germany. She will remain in the UK so if anything unexpected crops up, we have a senior officer who can organise things a bit sharpish at this end.'

Jane Cannon acknowledged his comments with a nod of her head.

And with extreme efficiency as well, thought Stenhouse, returning her nod.

'In Germany, a contingent of Royal Engineers will have set up a portable workshop for any work that may be needed on site for any of the equipment we are taking. They will also fix up a Chinook helicopter with special fixings for the weapon under the direction of Ben Blackwater, who is the project leader here at DARE in charge of building and testing the weapon.

'We will be using two long-range Chinooks on this exercise. They will take the forward party into Khazatan, be used in the fly-over, and one will be used as an overnight hotel if the test runs into two days. We are not asking for accommodation in Khazatan for security reasons, the locals will be very interested in our activities so we do not want to be separated from our hardware.

'If we stay over in Khazatan, there will no doubt be an invitation to the officer's mess for drinks. As usual, this will not be for socialising but to find out what we are doing, so the drink will flow very freely.

'To avoid this, we will be involved in working on the weapon until lateish in the evening and then only one designated officer will take up the invitation so diplomacy is not offended.

'If the Khazatanis hold us up for any reason so the forward party does have to stay overnight, I have to point out that facilities on the Chinook are pretty basic. There will be plenty of tea, coffee and cocoa but food will be from standard self-heating army solid rations. You may want to take something of your own, provided your baggage does not exceed the weight limit.

'The forward party will be led by me and will comprise one armed driver and two armed soldiers from the SAS for each of the

271

three Land Rovers; three film crew and one stills photographer; two interpreters; Mr Ben Blackwater and one other engineer from DARE; and several others whose names and functions are not being released.

'Regarding the SAS presence, we do not expect any aggression or undue interference with the exercise from the Khazatanis, but carrying insurance is always good practice.

'The situation at the moment is that we will be assembling at Lyneham in a matter of days and I have just carried out a recce in Germany and Khazatan. The Khazatanis are very friendly and should be good to work with. I don't expect the obstructionism we used to get from the USSR in the old days. But they are as keen as anyone to find out other countries' secrets, so no loose talk, please.

Stenhouse didn't add that he had delivered the single block of terratanium while he was there and several more would be taken by the forward party as agreed; nor that he would be the designated officer to receive any Khazatani hospitality.

'Now, any questions?'

'Yes,' said Cannon. 'What does this weapon look like, how much does it weigh and how much gear has to accompany it?'

Major Stenhouse clicked through several slides until he came to the Stop machine, with all its detail hidden behind protective screens.

'That's the only picture of it at the moment. Mr Blackwater, could you fill us in on the other details, please.'

Ben Blackwater gave some details of the machine's size and weight and how it would be fixed onto slides on the Chinook's floor so it could be moved outside the helicopter before it was switched on.

'There's also its power supply, which can go anywhere in the helicopter. We have developed it here at DARE but it is still on the secret list as it is atomic powered. It is smaller than the Stop machine but a lot heavier and ruggedised so it would survive a plane crash, for example, without releasing any radioactivity.

'There will be sufficient power to run a microwave oven to save running up the Chinook's engines at mealtimes. But it won't be able to run any heating as such. So sleeping bags will be definitely needed during a night stay in the helicopter.'

'Any other questions?'

No response.

'Have you all checked your Operation Layabout dossiers? Especially the contact details?'

Nodding heads.

'Very good. Any problems, get on the blower immediately, this exercise must go smoothly as I understand it could be difficult to set it up again at a later date. You will all have to be ready to go to Lyneham at a few hours' notice and I expect a call in the next few days. Squadron Leader Cannon is the authority for issuing travel documents to the base. In the meantime, DARE says we can use the canteen here for lunch for those who'd like to stay. Mr Blackwater will show you the way. So, good luck.'

As soon as Roger Wishart heard that the test session had been set up he called Lazio Palfrey.

'And what do you want now?' asked Lazio.

'I just wanted to keep you in the picture, that's all,' he said. 'A full blown test session has been set up with your Stop machine. Don't tell anyone else, please, it's all highly secret. But I thought you ought to know that things are progressing very well.'

'Thank you for that,' said Lazio. 'That's appreciated.'

* * * * * * * *

Chapter 18

'Something seems to be going on at Sandrapoor Steel Mills,' said Bill Oadby to Charles Thurmaston. 'The share price has gone up significantly on each of the last two days.'

'What's your analysis as financial director, then?' asked Thurmaston.

'Someone is showing serious interest in the company. But for why, I can't say yet. I've got our stockbrokers looking into it but it will take them some while to get the information back from the country. It's an awkward time difference.

'I just wonder if it's connected to the lack of information we've had from them over the last few months. We've said once or twice that the joint venture seems to be stalling. Sales are flat, future predictions are bland and I think you've had fewer calls from their managing director lately, haven't you.'

'Yes. You're right,' said Thurmaston. 'We've had so much going on elsewhere I had rather pushed Sandrapoor to the back of my mind. I think I was waiting for Alan Birstall to go out there before taking any action. When we first signed them up, they were on the phone every few days.

'But now David Bearing has come on the scene, maybe we should get him out there a bit sharpish as we discussed a couple of days ago. He's coming in a bit later to finalise his agreement to work for us. I got a copy faxed to him yesterday as we all agreed and there isn't going to be much room for alterations, so the meeting shouldn't take too long.'

David Bearing had been quite pleased with the agreement he'd been sent. He'd discussed it with Madeleine who was all for signing it there and then.

'You mustn't rush these things,' said David. 'A man in a hurry is a man to beware of, so they say when negotiating. This deal won't evaporate overnight, don't worry.'

'It's fine saying that but we're so dependent on your income. If this offer goes, what are you going to do then? To get a decent job you need a reference from your last employer and what's the university going to say in that? And if you get a job as barman in a pub somewhere round about, how would we live on that sort of income?'

'Well, we'd have free nights out from time to time and you'd have to come to the back door in between times and I'd arrange food parcels.'

Madeleine exploded.

'You stupid bugger. You want your arse kicking. What a bloody silly thing to say. We're in the shit and all you can do is joke. What about the kids?'

She started to cry.

'Sorry, love,' said David. 'If we don't look on the bright side we'll just go under.'

'Well there's no need to be so flippant about it.'

'Look. I'm as worried sick about it as you. But if I let it show, the people at Glen Parva will spot it right away and screw me down even more with the deal. I've got to go in there with my head up as though there's all the opportunities in the world to go for if they don't deliver what I want.'

'Oh, David. Just be careful. If you take that attitude it might make things worse.'

'Leave it to me. OK? Just keep your fingers crossed tomorrow morning. Now, grab this hankie and give a big blow.'

When David arrived at Glen Parva's office, it was after a night of tossing and turning, balancing his options so that he got the best deal without losing it.

In the event, he agreed to the deal without any amendments.

Charles Thurmaston had been very clear about the background to the deal.

'Our reputation comes above everything else right now. Next comes the sponsorship with Burnstone University. Anything or anyone that affects either of those two will be dealt with quickly and very effectively. Is that clearly understood?'

'Yes.'

'Good. So I must stress that you do not come into the office without prior agreement in case Professor Palfrey is on the premises. If you need anything else to help you set up an office at home, let me know. Now, we think it a good idea if you keep your head down for a week or two. Let the dust settle at the university and let the admin here get sorted out so your appointment is no longer newsworthy. It is absolutely vital that we go a bit further with Professor Palfrey before he finds out that you are working for us. You take my meaning?'

'Indeed,' said David. 'Don't worry. I shan't do anything to jeopardise this arrangement, it's been very good of you to take me on.'

'Well don't forget that we're both losers if it goes wrong. Now, let's activate the agreement here and now. We'd like you to visit our Mumbai office right away. The visit might last two weeks and we've made a reservation on the 1015 flight out of Heathrow tomorrow morning. Any problems?'

David sat speechless.

'No, no. Great stuff,' he said eventually.

'I think Alan Birstall has also got a hotel sorted out for you. He's been there a couple of times and can tell you what to wear, where to eat and all that sort of stuff. You won't need injections if you're very careful but he'll fill you in on that as well. Go private if anything needs attention.'

He picked up the phone.

'Hello, Alan, Charles here. David has just signed up with us and is OK for Mumbai tomorrow. Can you come and collect him and give him all the background info. I'm just going to call Vishay Bhopari and put him in the picture. It'll be about mid-afternoon there, won't it?'

'Yes. Four and a half hours ahead of us in the summer. What are you going to say about the short notice?'

'Good point. I was going to tell him that David is going round all the Glen Parva outposts so I'll say there's been a change to the schedule and we might as well fit Mumbai in now. We don't have to say why.'

'OK. I'll come up.'

'Thanks. Well, good luck, David, and you'd better start learning your own way around the place.'

* * * * * * * *

While David Bearing was flying to Mumbai, Lazio Palfrey was motoring across to Glen Parva to see the new quintahertz machine powered up for the first time.

'Here's the test results from the turbine blades you gave me,' he said to Geoff Aylestone. 'That gives us a comprehensive data base to compare our future results against. I can't say which technology has been used in particular because the hardening is only of a general quality but it will definitely be better after quintahertz treatment.'

Geoff studied the computer printouts.

'That looks good stuff to me. And it confirms the findings from our lab tests. What I'd like to do is to harden some raw blades and then harden some that have already been treated in the usual way. I've had a great pile sent over so we can keep some ourselves for testing and then give the customer the rest so he can put them in his test engine and run it up.

'We're ready to switch on the new quintahertz machine as soon as you are, so shall we go down to the lab?'

Lazio was delighted to see the new machine ready to go. It was like meeting an old friend. He had staked so much on it that he felt more nervous than he had for a long time.

'Can you tell Jean here what you are doing at every stage,' asked Aylestone. 'She is our technical writer and will produce the operator's handbook to go with the machine.

'Hi,' said Lazio.

Wow, he thought. This is getting exciting.

Lazio checked the software had loaded properly and then set up the test equipment to measure the radiation level that was outside the machine.

'What's it pointing at?' he asked.

'What do you mean?' asked Geoff.

'If the radiation beam goes a long way, what will it hit?'

'I'm with you. It's OK we've checked on that. This is an outside wall, then there's the road and the canal and a fairly big field on the other side. Then the houses start. We're about five hundred yards away from them and about fifteen feet above the road and towpath. You can check it's clear from the window next door.'

'That should be OK. Let's load a sample and see what happens. By the way, is the sample table interlocked?'

'Yes,' said Geoff. 'We've put a microswitch under it as you suggested so if there is no sample in place to press the table down, the circuit is not made and you can't apply power.'

Jean was writing furiously.

'Ready to go,' said the technician.

'All yours,' said Geoff

'I think I ought to make a speech or something,' said Lazio. 'This is quite an important occasion. Let's just hope that this machine makes both our fortunes.'

There was a ragged round of 'hear, hear' and someone clapped. The lab staff all seemed to have found a reason to stop work and a small crowd had gathered.

Nothing like an audience to work to, thought Lazio.

'Can you all move behind the machine, please, just to be careful. We don't want to make you into a load of hard cases. And can one of you watch the radiation meter. If the needle gets towards the end of the green section, shout.'

He stepped forward and pressed the two start buttons.

There was a clunk as the main relay switched power on to the radiation generator and a low hum.

'How's the radiation level?' he asked.

'The needle hasn't moved.'

'Can you move it in towards the machine until you get a reading, please.'

The trolley carrying the radiation meter was pushed to within about a foot of the machine.

'It's just come off the end stop.'

'OK. Leave it there, please.'

The hum stopped, the relay clicked off and the 'All Clear' light came on.

The lab technician opened up the machine and lifted out the turbine blade.

As Lazio expected, it looked exactly the same as when it went in. But someone clapped and someone else said they had expected the sample to be too hot to touch but in the absence of any pyrotechnics the group melted away.

'I've got the hardness tester set up over here,' the technician said to Lazio.

'Let's have a quick look, then.'

The technician put the blade on the tester and brought down the probe until it touched the blade. He pressed the 'On' switch and the machine pushed the probe against the blade until a steady reading showed on the dial.

'Wow,' said the technician. 'That's shot way up from the reading before. What have we bred here?'

Lazio rubbed his hands together with great satisfaction.

'What have we bred indeed?'

* * * * * * * *

'I see a plan coming together,' said Alistair Wyatt to his wife over dinner. 'And I think this one could be good.'

'You and your plans,' said Morag. 'You're always scheming.'

'Yes, but look where it has got us. That's not so bad is it?'

'No, of course not,' Morag smiled, thinking of the influential people she had helped Alistair to entertain, the many top tables she had sat on and the many opportunities that simply demanded a new hat and dress.

'So how do you fancy being Lady Wyatt?'

'Och, Alistair, give over. Don't you go scheming too far, you might come unstuck.'

'Don't worry, it's a long term aim. But just wait and see. There's some interesting things going on in the human biology department just now. We've taken on board a very ambitious sponsor and they want to do some exciting things.'

But Morag still retained her natural Scots reserve.

'Well, still take care. Make sure they don't use you for their own ends.'

Some chance thought Alistair, rather offended by his wife's lack of confidence in his carefully nurtured abilities.

He dreamed on over his roast beef. Alistair Wyatt, discoverer of the AIDS cure, saviour of the world. He liked that. Knight in shining armour, that's better, especially the knight bit.

'Have you finished, then?' Morag broke into his train of thought.

'Er, no. Er, yes. Thank you.'

'You were miles away, I hope you know what you were eating.'

'Yes, thank you dear, that was really good.'

What was? Morag was tempted to ask him but was perhaps afraid he'd give the wrong answer. She was not one to work in a kitchen only to find her efforts unrewarded but when Alistair was thinking through some plan, he would not have noticed a live hand grenade amongst his potatoes.

Next morning he went over his ideas with the Vice Chancellor.

'I like this threefold approach very much, Alistair,' he said. 'It shows a great deal of academic rigour and that should add considerable weight to your findings. And this seminar at the end should give us some additional publicity.

'I take your point that the approach will be microbiological rather than medical. The new angle could produce the winner. There's obviously a solution somewhere, there's no human condition that can't be altered one way of another, but a fresh approach at this point in time could prove the breakthrough.

'And if it brings in some European grant money and extends our web of influence to Mumbai University, they're all plus points.'

'I'm also looking very long term here,' said Alistair. 'If we can create a reputation for research at this level, the government should look on us very favourably and that will help if we have a particular need in the future.'

He didn't say what his particular need was, but that could wait.

'It also fits very nicely with the government's current plans to raise Britain's profile in high-tech research. If the plan comes together, I mean when it comes together, there will be someone outside the UK to take the risk of manufacturing, which is what the government really wants as I gather off the record from one of my contacts.

'And then we have a ready source of material in India to experiment on. If there are problems during the experiments, at least they're several thousand miles away and not on our doorstep.'

'Well, the whole plan seems quite excellent. Keep it going and keep me updated.'

Alistair had been patted on the head by the Vice Chancellor. It may have been a metaphorical pat, but that's what kept Alistair going.

Just before lunch, he telephoned Grover Wisden and asked for his secretary.

'Can I leave a message for Professor Wisden to call me, please?'

'Yes, but he is free if you want to talk to him now.'

'No. It's OK. He may need more time before we discuss the matter in hand. I don't want to harass him.'

But I do want him to come back on his mobile, was the unspoken thought.

About ten minutes later Wisden rang him back.

'Hi. Sorry for the delay, but I thought I'd take an early lunch and talk to you from a park bench that happens to be bathed in rather glorious sunshine.'

'Excellent,' said Alistair. 'You can soon forget what this summer is like when you're cooped up in an office all the time. Anyway, I just wanted to thank you for giving me the contact in Drakon Pharma.

'This AIDS project is coming together very nicely now in the way it fits in with government thinking. At Burnstone, we will just be doing the research bit. Drakon Pharma says that it is happy to come in and provide the manufacturing input to keep the research on commercial lines, so that takes the production risks out of the UK as you mentioned.

'And I'm pretty certain that Mumbai University will co-operate in providing experimental facilities and sources of research material, so that keeps any human problems out of the UK as well. It just leaves us to convince Europe that the project is good for funding.'

'I don't see any problems there,' said Wisden. 'The project is addressing a key global concern so there can be none of the problems that we have when we think companies are trying for funding just to feather their own nest. I'll keep an eye out for your application.'

'Thank you very much,' said Alistair. 'The application will be handled by my head of department, Professor Richard Daly. He'll be the man doing most of the work. And if there's anything we can help you with, you know where to come.'

'Thanks, I'll remember that. I suppose it's possible the application may mean someone like me has to go out to India to check on the situation there.'

'Consider it arranged,' said Wyatt.

So the next call was to Professor Richard Daly, Head of Human Biology. Although he was designated head of the department and so the equivalent of Lazio Palfrey in Combined Engineering and Luke Verity in Electronics, Alistair Wyatt had a large say in how he ran the department.

Alistair still felt that he had to have an active role in research as well as carrying out his function as Dean of the whole faculty. It kept his options open, he felt, so he could take greater advantage of any situation that might advance his ambitions.

As a microbiologist himself, and the previous head of Human Biology, he had a large say in whom should replace him when he was promoted to Dean. Richard Daly appeared the complete researcher, non-political and living just for his research, which suited Alistair down to the ground.

Wyatt kept him happy with crumbs from his table and Daly did what Wyatt wanted. Daly did not admit to any ambitions beyond his present position and became more comfortable as the years rolled by.

He gained status from the industrial and government committees he sat on, generally less important ones than those Wyatt belonged to. But Wyatt always seemed to bring in high quality research, which he appreciated, although when the research papers were published by the department, Wyatt's name would be included at the top of the most important ones although his input may have been less than important.

So Daly would spend the many hours it takes to compile a business plan to claim European funding. He would have to organise the descriptive write-ups from each partner and provide an easily-understood explanation of the project: why it was needed, the potential results and how the team would work towards the objective.

Wyatt would attend to bringing on board the other partners, but that was his strong point. He was very certain that the project would be approved and that money would be forthcoming, so it would be easy to persuade other partners to come along. They would be pleased to join a project they could benefit from while Wyatt would get the partners he needed before the application could be submitted.

So Wyatt and Daly agreed a meeting time to get the AIDS project under way.

＊ ＊ ＊ ＊ ＊ ＊ ＊ ＊ ＊

'I see a plan coming together,' said Vladimir Arbatov to Alexander Kasvanov. 'And I think this one could be good.

'We've got a quintahertz hardening machine working, extra terratanium to develop it, the British government in a position where they won't take any action and Professor Palfrey who can't afford to do anything by himself. We're on the way to getting Sandrapoor Steel Mills signed up, which gives us an excellent launching pad eastwards to China, Japan and that little lot and which will stall Glen Parva's efforts to move in there.

'Stavrol Rolling Mills gets a more modern set of machinery and Khazatan is paying for most of it. What a deal.'

'My members in the steel association will be proud of you,' said Kasvanov. 'Don't say I mentioned it, but make sure you jack up the price to Babrusk Steel Mill for handing over the quintahertz machine. They can afford it.'

'We'll do that all right. We'll also get a contract out of them for developing the machine further. And we've got the terratanium blocks as well. That's a bargaining counter we'll keep tucked away.

'But tell me, where will the association want to sell the machine and the extra steel that will come out of Stavrol in due course? Will they want to deal with Russia or the West first?'

'I don't know. I haven't thought that far ahead. The guys who run the companies in the steel association are just there for what they can get out of it. It's cash, not principles, that drives them. Why do you ask?'

'Well, this machine will mean a lot to whoever buys it. It's not just the better products they can make, there will probably be some subsidies from their own governments to apply for and it'll give the whole company a lift because it can offer this fantastic technology. Shouldn't your association persuade them to look after their own in Russia first?'

'I see where you're coming from,' said Kasvanov.

He suddenly realised why Arbatov was concerned. It was the old guard versus the new guard thing. Those who dreamed of the Soviet Union coming back together again and those who wanted to pursue the capitalist route and stay independent. The traditionalists against the modernists.

Arbatov was a traditionalist.

'I don't declare myself,' continued Kasvanov. 'I'm just a messenger really. There's not a lot I can do to convince the association as a whole. It's cash not ideals that's the driver, as I said.'

'We'd look on them very favourably if they went to Russian buyers first,' said Arbatov.

'I'll see what I can do. I really don't know what they each think privately. It's difficult and I just try to get on with my job of running the association. So many people would like to see communism back in operation, I think the idea is getting stronger. Perhaps things will change when the younger generation gets into power. I wouldn't mind betting the balance will move to capitalism then.'

Arbatov pursed his lips. He didn't like the way the conversation was going.

'Well just remember what I said when you report back.'

When Kasvanov had left his office, Arbatov rang his old friend Leonid Lebdev.

'Hi! How's things at the seat of power?' he asked Lebdev.

'How should I know? I only work here.'

Arbatov laughed.

'All the traditionalists say that. Half of them don't work anyway, do they?'

'Watch it. You're talking about my friends.'

'And my friends too, don't forget. Anyway, can we talk business?'

'Sure. What's on your mind?'

'This quintahertz business. The machine's up and running, we've lined up a foreign company to launch it and one of our steel companies is getting some new production machinery so it can make more low cost steel. I'd like to make sure it gives the maximum benefit to the people I think most of.

'It's a really great opportunity that doesn't come up very often. Now, we think the same way, so why should any capitalist company get hold of it? Fair enough, they've got the money to make a good offer for the package, but there's more to it than that, isn't there?'

'How can we help our friends, you mean,' said Lebdev.

'Exactly. And it's important to me because it was me who decided to pick up on the snippet of information from Sergei Danelski after he'd been to London for the last UK Technical Transfer Day.

'These developed countries, as they're so called, are wasters. They've got so much technology coming out of their ears that they're not using it all anyway. And there's a deserving cause in Russia that would appreciate it much more and would also do much more with it.'

'I think I get your drift and I couldn't agree more. What have you got in mind?'

'You must know how the land lies in the Khazatan government. Who's for us and who's against. Are there sufficient friends that could arrange a subsidy for the Babrusk and Stavrol Mills so Russia can get the technology and the steel at a price they can afford while the mills get the money they want?'

'All things are possible. It will probably come down to the sweeteners that are available to help people make up their minds as to what they stand for.'

'Do you think it would be possible to set up something before we hand over the quintahertz machine to Babrusk?'

'Now that could be difficult.'

'Well, these boys in the steel association seem to be a wild bunch. They go for the highest bidder no matter what. And, nowadays, no-one has any control over that sort of free enterprise any more.'

'Leave it with me,' said Lebdev. 'I've got a few strings to pull.'

'Good luck.'

So the scene was set for another skirmish in the battle between east and west. It may not be the Cold War as such, but the underlying principles were still there.

The British government may have been heavy handed with Khazatan over the theft of the quintahertz machine in the first place, but that was at the diplomatic level. Both sides appreciated that was inevitable. But it didn't affect relationships and strategy at other levels.

Western countries still wanted to pull eastern Europe over to their way of thinking. But there was still that old guard trying to pull Russia back together again.

* * * * * * * *

Things seem to be warming up in the steel business suddenly, thought Vishay Bhopari as he went back to his office to take the call from Charles Thurmaston. First a new company comes chasing us and now the first call from Glen Parva for a good number of weeks.

'Hello, Bhopari here. How are you Mr Thurmaston?'

'Very well thanks. Busy as ever but it keeps you young so I'm told. How's yourself.'

'Having to keep young as well, but it's hot, very hot here. We'd all like to be up country in the mountains in this weather.'

'Know the feeling. We're having one of the best summers here in Britain for a good number of years. But, to business. We are using an engineering consultancy to research the technical markets for steel, to see what technical help our customers want, to make sure we can offer the latest testing and analytical services and to check our equipment is state of the art.

'As part of that, we are arranging for an engineer from the consultancy to visit all our partners' laboratories around the world. We hadn't planned to visit you for a while yet but we've had to make one or two changes to the schedule and would like to send him to you next, is that OK?'

'I don't see any problem. Our labs are always ready in case any customer drops in without notice. We might want some time if you need any special tests setting up, if you want us to make any special samples for example.'

'There hasn't been any need for that so far but he'll be around for a while so there's no rush if he did want anything special. He's actually got two weeks before his next visit but we don't want him back here because we want him to be quite independent.

'Between you and me, I don't want my Technical Director telling him what needs to be done, I want his input fresh. My technical man tells me quite often enough what's needed but I want the wider view before we set up a budget.'

'Don't worry,' said Bhopari. 'I understand perfectly, we all need fresh blood from time to time to keep our companies progressing.'

'Indeed. So how is Sandrapoor moving on?'

'Quite well. Could be better, I suppose, but then that's always the case, isn't it?'

'It is with us. Shareholders breathing down our neck all the time. Which reminds me, your share price seems to have moved forward noticeably over the last few days. Anything we should know about?'

'Oh it's rumours probably. We've no new agreements to mention. Maybe we've been a bit sparse with the information we've been giving our stockbrokers of late. Once there's a gap in the information flow, their minds start working and they invent things. Or it could be just a revaluation of the company's fundamentals. We've a very secure financial base, someone must think we're suddenly a better bet.'

'Right. Well keep us in touch if there are any developments. And let us know if there's any problems with this engineer chappie. David Bearing's the name, he's got a doctorate in steel research.'

'OK, we'll watch out for him. Cheers for now.'

Vishay Bhopari accurately worked out that David Bearing was coming in on a spying mission. Coincidences rarely happened in the real world. So he decided to let David do all the running.

He welcomed him warmly when he did arrive at the Sandrapoor office.

'How's the hotel, did you get settled in all right?'

'Yes. I think I shall be very comfortable there, as long as the air conditioning keeps going. They booked me in the Hotel Kings International. It's only a few kilometres from the airport but it doesn't seem to be under any flight path.'

'You should be all right there but failed air conditioning is an ever-present hazard in this country. And if the equipment works, then the electricity will fail because everyone has turned on their air conditioning.'

Bhopari nearly choked laughing at his own humour.

'Anyway, I'll introduce you to my technical director and you can disappear off to the laboratory to see what we're up to.'

So David spent a couple of gentle days assessing the laboratory equipment and analysing the work that Sandrapoor customers were asking the company to do for them.

On the third day, David asked Vishay if he could visit some customers to have a look at what they were using the company's steel for.

'No problem. Would you like to go round with one of our salesman for a few days?'

288

'That would be brilliant. Yes, please.'

'Right. I'll see who is coming into the office next. But remember this is a big country and transport is not as good as in Britain. So always take an overnight bag with you and be ready to stay away for a couple of days. But, for now, what are you up to tonight?'

'I've been working my way round the restaurants so I'll probably do another one tonight. At least this visit is giving me a chance to catch up on my chess game. I seem to have got a bit rusty of late so I'm doing a lot of reading.'

Vishay's eyes lit up.

'Well, come and practise with me tonight. Try my wife's cooking and then we'll have a game or two afterwards. I haven't had a game of note for long enough.'

'OK,' said David. 'That sounds good.'

'Are you into curry?'

'Yes, but I much prefer them mild with a lot of flavours. I'm not a vindaloo man.'

'Don't worry about that out here. It's only the British that think curry has to be red hot. Many of our curries are mild and they're vegetable-based rather than meat. I know that British menus are virtually all meat-based, but that's somewhat of a luxury for us. My wife does a wicked Biryani, how about that?'

'Sounds good.'

'Right. I'll arrange a taxi to come to your hotel about seven. It's a firm that we always use so you will be quite safe and the driver won't go round Mumbai three times to make the fare worthwhile.'

Excellent, thought Vishay, we can now find a little more about this visit and perhaps Mr Bearing can carry a message back to Britain to prepare the way for us leaving Glen Parva.

So David Bearing faced an Indian meal that was quite unlike anything he had tried in any Leicester restaurant. It was after the plates had been cleared away that Vishay opened out the conversation.

'Tell me something about your consultancy. What sort of companies have you worked for?'

289

To all appearances, David was quite open about the work of his consultancy. He went through some of the projects he had been involved in over the last few years, but he didn't say they had been for Burnstone University. He didn't exactly say they were for his consultancy either, he left that to Vishay to infer.

'We've been working with Glen Parva for a few years now but things have changed in the world. We're probably ready for a change of partner ourselves now.'

David encouraged the line of conversation. He was getting his feedback without asking for it, that suited his cover very well.

'Between you and me, there's a lot of competition now and, frankly, there's other companies that would fit in with our operation much better.'

Vishay felt he had to be more direct with David than with someone from Glen Parva itself. David had given every appearance of being the independent consultant rather than the company spy he'd expected, so he probably was not so business wise. Vishay felt he would have to emphasise his message to get it across so David would be sure to carry it back.

'Yes. We had one the other day, for example. Offered us a very nice business package including some technology they said no-one else in the world had. It's a new hardening technique apparently. Didn't give us any details but it sounded interesting.'

'Who was that then?'

'Can't remember the name now. We're getting quite a few enquiries just now. We'll worry about it when they sound serious. Nowadays, everyone wants a launch pad into China and the East but Europe is really too far away for that. You'll probably know how long it takes to get set up in China but you can set up a base here very quickly and then you're virtually on their doorstep.

'We may suffer from lots of red tape and officialdom in India, we love administration, you know. But it's all the fault of you British when you were here. You gave us the flavour and now everyone wants to be an official.'

He wasn't going to say that some Khazatan companies in particular were showing a strong interest in Sandrapoor. All in good time.

'I believe Glen Parva has some new technology it is about to announce. Has anyone mentioned it?' said David Bearing.

'No. Charles Thurmaston didn't give any clue when he telephoned me to say you were coming. What are they up to then?'

'I don't know the details. It was just something someone said in passing. But I think it is also to do with hardening steel.'

'Well, if it is, I'm afraid the company will want an arm and a leg for it. And they'd be up against companies whose governments are subsidising these deals in all sorts of ways. Some packages are very tempting.'

'Thank goodness I'm only involved in technical matters,' said David. 'Wheeler dealing isn't for me.'

'We can't all be at it, that's for sure. So, are we going to engage in combat on the chess board instead?'

'Let's go for it.'

'Great. I haven't played for long enough. Chess was invented in the east, you know. I like to think it was India where it first started.'

Vishay set up an ornate set of chessmen.

'Solid ivory. Cost you a packet back home.'

* * * * * * * *

Chapter 19

'It always beats me how much stuff accumulates for just a simple test.'

Major Alan Stenhouse was standing in a storage hangar at RAF Lyneham, checking off the last items on the loading list with Squadron Leader Jane Cannon.

In front of them, lit by the harsh sodium lighting, was a stack of photographic equipment, food rations, sleeping bags and a pile of Bergens, suitcases and assorted bags containing the personal effects of the personnel now assembling for the flight to Germany.

Behind that, three Land Rovers were drawn up in line. To one side, a separate stack of equipment was piled beside the Stop machine and its atomic power supply. But that was all covered by a tarpaulin and watched over by two determined looking individuals armed with Heckler and Koch MP5 sub machine guns. The SAS always looked after its own arrangements.

Outside sat a Hercules transport aircraft, ominous in dark military paint, towering over the ground staff making their last minute checks and ready to take the whole shooting match to the Deggendorf airbase just inside Germany's eastern border.

'Right. It's all there,' he signalled to a corporal stood by a desk of papers. 'Can you go and collect your brood from the NAAFI and tell them we're loading the aircraft now.'

'I'll get the air loader to get the crew together then,' and Jane Cannon went to the telephone on the desk.

About an hour later, the loading ramp of the Hercules was closed and the engines started.

'This is where you find out the downside of being in the RAF,' shouted Major Stenhouse over the noise that filled the very functional interior of the aircraft. 'Extra marks if you brought your own seat cushion.'

He thanked the crew member handing out earplugs. Not that they were all that effective as the pilot wound up the four engines to maximum thrust for takeoff. The noise and vibration bounced off the unpanelled interior of the aircraft as it went down the runway. Then the vibration stopped as it lifted off and, a few minutes later, the noise level dropped as the pilot throttled back for the two hour run to Deggendorf.

The passengers relaxed. An uncomfortable mix of civilian and military ranging from the no-nonsense dress of the SAS, still holding their MP5s, through the casual wear of the film crew, Ben Blackwater and the engineers from DARE, to the blue and khaki fatigues of the army and airforce support crews. In between, several nameless men in shirts and trousers who could have been civilians or service types and who had not sat with the rest gathered in the NAAFI.

The cold gradually seeped through as people read books and newspapers, tried to sleep or just stared into space. Finally, a crew member came round to check seat belts and to say that the very warm evening in Germany was only twenty minutes away.

Once the aircraft had parked and the engines cut, Major Stenhouse gave out the arrangements for the stop over.

'I can now tell you we are on Deggendorf air base close to the eastern border of Germany. On leaving the aircraft you will be escorted to the hangar we have been allocated for the customs check. I have to say that you cannot go anywhere without an escort but someone from the base will be around all the time.

'You can take personal effects into the accommodation block. We are the only occupants for the next few days. There is a small canteen that will do the usual meals and a lounge area with TV but no bar, I'm afraid.

'Equipment for the test will be left in the hangar, including the Land Rovers. The base commander is providing a guard but I think our SAS contingent will help them out. Is that right?'

'Yes,' said one of the anonymous ones.

'Weapons should be left in the hangar according to local regulations.'

That wouldn't suit the SAS and Stenhouse knew it but he had no choice, he was as subject as anyone to the rules of the base while he was there.

'Who will look into our personal baggage after the customs check?' asked one of the anonymous ones.

'I don't think anyone will,' said Stenhouse. 'Why?'

'So if there are any weapons in our baggage no-one will bother?'

'You know the rules. That's all I'm saying on the subject. Tomorrow morning breakfast is at seven, local time. You will leave the accommodation under escort at eight. The two Chinooks will be at the hangar ready for loading and the portable workshop will be manned by Royal Engineers from about eight onwards.

'The timetable for the rest of the day is flexible and will probably be determined by our technical friends. We can't move until the equipment we've brought is fitted into a helicopter and tested. Remember that we may have to stay overnight in Khazatan so bring enough personal gear for one night. If it turns into a two night stop we may be able to send a Chinook back to collect anything vital. Any questions?'

'Right. Follow me.'

* * * * * * * *

On the following morning, Stenhouse saw all his charges into the hangar and then went to discuss plans with the two Chinook pilots.

'Morning,' he said on entering the operations office. 'What's the met report for our target then?'

'Good and clear,' said one of the pilots. 'There was early morning mist but it was very light and will have burned off by now.'

'Good,' said Stenhouse. 'Can we go somewhere private to discuss the schedule of events?'

'Yes. There's a briefing room that will be empty now,' the pilot led the way.

Stenhouse opened up his map on the table.

'Your flight plan for today should say that we fly at regulation height until we approach Khazatani airspace. Then we request permission to fly onto the target area. Hopefully that will be granted. If not, we land at Nodviran military base and see what nasty surprises the natives have cooked up for us.

'Then we fly at a thousand feet to the landing zone where we will unload the vehicles and personnel. We pick up an escort from the welcoming party there and drive the ten miles or so to the target area and carry out the first test.

'When we return, we load the Stop machine onto a Chinook and do the flyover, aiming to miss the Land Rovers that are waiting outside the village to do the follow-up. With the landing site so far out of the village, we should take them completely by surprise on the flyover. We'll try to fit that all in today. If not, we may have to stop over at Nodviran. It's all a bit fluid, I'm afraid.'

'Don't worry, we generally don't get such a good idea what's going on anyway. We're always prepared for anything out here.'

'Good,' said Stenhouse. 'Then I hope you're prepared for this.'

He pulled out a supplementary flight plan from his briefcase.

'This is an addition to the operation and is top secret. No-one here is to know, not even your immediate superior. Whether we let on later, I don't know yet. But we have to drop off two people en route. The grid reference is on the supplementary plan. It's an open grass field with no overhead lines or tall obstructions anywhere near so we can go straight in.

'The Khazatanis must absolutely not know that we are dropping people off. So you follow the flight path designated on the plan.

'At twenty four miles from Nodviran you notice the main gearbox oil level warning light come on in the cockpit. It flickers. You decide to land and check the oil level. It doesn't merit a Mayday call, we don't want anyone coming to have a look, but you advise Khazatan air traffic control that it is a PAN situation and you are landing immediately. You descend to a hundred feet and fly on for half a mile then land on the dropping zone.

'The reason for that is to disappear off Khazatan radar well before the dropping zone. At that distance, I'm told, their radar doesn't pick up anything below two hundred feet so they can't pinpoint where we put down. You leave the rotors turning and do a visual check for oil leakage outside the aircraft while your co-pilot checks inside.

'You decide there is no leak and can continue. You take off again, stay at a hundred feet for a mile or so, then tell air traffic it's OK to run the remaining 70 miles to the landing zone.

'They will tell you to pull up to a thousand feet so they can see you on radar again and off you go. That will confirm our intelligence reports about their system. The following Chinook has to follow the same flight profile and land as well.'

He turned to the second pilot.

'If you stooge around upstairs waiting for your partner, the radar will pinpoint your position. We definitely do not want that. So follow your leader down.'

'Understood.'

'Any problems?'

'Not for us. It's all good stuff. But there's two problems for you. First, operations back at Deggendorf will monitor all our wavelengths continuously. We'll probably be out of touch on UHF but the satellite link will still work. As soon as they hear the PAN message they'll go potty.

'Secondly, the cockpit voice recorder will pick up all the stuff. So I will have to answer a pile of awkward questions about the light when I get back. I can't lie as you'll appreciate and, anyway, the maintenance boys know that sort of thing doesn't happen. The light's either on or off. So they'll be quizzing me.'

'OK,' said Stenhouse. 'That decides it. I'll talk to whoever as soon as we get back.'

'Anything else?'

'Nope. We'll brief our co-pilots when they turn up and they'll talk us through the supplementary when we arrive.'

'Good. And remind them about the security rating for the operation. It's the highest. See you later.'

* * * * * * * *

Work was well under way when Major Stenhouse returned to the hangar. Ben Blackwater's design for the Stop machine had worked first time. Two sliding rails within rails were bolted to the helicopter floor and Stop bolted onto the moving rails. At the target site, the helicopter side door would be slid back, safety pins would be pulled out of the rails and the machine would be slid right outside the aircraft, clear of men and machine.

For now, the Stop machine was in the back of the Land Rover with its power supply ready for the first test.

'Ready to go,' said Ben Blackwater.

'Right,' said Stenhouse in a voice that carried throughout the hangar. 'Let's roll.'

The film and photographic gear was already aboard the second Land Rover and personal stuff had been stowed on the third so it was just a case of driving them into the Chinooks.

Within ten minutes the hangar doors were closed to the sound of the disappearing helicopters and the loaders and workshop engineers stood down.

Life was less spartan on the Chinooks so most people dozed. After the wearing trip in the Hercules and the early start, the steady drone of the Chinook engines soon sent people off to sleep.

Major Stenhouse was woken by the co-pilot.

'About 15 minutes to Nodviran, sir. And air traffic control have ordered us to land at the base for customs clearance.'

'I thought they might. Anyway, I have some boxes to deliver so it will get those out of the way at least. Don't lower the loading ramp when we get there, I'll go out of the side door and the customs can come aboard that way as well. Can you tell the other Chinook to keep all doors closed and only open up on my command. I've really no idea what sort of welcoming party will be there and I don't want to take any chances. Can you also pass a message across for the loader to check that the Stop machine is very well sheeted down.'

In the event, the customs check consisted of just a head count. But they were much keener to get hold of the boxes of terratanium that Stenhouse had brought. They checked that Stenhouse had the right grid reference for the landing zone and told him what sort of vehicles the escort had at the site.

Within twenty minutes the helicopters were airborne again.

Stenhouse went over to the two men who were to be dropped off.

'All OK?'

'Yes. No probs.'

'Right can you come over to the seats beside the door with your stuff so you can make a quick exit. And good luck with whatever it is you are up to.'

Stenhouse's tone was genuine. It may have been peacetime in most of the world and Khazatan may have been a friendly country, but men were still being sent on missions that might be their last.

He chivvied the men sitting in the door seats to make way as the intercom light came on.

'There's a red vehicle, looks like a pick-up truck, stationary on the road beside the drop zone, do we still go in?' asked the co-pilot.

Stenhouse asked the two.

'Yes,' said one. 'That's the description of our taxi.'

The answer was passed on and the Chinook suddenly dived as the pilot radioed his PAN message, the international signal that an emergency had occurred but it was not life threatening or as serious as a Mayday situation.

As the passengers woke up to the sudden movement, Stenhouse mouthed 'It's OK, it's OK.'

There was a bump as the Chinook touched down. Stenhouse opened the door and the two were out and legging it across the field in seconds.

The pilot came back to see Stenhouse.

'Customers dropped off OK?'

'Yes. No problem.'

'Good. I'll give it a couple of minutes, then we'll take off again.'

He disappeared forward and after a few minutes, the engines were put on full throttle and the helicopter lifted off.

Another half-hour and the Chinook was down again.

Stenhouse went out to meet the escort, which consisted of a battered black Mercedes with a soldier in the driving seat and three suited men who could have been scientists, engineers or secret service, and probably were.

'Good morning,' said the suited individual leaning against the car. 'I gather you had a problem on the way. Is it sorted out?'

'It seems to be,' said Stenhouse. 'The pilots will have a good look at the gearbox while we are away running our tests but they think it might be loose wiring.'

'Ah, so. Helicopters get like us, we all suffer from old age although I hope I don't suffer from loose wiring.'

Stenhouse laughed at the joke. It had relieved the tension that was probably being felt on both sides.

'We will follow behind your convoy. I gather you will drive up on to the ridge and then look for a target.'

'That's right,' said Stenhouse.

Suddenly, the idea of firing Stop at some innocent peasant harmlessly working in the fields seemed a bit cold blooded.

He shook off the uncomfortable feeling, jumped in the lead Land Rover and waved the convoy off.

By now it was midday and the sun was well up. The double-cabbed Land Rovers with six people inside grew hotter and hotter. Those sat in the pick up section were cooler, but covered in dust. And as the road dipped and bumped, the SAS MP5s got in everyone's way.

'I hope you travel with the safety catch on,' said one of the film crew to the SAS soldier sat next to him after the MP5 muzzle had inserted itself between two of his lower ribs for the umpteenth time.

The soldier didn't reply, he just gave a scathing look that said the safety catch was not on. That didn't help further conversation.

Up on the ridge, Stenhouse asked the driver to stop and got out with his binoculars. After scanning the fields below he pulled out a rangefinder.

'OK. We've got a target at sixteen hundred metres. That'll do for starters. You'll need to be fully zoomed in, I think,' he said to the film cameraman.

He then signalled to the second Land Rover to turn round so the Stop machine pointed at a small figure hoeing a field of what appeared to be turnips.

The power supply hummed in the still air and the DARE engineers fussed round the machine.

'OK,' said Ben Blackwater.

'OK,' from the film crew.

'Press the titty.'

The power supply hummed louder for a couple of seconds. The figure immediately jumped across two rows of turnips and flapped at his backside with his hat.

'He'll think he's been attacked by the world's first silent wasp,' said one of the onlookers.

'It's a world first anyway,' said Alan Stenhouse. 'Pity we can't go and tell him. Right, there's several people working a bit further on. We'll get within five hundred yards of the next one.'

The effect on the next target, at four hundred and seventy yards, was less dramatic but had a greater effect. The worker fell faster than his hoe, which then fell across his body. He lay still.

'Poor sod,' said one of the SAS.

'Just go and keep those Khazatanis away from the Stop machine, will you?' said Stenhouse. The tension was getting to the whole group.

'You can save your video tape for the next few minutes,' he said to the cameraman. 'But stay with it. As soon as you see him twitch, start filming again.'

The group stood for over a quarter an hour before the figure stirred. Then it picked itself up, put its hat back on and stood staring about. Seeing the hoe laid on the ground, it picked it up and carried on where it had left off.

'I'd love to be a fly on the wall when he gets home tonight. I wonder what he'll tell his wife?'

'He won't say anything,' said another. 'Do you tell your wife when you fall asleep on the job?'

'My wife would slaughter me if I fell asleep on the job,' said another of the group and the ribald laughter that followed broke the tension.

'OK,' said Stenhouse. 'That's it, back to the ranch. If there's no problems fitting the machine to the Chinook then we'll do the second test as well today.'

At the landing site the two Chinooks sat silently glowering. In their shade the pilots had put up a trestle table with cans of Coca Cola set out and piles of foil packets of self-heating personnel rations.

'Welcome to the Savoy.'

With breakfast seven hours in the past, hot plastic food was very welcome, thank you.

So Stop was transferred to the Chinook and the three Land Rovers sent off to wait about a mile outside the target village. Comprising about twenty houses, it meant that each person had two houses to check and report on while the cameraman and photographer were to cover as many unconscious bodies as they could. Ten minutes were allocated. No-one wanted to be around when the village came to life after the flyover.

When the people did come round, the Land Rovers were well out of earshot and the whole contingent was on its way back.

Stenhouse had told the escort that the helicopter did have a slight oil leak in the gearbox and the pilot would like to fly straight back to Germany. Could they clear that with air traffic control.

In fact, there wasn't much that the Khazatani military could do to stop the helicopters leaving the country's airspace. At least their spies had had a good look at the Stop machine and its results.

So the group landed back in time for dinner with a very successful result under its belt.

* * * * * * * *

'You couldn't have wanted a better result,' said Ben Blackwater at the debriefing in Grant Hawley's office back at DARE. As you saw on the videotape, everything worked as predicted and we've got some good pics from the digital camera that we can use in marketing the machine.

'The MoD bod was impressed but I have to say that, having seen it in action in the field, I don't think it could be used in a battlefield environment. You've got to get too close to the target and it's big and heavy, especially with the power supply, which is actually heavier than the machine itself.'

'We discussed this after seeing Professor Palfrey, didn't we?' said Liz Ewshot. 'I suggested putting it in a fast jet to knock out gun emplacements - until we found out how much the total package weighed.'

'Well, we've got to let the MoD evaluate it. But there's nothing to stop us mentioning it to an organisation like WorldForce in the meantime. They were sniffing round only a month or so ago to see what we might be coming up with,' said Roger Wishart.

'You've got to remember that their brief is to provide solutions that domestic police forces and the secret services need. They're not military. They've also got lots of money and they won't take ten years to evaluate an idea like our own MoD. As business development manager I feel that direction would produce our first sale. And as the outfit is financed by so many countries, Stop would come to the attention of a lot of military types anyway.'

'It would certainly help them with one of their key problems,' said Hawley. 'They're into drug prevention more than any other area at the moment but no-one has yet come up with a way to stop the stuff being grown at source.

'All anyone can do at the moment is to send in a squad of military to try and catch the leaders. But these barons have everything so sewn up that they know when an attack is going to take place, probably before the military do. And when the military do arrive, the workers are better armed and soon see them off.

'With Stop in a long-range Chinook, action could be planned miles away from the fields to be attacked. Well outside the barons' sphere of influence. Two would fly in low, so they're on the target before anyone realises. Number one lays out the workers, number two drops the troops to clean up the site before anyone recovers.'

'And where that would help is in demoralising the workers on these drug growing farms,' said Wishart. 'Once they know there's a way of beating the barons, word will soon get around and there'll be no-one willing to help grow the stuff.

'Because Stop is silent, all people hear is a chopper flying around. No-one takes much notice of that these days, so you can do another operation perhaps a mile or two down the road. A very efficient sweeping operation.'

Hawley had his personal organiser open.

'I've met the WorldForce chairman and got her number here. Shall I start the ball rolling and give her a call?' said Hawley.

The group agreed.

* * * * * * * *

Chapter 20

'Ah. Found you at last,' It was Geoff Aylestone. 'Are you busy right now?'

'Fraid so,' said Lazio Palfrey. 'I always tuck myself away at home when I've a paper to write and the deadline's too close for comfort. But as you've tracked me down, what can I do for you?'

'We've some problems with the samples we're putting through the quintahertz machine. They're not standing up to the dynamic tests.'

'In what way?'

'We can see a fine network of hairline cracks spreading through the sample very deep down when two pieces have been rubbed or banged together for several hours. And the turbine blades we hardened are showing the same signs. The customer says they showed up after forty hours running on their test engine.'

'But the static tests were fine, weren't they?' asked Lazio.

'Oh, yes. There's no apparent problem there when we look at the results of surface hardness, resistance to impact and flexibility tests. It's just when components are put to work. You couldn't pop over today and have a look, could you?'

'Yes, I suppose so. Can I have a couple of hours just to crack this work here and I'll come over after lunch. See you about two if that's OK?'

'Yes, that'll do fine. Thanks.'

Lazio dragged himself out of his chair. He felt life was becoming a physical millstone that he could actually feel the weight of. He went into the kitchen and flopped onto a stool.

'You don't look too good,' said Helen. 'Do you feel OK?'

'I feel bloody knackered to be honest with you. And we'll have to scrap lunch out on the lawn, I've got to hurtle off to Glen Parva. Can you bring it forward to half twelve?'

'Yes, that's no problem. But go and lie down until then.'

'I can't. There's this paper on tailored blanks that's promised for tomorrow, I'm miles behind with that.'

'Oh, Lazio, you're not doing yourself any favours with all this work.'

Helen went to the medicine drawer.

'If you can't lie down, take an extra blood pressure pill to be on the safe side. I'll make lunch into sandwiches and bring them into the study so you can carry on working. Get the window wide open, at least you'll get some fresh air.'

'God, I'm going to die rattling with all these pills inside me,' said Lazio.

'Well just lie still when the time comes and then you won't disturb anyone with the noise. Do use your head.'

Helen covered up the concern for her husband with this banter. But it didn't hide the fact that Lazio was not a hundred per cent fit. He was still overweight and didn't seem able to shake himself out of the routine that had brought him to this situation. If he couldn't, he would worsen and Helen didn't choose to think any further.

Lazio needed a sabbatical to get right away from the university. But there just wasn't enough money to keep them for a year's unpaid holiday. DARE had made a down payment on the Stop machine and that was very welcome. But it was soon swallowed up by the new engine for the Maserati and the roof repairs on the house.

This agreement with Glen Parva didn't help. It was creating more work but not much more money and Lazio couldn't just walk out and leave the department. If only his machines would get on and generate the sort of money Lazio wanted, they'd be OK. Helen sighed. She just felt utterly powerless. It took time for things to happen in the business world, but they wanted the money now. She busied herself with the sandwiches for lunch.

At Glen Parva, Lazio studied the deep X-rays and ultrasonic maps of the problem samples.

'This is not an unknown phenomenon,' he said. 'It's just that the process needs balancing between the type of metal and the degree of hardening. On the one hand we could be overgilding the lily and making the samples too hard so they're less resistant to vibration; on the other it may be that the core of the sample can't be as low quality as we hoped for. It may have to be of a higher standard so it can cope with the quality finish the machine is putting on it.

'Running a series of tests may take some time but if I work out a schedule, you could do some work here and I can do some at the university to shorten the time. You have to remember that we're all working in uncharted waters with this technology.'

Charles Thurmaston had been hovering in the background and he came over to greet Lazio.

'Heard you were here, how's things?'

'Fine. And yourself?'

'Can't complain. I gather there's a slight prob on the machine. Have you had a look?'

'Yes. The machine is fine, it's just that we need to juggle the type of material we're hardening with the strength of the process. If there's a problem, it's that the machine can achieve much more than steel can handle in certain circumstances. We'll soon have it sorted.'

Lazio went home with a box of turbine blades to work on, relieved that the problem could be solved but bothered that it added to his workload.

Charles went to find Alan Birstall.

'Can you get Kate Bellew to put out a press release saying that we've discovered a new process that provides an extra hard surface on steel at low cost and is ideal for jet turbine blades as just one example?'

'Sure. But isn't there a problem with the machine? We don't want to announce something we can't deliver, we'll be made a laughing stock.'

'Lazio says it's just a case of balancing machine and metal so there's no problem we can't handle. We're obviously going to have to tailor the process for different applications so there's no point in spending time finding solutions for every possible application. Let's find someone with an actual problem we can work on. We'll just have to let them know that it may take some time. That will cover us.

'But let me see the release before it goes out. More importantly than saying how good the process is, I want it to convey a particular message and the wording has to be right.'

'What's in your mind?'

'Those thieving beggars in Khazatan, whoever they are. They will have the same result as us when they run their dynamic tests. So if we say our machine worked brilliantly first time and orders are piling in, it will demoralise them that they haven't got it right. They may not be able to afford the quality of analytical instruments that we have so they may not be able to solve the problem anyway. But if we tweak up the pressure, it could force something out of the woodwork. The machine can't be hidden for ever.'

'Good thinking. I'll call Kate right away.'

* * * * * * * *

David Bearing called Charles Thurmaston as soon as he arrived back from his Sandrapoor visit.

'Vishay Bhopari definitely wants to end the joint venture with Glen Parva, I'm afraid. It's not just commercial reasons, he says, it's the way the two companies think as much as anything.

'I said we'd noticed the share price had gone up after a quiet run but he didn't offer any explanation. What I did find out was that they have had a number of approaches from other companies and one that Bhopari seems to favour I think is based in eastern Europe. He also said it was offering a new hardening technology that could be worth a lot of money to Sandrapoor and was the first of its type in the world.

'He wouldn't say who the company was or how the hardening system worked. I think it will take someone with a bit more clout than me to prise it out of him. He also said they might take some surplus plant off the company as part of the deal.'

Charles started putting it all together. Whoever had approached Sandrapoor had made a very good offer. It had been received favourably and so the directors of both companies and their friends were buying sufficient shares to jack up the price in anticipation of a signed deal.

It was more than coincidence that they were offering a hardening technology and when David had said the company was based in eastern Europe, it had to point to a Khazatani company.

Sandrapoor had to be brought back into the Glen Parva fold very quickly and decisively.

'Thanks for all that,' he said to David. 'Take a few days off and I'll give you a call when I've thought all this through.'

He sat back for a while and then called Alistair Wyatt.

'How soon would you and your wife be available to fly out to Mumbai? The reason for asking is that we need a high level meeting with our partners quite quickly, within a matter of days in fact, and we would like to introduce your good self to them at the same time.'

'How long do you think the trip would take in total?'

'At least five days. It's a long trip and it knocks the stuffing out of you a bit. When you take the time difference into account, you lose about five days productive work whichever way you look at it. But if you want to stay on for longer, feel free. We said we'd give you time to look round Mumbai and the university so even if our directors come back to the UK right away, there's no need for you to do the same.'

'If you could give us, say, three days to get packed and sorted, I can fix up some meetings at Mumbai University in that time, I'm quite sure. If we could have about ten days out there, that would suit us nicely and then we'd be back before the Christmas term starts, which is quite important. I'd like to mention it to Morag first but I'm sure there'll be no problem.'

'Right, Thank you very much for that. I'll get some bookings made and let you know the details as soon as possible.'

* * * * * * * *

Grant Hawley switched off the video machine as the television screen went to black.

'Well, gentlemen, a convincing demonstration I'm sure you'll agree.'

There were murmurs of assent from around the room.

The chairman of WorldForce had asked for a team to visit DARE as soon as possible after Hawley had told her about Stop and the trials in Khazatan. So he faced questions from a technical assessor, an operations manager and two members of the organisation's strategy committee.

To match that, DARE fielded its Stop team.

'Stop is a unique weapon that is ideal in a guerrilla situation. Totally silent and not too difficult to conceal, it is absolutely clean,' said Hawley. 'We say it has a great future in cleaning up drug growing operations as just one application.'

'What worries me is that it does not differentiate between civilians and terrorist targets. It could create some very negative PR. I'm not happy at the idea of knocking out people who may be doing all sorts of things that are safe at the time, such as carrying hot cooking pots, ironing or carrying children but that pose a danger if the person goes unconscious,' said one of the strategy committee.

'Whatever weapon you use, can, and probably will, harm a civilian at some time,' said Roger Wishart. 'But at least this weapon is not fatal and leaves no lasting effects. We're not claiming that it is the ideal weapon but we are saying it is more effective in the guerrilla situation than conventional weapons.'

'Its strength lies in its silence and the fact that it is not messy. By comparison, a gun battle is noisy, time consuming, creates a strong reaction from the other side and is not always successful,' said Liz Ewshot.

'Any unintended casualties of Stop will be very small in number, probably less than in a conventional confrontation. But once its reputation spreads, ordinary people will be quite afraid of it so they won't want to work on a drug farm. The drug barons will simply lose their workforce.

'It also has the element of surprise. Stop can be mounted in many types of helicopter, even the types that the drug barons use. So it can fly around all day without arousing any suspicion. There's no noise from Stop to alert people on nearby farms. Dogs are knocked out so there's no barking. You just follow up with a military helicopter that drops the clean-up troops,' said Wishart.

'Compare that with current operations. Firstly you have to assemble a small army and word immediately gets out that an operation is under way. Then the troops are probably outgunned when they arrive, besides having to face protected gun positions and pre-warned fighters. You've got to admit that Stop is much more effective.'

'There's also the problem of land troops needing local knowledge,' said Hawley. 'They need to know what sort of terrain they have to cover to get to the target site. But a helicopter fitted with a global positioning system just flies to a pre-set co-ordinate, turns onto a pre-set course and tells the pilot when to fire.

'The helicopter could be flown entirely on auto-pilot and Stop fired automatically, all with an accuracy down to a few inches. That means you can use units based well outside the target zone and then there's no fear of someone pre-warning the target. The pilot doesn't even have to know where he's flying to, he just follows the GPS out and home.

'And if there's a problem, the GPS tells him exactly where in the world he is so he can fly the aircraft manually to wherever he wants. The back up helicopter containing the troops flies with the lead helicopter and comes in immediately the lead machine has passed over the target.

'These drug growing areas always have a landing strip where troops can be dropped and the warehouse is always close to the owner's house and the workers' living quarters so if the lead helicopter comes in from the right angle, it will probably cover all the buildings in one pass.'

The room was silent as the WorldForce team thought that through.

'And if the raid was made at first light, the troops could clear up and then disappear off leaving a small group to intercept the people who came in during the day without realising that the place was in new hands,' said one of the visitors.

The WorldForce team was selling Stop to itself.

Hawley played the moral card.

'There is never success without cost but think of the cost to the whole world of drugs being so widely available. Some human

310

lives may be lost on these drug raids but you have to think of the bigger picture. How many deaths around the world is one drug farm responsible for?'

'You've certainly given us food for thought with this presentation,' said the spokesman for the WorldForce team.

'It fits in with our remit to provide non-military forces with solutions to their problems in maintaining law and order. When could we have one to try?'

'There is the one you saw earlier although I don't know if our technical boys will want to keep it here. They've a number of ideas for improving it that they want to work on. But we can always build another. We've got to think about going into production one way or another.'

'Well, I've got to report back to several WorldForce committees before I can commit us to anything. But I think I can say we'd like to move quickly towards a test session with Stop. See what you can do here, let me know as soon as a machine could be ready and then we'll discuss the fine detail.'

* * * * * * * *

'Let's see what they have to say, it can't do any harm,' said Vishay Bhopari to the other directors of Sandrapoor Steel Mills when he told them of Charles Thurmaston's proposed visit.

'Several of Glen Parva's board are coming and as they must have been pre-warned by David Bearing, they will know what the score is. So I would expect them to have cooked up a decent proposal. They are also bringing someone they sponsor to have a look round, but I don't know what that will do for us. My wife might pick up something from his wife because the two are going to have a look round Mumbai while the Glen Parva party are here.'

So Alistair Wyatt was introduced by Charles Thurmaston along with Alan Birstall and Geoff Aylestone. The preliminary chat was followed by a tour of the Sandrapoor factory and the group ended up in Vishay's office.

'I'll come straight to the point,' said Charles Thurmaston, 'We understand that you are looking for another partner, is that right?'

'Yes,' said Vishay. 'But it's early days yet. We are not committed to anyone or anything and we do not intend to break the terms of our joint venture agreement. And it is up to the whole board to decide the company's future,' He indicated the other board members sat around his office.

'That's as maybe, but your share price says otherwise, doesn't it? Stationary for months and then rises on three successive days.'

'These things happen.'

'Look, we've both put a lot of time and effort into setting up this joint venture and it seems a shame to throw all that overboard,' said Charles. 'Can we at least explore the possibilities of our continuing to work together?'

'Sure,' said Vishay. 'That's what we're here for today, after all. What do you propose to offer us?'

'Firstly, a global sales force. Your shareholders will press you sooner or later to go international with your sales, if only to spread the trading risks over several markets so you are not tied into the fortunes of the Indian economy alone. Doesn't it make sense to use a tried and tested network rather than to spend money on setting up salesmen of your own?'

'It would appear so on the surface,' said Vishay's sales director. 'But we may not be able to service all the sales orders that come in. We may need more production capacity and we will certainly need more money. Perhaps more than we could raise in the money markets. I think we would be better off working with a company smaller than yourselves. Our sales would rise slower, no doubt, but we would be in a controllable situation.'

'But to achieve a breakthrough in world markets you need substance behind you. We can offer a solid track record of international expansion. And you mustn't forget that we have the public relations clout that is needed to get into new countries. That is why we invited Professor Wyatt on this trip. We have sponsored his department at Burnstone University to research a solution to the problem of AIDS and after this meeting, he will go onto Mumbai University to set up an academic link with their microbiology department.

'Now, you know how much politics gets in the way of breaking into new countries. You don't just have to sell better products, but you have to convince the local government that you are good for them. If you are involved with a group investigating this important subject of AIDS, it can only be good for your business.

'We have also negotiated a new deal with the University's steel research team so we can offer some new technology, steel hardening in particular.'

Charles Thurmaston was on his sales soapbox again and went on at some length.

Eventually, Vishay broke in and said. 'We hear what you say and we cannot disagree with your arguments but let's move onto what all this means in terms of money. We all want extra profit out of any deal so what is all this going to cost us?'

'Well, it all comes down to commercial good sense. We can't undersell our side and we don't want to overcharge you, but we both have to make some profit out of the arrangement.'

'Are you able to offer us subsidised research facilities, a grant towards your new hardening technology and help with our rationalisation programme - which means helping us get rid of excess production equipment?'

'That is a tall order,' said Charles, rather taken aback. 'I can find out what export grants we can get from the UK government as a start.'

'That's all very well,' said Vishay. 'but we have been offered that package already. And, as you know, any first offering can always be improved on in later negotiations, so you have to admit your proposal is way off the target.'

There wasn't much Charles could say against that and his fellow directors weren't much help either. Sandrapoor was critical as a launch pad for Glen Parva and losing the joint venture would set back its strategy a long way. But there was only so far he could go. He wouldn't be allowed to put the amount of money into the deal that Sandrapoor wanted, that was for sure. He decided to play for time.

'Can we leave the matter there for the time being then? There is a lot to be thought of and I don't think now is the time for either of us to make a decision.'

Vishay smiled in agreement. He could be magnanimous in Glen Parva's defeat. His side had already made their decision.

* * * * * * * *

Chapter 21

'We're ready to roll out the publicity machine for the first part of the sponsorship deal with Glen Parva,' Alistair Wyatt was in the Vice Chancellor's office having just got back from Mumbai.

'I had an excellent time at the university and they're very keen on this new approach to find an AIDS solution from the microbiological angle. The Indian government is totally behind them and, of course, there's plenty of research material on their doorstep. Drakon Pharma are also very keen to jump on the bandwagon. They think that research into a solution has stalled and a new approach could now produce a significant result so they want to get in on the act. A couple of their people will come over and see us before long.'

'That's excellent. But weren't you going to apply for some European funding to help things along?'

'Yes, that's all in hand. But that will be worth some publicity in its own right. The next thing is to get the fair Kate Bellew to write up a press release for this bit and away we go.'

The telephone rang.

Alistair Wyatt rose in preparation to leave the Vice Chancellor alone with his call. But no sign came.

'Oh my god. I'm so sorry. We'll both come down right away.' The Vice Chancellor rose.

'Bad news, I'm afraid. You seem to have lost your sparring partner. Lazio Palfrey has collapsed in the workshop. It doesn't look good.'

* * * * * * * *

Away in eastern Europe another bombshell was about to drop.

At the Khazatan Research Institute one of the nightwatchmen glanced up from the naked beauty draped across the centrefold of the country's version of Penthouse. He watched as a set of headlights slowly came up the potholed drive.

About half way up, the night identification camera automatically checked the number plate and the shape of the vehicle. A message flashed up on the screen in the security office confirming the visitor as Vladimir Arbatov, the institute's main director. It was followed by a green light to indicate the car park barrier had opened.

The nightwatchman warned his partner, put away his magazine and started tidying up the remains of the pizza they'd had for supper as they waited for the boss to present his pass at the window.

But the director was not going to do that. He couldn't. He had just got into bed at his home several miles away.

The driver of the black Mercedes backed the car up to the Institute building and left the engine running as he got out and went round to the boot. He pulled out a large hosepipe and used the heavy brass fitting on the end to smash the nearest window. He fed the hose through the broken glass, operated a switch in the boot and ran away across the car park into the darkness of the bushes.

He watched the seconds pass on the luminous dial of his watch. The car had been modified with false number plates and, more importantly, a huge tank, which took up the space of the boot and where the back seat should have been.

The pump he had switched on was emptying the tank at a gallon a second - of high octane petrol. There was the best part of three hundred gallons waiting to go into the building. Just over five minutes to empty the tank completely. But already there were thirty gallons or more swilling about on the floor of the Institute. The pungent smell of neat petrol reached him across the car park.

A few seconds later the smell reached under the door of the security office. The nightwatchmen were lost. To chase the smell or to wait for the director? Where was he?

They went into the corridor and started switching on lights.

That was the cue for the man in the bushes.

He pressed the small box in his hand. A remote controller. Immediately a huge explosion rocked the building as the petrol ignited. A hot blast of reeking air hit him with a stinging blow. Flames poured out of the broken window, engulfed the Mercedes and licked upwards to the rest of the building.

The man ran to the rusted fencing, jumped through a gap and leapt into the passenger side of a red pick-up truck that had just pulled up.

'Don't you just love it when a plan comes together?' he said as he was driven off. 'Even if security realised what was going on, they'd never be able to get near the car to switch off the pump with that inferno going. Just think, three hundred gallons and no stopping it,' He positively rubbed his hands with glee.

'My lips won't let me forget in a hurry,' said the driver. 'I never siphoned so much petrol, even when I was a kid without any pocket money.'

As the driver took the truck in to the city centre, the glow from the fire rose high in the sky.

'The fire brigade may take their usual two days to get to there but at least they shouldn't get lost,' he said.

They entered what had been a high class residential area of the city. Large, square mansions, set well back from the road in huge gardens behind high walls. Now, the buildings housed government offices, headquarters of commercial companies and foreign embassies. The driver pulled up outside one, went to the gate and pressed the intercom.

'Yes. What do you want?' A tinny, disembodied voice came out of the loudspeaker.

'We need to speak to the security attaché immediately and we want our vehicle taken to your garage now. We're British Army, SAS, it's top secret and bloody urgent.'

After a couple of minutes a side door opened and a dark suited man appeared. Behind him stood a figure with an MP5 at the ready.

The two showed their passports and Army identification cards.

'Here's the contact who will vouch for us.'

The driver passed over a piece of paper.

'The main thing is we need to get this vehicle out of sight bloody quickly.'

'OK. Come in.'

They went into the reception area of the embassy and stood under the watchful eye of the man with the MP5. He was in combats but there were no regimental flashes at his shoulders.

'You're making me nervous with that thing,' said the driver. 'And we're on the same side, aren't we? What are you? Marine Commando?'

The question was ignored.

Dark suit came back with a young man following.

'Where's the keys?'

'Here,' said the driver. 'The arrangement is that the pick-up is resprayed ASAP. Any colour other than red. Hub caps are to be changed and the number plates as well. It's to be kept completely out of sight and in a few days someone will call to collect it. As identification, they will have an exact duplicate of this set of keys, including the corner knocked off the plastic key tag. The bill is to go to the contact on that piece of paper.'

'OK,' said dark suit to the young man passing over the keys. 'Drive carefully and don't get picked up or we might disown you.'

He turned to the pair.

'You stink of petrol, what have you been up to?'

The driver just pointed out of the window where a red glow could be seen over the house tops.

'Bloody hell, that's a big one. Don't tell me. I don't want to know, but I suppose it's a pity if you can't have some fun once in your lifetime. Now, I see two bags on the floor there, are you wanting a bed for the night as well?'

'And a long, hot shower please.'

'That goes without saying.'

Another dark suit appeared in reception.

'Hi. I'm the security attaché. What can I do for you?'

'We need to put you in the picture as to why we're here just in case there's a knock on your door from the local nasties.'

'You can see why they're here if you look out of the window,' said the first dark suit.

The glow was brighter than before.

'Wow. You've had some fun there, and it's not even Guy Fawkes' night. You seem to be pretty doused in petrol as well.'

'That came from the explosion, we both got caught in the blast fumes. We've also been siphoning petrol for the last week - about three hundred gallons. Not all of it went in the can, I'm afraid.'

'That's obvious. But you'd better put me in the picture first. And we'll do it out here if you don't mind rather than in my office. Don't want to be rude but...'

He indicated some plain plastic chairs in a corner of the reception area.

Dark suit brought him a faxed message and dismissed the MP5 carrier.

Dark suit two read it.

'Right, let's see your ID,' He checked the passports and cards against the fax. 'Looks as though we've got your boss out of bed,' he said, checking on the time difference.

'Don't worry. Hereford never sleeps. Our lot are used to working in the middle of the night,' said the driver, referring to the SAS headquarters.

'So, what's on fire?'

'The Khazatan Research Institute.'

'Boy, your lot don't mess about, do you? That's what it says in the fax but I didn't believe it. And what's inside it, rather, what was inside it, that interested you?'

'We don't know exactly but we were told it's a machine that has been stolen from the UK. There was no chance of the Khazatanis returning it, and it was deemed too risky to try and steal it back, so the powers that be decided to destroy it and give the K's a bloody nose into the bargain. The message is that no-one messes with the UK.'

'Well, you've got that message across all right. The details of virtually every military secret that the K's possess are, correction were, in that building. Every bit of secret research is done there as well. Let's hope they blame it on the dissidents. If the bill lands on our doorstep it'll probably bankrupt the UK.'

'Anything else I need to know?'

'That's it really. We've been staying at a house rented by some Brits for the ten days we've been in the country. We don't know what they do and we don't know who fixed it up, but the beds were bloody comfortable.'

He recited the address.

'The women were pretty good as well but they only came in the evening, when we had to go out siphoning petrol from everything that had wheels. We even clicked a couple of lawn mowers.'

'You can tell which houses they were, the grass is very long.'

And the two roared with the laughter that comes from a very silly joke told when people are exhausted, stressed and well short of sleep.

'OK. The fax confirms most of what you say. Come on then, the emergency accommodation is in the basement. I'll show you down. It's basic but there's plenty of hot water. There's machines down there for coffee, biscuits, chocolate and that sort of thing. The steward comes on at seven. I'll leave him a note to call you. He'll fix up breakfast. And then, under the circumstances, we need to get you out of the country pretty damn quick.'

It was two days before embassy officials could get the SAS men out of Khazatan through the diplomatic channel at the airport that avoided any exposure to local customs officials. Just before they left, dark suit number one brought them some pictures of the site where the Institute had stood.

'Point one, you haven't seen these, OK?'

'OK.'

'They're photographs from a surveillance satellite four hundred miles up. Can't say whose it is. The first was taken at midnight. You can see the huge fire, it's so bright it has blinded the camera. The next is twelve hours later. There's just a smoking black circle on the ground. Nothing more than a couple of feet high is left standing. Total devastation.

'The local paper hasn't mentioned it at all but other papers round the world say it's the result of an atomic explosion. So the Khazatanis have a lot of explaining to do. You might have got your revenge but you've also probably done the UK some positive good. The K's are going to want someone to help them carry on their industrial research at least, so we can help them, can't we?'

'At a price.'

'Nice one.'

* * * * * * * *

Helen Palfrey looked drawn and her pale face seemed to emphasise her greying hair and rounded shoulders.

'At least he died where he was happy, playing with his blasted steel.'

She dabbed her eyes.

'I sometimes thought he was as much in love with that stuff as he was with me.'

Saxon put his arm round her shoulders.

'Come on,' he said. 'But look what it brought you. And this place is yours totally now. You've more than enough now to keep it in good order. And Donnatella and I will need you more than ever now with the kids coming on.'

Helen pulled back sharply.

'But Donnatella hasn't any children.'

'Aah,' said Saxon, rubbing his chin.

'Come on. What's going on? Tell me. I'm not daft.'

Saxon grimaced.

'Look, I'm not supposed to tell you. Donna is preggers.'

'Well, why keep it a secret? That's really good news. Does that mean a wedding?'

Helen brightened perceptibly.

'I'm not saying any more. I'm probably in enough trouble as it is. But one assumes that Simon will do the decent thing and marry her now. They've been together long enough anyway to know if it's going to work.'

'Oh, Saxon, that has cheered me up.'

'Well, keep it quiet. She'll tell you herself this afternoon I should think. Pretend not to know anything or I'll get it in the neck.'

So Saxon made himself scarce when he heard Donnatella drive up.

'You're looking well,' said Helen. 'Positively radiant, in fact. Come and tell me all your news. And where's Simon?'

'He's just clearing up some business at work and then he'll come up in a day or so. I'm not feeling radiant anyway. Tell me first what happened to dad.'

'Well, he's put himself under so much pressure to develop his quintahertz machine and then to have it taken off him just about broke his heart. He had a real bad cold a few weeks ago, it was all due to that. Then there was this business with him having to sack his number two and he's been having problems with his blood pressure, his heart and he was overweight as well.'

Helen started to cry.

'Come on,' said Donnatella. 'Where's the whisky. I think we both need a shot.'

'Well, it was all my fault,' sobbed Helen. 'I shouldn't have fed him so well and I should have stood up to him and made him eat properly and I should have gone on more walks with him.'

'That's nonsense. No-one could have ever made him lead a sensible lifestyle. He lived life the way he wanted it and he wasn't going to listen to advice if it didn't suit him. You know that. Don't start blaming yourself. We all know what he was like - loveable and a pain in the arse. At least he could spot good whisky.'

Donnatella poured herself another good measure and topped up her mother's glass.

'You've got to look ahead - we all have.'

'Yes but what about those buggers like Alistair Wyatt, they go on for ever. He made your father's life a misery sometimes, you know that? He was looking forward to a lot of good times when the money came through for the machines he'd invented. They were such good ideas. And it was Wyatt's doing that Lazio had to do all the extra work for this new sponsor.'

'Come on. You won't do any good dwelling on that now. Let's have a look at the arrangements you've got to make. Will his parents come over from Italy?'

'I'm sorry. I shouldn't be burdening you with all this. Yes, they are making arrangements now.'

'So there'll be beds to make up?'

'Oh, yes. And for you and Saxon as well. Oh, there's so much to do.'

Donnatella poured out another measure of whisky for each of them.

'Well it'll just have to wait. Get that down you.'

The phone rang.

'I'll take it,' shouted Saxon, not realising that the two ladies were not as able as usual to hold a rational conversation.

There was a brief exchange then Saxon stuck his head round the lounge door.

'David Bearing would like to talk to you, mum, do you want to talk to him just now?'

'Wosh that?' Helen tried to focus on the doorway. 'Bearing to who?'

He looked at the glass in her hand and then at Donnatella.

'Hi. Didn't know you had arrived. Is she OK?' he indicated Helen.

'Wosh that?' said Donnatella, having obvious difficulty in focussing on anything.

He saw the glass in her hand

'Don't bother.'

He retreated to the phone.

'Hallo. Helen can't come to the phone just now, I'm afraid, she's out for a while. Can I take a message? It's Saxon.'

'I just wanted to say how sorry I was to hear about your father. How's your mother taking it?'

'Much as one would expect, they were very close.'

'Look, it's perhaps fortunate I've got you instead of Helen. I know I wasn't much help to your father at times, did you know that I'd left the university not exactly voluntarily?'

'I had heard something.'

'Well I'd really like to help Helen. She should get something substantial out of the steel firm that took over your father's hardening machine but if she doesn't do anything, they probably won't raise the issue. Now I know plenty about the machine and Glen Parva so if I can be of help to get some cash out of the firm. I'd really like to help.'

'Well I'm one of the executors of my father's will so I've got to do the best I can for the estate but it's also a personal issue so perhaps we ought to have a talk. Could you come over some time, please?'

* * * * * * * *

Lazio Palfrey's death had quiet but international repercussions. For much of his life he had helped influence the developments in steel industries around the world through his research, while his work on committees had helped improve product quality and working standards.

But now, that world was preparing to do without him. Like a pail of water whose surface is ruffled when something is pulled out, that surface was settling down. The ripples were disappearing and, soon, no-one would notice that any disturbance had happened.

Whatever Helen Palfrey and her family could do, life would never be the same again for them. But the organisations that they were linked to through Lazio had to continue.

Once word got around the security services that the Khazatan Research Institute had been handsomely razed to the ground and that the quintahertz inventor had died, MI5 closed its active case file, moved it to the archives and told the Leicestershire Police.

DI Wigston told Helen Palfrey they would do the same unless she wished to continue the matter personally.

'I'm afraid I'm not sure how you would go about it anyway,' he said. 'It may be that you have to ask your member of the European Parliament to take up the case.'

'We won't be going that far,' said Helen. 'The university will get something from the insurance and Saxon has arranged for them to reimburse the estate with what it cost my husband, so we think there would not be more to be had anyway.'

'Well I can tell you that the people who stole your husband's machine have paid very dearly for the privilege. I haven't been told the exact details but it appears that the machine ended up in the Khazatan Research Institute and they were going to sell copies of it through their country's steel association. Unfortunately, the

Institute has been razed to the ground by fire. The machine, all its details and lots of other secret research have gone up in smoke.

'There was a satellite picture of the site in Thursday's Daily Telegraph. The public story is that it was the result of an atomic accident. So instead of the Khazatanis blaming all and sundry, they been forced back on the defensive and have to explain themselves. Funny coincidence that it happened at this time, eh?'

Saxon then had to deal with DARE. But that was a more formalised affair. The company still used the form of contract that was used when it was a government department. The Palfrey estate would receive a lump sum less the advance that had already been made to Lazio. It would also receive a percentage of the money raised through sales of Stop.

DARE would have the machines built under licence by a commercial subcontractor and Saxon could audit the company's dealings through a mutually acceptable accountant or solicitor.

But he wanted the contract to extend beyond the prescribed three years.

'No-one else will come up with anything like this for a long time to come so there should be good sales for more than three years. It's only right that the estate should benefit from that.'

'It won't work quite like that,' said Roger Wishart. 'First of all we will be putting work into developing Stop to give it additional features so it continues to sell and so customers come back for updated versions. That will cost a lot of money and that will be out of our purse.

'Secondly, if there isn't an alternative in three years time, then one will be on the horizon. It always works out like that. A new device coming onto the market suddenly concentrates everyone's mind on that area. So customers for Stop will hold fire until they see what the new option has to offer.

'In the meantime, you should do well from the deal. An organisation called WorldForce is already talking of buying several Stop machines. It has tried one very successfully as an anti-drugs weapon in South America. It seems to be the definitive answer in the battle to eradicate drug growing farms and that has been a sore problem for long enough.'

So Saxon had to be content with the standard contract although it would add up eventually to a large sum of money.

But with Glen Parva, David Bearing had proved very useful with his background knowledge of the quintahertz technology and his inside knowledge of the company's plans.

'They suffered a setback when their Indian partners wanted to move to another company. But that was largely dependent on the new partner offering subsidised research facilities and a cheap hardening machine. Once the Research Institute was burned down, that offer didn't look half so good.

'The Glen Parva directors are now talking to the Khazatan steel association and offering them technical help and the chance to buy the quintahertz machine legally. Glen Parva are also back in the frame with Sandrapoor so the company could do very well out of all that hiatus. So when you talk to them, remember that they stand to do very well out of your father. Make sure the estate gets its cut.'

* * * * * * * *

At Burnstone University life also started to settle down. Ann Whittaker took down the poster of Vesuvius from her office wall.

'I was wrong about that. There's been no warning of a possible eruption on the news. I always said the two would blow up together. I wish I hadn't now.'

'Well just look at this picture in the Telegraph. That could almost be a volcanic crater couldn't it.'

She and John Fleming were looking at the satellite picture of the Khazatan fire.

'It's a black circle and you can't really tell how deep it is. And there's wisps of smoke coming out of it. If the rumours are right, then his machine's in there somewhere. It's allegorical, I tell you. It may not be Vesuvius itself, but it's an allusion. You were right in principle.'

Alistair Wyatt poked his head round the door.

'Hello, Ann, can I have a word with you, please?'

He moved towards Lazio's office.

'You might as well come in as well,' he said to John Fleming.

'As you will probably appreciate, Combined Engineering is suddenly in a very difficult position. Term starts soon and we've lost our numbers one and two. We're also just settling down with an important sponsor and we have to take care of them.

'I've got to move fast so I have asked Professor John Smithson from Empire University to come in and take over the research work so there is no break in teaching or in student project work. You've both heard of him, haven't you?'

'Yes, Professor Palfrey often described his work although it wasn't in the most complimentary terms.'

'Well I'm asking you both to give him maximum co-operation. He may only be here for two terms as he is in the process of retiring and handing over his chair to his deputy, so that is very convenient for us. But it will increase your workload, I'm afraid.

'That brings me onto a rather sensitive area. Dr David Bearing. I've run over this with the Vice Chancellor and we are inclined to bring him back. It will be on a one-term contract only and he's straight out the door if there's any old malarkey. But will you both work with him again?'

'I don't see a problem,' said Ann. 'We're still not really sure why he went, but there was never any problem with working with him before. I suppose it might be a bit awkward at first but things should soon settle down. Once the students are back, there's no time to dwell on these things.'

'And you, John?'

'Same goes for me.'

'Well, thank you both very much. If there's any problem let me know through Jenny. Now I have to dash off to London so I'll be away all tomorrow as well but nothing should happen before then.'

What Wyatt didn't say was that he had to look after himself as well. The university had to run smoothly but so did his own career. Keeping Glen Parva happy as a sponsor meant that his own private research moved forward, and that would move him forward. The next step was very close, that same evening, in fact.

The Scientific Research Council had approved in principle a grant to Burnstone University and Grover Wisden had managed to get Alistair Wyatt onto the tail end of the guest list of a reception at 10 Downing Street in London, where the Prime Minister would be introduced to the major captains of industry. The sort of gathering that had excited even the hardened arch schemer.

But it was a two way deal. An envelope in Wyatt's pocket contained two air tickets and hotel reservations in Mumbai for Grover Wisden and his wife. Some things would never change.

At Glen Parva, the monthly board meeting discussed the ups and downs of the last few weeks.

'I don't think we've lost too much when all's said and done,' said Charles Thurmaston. 'In fact, if these latest developments move forward as we expect we'll have Sandrapoor back in the fold, but on a stronger footing, plus the benefit of the opportunities that must come from our link with the Khazatan Steel Association. So the overall result should be better than we first planned.'

'We could also benefit from the contacts that this chap Sergei Danelski has offered us,' said Alan Birstall. 'I should explain to the board that Danelski has apparently been an eastern European fixer for some time. He's well in with the Khazatan men of steel, that's how he knew about us. He travels to the UK a lot and once I've checked out his credentials I'll fix up a meeting.

'But that won't be for two weeks at least because I've got a spot of leave booked. And that leads me to a matter that I think the board needs to discuss. Kate Bellew and Hoogen, Bellew Cutler. Do we think they're doing a good job?'

'The results so far have been good,' said Bill Charnwood. 'I know they're working for us behind the scenes through one or two snippets I've picked up from my other directorships.'

'It's all been good publicity so far, but you have seen that for yourself, so why do you ask?' said Thurmaston.

'I'm going on holiday with Kate Bellew and if I'm lucky, we could be engaged when we get back. Would the board be happy to continue working with her under those circumstances?'

'Well, lucky you,' said Charles. 'That's a nice catch. Congratulations. I suppose there could be a conflict of interest at some time, but, there again, you'd both be on the company's side, so I don't see a problem. What about anyone else?'

'Same goes for me,' said Bill Charnwood. 'I wouldn't want it broadcast, of course, you don't know what others might read into it, but Kate seems extremely professional and discreet so I'm sure she'd handle it very well.'

'I agree,' said Geoff Aylestone. 'Congratulations.'

Bill Oadby echoed that comment and a very self-satisfied board moved on to the next business.

The headline in the Leicester evening paper summed it up.

'Late Professor Built His Own Monument.'

The article recorded the success of Stop in South America and its future as a leading force in the war against drugs. It also listed some of the ways the world's steel industry had benefited from Palfrey's work and would continue to do so through quintahertz.

It mentioned that Saxon was the new Lord of the Manor and concluded, 'Professor Lazio Palfrey was larger than life and the life of the world benefited.'

'That's his epitaph,' said Helen when she read it. 'That will go on his headstone.'

* * * * * * * *

329